BENEFIT OF THE DOUBT

BENEFIT
OF THE
DOUBT

LES COWAN

Published by Lion Fiction
an imprint of
Lion Hudson IP Ltd
Wilkinson House, Jordan Hill Road
Oxford OX2 8DR, England
www.lionhudson.com/fiction

ISBN 978 1 78264 251 0
e-ISBN 978 1 78264 252 7

First edition 2017

Acknowledgments
Scripture quotations taken from the Holy Bible, New Living Translation,
copyright © 1996, 2004, 2007 by Tyndale House Foundation. Used by
permission of Tyndale House Publishers, Inc., Carol Stream, Illinois
60188. All rights reserved.

Cover images: Fedora © blackwaterimages/iStockphoto.com;
Figure © PeteSherrard/iStockphoto.com;
Edinburgh © Arcangel Images Ltd

A catalogue record for this book is available from the British Library

Printed and bound the UK, May 2017, LH26

For Fiona

ACKNOWLEDGMENTS

Grateful thanks are due to those who have helped in one way or another in the evolution of David Hidalgo and *Benefit of the Doubt*.

Firstly, to those who took the time to read and comment on excerpts, early drafts, or entire texts and who provided crucial encouragement: principally Fiona Cowan, Angus Mackay, Gillian Morrison, Mija Regoord, Jan Gordon, Dot Hanson, Janet Burgon, Ron Ferguson, Andrew Greig, and Morag MacInnes.

Secondly Tony Collins, Jess Tinker, and the team at Lion who were willing to take a chance on something a bit different. Also Julie Frederick for her zealous editing and amazing attention to detail.

Thirdly special extra thanks to Morag MacInnes for her inspiring writing groups in Kirkwall and Stromness, which unfailingly gave me energy to keep going.

Finally, thanks to the many wonderful friends we have made in Madrid, Galicia, and elsewhere in Spain over the years, for their kindness and generosity in sharing their culture with us.

PROLOGUE

An ordinary day – phone calls, messages, *oficina de correos* with the post, last-minute copying for Sunday. Tidy up and it's time to go. Then Marisol from the rehab programme turns up and wants to talk. She's fallen out with her boyfriend who doesn't approve. He wants her to drop out and move with him to Malaga. She needs an older sister to help her say no.

Finally, bus stop in the dying light. It's late and the streets are deserted. First a push – *"perdona Señora"* – then two dark-suited men she doesn't recognize – one on either side. A black 4x4. She can hardly cry out before she's shoved in the back, a fat strip of sticking plaster on her mouth and arms wrenched behind her. A searing blow on the head puts the lights out.

* * *

A routine appointment for a busy pastor, taking calls about his work. Then the last caller he expected. A sound like the cracking of dry twigs. A frantic drive to the hospital. "I'm so sorry," the doctor says. "Can you come this way?"

That's when the nightmare began.

Chapter 1

BRUNTSFIELD

David Hidalgo leaned forward in an attitude that could either have been prayer or desperation. He took off a pair of gold-rimmed glasses and dropped them on the desk, rubbed his eyes, and ran his hands through what was still a fairly full head of sandy hair. How on earth was he supposed to finish a sermon – now getting distinctly urgent – in a freezing cold flat, surrounded by boxes, not a clue where his books were, the constant rumble and hiss of Edinburgh buses outside the window and an equally constant stream of interruptions? Neighbours, his new landlady, market surveys, political canvassers (preserve us), even someone encouraging him to carry a post-mortem sperm donation card. Where did these people come from? For a second he felt the inner toddler whinge *it's not fair*, then caught himself. Of course it wasn't fair. Who said life was fair? Brutal and clichéd but direct and to the point. And only a cliché because countless generations repeated it to each other in the face of what definitely did seem unfair. Everything from a slightly overdone Sunday lunch to bereavement and ruin.

Indeed it was not fair. And the next point please.

He put his glasses back on, ripped the half-written page from the pad, crumpled it up, dropped it in the cornflakes box doing duty as a wastepaper bin, and wrote Sunday's date yet again in small neat script at the top of the page – *19th February. AM. Luke 10:25–37: The Good Samaritan* – then leaned back and tried to pull his thoughts back together again. So a sermon is basically biblical explanation and application – ok. But what had originally meant something to near-eastern farmers, fishermen, builders, and bored teenagers (presumably teenagers have been bored throughout history) in a minor province of the Roman Empire was still supposed to mean something to Edinburgh teachers, students, account managers, nurses, secretaries, and harassed mums with two squirmy kids under five all in the second decade of the twenty-first century. Then it was recommended to be actually *interesting* as well as informative and moral. Who would want to hear twenty minutes of Kant's *Critique of Pure Reason* on a Sunday morning? Or indeed at any time. So maybe a bit of humour as well – but surely not stand-up. Finally, something that actually might prove a bit of help on Monday morning as well in the face of dreary repetition, deadlines, slimy bosses, and sweaty colleagues. Probably pompous to call it wisdom but the aim was somewhere in that ballpark. Some little pearl that might make a difference to somebody's chaotic universe. And this week we're up to Luke 10. What on earth could be said about the Good Samaritan that hadn't been trotted out a thousand times before? And probably there'd be those present who'd heard it a hundred times.

He dropped his pen again, got up, and went through to the tiny kitchen, blowing fog in the freezing air. He'd forgive an interruption now if it was somebody from Scottish Gas to turn the heating on. He filled the kettle, then a hot water bottle, and made a pot of Russian Caravan tea – a small though rather expensive treat from Whittard's on Princes Street. He took a sip, breathing in the smell of bonfires on the Silk Road, and shuffled back through. So where were we?

The ancient, burned, chipped, battle-scarred antique that was more or less a desk had an A4 notepad on it, a couple of Bible translations, the one commentary he'd been able to find in the mess, and a single framed photo. It was the girl in the raspberry beret. His favourite – photo and girl. She was sitting at a table in the Plaza Mayor, a glass of Rioja or Ribera in front of her and a Zara bag propped up alongside. She was holding up a new silk scarf and looking as pleased as if she'd just been voted cutest in Madrid. Actually not an altogether unlikely event. A busking jazz quartet was frozen in the background, their double bass player the size of a prize fighter grinning at a tiny trumpeter whose cheeks looked like they were about to pop. They seemed to be playing just to each other, the mixed crowd of Madrileño natives and tourists milling around behind just a good excuse, not really part of the joke. Behind their heads the murals round the square were vague splashes of earth colours: orange, red ochre, and shades of beige. A line of dark rooftops was sharp against a firmament of solid blue. The girl in the raspberry beret was grinning as well and he knew the cameraman was grinning too. Himself. Everyone was grinning as if they'd put something in the water that day. Then another cliché came to mind: *if I'd known then what I know now...*

The harsh clanging of the doorbell broke into his thoughts but this time he welcomed it.

"Southside Seconds, mate. For..." the delivery man pulled a pink flimsy chit out of his top pocket and peered at the address. "Eh... Reverend David Hidalgo." He looked up. "That you then?"

Together they hauled, slid, walked, and carried a sofa, two armchairs, bookcase, standard lamp, and wall unit up the stairs and into whichever room they were destined for. Then some individual boxes with pots and frying pans, Pyrex dishes, an old brass candlestick, a set of chipped wally dugs, picture frames, and a white china chamber pot.

"House clearance," the driver said. "Never know what you're gonna get. I can keep some o' that if ye want. Somebody's dead granny must've liked it 'n' tha' but that disnae mean you huvtae."

"Right," said David. "We're not quite in the land of chamber pots yet." So half of the last box box was sorted out and repacked.

"Ok." The process complete, the driver fished out his chit again and scanned down it, leaning on the door jamb. "Two hundred and fifteen, seventy five. Cash on delivery." He didn't offer to let David check it and stood waiting.

"Right. I wasn't actually expecting you'd need paid right away..."

"Naw? Well that's how it works. That's how we keep the prices down. Ah telt the wife tha' phoned." Just then a commanding Morningside voice well used to tradesmen and the like echoed up the stairs.

"Driver! Just a minute. I'm coming right up."

"Short shrift" was the phrase that came to David's mind over the next few minutes as the awesome Mrs Marjorie MacInnes swiftly and efficiently dealt with items that had never been ordered ("That's not ours; nor that one"), some that were but proved unacceptable ("I don't care if it is second hand. There's good second hand and bad. This is not fit for sale"), some that had been ordered but hadn't appeared ("Monday morning. First thing. I'll be here"), and a few extra items that were clearly needed though not on the list ("And a decent chest of drawers if you've got one. Good condition now. And no more than twenty pounds"). Then a carefully counted out pile of tenners and some change out of a stout, serviceable handbag that would probably have survived trench warfare. No wonder she dealt with church finances with such ruthless efficiency. But in that case the aim was keeping the lights on, a decent Christmas for struggling families, some of the more expensive books for penniless students, and above all proper care of the pastor. So once Southside Seconds had been packed off with a flea in their ear and she'd apologized for the third time for arriving a bit late in the middle of a potentially awkward situation, she took an unbidden tour of the flat, shaking her head and tutting in every room.

"Señor David, I am so embarrassed." The nickname had been given by some of the church teenagers and seemed to have stuck even among the adults. "When we signed the lease I was promised all this would have been taken care of – the heating, decent crockery, the phone, furniture, bookshelves. None of it done. I'm so sorry."

"Well, I'm sure we can get things sorted out. At least one warm room would be good though." However, Mrs MacInnes was not in the soft soap business.

"Very kind of you to put it like that but nevertheless… I'll get on to the powers that be and we'll get things knocked into shape. Never you worry." David thought he wouldn't care to be among the powers that be. "And in the meantime, you can't possibly work in *this*." She glanced around with obvious distaste and gave a shiver, whether from cold or an allergic response. "So what I suggest is you take yourself off and have a nice lunch somewhere. Then with a bit of luck – or should I say God willing – we'll have things sorted by the end of the day." Five crisp fivers were thrust into his hand – he felt like a twelve-year-old sent off to the pictures to let Mum get on with the spring cleaning – but he was grateful. "I recommend the restaurant at Jenners. Not particularly cheap of course but quality and good-sized portions. Or John Lewis of course. Anyway, what am I saying? You know Edinburgh as well as I do and you'd probably want something a bit more... well... exotic, I suppose."

"No. Not at all. I'm sure either of these would be fine. Anywhere with the heating on." They shared a companionable smile.

"Right. Off you go. Leave it to me. After everything that's happened you surely deserve a warm house at least."

Up to that point David had been feeling somewhat relieved and relaxed. Some movement on the heating, the prospect of a nicer lunch than he had been planning, and a more robust state of mind taking over on his behalf. Then that "everything that's happened" brought him back down to ground zero. It had certainly happened and it did seem to be "everything". Because of "everything that had happened" he now found himself in Edinburgh, not Madrid. Pastoring a congregation of sleepy conservatives instead of in the thick of it with people who really did need a higher power. And in the bitter damp east coast cold instead of winter sunshine and crisp clear days. Also, not to be forgotten, on his own. It was so much better not to think. To be distracted by a furniture delivery, a sermon outline, a kindly church treasurer or even lunch with the middle-income, middle-class, middle-aged ladies of Morningside or Corstorphine. It didn't really matter. It could have been fish and chips in the Rapido Fish Bar. Anything was better than the one thing that wouldn't go away.

Anyway, he had his marching orders so he climbed into an overcoat, screwed down a battered blue fedora, tucked in a faded grey scarf, and left Mrs MacInnes perched on the arm of a chair between the crates and cases deploying a very "Don't take that tone with me young man" approach to Scottish Gas Customer Services in Bangalore.

* * *

Even at 11.00 am there was still frost on the slopes of Bruntsfield Links as David headed briskly downhill, then over the Meadows, up through university land round George Square (nice to be here without an essay to write), then along Forest Road and up George IV Bridge. He paused for a minute to listen to Javier hooting and tooting his alto sax at the top of Cockburn Street, waited till the end of "Honeysuckle Rose", then dropped one of the fivers into the makeshift collecting case.

"Hey. Muchas Gracias man! Qué tal David?"

"Bien. Surviving. And you – still making a living?"

"Yeah, well, you know what it's like. I'd rather be back in Bogota but at least here the dealers don't hold you to ransom in the street." Javier stamped his feet, blew into his cupped hands, and shivered from head to toe.

"Sure. I guess they're here though. Just maybe not so obvious."

"I know. I try to keep out of their way and hope nobody from the Medellin Cartel comes to the Edinburgh Military Tattoo on their holidays."

"Ok. Take it easy. Buy some gloves. Your hands must be freezing."

And so down the hill, over Market Street, along Waverley Bridge, sidestepping queues for the next open top tour and the lone piper mournfully screwing out the "Flowers of the Forest", then a left onto Princes Street, past Thunderbird Three cunningly disguised as the Scott Monument, and finally to the doorstep of Jenners. He pushed open the heavy swing door, took in the number of people, the perfume-saturated air, a Dante-esque vision of chrome, glass, glaring lights and assistants who didn't consider too much make-up a possibility, then fled to a hot dog street seller across the street and a park bench in the gardens.

It took at least ten minutes till his heart rate dropped back to normal and he was breathing calmly again. Just when he had thought he might be on what they called the road to recovery his autonomic system coughed politely and informed him that as yet nothing had changed. So he tried to clear his mind and think positive, calming thoughts instead of – well, just instead. But it turns out this is another of these little things you have as much control over as your thumbprint or blood group. Distraction, like beer, proves to be only a temporary solution, and just when you drop your guard for an instant Reality jumps up and gets a grip like White Fang. This wasn't where he was supposed to be and this wasn't what he was supposed to be doing. "Let's go round again" the Average White Band used to sing the last time he lived in Edinburgh. A nice trick if you can master it, but not so easy in your fifties as when you're twenty-two.

He dropped some crumbs of stale burger bun for the squirrels and watched them squabbling with some starlings for the biggest share. A couple of Goths wandered by snacking on each other. Appropriate for vampires somehow. Winter was a lean time for everyone around here; you had to take what you could get. And here he was, getting what he could like the rest. The people he should have been with and who maybe needed his help were two thousand miles away. But what help could he be in this condition anyway?

So he'd taken up the invitation from an old Madrid amigo now running his own restaurant in Edinburgh to come back home. "You can help with the church for a bit," Juan had said. "You'll feel at home. And you can eat with us for free. Just till you get back on your feet. The church can probably pay you a little. Maybe some Spanish teaching for the rest. We need a pastor. You need a break. Think it over." So he did, and for lack of a better offer packed what he could, sold or gave away the rest, politely declined any public send-off, handed back his library books, chopped up his Caja Madrid cards and caught an EasyJet to Edinburgh. Juan met him at the airport and took him home. The next day they met Mrs MacInnes at the church building on South Clerk Street, dealt with what she called "the practicals", then went for coffee. She was well briefed and avoided any reference to "unfortunate events" though she did find it difficult not to want to take him home and feed him up on some wholesome Scottish home cooking, Morningside's answer to all difficulties moral, physical, emotional, and spiritual.

Next day they went looking for flats and found 112A Bruntsfield Place, a nice flat in a nice area full of nice shops and nice open spaces. Very nice if you're feeling nice. It didn't take much effort to carry a couple of cases in and arrange for the transport company to ship the rest. So that was that. He met the leadership of Southside Christian Fellowship, such as it was, then spoke the next Sunday morning and stayed for a cup of tea to meet the congregation. "Say something Spanish," Trevor, the precocious eight-year-old, asked him. So he did. Not all the questions were as easy to field but Mrs MacInnes had it covered. Nobody asked why he'd left Madrid. Nobody referred to his previous church. Nobody asked about young people and drugs. Nobody mentioned inner city violence. And particularly, nobody mentioned the girl in the raspberry beret. It was as good as he could have hoped and not so bad as he had expected. If that's not a tautology. Now after two weeks with Juan and his wife Alicia he was ready for his own space even if it was filled with ghosts. If he could just get that confounded heating turned on.

Chapter 2

LA MOVIDA MADRILEÑA

It had happened at last: the day everyone knew in theory must come but, like Christmas for five-years-olds, just never seemed to arrive. Now, finally, Francisco Franco Bahamonde, victor of the Civil War and dictator for thirty-six years, had made his final exit. Wonderful wasn't the word; unbelievable more like. There should have been dancing in the streets but everyone was still too uncertain of what might come next. When Juan Carlos, son of the passed-over monarch, arrived he did what few had expected and oversaw the new constitution, new elections, new civic freedoms and resisted the attempted coup. So maybe a little dancing in the streets might be in order after all.

David Hidalgo, aged twenty-two, stepped out of the Iberian Airways DC10 into blazing sunshine and contemplated Spain in 1980 – a country he had never lived in, that his father had had to flee from, that he had experienced only from holidays with his grandparents in Galicia – and knew he had come home. First on the agenda was renewing some old family connections in the posh Salamanca district of Madrid to get him settled into society then a well-furnished *piso* that wasn't too expensive, in up and coming Santa Eugenia. Next a pretty reasonable job thanks to honours in International Business from Edinburgh University, not to mention fluent English and the all-important *enchufe*, literally connections like a plug in a socket, but in practical terms that inextricable tangle of interrelatedness that Spanish society runs on. So with a place of his own, enough traction to make ends meet, and a couple of supportive relatives, the next-level priorities weren't too hard to work out: a cool car – anything other than a SEAT please; a sharp suit from *El*

Corte Ingles, and lots and lots of sex. Nineteen-eighties Spain was good to go on all three.

La Movida Madrileña. A movement but also literally meaning *movement.* Suddenly all the sweets in the shop were out on the street. Like children starved of fun for thirty-five years – which is more or less what they were – Spaniards were determined to cram as much in their mouths as they could and worry about the stomach ache later. New music, new movies, new morals. Contraception was in and Catholicism out. David got himself into a band doing covers of the Pistols and the Damned, translated Leonard Cohen for his friends, and drove to Segovia or Avila at the weekends to chill out with some *amigos* and *amigas* on Rioja and reefers. Perfect.

As a Scottish Spaniard with fluent English and cool credentials (his journalist *Papa* had fled Spain to avoid the likelihood of bullets in the back), David Hidalgo was an interesting animal in the *Movida* world. Riding on his credentials and a naturally sociable personality, he gained entry to artistic circles, rubbing shoulders with the young Almodevar and Moltalbán. More importantly that introduced him to Alicia (very nice), Sara (friendly but a bit possessive), Bea (small but *perfectly* formed), Mayte (argumentative but eventually worth the effort), and even Kurt from Hamburg (turned out to be not his thing at all). But for some reason he never seemed to make the headway he hoped for, indeed almost felt entitled to, with Rocío.

Rocío. The dew. Fresh, funny, sparky, creative, completely unpredictable, full of crazy ideas. Tango in the Plaza Mayor at 3.00 a.m. *Let's sleep overnight in the Prado. It's easy. You can sneak in, hide in the toilets, then sit staring at Zurbaran's St Peter being crucified upside down without the crowds. Why not? Come on!* Diminutive but seemed to fill the room. She certainly filled his imagination. Even when honestly trying to concentrate on Alicia, Sara, Bea or some other beautiful body he would open his eyes and be disappointed for an instant that the face below him did not have Rocío's short chestnut hair, dark eyes, pale skin, and a look that always seemed to say, *if you hold still long enough I'm going to burst that bubble.* Despite the Spanish genes he was Scottish enough to know this was extremely bad manners. But she managed to twist and turn out of every attempt to box her in. He knew – or thought he knew – that she liked him well enough. And God knew she wasn't a virgin. So, c'mon then. Why not? What's so precious? It's only sex. But Rocío didn't do casual. She'd been with Roberto for two years before concluding he wasn't playing for keeps so pushed him out firmly and politely. Roberto cried on David's shoulder while David said comforting words and tried to keep a note of celebration out of his voice. That would also have been bad manners. But it made no difference. With Roberto or without him Rocío wasn't interested. No, actually not that. She *was* interested. They went to the movies, cruised Recoletos for the best tapas, wandered up the hills of Casa del Campo, but that was definitively, pointedly, as far as it went.

"What is *wrong* with me?" he finally asked her in exasperation after she'd turned him down yet again.

"What do you think's wrong with you?" she fired back, twinkling with amusement.

"Well – nothing I can think of."

"There you are then."

He pondered this for the rest of that night and three days following till they met again.

"And what's wrong with that?"

"David," she said, addressing a nice but not terribly bright *adolescente*. "I'm waiting for you. I really am. You're just not ready yet."

He took umbrage at that. He absolutely was ready. He was so ready he couldn't sleep at night. What was she on about? It was infuriating. He wanted her, though better to say, wanted to be *with* her, not *have* her. To be together, not take possession. To move into her orbit, not capture her into his. But all to no avail. She said she was waiting. Well, waiting for what? For when? How could he know? *Madre mia! Tela marinera!*

Three years later he found out. Alicia, Bea, Carmen, and the others had all come and gone. He'd left the band. Somehow he'd come to prefer cooking to carnality – how did that happen? – and went to Toledo to stare at the cathedral ceiling instead of lying stoned on the opposite hill watching the skyline transform into what El Greco saw. Rocío was still friends with everyone but belonged to no one. She was funnier, sharper, less forgiving of hypocrisy, but also quicker to forgive and comfort than anyone. Then, when he wasn't looking, had almost forgotten their enigmatic conversation and was focused on just being friends, she bought him a beer one night.

"Now you're ready," she said.

"Sorry?" He thought she was for moving on to another bar.

"You heard. You're ready. It's time."

"What?"

"Get your coat. I'll show you." So they left early, went to her place, and made love till the night owls could be heard coming home and the early birds were just getting up.

David left Sta. Eugenia like a young offender on early release and moved into Rocío's place in Chamartin. It was like *El Dorado*, the place of gold, where they lived, loved, laughed, cooked, cuddled up, dreamed, confessed all, and forgave all. Each one with the *otra mitad de la naranga* – the other half of their orange.

But there was a serpent in paradise.

"Hey David," she said one night in the afterglow while they were listening to Stan Getz and sitting up in bed with a glass of Ribera del Duero. "Do you think you might like to try a change of name?"

"What? You think I look more like an Alfonso or Pablo? What's wrong with David anyway?"

"Nothing. But you're partly there. It does begin with a P."

"Eh? So, Paco, Pedro, Patricio, Paulo, what?"

"Actually, I was thinking of Papa…"

In a moment of extreme surprise he reverted to the Midlothian patois, "Stone the crows! Magic!"

So there were baby clothes, decoration schemes, lists of names, visits to the family to share the good news – hers in Jaen, his now in Malaga after years of freezing Edinburgh. So normal, so natural – almost inevitable but wonderful too. *Papa*. He definitely liked the sound of that. That would complete his growing up and give him a reason to go back to the beach.

Then one day a bump in the road that wasn't meant to be.

"David. I think we need to get to the *Centro de Salud*. Now."

Apparently a bit of bleeding at twelve weeks isn't too uncommon. But a bit is different from a lot. Then there were the stomach cramps and sickness. The next visit to the *Centro de Salud* became a blue light run to the hospital at *Ramon y Cajal*. Medication and comforting words, then a surgeon in scrubs who told them the worst before shooting off for lunch.

"No reason not to try again, though," he added on the way out the door. "It's not that uncommon."

So they did.

How many times can a young woman miscarry before losing hope entirely? In her case it was six. She would sit for hours staring at nothing – ignoring questions, not eating, not sleeping. The twinkle was dying.

He never did find out what made him leave work early that day. There was plenty of paperwork to do, customers who could do with a call. For no reason at all he just decided he'd had enough, flipped his filofax shut, told Monica to take messages instead of calling him, and wandered out into the car park. On the Chamartin doorstep he spent almost a full minute fiddling with the lock. *Got to get that changed; one of these days it won't work at all.* A bag of groceries was threatening to tumble out of his other hand. Maybe something tasty could tempt her. On the other side of the door something clattered. Then whimpering like a puppy and some kind of scratching and banging. At last the key connected. Phew. A surprise lunch then maybe off for Cuenca to see the *Casas Calgadas*. A night in the Parador was always special. Something. Anything.

There, in the middle of the hall, suspended from the ceiling, she hung, slowly turning like a Christmas decoration.

"You're a very lucky man," the doctor in *Urgencias* told him. It didn't feel that way. Rocío was in a hospital gown with drips in, oxygen attached, and dressings round her neck. She wouldn't look at him. No point in asking why. The next day he took her home, saw her into bed, then went out and bought a bottle of vodka. They passed the next couple of weeks in a fog like strangers too frightened to talk, as if that would set off the bomb under the bedroom floor. There was nothing to say that wasn't a meaningless pleasantry, the spark between them as dead as the *Reyes Catolicos* Isabel and Fernando but no Columbus coming to bring them to a new-found land.

"So what do you want to do?" he asked one Saturday afternoon without enthusiasm. "Shopping? Drive somewhere? Your brother's?"

She shook her head.

"Well, I'm not sitting here waiting for something to change," he said. "I'll see you some time." He picked up his car keys and jacket.

"David…" she stopped him as he was heading for the door. "It's not fair."

"I know." He sighed. "We've been through all that. Life's not fair. You can move on or not. You have to choose. I can't do it for you."

"That's not what I mean… It's not fair you should come home every day and not know what you'll find. I'm going back to Jaen. I'll stay with Mum for a bit. Look for work. You can have the house. Bring Bea here if you like. I don't care. I'm sorry." Her eyes were bright but she was cold and totally calm.

Well, if she thought he was going to beg her to change her mind she was wrong. He'd done everything he could. Comforted, consoled, cajoled, flattered, pampered, jollied her along, joked when he didn't feel like it, persuaded, raged, waited, hoped. Now there wasn't anything left in the tank. *So go to Jaen. What do I care?*

They tell you not to let the sun go down on your wrath, David thought on the way down to the *plaza de garaje*, but they don't tell you what happens if you do. Now he knew. It's actually no different to the sun going down on your barbecue. It gets cold. The pain inside turns to anger then grows cold and bitter. He flicked the central locking on the new BMW the company had just bought him, which he thought he'd enjoy but wasn't nearly as much fun as he'd expected.

"*Hasta cuando* – see you whenever," he said to nobody and got in.

The *Sierra de Guadarama* circles the north of Madrid like a grandstand overlooking the drama of the city. *Sierra* means "saw" and that's what it is: jagged and uncompromising. He drove up into the falling dusk as, one by one, the *pueblos* below lit up, mirroring the stars. The smell of the pines filtered into the quiet and comfortable cabin. Cries of the midnight birds could just be heard along with the cicadas, backing track to the night. It was a steep drive with lots of turns. He had to concentrate. A load of timber coming the other way round one of the hairpins could mess things up quite a lot. Well, maybe not. How much more messed up could it get? Like the good atheist he was, he was seething with an infinite rage against no one in particular. God was still a living and useful part of the Spanish language. *Dios mio. Gracias a Dios. Si Dios quiere.* But anything more than that seemed to be expiring from the culture like the last breath of a corpse. Now who was there left to scream at?

Higher and higher he drove, the night a field of dark velvet with stars like diamonds on a jeweller's cloth. He reached the summit. Somehow it seemed too final to continue driving, plunging down the road on the other side as if he really wasn't coming back, so he simply pulled onto the viewpoint, switched off the engine, got out, and looked out over the valley to the city beyond.

Madrid – an idea as much as a city. In the past an idea of monarchy, then ruthless repression under Franco. Now almost overnight it had become a city of excess, with heroin and herpes running rampant. Somehow David had always managed to keep one step ahead, maybe because he knew he was waiting for something better. Rocío had said she was waiting for him but maybe he was waiting for her as well. Now they both seemed equally damned.

He picked up a stone, weighed it, and hefted it into the night, not caring where it landed. He stood up and shouted into the black, then sat back down and wept. No one either shouted or whispered back.

Why should they? There was nothing out there. Finally, the storm blew itself out and he started talking into the darkness.

"So just to be clear, I don't believe in you. Whoever you are. Wherever. Whatever. I don't believe in you and I don't expect anything... But just in case. Can't you see we're dying? You're supposed to be the lender of last resort. Is there anything left for us? If not for me, then for her? She's the good one. You know that. She does not deserve this. No way. So if there is anything there. Just for her. A miracle would be nice."

Suddenly, breaking into the silence there was a screeching of brakes and tyres and a bang that shook the trees. He turned round to see a Fiat 500 half on its side, wheels still spinning, half on top of the boot of his beloved BMW.

Fantastic, he thought, absolutely perfect. That's what you get for trying to converse with the universe. He covered the 50 metres to the tangled mess in a few seconds and jumped up onto the side of the Fiat. The interior light was on. That meant electricity. He could smell the gasoline already. It looked like an elderly man with neat grey hair and a suit was slumped on the side of the compartment. The door came open easily enough but unless he was careful the car would tumble onto its roof, pinning him underneath as well. The old man groaned.

"Oh. I'm so sorry. So sorry. Can you help me? Can you... oh..."

"Of course. You'll be fine. It's ok. How do you feel?"

"Ay, ay, ay... not so good..."

"Can you move? Can you move your legs?"

"Yes. Yes, I think so."

"Ok. So long as you can move we'll get you out." David pinned the door back and stepped down with one foot on the steering column. He caught the old man by the lapels. He was surprisingly light. Together they did a half turn that would have looked good on the dance floor till the old man got his legs under him against the driver's door. He slowly stood up, head level with the sill.

"Here. Foot against the edge. That's fine. Now push. Ok. Up now. Hold my arm. That's good. Take it easy. Now sit on the edge."

It took a couple of minutes but felt like an hour, the vapour of spilling petrol growing stronger by the second. David jumped down, then helped the older man slide down the coachwork onto the ground.

David walked him over to a rock some way away and sat him down, and then, aware of a now almost overpowering smell of fuel, ran back to his own car. It was probably not the smartest thing to do but before he knew it he had turned the ignition, slipped it into "drive" and pulled forwards to the sound of tearing, shearing metal. He left the car 50 metres away then jogged back to the old man. Just then night became day with a whoosh as the Fiat transformed into a bonfire, bits of debris pinging into the trees. David instinctively hit the ground while the old man was blown off his perch. *Fiat Lux.* Let there be light.

It all turned out to be mainly cuts and bruises, a twisted ankle and shock. The old man wouldn't stop saying sorry which David found almost as annoying as the damage to his car. He wet a handkerchief from his windscreen wash and dabbed the old man's forehead and cheeks in the light of the Fiat's blazing remains, pulled at his tie, and loosened his shoes. By then a couple of other cars had stopped. A retired football physio gave the old man a quick check over and pronounced no broken bones. Still, you need to get to *Urgencias*, he suggested.

"Just where we're going," David agreed. "Ok," he continued, crouching down in front of his new responsibility, "having saved your life, maybe I should know your name."

"I'm so sorry, I…"

"And stop saying that. I'm David Hidalgo. You are…?"

"Francisco. Francisco Garcia Morales. At your service, Señor."

"And at yours – as we've already seen. Francisco or Paco?"

"Well, Paco to my friends. Paco."

"Ok then, I guess it's *Urgencias*. Where do you live?"

"Congosto. Madrid. Villa de Vallecas. I was on my way home."

"Ok. I know it. I have a place in Sta. Eugenia."

"Ah. Very nice."

An hour later, after a phone call to police, they were in the waiting room in Calle Sierra Gador watched over by a sleepy receptionist in a dirty white coat.

"Yes?"

They were pointed to another row of seats. As they sat Paco squinted round.

"David Hidalgo," he said quietly.

"Correct."

"David Hidalgo Rodriguez – *Rodriguez* for your grandfather, because your mother isn't Spanish. Father: *Ricardo Hidalgo Espina*. Mother: *Helen*. I'm sorry, I forget her Scottish family name. Yes. It's you. You have your father's eyebrows, you know."

Chapter 3

BUCCLEUCH

The heavy door of the common close slammed hard as David stepped out onto Bruntsfield Place, the sky thick and dark almost to the point of deep purple. Snow was on its way. Shoppers bustled along, muffled against the wind, not wasting time. The bus queue stamped, shivered, and moaned about the cold, the late buses, the chance of a heavy fall. Everyone seemed to have ice in their bones. For some inexplicable reason however David felt a lightening in his spirits, even a sense of elation. The heating was more or less on upstairs. Everything had finally arrived from Madrid and he'd unpacked most of it – at least the important stuff – pots and pans, books and music. Now he could listen to the lyrical Chet Baker over breakfast in a warm kitchen, as he'd been doing for almost thirty years. And there were compensations: the Edinburgh skyline, the maroon liveried buses, even the penetrating east coast wind – they all took him back to his youth, before what everyone around him referred to euphemistically (but never in his hearing) as "recent events". They call the seventies the decade that fashion forgot but it wasn't all bad. Back then things seemed more reliable somehow, whether it was leaving your bike out or having a family around you. Or maybe that was just his experience and his memory. Nowadays it felt like he'd been mugged and every item of value taken. He was like the bewildered American tourists deftly relieved of their wallets in the Puerta del Sol, blinking, groping and looking round in disbelief.

Anyway here, back home in Edinburgh, there was still some memory of who he used to be resurrected out of the mists. And still a few things he could do. Looking after the spiritual welfare of a clutch of respectable Caledonian nonconformists surely wouldn't be too taxing. Some Spanish teaching to pay the bills. That was something he'd always enjoyed – but not high school pupils cramming for exams they didn't want to sit and would instantly forget. This was sharing something you'd discovered with others who wanted to discover it too. He turned up his collar, tucked in his scarf, pulled on a pair of brown leather gloves, screwed his battered fedora down a bit tighter, and headed off down the hill.

Today was Friday. Mondays, Wednesdays, and Fridays from five to six-thirty was Spanish conversation. He might have eighteen-year-olds struggling with first-year degree exams, or ladies from Colinton Mains planning a holiday in the sun. He didn't mind. He still loved the language, the culture, the music, the food, the climate, the people. It was like popping open your favourite bottle of wine and sharing it round. Today would be a new group, though, which added some interest. Diligent students or lazy ones? Engaging people or boring ones? Those he would learn as much from in other ways or those that made you feel like you were tipping the beauties of the language of Cervantes or Lope de Vega into a bucket of sludge? He'd soon find out.

He strode past puffing and shivering shoppers. Down Bruntsfield Links by the Chinese restaurants and charity shops towards the Barclay Church with the spire about to head off into orbit. Along Melville Drive, up Middle Meadow Walk, leaving the clogged up arteries of teatime traffic behind, as the first few flakes of snow began to swirl through the branches of the cherry trees. Finally, skirting the back of where the old Royal Infirmary used to be – now studio flats, bistros, and upwardly mobile youngsters – then onto the old Edinburgh cobbles of Buccleuch Place.

Buccleuch was a street with two faces. On the left, the modern ugliness of George Square university buildings; on the right, the fantastic towering old tenements, bought over in the fifties and now a labyrinth of tutors' rooms and seminar spaces. Filthy and crumbling outside, but inside narrow, winding stairs spiralled up to high-ceilinged rooms with deep skirting boards and intricate plasterwork cornices. They reverberated with generations of teachers, learners, brilliant academics, dull nonentities, enraged anarchists, bored middle-class Oxbridge rejects, and ordinary kids just trying to pass their exams. The ghosts of the bright, the enthusiastic, the naive, and the impressionable mingled with those of lecherous, ageing, beery tutors and readers. All, in fact, exactly as it should be. David puffed up to the top floor flat of number 17 and knew – despite how it had all happened – this was where he was meant to be right now, and at least for this instant he was content.

About a dozen had gathered already – hairstyles, dress codes, backgrounds, and abilities as widely mixed as he'd expected. The largest group were upper teens and twenties – the struggling students. Then a gap up to the over-fifties. Apparently only one in between. She looked thirties or maybe more and sat slightly apart in a middle row next to the wall. She was undoing the ties of a black velvet cape and taking off a matching floppy hat with flakes of snow still clinging to it. Jet black hair framed a pale elfin face. She smiled as he glanced around, and mouthed a silent "Hi". He nodded self-consciously, cleared his throat, and took in the rest of the scene.

"Good evening everyone. Looks like that's all of us. *Buenas tardes.* Welcome to Spanish conversation. I'm David Hidalgo." He wrote it up on an ancient chalkboard, then turned back, scanning round for hints of interest and enthusiasm. "Spanish is a fantastic and a very romantic language – *es un idioma estupendo y muy romantico* – I hope we can enjoy it together. Could you all just put your names on the list while we do some introductions?" He handed out a clipboard and nodded towards an elderly gent at the back to start the ball rolling. Most were as he'd expected, but halfway round he became dimly aware of only partly listening as contributions drew nearer to the girl with the velvet cape. Finally her turn came.

"Hi. *Buenas tardes* everyone." It was a soft Scottish voice, cultured but not highbrow. She hooked a long strand of dark hair behind one ear and looked round with an expression of openness and warmth. Despite himself he found it completely engaging. "I'm Gillian Lockhart. I teach in the Scots Language Department. I've got some family connections with the Basque region near San

Sebastian." David turned and wrote "*Pais Vasco*" on the board. "I've been dabbling a bit for a few years but I'd like to improve and make myself better understood."

David nodded. "*Gracias, Señorita.* To 'improve' in Spanish depends on what you're improving. For most activities it's '*mejorar*'." He wrote it up. "Literally – to make better – but for language study we use '*perfeccionar*'. So," he turned back to Gillian, "*I would like to improve my Spanish* would be…"

"*Quiero… perfeccionar… mi Español…?*"

"*Absolutamente. Perfecto.*"

The next hour followed the usual first night routine gauging levels of ability, picking up points of interest, and scrawling up some vocabulary. One or two, he reckoned, should definitely be coaxed in the direction of a beginner's group but most seemed up to it. Mrs McGregor in the fur coat wanted vocabulary for foodstuffs and cooking. Baz in the Caftan needed guidance on prepositions. Julie, halfway through first year Spanish, had a note of incipient despair in her voice when David asked how she was doing.

"*¿Y qué te resulta mas difícil?*"

She stared out of the window towards David Hume Tower where Spanish lectures took place – apparently a scene of both terror and torment.

"*Todo,*" she replied miserably. "Everything…"

"Well… *bien*…" He tried to sound encouraging. "I'm sure we can do something about that…" Julie didn't look convinced. Her expression of misery only deepened. She seemed close to tears.

"I'm sorry," she muttered. "I just can't keep up." She paused, then seemed to gather courage till it all came out in a flood. "I can read ok and… and… more or less say what I want… but I just can't understand a word anyone says to me. So I can't follow the lectures, I've got no idea about the grammar. I… I… I don't know what to do…" Then, to everyone's surprise and embarrassment, young Julie completely lost it, buried her face in her hands, and sobbed. There was a stricken silence. For two or three seconds nobody moved – least of all David, who seemed struck dumb and rooted to the spot.

Suddenly Gillian – now with the cape draped over the back of her chair – got up, slid out past a row of stunned Morningside matrons, glanced slightly reproachfully at David, gathered up the stricken Julie and got her out the door, all in a matter of seconds.

"Yes… well… ok…" David stammered. "*Bueno*… Eh… someone was having problems with *por* and *para*? Baz?" He turned and started studiously listing various uses and meanings while everyone did their best to pretend that nothing had happened. A few minutes later, just as he was pointing out *por aquí* as an exceptional use meaning "around here", Gillian came back in.

"She had to go," she whispered and slid back into her place. The rest of the time was taken up with an activity based on "what would you do if…?" till finally a clock chimed outside and David looked at his watch. Six thirty. Not a moment too soon.

He wiped the chalkboard clean, as students gathered up their papers, chatting loudly in the release of tension. He sensed someone behind him and turned. Gillian had paused with the cloak slung loosely round her shoulders and the floppy hat in hand.

"I managed to get her calmed down. Poor thing. She's at her wit's end. I get students like that sometimes. She really is about to pack it in. I can tell. I don't suppose there's anything else you could suggest? She told me if she can't get past this term she's going back to Cupar to work in Boots the Chemist. What a fate." They smiled as David paused, wondering if there actually was anything that might keep Julie out of the High Street pharmacy.

"Actually, I think I do know something that might help. I'm in touch with some Spanish people in town. My friend Juan's wife Alicia is a really clear speaker. Maybe she'd be willing to help – just informally." Gillian's face lit up and seemed to David to light the whole room.

"That would be good. The sooner the better though. She's definitely on the ropes. She's probably away back to Halls to worry all night."

"Or the Union to blank it out."

"Sure – more likely. So how soon could you set something up?"

"*Pronto. No hay problema.* I'm going to see them now actually. Juan runs the Hacienda restaurant. I quite often eat there after classes."

"Hacienda? South Clerk Street?"

"Sure. Do you know it?"

"I love it – I've been with friends a few times."

"Well – em..." He was about to plunge ahead then stopped himself. Then started and stopped again. There was a second embarrassed pause of the evening. Then, as if it were someone else speaking, he heard himself say, "If you haven't eaten... would you like to meet Juan and Alicia?" *How had that happened?*

Equally against the odds, the girl in the velvet cape didn't seem surprised or hostile.

"*¡Como no!*" she said. "Why not!"

The air outside was freezing and a chilly draught blew round the half-open door but this time he didn't notice it.

"*Muy Bien.*"

Chapter 4

VALLECAS

"What are you talking about?"

David Hidalgo spun round to examine the old man more closely. In the frenzied moments spent pulling him from the wreckage of his car, then driving the hour or so into Madrid, and now checking in at health centre reception, he hadn't really taken much notice. Another casualty. Another pain in the neck sent to make his life more complicated. Now the old man – Paco – claimed to know who he was, to know his father and mother plus whatever else. David took a closer look. For starters he wasn't even that old, maybe mid to late sixties. A bit thin on top with long strands of steely grey hair carefully folded round and grimly holding on despite the events of the night. A light complexion and a squarish face with thick, dark-rimmed, bottle-top glasses. The overall effect was distinctly owlish. Collar and tie had both seen better days but were neat apart from a few spots of blood. *Dapper*, David would have said in English. *Elegante* or *sofisticado* didn't quite have the same nuance. Dapper, owlish, and surprising.

"You knew my father?"

"Well, probably I still know him unless something's happened since last Thursday."

"Sorry." David shook his head. "This is getting a bit weird. You saw my father last Thursday?"

"It might have been Friday. Normally near the weekend but never on Saturdays. That's my preparation day and Sundays I work."

David glanced around looking for some fixed point of reference. He tried again.

"You know my father."

"Yes, I think we've established that. You're a lot like him but maybe not so quick on the uptake."

David frowned.

"I think I'm entitled to an explanation before you start insulting me."

"Of course. I do apologize. That was quite unfair. You've had a rough night... and a rough few months I gather."

"Let's leave my private life out of it, shall we? How do you know my father? We'll start with that."

"By all means." The old man was enjoying himself now, pulling rabbits out of a hat. "We studied politics and philosophy together at Complutense in the fifties."

"Now you're wrong. My father never studied at Complutense. He went to Alcalá de Henares."

"Ah yes, that's what he liked to say." Paco chuckled, enjoying himself immensely, not suffering from shock as he should have been. "You know Complutense was founded in Alcalá by Cardinal Cisneros. *Complutum* – that's just the Latin name for Alcalá. Your father was born in Alcalá – you know that of course. He always resented the fact that the university had been moved to Madrid so he used to call Complutense the real Alcalá University. It was his joke. Though maybe right and proper too."

"And you've kept in touch all these years?"

"Off and on. We were closest at university. Lost touch a bit when he had to make a run for it. I only visited Edinburgh the once when I happened to have a conference there. Now he's back from Scotland we meet up now and again. Last week I was in Malaga for a meeting. We had lunch together. Caught up a bit. He's quite worried about you, you know, but he wouldn't want to interfere." Paco gazed up at the dingy ceiling of peeling paint and drifted back through the years. "When your father was on the run from Franco for publishing something he probably shouldn't have he lived with Marisa and me for three months here in Vallecas. Oh, the arguments we had. Wonderful times."

"What did you argue about?"

"Everything really. Your father is an argumentative man. You know that, I suppose. But that's because of his principles. He was a free thinker. I like to think I am too but my thoughts took me in another direction."

"How so?"

"Look," Paco said, slowly standing up. "I'm feeling fine now. No broken bones. A bit shaken up but no worse than when *Raya Vallecano* lose to *Real*. Which is nearly every time. Let's get a drink. A little lubrication always helps big speaks. By the way, I must say I am very pleased to make your acquaintance – as a grown up that is. It's a few years now since I gave you your baby bottle!"

It was David more than Paco in shock now as they headed out into the balmy Madrileño night and pulled out a couple of chairs at the bar across the *Plaza*.

"So you and *Papa* were friends. You studied together. He went into journalism – what did you do?"

"Teaching."

"Teaching what?"

Paco switched effortlessly to perfect English with a slight 1950s Home Service accent.

"English is such a simple, direct language, don't you think?" David nearly choked on his San Miguel then smiled in spite of himself. Something about the older man was growing on him.

"Maidenhead for six months – Spanish teacher in a small secretarial college. Then Bournemouth for another six months. While I was safe on English soil your father was getting into more and more bother here."

"I know. He told me about those years. But he never mentioned you. Why not?"

Paco smiled again and took a sip of his Rioja. "I'm afraid we had what you would call a 'falling out'. Over ideas of course. Nothing personal. And temporary, I'm happy to say."

"What ideas?"

Paco paused before answering.

37

"David. You are a modern – even postmodern – man. You are not fooled by tradition and culture. You know the church here was hand-in-glove with Franco, sustaining the dictatorship. And before that propping up the aristocracy, maintaining the status quo – all that 'keep us in our proper stations' nonsense. Social order is not a bad thing, but when it's an unjust order then it is. Your father hated that. I did too. We rejected the faith of our fathers and mothers. It was natural for young men searching for a new way. So your father found Marx. I found another way. He didn't accept my choice as legitimate so we were never as close after that."

"But that's what I'm asking. What *was* your way?"

Paco took another sip and looked around him with interest at the few other drinkers, late night revellers just having one last drink on their way home, an elderly couple supporting each other out of the metro entrance.

"You'll forgive my hesitation. Prejudice is not a nice thing. We've had a lot of it in Spain. You think you're not prejudiced but when I tell you what I do you'll find out whether you are or not."

"Try me."

"Ok." Paco looked him straight in the eye with a hint of the hunting owl in his expression now. "I am the pastor of an *iglesia evangelica*. An evangelical church. It's just along the road, just past Congosto Metro."

"But you said you were a teacher?"

"I am. At the present Alcalá University."

"So you lecture in English?"

"Not as much as I used to. If you stop teaching and spend all your time on committees, they call you a professor. But I am also a pastor. That's my calling."

"So a Protestant?"

"*Si, claro*. But not just by designation – you know, what you have to put on the forms. It's my conviction. I believe it. I follow the founder."

"I see." David was thoughtful, taken aback in spite of his determination to be open-minded but also intrigued. "So I can see why you and Dad would fall out. He hates religion."

"Ah well. That's a misunderstanding, if you'll permit me. For me it's entirely relationship and nothing of religion." He drained his glass and set it down. "Anyway. Enough. We've had a taxing few hours. Both of us. If you would be good enough to run me home perhaps then you can get back to your own life. I'll call the insurance company in the morning. I owe you a debt of gratitude, *caballero*. I have no idea what happened on that bend. One minute singing along to Silvana Velasco then upside down with a briefcase on top of me. Pity. I was quite attached to that little Fiat."

David dropped Paco off in one of the maze of back streets behind Congosto, surprised to find a university professor living in such humble – not to say somewhat rough – surroundings.

"You're a lot like your father, though you maybe don't think so," Paco pronounced, holding the open car door.

"I *don't* think so," David replied with almost a laugh. "He was a campaigning journalist. Maybe you've heard? I sell whiskey and cheese to the middle classes."

"But you pulled me out of the wreck with petrol fumes all round. No thought of the risks. There might be some point of connection there, don't you think?"

David didn't argue but neither was he convinced. Political corruption and cottage cheese – not much obviously in common. Was his father disappointed? Probably, but then he had lost his cutting edge too now. He had partly chosen Malaga for the golf, for goodness sake.

Leaving Paco behind he threaded his way up ontó the A3 to Valencia in one direction or back to Madrid in the other. *Avenida Mediterránea*. Valencia was definitely tempting. Somewhere warmer in winter and cooler in summer. And more relaxing, less stressful than Madrid. Less fraught with nasty surprises. Suddenly, on the take off to the M40 ring road heading north towards Chamartin it struck him. For the first time in months he had spent a happy, engrossing couple of hours interested in someone else's problems rather than his own. Rocío and her constant cloud of sadness hadn't entered his mind. Was that a bad thing? He felt oddly revitalized from the evening. Paco was full of surprises. David had called out to the void for answers and heard nothing back – well, unless you counted a careless driver wrecking his nice new BMW as a transcendental response. But at least the Fiat 500 and its inattentive driver had taken his mind off things for a bit and that was worth something.

Ok. Deep breath now and back under the water. What would be behind the door this time? He almost hoped for nothing and no one. Cases packed and gone, maybe a note on the table. No more marriage – though they weren't even married. But no more madness either. What a relief. He could surely rebuild; he wasn't even thirty yet – plenty of time. What had happened to them was nobody's fault. Just one of those things. *Es lo que hay*, the wonderful, utilitarian Spanish expression there was no exact equivalent of in English. Literally, "it's what there is" but meaning more "that's the way it is" or "take it or leave it". An expression of Spanish stoicism born of centuries of decline and exploitation. When the landlord jacks up the rent, when your child dies of diphtheria, when your woman leaves you and goes back to her mother in Jaen or just when there's only hard, day-old bread left. *Es lo que hay*.

He parked the car and got into the lift, his stomach having that momentary sinking feeling on the way up, physical equivalent to his mental state. Keys in the lock. Fiddle and fumble. A turn and a push. Then a shout from the kitchen.

"Hi. You're back. Dinner's just ready. Chicken with paprika, your mum's recipe. Want to open the wine?"

Rocío didn't explain and David didn't enquire. They ate. She seemed relaxed and normal – or what used to pass for normality among normal people. Nowadays that made it *abnormal*. They washed up tiptoeing round, just chatting about nothing in particular. They were on their way to bed before David even thought to tell her about the accident and the ghost he'd met from a past he didn't know existed.

"He knows *Papa* and says he used to help feed me when we lived in Spain. Before we went to Edinburgh. How weird is that?"

"Sounds interesting. Can you introduce me?"

"Sure. Why not?" David thought for a moment. "Actually no – I don't know where he lives and I don't have a number. I just dropped him off in the street."

"But he told you he was the pastor of a church near Congosto."

"Right."

"So we'll go to his church."

"Ok." David shrugged. "No problem." How many weird events could happen in twenty-four hours? "You'll have to confess though. You know – 'no idols nor false gods'."

"I can add that to the rest."

The remainder of the week seemed to pass in a blur. An unspoken truce was characterized by ordinary things ordinary people do but that they hadn't done together for months. Shopping at the local Mercadona. A walk in the *Retiro*. Washing and ironing. Even sex for the first time in months. Afterwards David chatted about some new customers that might prove quite remunerative. She dropped into her office to talk about coming back to work and told him all the gossip. It was like a thousand tons of snow piled up at the head of the slope. Nobody speaking too loudly for fear of setting off the final vibration that would set everything careering down the hill destroying anyone in its path. But so long as it was staying where it was...

They decided to try to find Paço that Sunday evening and spotted the premises after a short search. The service seemed to have just got going as they tentatively edged in at the back. Thirty or so middle-aged and older Spaniards in pews faced a low platform in a poorly lit hall. There were one or two darker Latinos and a few gypsies in black from head to foot, and a gaggle of teenagers smirking and fooling about at the back. Everyone was standing singing so they found a space and tried to catch up. Paco, up on the platform, spotted them but only gave the slightest twitch of a eyebrow. The congregation sang with surprising enthusiasm and energy while the old man was hopping about, waving his arms in a kind of manic mix between cheerleading and conducting. Eventually it came to an end; everyone sat. Paco opened his Bible and read.

David had little to compare it with coming from solid, respectable atheist stock on one side and "Christmas and Easter" on the other, which practically amounted to much the same thing. Still there had been school assemblies his father had tried to get him out of but he had tolerated or ignored like the rest of his peers. *Blah, blah, holy blah* they called it and that was all the impact it made. Paco was different though. He read, then *explained*, not as it related to Roman Empire provincial Jews but for twentieth-century Spaniards. No cheap jibes at the Catholics, lots of personal anecdotes and a couple of jokes that made David smile in spite of himself and glance at Rocío. She was sitting forward as if she was watching the final of the *Copa del Rey* with Real 2-1 down to Barça and ten minutes left. Engrossed. After a final summary, a closing song, and a benediction of sorts the tea trolley was wheeled out by an ancient *Señora* in a pre-war headsquare and people began to shuffle forward. David took a coffee and looked round but Rocío had already cornered Paco and was explaining something – doing that Spanish thing where the import of communication seems to be more in the gestures than the words. He was listening attentively then talking back in a way both earnest and pointed. It looked like father and daughter, or maybe like an uncle and a niece. For all his distrust of clergy David felt he somehow – surprisingly – trusted Paco and whatever he was saying.

They went the next week too, then the one after that. Then it became sort of accepted but not talked about, in the same way that there was a cessation of hostilities in general. What Paco preached about each week and the mysterious fact of persistent religious observance – when Marx, Freud, Mendel, and Feuerbach had made it all so patently ridiculous – was carefully skirted around. Rocío got back to work. David stopped worrying about what was going on behind the door when he came home. By now it was obvious that at least one of them was living more and more for the weekend but not in the usual way. And it wasn't David. The only jarring note came one day when he once referred to her sudden interest in religion.

"It's not religion," she fired straight back. "I'm not sure where it's going but I need to find out." Almost exactly what Paco had said to him that night in the bar. Maybe he was more prejudiced than he thought. Still, no harm done. They weren't Moonies or Mormans at least. Personally he would have preferred some sort of mild Buddhism if they had to be religious – sorry *relational* – but neither Chamartin nor Vallecas had many ashrams open to the public. In any case Paco was the draw, not dogma.

"Just watch him. He's a sly old fox," was his father's only response when David spoke to him about it briefly in one of their very rare phone calls. "He's not a liar though. He really believes everything he's saying. You can be sure of that." That was maybe something.

It was during a Saturday wander round the gardens at Aranjuez that she dropped her bombshell.

"I've decided to convert."

"From what? I didn't know you *were* anything."

"That's true, but I don't know how else to say it that doesn't sound American."

"But Protestant?"

"I prefer *Christian*."

"I thought Catholics consider themselves Christians too, don't they?"

"Of course. But this is different. I just don't know how else to say it. I said a prayer when Paco was preaching last Sunday. I want to follow a different way, that's all."

"Ok – fair enough. I won't get in your way. I respect Paco and his little flock. Just don't expect me to follow you."

"Of course not. You must decide for yourself," Rocío added in such a matter-of-fact tone that David knew she had rehearsed the line.

"Do you mind if I ask why? I guess it must be to do with what you've been through the last few years."

"What we've *both* been through," she corrected him. They were holding hands, walking round the fountains and flowerbeds, the traditional summer palace of the Spanish monarchs spread out behind them. "Well, yes and no. It's not been easy. On you too. But it's not just that. I want something to live for that has a meaning. Politics is beyond redemption. We've all lost too many friends in *La Movida* to think that just getting wasted is what it's all about. I just think it all makes sense. Human weakness. The need for some sort of solution from outside. We need something outside the resources we've got."

They walked on in silence.

"You're impressed by Paco, aren't you?" David asked.

"Of course, but it's not just him. There are stories of people coming to faith just from reading the Bible or praying on their own. Even through dreams. No human input at all. It just makes me think there is a power beyond us and it's got something to say."

"What happens if Paco lets you down – feet of clay and all that?"

"I don't know. We'll cross that bridge when we come to it." David stopped and kissed her lightly on the forehead.

"Just one more thing: I've got to ask you about the night I came home after the crash. What changed? You were suddenly so different."

Rocío stared into the distance, shaking her head. "I can't really say for certain. I was packing a case and came to the photo albums. I sat down and started looking through them. I just thought we've lost six lives in the past few years – is that any reason to lose two more?"

Chapter 5

HACIENDA

By the time they stepped back onto Buccleuch Place the snow was heavy and constant, covering the cobbles in a puffy undulating layer like ripples on a duvet. An amber sheen reflected from every flat surface in the glow of the streetlights. The faces of the tenement buildings had softened with what looked like aged overhanging eyebrows on every ledge and crevasse. Up and down South Clerk Street the early evening traffic was beginning to build.

Hacienda was not part of a trendy chain of Spanish-themed restaurants designed for young people just back from Ibiza and did not have strings of plastic onions, garlic bulbs, and peppers hanging from glass fibre ceiling beams. There were no bull-fighting posters and no plastic vines up the pillars. Instead it had the atmosphere of a small family restaurant in a country district. The floor was red tiled, the walls white, the dozen or so small tables covered in bright cotton cloths, and prints of rural scenes hung on the walls. Groves of olive and almond trees on sun-baked hillsides were overlooked by Moorish castles and the white-topped Sierra Nevada in the distance. A bit of the warmth of southern Spain enveloped visitors whatever the weather was doing outside. David and Gillian pushed open the door with a swirl of snow behind them.

Juan – owner, head waiter, maître d' and odd job man – looked up from behind the bar, spotted David, dropped the dishtowel he was polishing glasses with, and came striding out with a broad grin.

"Señor David. *¡Bienvenido! ¿Como estas?* And your companion? *Encantado Señorita.*"

"*Hola, Juan – te presento* Gillian, one of my language students. Gillian – Juan – maker of the best *rabo de toro* outside the peninsula."

"*Tan amable* Señor David. Alicia! Señor David is here. With a companion." A petite, dark-haired, golden-skinned young woman emerged with a look of pleasure and stood beside her husband.

"Señor David – you are neglecting us. We've hardly seen you since you got your own place. And there are so many people at church nowadays, we never get to speak properly. Though we're enjoying the sermon series. Anyway, it's good to see you now. And welcome to your friend. *Bienvenida a Hacienda*. First time?"

"No – not at all – quite a few times. I love your paella!"

Juan was studying Gillian's face now she had taken off her hat and cape.

"*Por supuesto*. I thought I recognized you. Come." A little table in an alcove out of sight of other diners had a reserved sign on it. Juan snatched it up, stuffed it in his pocket, ushered them to their places and swept off to get the menus, which he produced with a flourish.

"Something to drink? *¿Qué quieres?* What would you like, *Señorita*?

Gillian ordered manzanilla with iced lemonade. Juan noted it on his pad with slightly raised eyebrows.

"I'm impressed, *Señorita*. That's not a common order."

"I was at the *Feria de Abril* in Seville two years ago and got the taste. It's what they drink in the *Casetas* – the marquees on the showground."

"I know. Sevilla is my home town. We went to the *Feria* every year. Señor David – why is she studying? She should be teaching!"

"So it appears." He made it two of the same and Juan went off to look out the Manzanilla Gitana.

"What did you think of Seville?"

"Fantastic. It's a beautiful city. We were only there for a couple of days though. Not long enough. You know it?"

"Sure. Not as well as Madrid but I know it. I worked for an importer for a time, so I had to travel to retailers throughout the south." Juan returned, pad in hand.

"*¿Estáis listos?*" Gillian nodded and ordered mixed tapas, paella de casa, and a single glass of chilled Albariño.

"*Perfecto Señora*. Señor David?"

"Can you make that tapas for two? Then Rabo de Toro. And…"
He looked across the table. "Shall we make that a bottle? Ok. A
bottle of Albariño. The Paco y Lola if you have any left? *Gracias*,
Juan. And one other thing before I forget. The main reason we're
here. Would Alicia be willing to help one of my students who is
struggling a bit and needs some extra conversation – from a clear
speaker."

"And I'm not? I'm offended. Of course she'll help. Call her
during the day tomorrow. I'm sure she'd be delighted."

Omara Portuena was singing *"Flor de Amor"* in the background
as they sat thinking about a surprising turn of events for both of
them. Gillian spoke first.

"Sermons. She said they liked your sermons…" David inclined
his head and grimaced.

"Alicia is a kindly woman. I could talk about pig farming in West
Lothian and she would still be complimentary."

"But sermons? I thought you were from the Spanish Department
at the university."

"No, not at all. I just teach a bit to pay the bills. The 'job', if
that's the right word, is part-time pastor at a small church near here.
Southside Fellowship. I knew Juan and Alicia in Madrid. They had
a hand in me coming back to Edinburgh."

"Coming back – from Madrid?"

"Yes. I'm afraid it's a bit complicated. My dad's Spanish and my
mum's from Edinburgh. They left Spain during the Franco years
before I was at school. So I did all my education in Edinburgh –
Gillespie's, then Edinburgh University. When Franco died I went
back to Madrid and picked up a load of old family contacts. We
ended up in Torrejón de Ardoz, just outside Madrid. I was founding
pastor of a church there. Juan and Alicia were our staunchest
supporters and friends."

"What brought you back?"

"Change of circumstances almost two years ago." He took off
his glasses and gave them a wipe.

"Oh I'm sorry. I didn't mean to pry."

"*No pasa nada*. What happened happened. Juan and Alicia had come to Edinburgh a bit before to start something new. I think it was because I used to talk about my childhood here they thought it might be a good place for authentic Spanish food. I tried to keep going afterwards but it didn't really work so I came back home too. They'd found the church and liked it. They told me there was a space for a part-time pastor till they could afford someone permanent. They thought I might fit the bill. So we're back together."

There was an uncomfortable silence for a few seconds then suddenly David got up. "I'm sorry. Can you excuse me for a second?" He disappeared abruptly outside. Gillian could see him standing on the pavement, stamping in the falling snow. Juan looked up as he passed, then came over and sat down.

"He was speaking of his wife?"

"I'm not sure. He just said a change of circumstances. I just asked why he came back to Edinburgh."

"Ah yes. Well it was certainly a change of circumstances. How could you know? It's still very fresh in his mind. You must forgive him. How do you say it? It's still an uphill struggle. David is a remarkable man. He will recover. But he loved Rocío very much."

"Rocío. What a lovely name."

"*Sí*. It is lovely. It means 'the dew'. She was a remarkable woman. And beautiful – like her name. She had a strong spirit. But it was too much in the end."

"What happened?"

"Well, maybe I should leave that till David feels ready to tell you himself."

Gillian nodded and gave a nervous cough. "Oh, of course. I'm sorry – none of my business."

"Enough to say he was trying to help those that couldn't help themselves. Or better to say his job was connecting people to the power they needed to change. What David did brought us some, how can I say it, negative attention as well as the positive. There were those that wanted him to stop but he wouldn't. He paid the price. So did she."

"That's horrible! What a thing to happen. You loved her too, didn't you?"

"I did, *Señorita*. She was my sister."

David reappeared before long, brushing snowflakes off his collar. Juan jumped up and disappeared to clear some tables and make up a bill. He pulled out his chair and tried for a smile.

"Forgive me dragging you into my problems. It's been a difficult time. I'm sure you can understand."

"Of course. I'm sorry," Gillian agreed, feeling she didn't understand at all. He'd been married; now he was on his own. Something terrible had happened that forced him to leave his home and job and friends. That seemed to be enough to know.

"Juan and Alicia were my first-aid team. I wouldn't have managed without them."

Gillian was silent so David refilled both glasses and changed the subject.

"So why Spanish – really?"

"Just what I said in the class. I wanted a new interest. I've had some holidays in Spain with an uncle and aunt in San Sebastian. I thought speaking a bit might come in handy." She paused as if weighing things up and coming to a decision. "And I've just divorced. Anything to take my mind off things would be welcome."

"Now we're both sorry. I won't say I know how you're feeling but I think I know about the need for a bit of distraction."

"*No hay problema.*"

They both waited till they felt the air clear. David tried again.

"You teach at the university?"

"Scots language."

"Burns?"

"Not so much. He's mainly in literature. I teach about the sound systems of Scots, and my research interest is how the language changes, particularly in urban settings."

"I thought they said Scots was dying out?"

"That's what everybody says but it's just changing. Scots is just what people in Scotland speak. A few years ago everybody started saying 'magic' and 'cheers' instead of 'braw' and 'cheerio'. Nobody now uses the words Burns used – except at Burns suppers of course – but then he didn't speak the language they spoke three hundred years before him. It's just constantly changing. That's what language is."

Juan appeared with the tapas selection, announcing each as he set them down. David cleared space as they arrived and they took in the fantastic mix of colours, smells, and textures.

"Estupendo Juan. Muchas gracias."

Gillian took a deep breath over the busy tabletop.

"And it smells wonderful too. Thanks."

That evening seemed to pass like a dream. The food was good and the music evocative but they barely remembered it. Both found themselves spontaneously sharing things they didn't tell friends and family: past lives, present troubles, future hopes. David spoke about his father running into trouble in the Franco years and escaping with his wife and two small boys to his wife's home town of Edinburgh. They had always meant to go back when Franco died, but the old man had held on so long by that time they had put down too many roots. However, David did make the return journey as soon as he'd finished university. He met Rocío through mutual friends on a night out in Madrid.

She spoke about growing up in the Borders, with an alcoholic mother and a father who did his best to hold things together and protect the kids in between bouts of utter despair. Things were a great deal easier when Mum disappeared for weeks on end and life became slightly more normal. Then she'd dry out and come back and the cycle would start again. He always took her back, hoping things could be different. Eventually she wore herself out and died of renal failure. Dad was still pegging away in a nursing home at Silverknowes. For recreation she went sailing and he listened to jazz. When the neighbours didn't complain he tried to keep up his sax playing.

They both read voraciously – science, politics, and culture for him; crime and history for her. They spoke more about his journey and hers all the way through *patatas bravas*, calamares, little mouthfuls of crispy deep fried fish, mini chorizos, and tortilla, then the mains, followed by *arroz con leche* for him and torrijas for her. And more Albariño.

Finally she drained her glass and scooped up the last morsel of crispy sugared toast. They were both feeling relaxed and speaking more freely than a couple of hours' acquaintance would normally permit.

"One thing you haven't told me," said Gillian. "Your degree was in marketing, your job was in business. How on earth did you become a minister?"

"Good question," David laughed. "I didn't plan it. Honest. It's what some people call a God thing." She waited for an explanation. "You've got to understand," he explained, "Spanish people are still very suspicious of things outside the Catholic church. Numbers are dropping fast but it's still the devil they know – so to speak. Anything else isn't really Christian and more likely full of drug addicts and gypsies. So I wasn't interested. Then when Rocío seemed to connect I went along with it. And it seemed to have a big effect on her. We had been going through some problems. When she came to faith it seemed to make everything different. She wasn't upset or frustrated any more. It felt like she'd found something fulfilling, so I started to take it a bit more seriously. They weren't nuts or brainwashers. I began to find out about what they believed. That made me go back to think about what *I* believed. Turned out it wasn't very much."

Finally the coffee appeared and they knew things were coming to an end.

"You don't seem much like a minister," she said, "if you don't mind me saying so."

"Ah well, that all depends on what you think a minister's like." He sprinkled a little more cinnamon on the last of his *arroz con leche*.

"Like my Uncle Sandy, for instance," she added. "He's a minister too. Full of goodwill but not much grasp of how ordinary people think – not churchgoers, I mean. Well intentioned but a bit out of touch."

"I think that might be a fair comment sometimes. I've always wanted faith to be relevant to real life, especially for people who know nothing about faith outside the 'rites of passage' kind of religion. Remember, I was exactly like that."

"Well, maybe I'm still like that. I'm certainly more used to St Andrew's Parish Church in the High Street than anything like you've described at your place."

"I'm sure it's not just one or the other. There are lots of flavours and people with real faith in all varieties. And people with not much. Or not much left." He felt the need to be honest but hoped she didn't guess who he was referring to.

"Well. You're full of surprises anyway. And the church here in Edinburgh – is it much like what you had in Spain?" David made a sound halfway between a laugh and a grunt.

"Not at all! Most of our folks wouldn't have me in the door if they knew what we got up to in Spain. But they don't have to know, so that's ok."

David paused for a second, wondering whether to continue and how honest to be.

"Actually, when I left Spain, church and me weren't on very good terms. Likewise faith. I'd been doing what I'd been doing for about twenty years. Then the price just got too high. The tank was empty, as they say. Then the only way back here seemed to involve taking it on all over again. I wasn't wanting it at all. It's just how things worked out."

"Maybe you're good at it."

"Don't know about that. It's just that every time I put pen to paper or stand up to speak I end up asking myself what on earth I'm still doing this for. After, well, everything that's happened."

"That can't be easy. It would be like me nursing alcoholics. Too much baggage."

"This is funny, you know. It's a long time since I've spoken to anyone like this. And we've just met. You didn't expect this when you signed up for Spanish conversation."

"Well, it *is* conversation. And you're nearly Spanish. Can't complain."

The bill came and Gillian insisted on paying half. They thanked Juan, got their coats and were heading for the door when Alicia appeared from the kitchen looking slightly concerned.

"Señor David. A phone call. It's Mrs MacInnes from church. She's sounding quite upset." David glanced at his watch – 10:35.

"I wonder how she found out I was here?" He excused himself. Gillian said it was no trouble and she'd wait. When David came back, he had a worried look.

"It's our treasurer from church… about her granddaughter, Jen. She's gone missing. They think she's been abducted."

Chapter 6

PLAZA DEL ÁNGEL

David sat at his desk in a first-floor office next to Tirso de Molina metro and fiddled with his monthly sales returns. He couldn't concentrate. Paco had come at him out of the blue – almost literally. And now Rocío was a follower. What had she said? "I've decided I want to follow the founder." It sounded much like one of Paco's phrases. He had turned the chain of events over in his mind a thousand times. That life was better, calmer, more tranquil, there wasn't any doubt. But this new direction... somehow it seemed to change the agenda between them in a way that had never happened before. Like they were travelling roads that increasingly diverged. Trying to talk her out of it was out of the question and not just on ethical grounds. Rocío would do as she wanted and believe what she wanted. You might just as well try to influence an avalanche. Ignore it? But why? They had shared and talked about everything up to the time of the loss of the babies, when it became harder to address the painful realities. But this wasn't painful. She was undoubtedly more at peace and more contented than ever. That wasn't a bad thing. Maybe it was even worth being deluded for. The church didn't seem at all interested in their money and made absolutely no other demands on them. But talking about it might mean having to conclude she had stumbled on something he needed to be open to for himself. And that might force another painful decision.

On an impulse, right in the middle of his monthly returns, David grabbed the phone and called the University of Alcalá.

"Department of Modern Languages. Professor Francisco Morales please." A pause. The line ringing out. As it rang and rang he didn't know whether to be disappointed or relieved.

"I'm very sorry," the telephonist started, "there doesn't seem to be... oh, just a minute. Transferring you now." Then a brisk, businesslike voice.

"Morales. Yes?"

"Paco?"

"Who's this?"

"David Hidalgo."

"David. How are you? Just a minute. I'll call you back. Departmental minutes to be read and signed. For my sins. I'm right in the middle of it."

"Of course. Whenever you can." David put the phone down with a feeling of anticlimax despite himself. He was used to customers "calling him right back". It was almost official code for "Don't bother me; I've more important things to do." So he was quite surprised when half an hour later the phone rang again.

"David. What can I do for you, my friend?"

"That's just it, Paco. I'm not entirely sure. I'm confused."

"So you called me to tell me you're confused?"

"In a manner of speaking. There's a few things I'm finding quite hard to make sense of."

"Excellent."

"Why do you say that?"

"Well, I'm also very often confused. It's the men of fixed opinions we have to fear, don't we?"

"You may be right. I hadn't thought about it that way. Can we meet?"

"To talk about your confusion?"

"Indeed. Do you have an evening free?"

"Let me see. Oh – better than that. Johnny Griffin is playing at Café Central tonight. How does that sound?"

"Great. You have a spare ticket?"

"You don't know Café Central? It's a very civilized system. You turn up for drinks anytime in the evening then an hour before the show begins they come round selling tickets. You want to stay, you pay; if not you can go. I hate queueing for tickets. This is so much easier."

"Why not? Sounds good."

"So Café Central, Plaza del Ángel, let's say, half past six? Then we can get some drinking in before the music starts."

David was smiling as he put the phone down. To say the old man was full of surprises didn't really seem to cover it. He was like a jack-in-the-box. Every time he popped out wearing something different, doing something different, challenging your expectations in a different way. So Café Central and Johnny Griffin then. And a night out drinking which he hadn't done for years, with a man twice his age. He left a message on Rocío's voicemail and got on with the paperwork.

Café Central was in Plaza del Ángel, not Basin Street, but at least it was a smoky bar. Couples of all ages, a mixed group looking very studentish, a sharply dressed older man on his own, two women, maybe mother and daughter, all sitting round the rather cramped space, much of it taken up by a low platform and a baby grand piano. David liked the way jazz seemed to be accessible to all, regardless of age. It wasn't obsessed only with the young and the new like rock and pop. You could discover a Brubeck disc from thirty years ago and for you it was new. In Scotland he'd grown up with Matt Munro on TV and Petula Clarke on *Top of the Pops*. Nobody was going to discover some new bit of crooning from Mr Munro circa 1958 and consider it cool in the 1980s. But with jazz you could. The Modern Jazz Quartet were anything but modern but sounded as up-to-date now as the moment Heath, Kay, Jackson, and Lewis first played at the Savoy in 1956.

David arrived promptly but found Paco already there, already nursing a *caña*.

"Just keeping it company," he beamed. "What do you want?"

"Well, since we're being cool and sophisticated, I'll have a malt."

"How very Scottish. Bowmore?"

"Laphroaig. Ten years old if they have it."

"Of course. An evening of sophistication. Let's make it two."

Paco shuffled along, letting David into a space as the waiter came over, scribbled their order, then continued his progress round the tables as the seats filled up.

"I discovered jazz when I was working in Maidenhead," Paco reminisced as they waited for their drinks. "And whiskey too. Equally unlikely but both true. Chet Baker came to the local town hall. Past his best by then of course and in and out of jail more often than the mafia. But still quality. Absolute quality. A bit like the Laphroaig, if you like. Baker is a specific taste. Not everyone's cup of tea. That's to say, not if you're into light speed changes and the more notes you can fit in the bar the better. Nothing against Dizzy and Bird of course, but as I get older I seem to like the more reflective style. So I went to see Chet with an English girl I was dating. She was tasty too. Before I met Marisa of course. It's sometimes not healthy to reminisce too much."

David looked down, trying not to smile. Paco was so *not* the model of an earnest evangelical pastor you might imagine if all you had to go on was what you heard on the metro or watched on American TV.

"And that was that. One night – two love affairs. Good value ch?"

"Cheers Paco," David said as the drinks arrived, "since we're being *Britanicos* this evening."

"Cheers." Paco rolled the spirit around in his mouth. David wasn't sure if he was savouring the flavour of the whiskey, the memory of Chet Baker's cool, educated trumpet style, or thinking about the English girl from Maidenhead. Better not to enquire.

"So, David. Much as I enjoy a good malt and cool jazz, we'd didn't come here just for that. You're confused. What about?"

David hardly paused. He had his pitch ready.

"*You*, for one," he said. "You're an educated man yet you believe things educated people think are nonsense. You must be well paid but you live in the backstreets of Vallacas with the gypsies and the junkies. You have sophisticated tastes," David raised his glass and Paco reciprocated smiling, "but you spend all your free time with gullible people who seem to have swapped one set of superstitions for another. I just can't make it out."

"And now your girlfriend has made a deal with the devil and joined up with the legions of the gullible. Is that it?"

"Well, I wasn't going to put it that way, but yes. That is it. What is it all about. Where's the sense?"

Paco took another sip from his glass, rolling it around. He took his time and seemed to be savouring the question as well as the spirit.

"Gullible," he said at last just as David was wondering if he'd overdone it. "Uneducated. Superstitious. Strong words, my friend." He paused again, looking round the clientele as the café was beginning to fill and waving to a couple just taking their seats across the room. "Tell me, what do you think of Miles Davis's later work? Say, *On the Corner* or *Big Fun* compared with *Kind of Blue* or *Birth of the Cool*?"

Now David was stumped.

"I've no idea. I know *Kind of Blue* of course but the others, not so much."

"Well, everyone has their opinion and Miles is the master, so who are we to criticize, but there are some that say there was a marvellous simplicity in the earlier work that he lost later on. Studio tracks that were never actually played complete. Stockhausen and funk and a group of musicians who didn't even play jazz. Maybe it was all bold and adventurous, but maybe on the other hand he lost something as well. Do you know he hasn't played in public now for the last six years?"

"And your point, Paco?"

"Just that education and sophistication might be a bit overrated, don't you think? The words of our founder have been changing lives for two thousand years now. Sometimes simple words. Why should you need a higher degree to understand 'love your enemies and do good to those that hate you' or 'render to Caesar what is Caesar's and to God what is God's'? My congregation are simple people on the whole, I agree. But their stories aren't simple. Pablo spent three years in prison for his faith under Franco. When Daniel and Rosa married, the church wouldn't recognize a Protestant ceremony, so they were thought to be living in sin and their children were all called 'bastards' at school. Do you know that when they lost the youngest, the church wouldn't even let them bury the body in the town cemetery? That was holy ground and they were all heretics. Javier wouldn't take an oath of allegiance to the Virgin when he was called up for national service so he did his entire *mili* digging ditches and cleaning sewers. Simple people, yes. But not gullible. Not deceived. Not to be pitied or patronized." Paco's tone had taken on an edge David hadn't heard before.

"You know the parable of the pearl merchant, I suppose?" he continued. David nodded, hesitant now to say more. "Well, it's about what we most value in life. Javier, Pablo, and the others – every one of these uneducated people has a story. They would say they found something better – the perfect pearl. So in a sense they couldn't be intimidated any more. And you could never say they were in it for the money or the popularity or the fashion. So what about Spain today? All the education and sophistication. We've seen the corruption of the last fifty years and every week we hear something new. Now it's priests who've been abusing children and babies stolen from unmarried mothers and passed on to good, respectable Catholic families. The church is a human institution. The Catholic church. My church. Whatever. But God's church isn't a matter of cardinals and conclaves, or the membership role in Vallecas for that matter. It's those who have a relationship – a personal connection – with something bigger than themselves. Something that rescues, renovates, reinstates."

"Or *someone*, I suppose?" David muttered. Paco inclined his head.

"Or someone, indeed. That's our belief. And our experience. The universe has a voice. It has a personality. However unlikely it may seem, there is someone seeking us, wooing us. Do you know the Englishman Francis Thompson? He was addicted to opium, lived as a tramp in London, then died of TB before he was fifty. But he also wrote *The Hound of Heaven*." Paco cast his eyes up to the ceiling and recited, "'I fled Him, down the nights and down the days; I fled Him, down the arches of the years; I fled Him, down the labyrinthine ways'. He was writing about what our 'gullible' congregation have themselves experienced. What he's saying is that God is seeking those who are honest enough to listen and brave enough to respond. Education and sophistication don't have any bearing on that."

Paco seemed to have said his piece. He sat back, dabbed his brow with a large white handkerchief with saxophone motifs, and took another sip.

"And Rocío," David said, tentatively. "I just feel confused about where we are as a couple. We've always more or less seen things the same way. Forgive me, Paco, but this is something new. It's something we don't share and I can't imagine we will. It worries me."

Paco half turned and put his hand on David's arm.

"David. My friend. Son of my best friend. Please forgive me."

"What for?"

"I've been talking about other people's experience. That doesn't matter to you. Nor should it. This is personal. The one you love – can I say that?" David nodded. "She's taken a turn in the road you feel you can't follow. Correct? And the question is, what happens if there are further bends ahead and you lose sight of each other. That's the issue, no?"

"Of course. And what happens then? It's like I've just got her back and she's about to slip through my fingers all over again." David felt something worryingly like pricking in his eyes.

The café was filling up in earnest now. One of the waiters had started going round with one hand full of tickets and a biscuit tin of cash in the other.

"We're staying?" Paco asked.

"Of course. Why not?"

"Well. We haven't long then. I'll just say this. Do you prefer the new Rocío or the old?"

"You mean over the past few years? Well, the new, of course."

"Ok. Let that be enough for now. Let her follow her own journey. And you follow yours. But don't let a prejudice get in your way. Be open – to me or others. Open the window and let in some fresh air. Open a door and see who's behind it. Read, think, study, talk. Now, here's what we've been waiting for!"

A middle-aged man in a white shirt, black waistcoat, thick black beard, and a scrappy note in his hand hopped up onto the stage.

"*Señores y Señoras.* The moment you've been waiting for. For your listening pleasure. Please, a warm welcome for – Johnny Griffin and friends!" There was a warm round of applause while a diminutive African American with a large tenor saxophone round his neck and three significantly larger companions tiptoed out of the back room. A brief acknowledgment of the applause. A word of thanks in careful Spanish, then one at the piano, one on drums, and the third picking up a double bass left on the stage and they were off.

"'Hush a Bye' – my favourite!" Paco whispered, still clapping.

Chapter 7

MORNINGSIDE

When ladies from Morningside phone their minister late in the evening it can mean a variety of things. One, that they won't manage Sunday school in the morning because their sister from Winnipeg is visiting and they're going to take a picnic to the Botanical Gardens. Two, would the minister mind announcing that more names are needed for the flower rota which is due to expire next month? Or three (in some cases), that Auntie Jessie has just died and would it be all right if something appropriate goes in the notice sheet? Ladies from Morningside are brisk, businesslike, and self-reliant and obtain what spiritual comfort they need from *Songs of Praise*, not late-night pastoral visits. So it was with considerable embarrassment and confusion that Irene MacInnes was pacing the floor fully ten minutes after eleven o'clock waiting for the doorbell to ring. It wasn't just "what would the neighbours think"; she had no idea what to make of it herself. It had never happened before to her or anyone she knew. Dealing with troublesome tradesmen was one thing, but the minister? At ten minutes past eleven? Think of it. In this case, however, a lack of anywhere else to turn had overcome Morningside respectability. The doorbell chimed softly and she ran to answer it.

"Oh, Mr Hidalgo. I mean Señor David. Thank you *so* much for coming. I didn't know who else to speak to. Come away in. Would you like a cup of tea?"

"That would be lovely, but perhaps you should tell me what's happened first and why you think there's anything wrong."

"Of course, of course. And so late at night too. Taking you out of your way. I just want you to know I don't make a habit of this."

The calm, totally-in-control woman of practical affairs and the resolving of problems seemed quite distant from the troubled elderly lady David had before him now.

"I'm sure you don't. Now what's going on?"

They made their way up the hall and into the front room. It was dominated by heavy red drapes, firm upright furniture, and such a combination of clashing wallpaper, cushions, carpet, and rugs as to make anyone of more modern tastes feel giddy and need to sit down for a bit. David sat down.

"Well, as I said it's about my daughter Alison. You've met her I think. She came on the Sunday school trip to Dunbar last August. You know, when it rained all day and we couldn't have the races or anything?"

"I think that was before I came, but yes, I've been told. What about her?"

"Well she has a daughter, Jennifer. My granddaughter. Well, that's obvious I imagine. You know, this has just got me all upset." She perched on the edge of an upright chair, took a deep breath and carried on. "Well, Jennifer – that's Jen, that's what she calls herself, though Jennifer is a perfectly lovely name if she would just use it. Anyway, Jen is not quite sixteen and she's been keeping some quite unsavoury company." David nodded. "You know Alison and her husband split up two years ago now and what with having to divide the house and everything she had to take a council flat, down in Muirhouse. Terrible. I would have had her here of course but you know I just don't have the room and Jennifer wouldn't have liked it at all. Why she couldn't keep the house and have that man of hers live in a council flat I don't know but there you are. You've got to keep your nose out of it. That's what I always say. I say that to Mrs Buchanan all the time you know. You've just got to bite your tongue and keep your nose out of it and let the young ones get on with it. Now, where on earth was I?"

"Jen…" David prompted, wondering how long it would take to get to the point and why it couldn't just have waited till morning.

"Yes indeed. Jen. That's right. Well. Did I say she had been keeping some not very suitable company?"

"You did."

"Well, it turns out it's not just the company. She's actually been taking... well... taking the drugs... actually. Yes. The drugs, I'm afraid." Mrs MacInnes had lowered her voice as if the neighbours might be listening and saying it in a whisper might yet keep her reputation intact.

"What sort of drugs?" David asked in a normal tone, to Mrs MacInnes's obvious discomfort.

"Well, I don't entirely know. But Alison thinks it started with that stuff you smoke, what's it called – Margarina?"

"Marijuana."

"That's it. About two years ago. Not long after the break-up. But then she's been going on to stronger stuff. I don't know what you would call it all but her mother was finding teaspoons, matches, silver paper... even a syringe in her room, and seemed to think it was all connected. Though what you would do with a teaspoon, matches, and silver paper I can't imagine." David could imagine perfectly well and was beginning to feel there might be something to worry about after all.

"You said she had gone missing."

"Yes, I was just coming to that. It wasn't just the drugs and the company, but she'd been coming home later and later. Then she'd started not coming in at all and saying she was with a friend. What do they call it nowadays – a sleepover? Yes, that's it, she kept having these sleepovers and not coming in at all. Then last weekend she didn't come in on the Saturday night. Or the Sunday. Now she's been gone the whole week and Alison doesn't know where she is at all."

"And how did you find this out?"

"Well I was over there at teatime today. It's Alison's birthday on Tuesday so I got her a wee something and I went over there on the bus. She tries to keep up appearances, you know, but I could tell. I can always tell with Alison. So I just asked her straight out. I said, 'What's the matter Alison? There's something upsetting you and you'd be better just to tell your mother, whatever it is.' And then she just broke down entirely. Just about screamed the house down in fact. Like a banshee, she was. I suppose they're maybe used to that sort of thing in Muirhouse, but I can tell you Señor David, I wasn't prepared for it at all."

"And what does Alison think has happened? Has she heard from her at all?"

"Not a dicky bird. Alison thinks she's run away but I think she's been abducted. Mrs Buchanan thinks she's probably taken an overdose and ended up in a coma at the Western General but I said they'd have had something in the *Evening News* if that had happened and I would have seen it. No, you can rest assured, she's been abducted by someone. One of her druggy cronies I'll be bound."

"And what do you think I might be able to do... exactly?"

"Well I don't rightly know, Señor David. But I do remember you telling us at the vacancy committee, and when we were speaking the other day – I remember you saying you used to help young people who were using drugs and things. I just thought you might be able to do something."

"That was in Spain, Mrs MacInnes. Really I have no connections in Edinburgh at all. I don't think there's anything I can do that the police and the social work department aren't doing already." Mrs MacInnes looked at David in silence for a second then leaned forward and lowered her voice still further.

"That's just it. I'm not allowed to tell the police. Or the social people. Alison made me promise. She says we can't let anybody know or Jennifer might be in danger. I don't know what to do. You've got to help us, Pastor David. I don't know where else to turn."

By the time David had calmed her down, assured her that everything would probably work out ok, that it was probably nothing more than a bit of teenage rebellion and made her promise to try to bring Alison along to church in the morning, it was late. However, to the anxious Mrs MacInnes's credit, by this time all she wanted was her granddaughter back in one piece and what the neighbours might think didn't seem as important as it had an hour before. Finally, well after midnight, David managed to excuse himself and

Mrs MacInnes managed to get her cup of Ovaltine before tucking herself up in bed and dreaming of Rudolph Valentino. Señor David would surely take care of everything.

The snowfall had come to an end by the time David came out. The sky was studded with stars and a full moon made everything sparkle and glisten. Late-night partygoers crunched home and such traffic as there was crept along, engines, gears, and tyres muffled by the dampening effect of the fall. In the moonlight glow it was tempting to think that life *was* beautiful, people were kind, intentions were good, and things that went wrong were unfortunate misunderstandings – like the missing Jen – to be cleared up in the morning. But for David the illusion held no significance. Despite all his assurances, a vulnerable teenage girl plus drugs, users, and dealers was never a good combination. Worse still it brought the past crashing back into his present again like a railway wagon hitting the buffers. Far too often he had seen youngsters with everything to live for gobbled up and sucked dry of all their hope and humanity. He had also seen a supernatural power transforming lives, but the monster rarely seemed to be entirely slain. It was a perfect fit for the apostle Peter's vision of the devil prowling around like a roaring lion seeking whom he might devour. Did he have his jaws gripped round Jen right now? No doubt they would soon find out.

He felt like the cancer care doctor trying to assure a newly diagnosed patient that recovery was possible when he had just lost a loved one to the same condition. If Jen had really descended into the shadowy world of drugs and dealers, there was no telling what might be going on. He could feel his heart sinking. What was the point? The men with the guns, the muscle, and no conscience always won. No one in Madrid was lying awake at night haunted by his tragedy. After this last two years, he had sworn to have nothing more to do with drugs, addicts, dealers, violence, and drugged-up lives. Instead of being in the life-changing rescue business, he had chosen Southside Fellowship. In place of a bustling, lively, modern church of transforming lives and real issues he had opted for the sleepy, staid and resolutely respectable, the prosperous middle aged, the devout and dutiful elderly, one or two reluctant youngsters, and the usual sprinkling of oddballs, misfits and the simple minded. That's it, he thought. Let's stick with disputes about the hymn book, the notice sheet, and redecoration of the vestry. Leave the real problems to those who still have the energy, the compassion, and the hope. Leave it to the true believers.

Just as he was beginning to feel the icy cold penetrating his shoes and his bones he got to the door and started fumbling for keys. He felt more settled in his mind and was looking forward to a late-night snack, Stan Getz playing "Nature Boy", and maybe one last look over his notes before a hot water bottle and oblivion. Suddenly a shadowy figure lounging against the bus shelter outside the close stepped forward into the light and startled him.

"*¿Cómo estás Señor David? ¿Qué pasa?*" David almost leapt out his skin.

"Juan! What are you doing here? You frightened the life out of me!"

"We closed Hacienda a little early. I thought I would stop by and see how things are. Did you find out anything about the girl?"

"Well, nothing good anyway. She's been shooting up for at least a year. Hanging about with junkies and dealers. Taken to staying out all night, sometimes a couple of days at a time. This is more serious though. The mother hasn't seen her for a week. Nobody knows where she is. Irene managed to worm the truth out of Mum this afternoon. Now she's up to high doh."

"High doh? *No te entiendo.*"

David laughed with a release of tension.

"*Lo siento.* A Scottish expression. She is *muy preocupada* – very worried." Juan nodded.

"*Y tú* Señor David. How are you?"

"Well… not great, to tell you the truth. Thanks for looking out for me. Come in before we both freeze to death."

* * *

Juan started rummaging through drawers and cupboards in the chilly flat as David took off his coat, lit an ancient gas fire, and put the kettle on. He was looking serious and disappointed by the time David came back.

"Señor David, this is terrible. You are not looking after yourself. Cheap American rice, no fresh vegetables, instant coffee, horrible Scottish sausages. This will give you a heart attack. You cannot feel good eating this… this…*basura*…" – he searched for the right word in English – "this rubbish!"

"You're right. I've a lot on my mind. I'll never equal Rocío's cooking so maybe I feel there's not much point in trying."

"Now you know you can eat free at Hacienda any time. We've told you that a thousand times. Alicia wouldn't let you eat this stuff if she knew!"

"I know. It's very kind but you have a business to run. *Gratis* for me is not so *gratis* for you. You don't have enough customers yet that you can afford a non-paying guest." David was spooning instant coffee into two cups. Juan pursed his lips then decided to speak up anyway.

"Señor David – it's not like that. You are family to us. Closer than family. Rocío was my sister but you're family in a deeper way. You found me on the streets when I was nothing. What was I? I was running errands for the dealers. I was learning the ways of the gangs. I had nothing. I was taking my first steps to hell. You picked me up. The church became my home – my family. You were my *padre*. You cared about me when no one else knew who I was. You got me my first job. You introduced me to Alicia. You brought me to know *El Señor*. How can I repay this? It is our job to keep you strong so you can help people the way you helped us."

There was silence in the tiny kitchen except for David stirring the coffee and putting a half-empty carton of milk back in the fridge. He handed Juan a cup and sat down in a threadbare armchair. He took a sip and said nothing. At length he looked up and spoke very slowly.

"Juan. I love you too and I love Alicia. You are more than family to me also. In fact you're about the only family I have left. But the David Hidalgo you met in the Plaza Mayor in Madrid ten years ago was a different man. You've grown up since then. You're not the same kid that tried to pick my pocket but you've grown in a good way. I thought I could take them on and win. I was wrong. We paid the price. I came here to get away from it all, so I would never be faced with the same dilemmas and make the same mistakes. I'm sorry if that disappoints you but it's the truth. I haven't got anything left. It's all gone and I can't go back to the battle. I'm sorry."

"So what are you going to do to help the girl? Maybe to give her a life the way you did for me?"

"Nothing, Juan. I'm going to do nothing." He spoke very slowly, taking time over every word. "I'll meet the mum if she comes to church. I'll talk to her and tell her to report her daughter as missing. I'll encourage her to put up posters, to go on the news, speak to the papers. And I'll pray for her and sympathize with Granny, Mum, the neighbours, and the dog. Beyond this I will do – nothing. I'm sorry."

Somewhere there was the muffled sound of a late-night party. The brakes of a night service bus hissed and squealed outside. Juan swilled his instant coffee round the cup but didn't drink it.

"How can you say that? After all the lives you touched in Madrid – not just mine. It was the power of God but it came through you. You did what had to be done. People with no hope found it through you. Warehouse 66 was your invention. Lives were changed but you were the one with the vision that made it happen. How can you say you're not going to help? That girl could be any one of the hundreds we know in Madrid – in trouble but ready to change. This is a chance to make a difference in her life too. How can you say no?"

David didn't drink his coffee either. He got up and poured it down the sink. Instead he took a bottle of Lepanto brandy out of the cupboard. Three times the price in Scotland as in Spain but he felt he needed it. He poured two glasses and handed one to Juan then sat down again.

"I've always believed in the contract," he said slowly. "I know you don't make deals with God but I've always believed that if you did what God was calling you to do then he would look out for you. The Old Testament is full of it – the children of Israel going into the promised land, David in the psalms. It seems pretty clear. You follow my laws, my teaching, my ways, and I will protect and deliver you. Though a thousand fall at your side, ten thousand at your right hand, but it will not come near you. Remember? That's what I believed. But I found, in the end, it didn't work. I did everything I thought I was supposed to do. I took risks. With my life. With Rocío's life too. But it turned out God did not protect us. God did not preserve us. I may be here but she didn't make it and that means I've got nothing to offer to anyone else. None of the certainty I used to have. I didn't have too little faith; I had too much. I'm not the same man. I'm sorry."

The clock on the boarded-up fireplace ticked. Juan stood up and put on his jacket.

"Do you think you're the only one who's lost something? Don't forget she was my sister. I lost something too you know. What do you think Rocío would be saying to you now if she were here? She'd say we always knew the risks. There are no guarantees. The Bible is full of the blood of the martyrs. Paul was nearly murdered a hundred times. I suppose lots of people he knew never made it either. She's one of that community. The ones that kept on giving till they gave their lives. She gave one life but she saved many. So did you. And don't forget the story isn't finished yet. You don't know how it's going to end. How can you say you won't do anything because God let you down? Jesus was a martyr too. He gave up more than you. You're right, Señor David; you're not the same man. Please God you will find that man again. I can see myself out."

Chapter 8

RADIO DYNAMIS

David Hidalgo parked his old, off-white Peugeot 206 with almost 300,000 kilometres on the clock, locked the door that was still lockable, and checked the time. Just after five. He wasn't absolutely needed till five thirty but he liked to be prompt. Getafe was out of town – an industrial suburb to the south of Madrid – but parking anywhere even near the city was never straightforward and it was probably still the Scot in him that liked to be early – even after almost thirty years in Spain. Besides, he'd never been to the Radio Dynamis offices before and didn't want to find it up four flights of stairs and no lift. His recent fiftieth had brought it home he needed to pace himself just a little bit more than he had in his thirties. Rocío kept on at him to join a gym, go swimming, take up Tai chi – anything to slow the inevitable – but he always put it off. There were always other more important things to do. While not entirely going with Warren Zevon's "I'll sleep when I'm dead", he had to admit there was a bit of that in him. That was how God had made him – or circumstances of the last twenty years had determined. So be it. Amen. There was still a bit of life, energy, and thought left. Presumably that was what they were going to ask him about on Ortega's early evening "Meet the Pastor" show.

There it was. Ground floor. No sweat. Literally. So, time for a coffee. Arriving *too* early wasn't very Spanish but these were Latinos – like the Spanish but more so when it came to timekeeping so best not embarrass anyone by turning up too promptly. Luckily you're never far from a bar in Spain so he found a couple of chairs on the pavement just round the corner. *Café cortado*, a rather stale chunk of *marguarita*, and a seat in the sunshine. A replay of last night's champion's league

Liverpool versus Real was blaring on the TV above the bar but he didn't pay attention. Radio Dynamis (Power of God) listeners were going to meet the pastor this evening. He ought to give them their money's worth. Who exactly were they going to meet?

Perhaps they should be speaking to Paco Morales, not him at all, if they wanted to find out about David Hidalgo. Paco had been such an influence, guide, mentor – not to mention a drinking buddy and fellow jazz fan. But Paco had been dead for more than ten years now. Heart attack right in the middle of a Bible study on the Song of Songs. *All night long on my bed I looked for the one my heart loves. I looked for him but did not find him.* Well, he'd found him now. Paco's challenge had been to read, think, study, talk. So he did. Whatever this was all about it had brought his girlfriend, lover, best friend, and later on wife, back – almost literally from the dead. It deserved fair attention. She deserved it. And she never pushed him. They continued at Paco's little Baptist church near Congosto. Rocío had gradually got more and more involved. A Saturday morning women's group. Bible studies. Helping with the food distribution and second-hand clothing. Even stood up the front and told her own story one week. He had made himself sit it out, expecting to be embarrassed, but found himself in tears. The loss of all these little lives that had brought her to the point of almost ending one life more. But now it seemed she was rewriting history. Not to deny it but to reframe it in a new, healthier way. Why had all these lives been lost? There were no easy answers. No hard answers either and Paco had never tried to fob them off with platitudes. But it was like a change in the light. The shadows had softened and no longer did she seem to be carrying round their tiny unformed bodies in her own, day after day. It wasn't denied; there just wasn't the anguish there had been. Life did indeed go on even though that was the most anodyne of truisms. Rocío had found something she didn't have before. That wasn't bad, it was good. So David took on Paco's challenge and did read, study, think, and talk.

"What's this I hear, David?" his father had asked him over the best Scottish style Sunday roast on one of his rare visits to the *casa de los padres* in Malaga. "Got religion have we?" Ironically that single phrase galvanized him all the more. Characterizing a serious journey like a three-day cold annoyed him – probably exactly what his father had meant to do – but he kept his cool.

"Well, not so much as to keep me in bed," he smiled back over the parsnips. Thanks to the acres of well-oiled English flesh tanned the colour of pigskin lounging around Malaga, like Southend in the sun, the shops stocked everything you could get in Stockbridge or Marks and Spencer's in the Gyle. "But if I have you'll be the first to know." He smiled sweetly. They both understood his father would be the last to know – at least directly. Paco was discrete and David only spoke to *Papa* when it couldn't be avoided. Mum was a different matter but she seemed to trust him to make sense of things on his own without the need to be browbeaten and mocked. So they met up sometimes when the old man was out whacking a ball round eighteen holes with a retired Edinburgh lawyer or some broker who had swapped Charlotte Square for the *Costa*.

"So long as you're happy, David," she said, another from the all-time top ten of family favourites. But Mum meant it and David took it kindly. She stretched up and pecked him on the cheek. "Love you, Davie," she whispered.

Under Paco's watchful eye and Rocío's rather more nervous observation he tried to make progress, at first treating the whole thing like a bit of perfectly calm research. What do this strange breed of non-Catholic Christians actually believe? Why? What do they do? Why? What was the source of what even David could see was a remarkable degree of commitment and tenacity? Could it all just be cultural group think by the simple minded and trusting poor? Paco himself was the obvious counter to that. But then how could a thoughtful, intelligent humanitarian like him inhabit the same ideological space as the fundamentalists who thought the will of God was taunting gays and fire bombing abortion clinics? Then there were the outright crazies who thought Jesus Christ was coming back next week but needed a bit of party planning from the faithful. So an internet virus to sabotage the banking system, Ricin in the post to the president or fundraising to rebuild the Jerusalem Temple and flatten the Dome of the Rock – that's what brought a smile to the face of the Almighty. Paco was unperturbed. He just shrugged and asked, "Is that what Jesus taught? *Si o no?* If not then they're no affair of mine. *Punto.*"

Then somehow it happened when David wasn't looking. The game he thought was solitaire turned out to be chess. His relaxed investigation was suddenly feeling more like the best of thirteen against Bobby Fischer. *Someone* rather than *something* was on the opposite side of the table. He didn't give up without a fight and there was always a choice – he could just have tipped the pieces on the floor and slammed the door but that would have been equivalent to closing his mind – what he had previously accused Paco's little band of doing. It somehow seemed no contest – that it was the kind of losing that was better than winning. The defeat that was better than victory. *Batter my heart, three person'd God;* was the way John Donne had put it *for, you as yet but knocke, breathe, shine, and seeke to mend; That I may rise, and stand, o'erthrow me, and bend Your force, to breake, blowe, burn and make me new.* Well he'd been broken and burned. But the overthrow was the new beginning. He chose to believe.

Not long after his change of heart he started going to a small group from Paco's church that met in the fourth floor *piso* of an unemployed builder and his seamstress wife. Then some evening classes at Sefovan Bible college. Then leading a new group linked to Congosto but independent. Somehow it just kept growing. *La Movida* continued to exert its open-minded, searching influence. Eventually the big one: he packed in his job to pastor full time. His colleagues mostly thought he was mad but one or two cornered him over coffee and asked what was really going on. "How long have you got?" he'd usually answer. The new group grew too. Then they got a bigger *local* that had once been a dance studio, between a tanning lounge and a lottery seller across from what turned out to be a brothel. Drugs trading all round them. Junkies in the underpass or hanging around for a handout after the services.

That's when the drugs thing began. A junkie – who was trying to get it together, with nowhere to go, and who needed a street address so as not to be sent down again – pleaded with him. *Please. Anywhere so I can say I don't live on the street. So I can stay out. There's more drugs in prison than out on the street. I'll never make it inside again.* So Ignatio – Nacho – came to stay for six days and left five months later. He would get so agitated for a fix he'd pace up and down the hall all day so they had to find practical things for him to do. He painted the living room three times and the hall six times because that was (marginally) less disruptive. Then he got sick with some new kind of virus the hospital had never seen before. But before he died he made his own new life commitment and passed away without a molecule of heroin in his body, and a smile on his face. Others heard about Nacho and also came knocking. Again the building wasn't big enough. Just around then the Americans were scaling down the NATO base at Torrejón and had property to sell. They bought a huge warehouse shed – number 66. So *Iglesia Evangelica* Warehouse 66 was born, and a cluster of addicts' halfway houses sprouted up around it. He and Rocío did it together. She didn't have a title and didn't want one. She was helping him – or he was helping her. It was never entirely clear and neither of them cared. They just went on getting the job done. Worship, Witness, Works, and Word, they said. And somehow lives did change.

Rocío's little brother Juan was getting into bad company and smoking far too much dope. Then he had to pick pockets or shoplift to pay for it all. He even tried to relieve David of his wallet one day in Puerta del Sol without realizing who it was. Finally the drugs tipped over from being exciting and fun to a monster that was strangling him. In the middle of his latest escapade he remembered his big sister and her man and phoned them up from a police station. They agreed to release him if he had a home to go to and a family to look after him. So Juan came to stay. And the mystery of God-given change came over him as well. One day he got down on his knees, admitted the truth about himself, and handed it all over to a higher authority. By the time he met Alicia –

daughter of a pastor from A Coruña – he was in charge of his own halfway house, and a man who could once again be trusted. And so it went on – another day, another deliverance. David would have to be very clear to the Dynamis listeners that this was not the result of a successful rehab programme; it was a something much deeper than that. Sometimes he felt like the lucky man standing under the window when a toddler falls out. Just be in the right place at the right time, trying to do the right things, and you get to stop a life from breaking. How cool is that?

On the TV over the bar, Real slotted in another one and the Liverpool players' heads went down. *Dios mio* – what was the time? Twenty-five past five. So much for arriving *a tiempo*. He dropped a couple of Euros on the table and ran.

"Pastor David. Thanks again so much for coming in today. We have lots more questions for you, coming up right up after this." The presenter, a young man with dark olive skin, jet black hair, wrap-around sunglasses perched on top of his head, a T-shirt with the station logo, and enormous silver headphones, sat behind his console. He pushed a slider up on the panel in front of him, hit a couple of buttons and slipped the headphones down round his neck.

"Well, that should hold them for a few minutes. We get all the Latin-owned businesses that want to advertise to the evangelical community. It doesn't cost much and it's perfectly targeted. Why do all the dentists come from Bolivia? I don't know. Anyway, feeling ok Pastor David?"

David slid his own headphones off and scratched the slightly greying hair round his temples.

"Yes. Fine. No problems. I've done a fair amount of radio over the years." The young presenter pushed his chair back and took a quick drink from a can of Aquarius.

"You know, I'll have a few questions for you myself when we've finished," he smiled. "Live phone-ins are always a bit hit and miss. Opening the airwaves can be a risky business. Sometimes we get really intelligent questions that come across really well. Other times it's 'What's your favourite Bible verse?' or 'Would you pray for my daughter. She's in love with a presbyterian!' You never can tell."

David smiled. No pastor of a growing church would fail to recognize the problem. But for every question you thought was a waste of breath there was someone who had a doubt, a fear, a dilemma, and that was a pastor's job – to take it all equally seriously and help people find an answer that works for them. Then the ads were done and they were back on the air.

"You've told us a bit about your own journey, Pastor David. How that night Pastor Morales challenged you – the late Pastor Morales, I should say, a great loss to us all. And how you eventually came to faith for yourself. Bringing things up to date now…" He glanced at the big clock on the studio wall – they were still ok. "… Warehouse 66 is one of the biggest churches in Madrid these days. Probably the fastest growing too. Your drug rehab ministry has been widely admired – some would say, copied. Aren't you worried all this attention is going to bring a backlash? You must have reduced the market for drugs in Torrejón by half just by yourselves."

David polished his gold-rimmed glasses for a second. "Of course it's an issue," he said at length. "We've had death threats. Property damaged. Someone sent me a dead rat in the post once. But when you think about the lives that have been changed, how can we stop? It's a mission, but the point is it's not *our* mission. It's something God gave us. We have to keep on. We don't pay for protection – we get our protection from another source. And it's free."

The presenter smiled, glanced quickly up at the clock, then deftly slipped the headphones on again, ran another slider up, and pulled the mike a little nearer on its boom.

"Radio Dynamis, 87.5 FM, throughout Madrid. And it's Luis Ortega on the sofa with Pastor David Hidalgo of Warehouse 66 in Torrejón, one of the fastest-growing churches in Spain. We have another caller on line one. Tell us your name and what you would like to ask Pastor David."

So the phone-in rambled on through the evening show. A few insightful, interesting questions among a majority of bland or predictable ones – wheat with the chaff, just like life – till about ten minutes before the end.

"So, just time for one more question, then a final track from the fantastic new album by Marcos Vidal. Caller on line two, what would you like to ask Pastor David?"

A pause as the caller drew breath.

"Caller on line two," Luis prompted, "You have a question…"

"Sure, I have a question," a slow dry, voice replied.

"And your name please, caller," Luis interrupted, charming but professional.

"David Hidalgo knows my name," the voice replied, smooth and unhurried.

"But we'd like to know too, caller," Luis was smiling at David and holding the boom mike to the side of his mouth.

"Shut up, Ortega," the voice intoned without a break in the rhythm. "And don't cut me off or I'll cut you off." Luis looked at David, eyebrows raised, gesturing across his throat the universal symbol for ending things. David shook his head.

"I know what they call you," David said into his table mike, staring straight ahead. "I don't know your real name though. Raúl *el Niño,* isn't it?"

"Full marks, *Pastor*," with heavy sarcasm on the "pastor".

"Do you have a question, Raúl?" Luis was now looking anything but relaxed.

"Sure I do. My question is this: do you love your wife, Pastor? Do you think she's worth more than your ministry? What do you think she would say?"

A confused mix of sounds. Maybe a scuffle. Then unmistakably a muffled scream.

"David! David! I…"

"That's enough!" Raúl barked, before the sound of a blow, a deeper voice with a Colombian accent swearing heavily, another blow, and a scream rapidly cut off.

"Stop that at once!" Raúl was shouting away from the phone. Not a finger. I told you. Miguel, sort it out!" Then an eery quiet.

"Still there, Pastor David?"

"I'm here."

"Well I'm here too. And so is your lovely wife. She must be such a blessing. So cute. So full of fun."

Luis was looking helplessly at David, hands and arms up in a "what do you want to do now?" gesture. David covered his mike.

"Can you trace the call?" A nod. "Then do it."

"Pastor? Pastor? You've gone all quiet. Not *losing the faith* I hope."

"What do you want, Raúl? Let her go. I'll meet you. Name the place."

"Sorry David." The voice was slow again. "Too late for that, I think. I'd have been nice to you, you know. I really would. Even though you've been taking my customers away. But talking to the police – I can't forgive that. You see *I'm* not even a *Christian*."

"We didn't call the police, Raúl. They came to us. We let them speak to some of our members. That's all. How could we stop them?"

"Well, that's your problem. And now you have another problem. There's a price to pay, Pastor David. By you and those around you. We call it the ultimate price, don't we…?" A sharp crack like a dry stick breaking, and then the line went dead. Luis turned off the open lines and pushed a button on the CD stack. Marcos Vidal started to sing that God would always make a way. David sat with his head bowed forward, forehead in his hands. His face had suddenly lost all colour. Beads of sweat were on his brow.

Chapter 9

MUIRHOUSE

When your parents get divorced it isn't necessarily a good thing in itself but there are definitely compensations if you play it right. Of course there's less routine money around – at least that's what Mum was always saying, usually pointing out why there wouldn't be any cakes, sweets, real Coke or proper ice cream – in fact, almost anything that doesn't come with a cheap "own label" supersaver wrapper slapped on it. But on the other hand there were definitely more treats. Jen didn't think much about the dynamics of post-divorce no-blame child rearing, but the fact was that Christmases and birthdays were usually massive. Whatever Dad gave you, Mum had to give you more, and the other way about. It was like a price war in reverse – and that made you popular at school. And free cash bought ciggies, alcopops, alco without the pops, and some other stuff with names you couldn't even pronounce. It was like steps on a stair. First *this*, which was fun, then *that*, which was better, then *the next thing*, which hit your brains like a frying pan till you couldn't remember why you'd been in a bad mood all week. So you didn't need to try to distract yourself to forget all the rows, the fighting, the accusations, and the hail of ashtrays and ornaments. You could just smoke, sniff, drink or poke it in your arm. No more hassle. Cool.

And that seemed to open the door to new cool friends as well. There was a new bunch of guys around Pilton and Muirhouse. They were funny. They could hardly speak English, some of them, and called each other *amigo* but there seemed no limit to the amount of money they flashed around. Cars, computers, clothes, whatever. And they seemed to be able to supply any sort of "substance" she'd ever been warned about at school and lots she'd bet her teachers had never even heard of. None of it was dear and sometimes they'd even give you stuff for free. When she was high there were other things that all the grown-ups warned her about as well, but they were fun too. And, after all, the grown-ups were so lying. They'd all done it too, except maybe Granny. Though she must have, at least once. So what was there to get so excited about? She had to do some things she didn't much enjoy, but so what?

Raúl was the most fun of all. He spoke perfect English, though with a bit of an accent, and he was always really polite. He said they spoke the best Spanish in the world in Colombia, so she said they spoke the best Scottish in Pilton, which made him laugh and she laughed along too. He never gave her a row for anything, unlike Mum who never stopped giving her hassle. So she ended up spending as little time at home as possible, which wasn't hard once Raúl said she could stay at his place whenever she wanted. It was a bit scary the first time. They had bought four flats in a block. She thought it was a bit strange that they had all been for sale at the same time, but Raúl said it was just a coincidence and that coincidences happened to him all the time. Anyway, they bought all four then got a builder in to knock through the walls. So outside it looked like any other four in a block but inside it was massive. She called it "The Mansion". She'd never seen anything like it – beautiful dark wood, heavy dark furniture, thick dark curtains and stuff. In fact they never seemed to open the curtains much so it was always a bit dark inside. All the guys had their own room with their girls, except Raúl who had two knocked together. Every time she went in it felt like entering a magical realm where Raúl was the magician. In fact, Raúl did seem a bit like a magician brought to life. He could magic up anything you wanted. He gave her a new laptop for her birthday, which she had to tell Mum came from a scheme at school refurbishing old PCs to help with homework. In fact it was the fastest, latest, with the biggest memory and an absolutely massive hard disc. So Raúl told her anyway. And the fastest internet she'd ever seen. They used to watch porn at The Mansion on the big computer upstairs and project it up on the wall. When she tried the laptop it seemed to be just as fast and it was portable so you could watch anything, anywhere. At first she felt a bit confused and upset by what they were watching, but the guys all liked it and their girlfriends (they called them *chicas*) didn't seem to mind. She didn't want to seem ignorant so she didn't complain. When Raúl wanted to do some of the things they'd seen in a clip it was sometimes uncomfortable or gave her an infection but he gave her so much stuff she didn't make a fuss. She told the doctor she caught it swimming.

Raúl was kind – at least he was kind to her, which is what mattered. She'd heard he could get angry, and people he got angry with seemed to disappear for a while. But he never got angry at her. Well, only once when she wouldn't stay overnight. *I've got to go home*, she'd told him. *Gran's coming for tea. I promised her.* He hit her so hard and told her to pick up her clothes and not come back. She didn't have time to get dressed properly before they threw her out the door. But next night when she came back after school everyone was just like normal. Raúl never mentioned it so neither did she. She knew Mum was probably worried but if she was she had a funny way of showing it. All she seemed to do was nag, nag, nag. *Do this. Don't do that. Be in on time. Go to bed. Get up. Why aren't you like your cousins?* Raúl was never like that. And neither was Granny either, actually. She'd have loved to go to Granny's when Dad left, but Mum said no. She knew they'd been invited. There was something between Mum and Granny she didn't understand. Anyway they came to Muirhouse instead of Morningside. Yippee. It was a total dump. But then she would never have met Raúl in Morningside.

Actually, it was wrong to say Raúl never nagged. He did go on at her to get her things and move in. But she was only fifteen; she couldn't live with a man of thirty-five. Or could she? Why not? Once he bought her a diamond on a chain. She tried it on and looked in the mirror. It was unbelievable. But then he made her take it off. *Yours when you move in*, he'd said. She really was sorry to put him off that time. He must really love her or else at least seriously fancy her to get her something like that. She said Mum wouldn't agree but Raúl just laughed. He said he had a way of getting people to agree with him and it seemed to be true. Even the police seemed to mostly leave him alone. Nobody bothered Raúl and all his friends seemed pretty rich and independent too. They were from Glasgow or Liverpool or London. He promised her a weekend in London. But only once she'd moved in. There was no point even mentioning it to Mum. She just kept on about homework and study and tidy your room and stuff. If she was with Raúl there wouldn't be any need to study or go to university or even get a job. None of the guys seemed to have normal jobs but they were never short of cash. Not like the usual Pilton crowd that didn't have jobs either but were always penniless. And there was even a *chica* that tidied your room for you. She looked at Jen in a funny way and once or twice tried to talk to her when Raúl wasn't about. She looked really serious and said *cuidado* a lot but Jen couldn't work out what she was on about so she ignored her.

She suggested Raúl might speak to Mum about things but he said, *no, that's your job*. Then once when she was out shopping with Mum for a new school top, they bumped into Raúl in the shopping centre. She was just about to introduce them when Mum stuck her face right up against his and said, *I know who you are you piece of crap. If I ever catch you near my daughter they'll have to scrape you off the street.* And some other stuff. Nobody ever spoke to Raúl like that but he just kept smiling and called her Ms MacInnes and didn't get upset at all. Actually, it was a bit awesome, but when she'd tried to tell Mum how cool she'd been Mum just said *if I so much as catch you even talking to that maniac I'll nail you to the wall as well.* Just as well Mum thought she spent all her sleepovers at Chivon's. Chivon was a pal and never grassed but it cost her a fiver every time. Lately she'd been asking for ten but Jen said that was too much. If she kept on about it though she'd probably have to hand it over. That or get grounded for the rest of her life.

All things considered Edinburgh was working out quite well, Raúl reckoned. Freeze the *cojones* off you of course but that couldn't be helped. Madrid had become altogether *too* hot and of course there was no way back to Medellin now Pablo was dead. Still, he'd learned everything the old man had had to teach him so that wasn't so bad.

Of course he'd started young. That's why they called him the baby –
El Niño. It had annoyed him at first but he'd got used to it and joined
in the joke. That was safest. If the man he'd taken to thinking of as
his *Papa* thought it was funny that he was the *niño* then it *was* funny
and you should just take the joke. Anyway, he'd learned the entire
business and more importantly the old man's style before it all went
wrong. It was important to leave absolutely no doubt in anyone's
mind about the important things, Pablo said. "Overwhelming
Unreasonable Force" was his expression. Any resistance, any
suggestion of reluctance and you replied with "Overwhelming
Unreasonable Force". A wounding costs a life. A life costs a family.
A family costs a village, etc. Once everyone understood that then
you didn't need to do it so often, which was better for everyone. And
you also needed to be nice to the poor people, who were your real
protection, even more than the judges and police chiefs you had to
pay off every month. In fact, if you were more often nice than nasty
then that was how people came to think of you. He remembered
how tickled the old man was when there was a campaign "Pablo
Escobar for President". The press thought it was a spontaneous
movement of the people and that amused him very much.

And all that effort – all the officials and politicians you had to
keep happy and well oiled, all the time spent in business meetings,
all the detailed meticulous planning and of course some inevitable
risks – it all paid off and made life very comfortable indeed. So you
could indulge yourself in whatever you particularly liked. And Pablo
had some tastes that he could never have indulged living an ordinary
life like the stupid *peones* Colombia was full of. Cars and clothes were
fine but that was more or less routine. The power over other people's
lives was definitely satisfying too, but sometimes all the effort to keep
the operation going made it feel like you were working for them, not
the other way round. No, there were some particular, specific tastes
that most men simply would never experience but that this life made
easy and abundant. It wasn't much spoken about, and of course no
one would dream of complaining, but sometimes you couldn't help
feeling just a little bit sorry for the younger ones. Sixteen or eighteen

was normal. Fourteen was a bit on the limit. Pablo had liked the twelves and thirteens. Well, that was his business. Raúl's business was to look after business. Then, when he became senior enough, he began to emulate his mentor in that as well and found he really liked it too. Like father like son. Pablo encouraged him even to the extent that sometimes they used to swap and compare. That's what all the risks and bloodshed bought you. What a good job there were so many nice kids from nice families and nice communities, in countries that thought themselves superior to a South American warzone, to keep up demand for the product.

However, all good things come to an end, and eventually this was no different. They finally got Pablo through some fancy mobile signal tracing, but still, 25,000 people came to the funeral. Against all the cheering and trophy photos from the police, the ordinary people loved him and missed him. There were many families who blessed his name, as well as those that gave thanks he was dead.

Raúl did think about going to pay his last respects, but he knew the old man would have told him not to be so stupid. So he gathered up those he could trust and they bought tickets to Madrid to start up something new. That had been fun, being your own boss and trying to put the principles of the business into effect in a new market. Unfortunately the key strategy that made Pablo so rich and so well protected for so long didn't seem to work as well in Europe. Many – maybe even most – policemen and judges seemed to have surprisingly little interest in getting quietly and quickly rich by making the famous *vista gorda* – the fat eye – to illegal activities. Politicians were easier, of course, but without getting law enforcement on their side there was a limit to what could be accomplished.

And there were also those that actively got in the way with an almost inexplicable disregard for their own well-being – like that stupid pastor from Torrejón – who had so many *chicos* coming off cocaine that it seriously affected the market. Something had to be done. Killing Hidalgo himself would have been the easy and the reasonable thing to do but that wasn't Pablo's way. So Raúl thought again about Overwhelming Unreasonable Force and tried to think what would be the most overwhelming and unreasonable thing they could do. So he decided to take the wife instead. Much more memorable. However, even that didn't work out like he'd planned. Instead of making everybody back off like it was supposed to, it turned out that the girl had been so popular there was a backlash. The drug enforcement chief – Rodriguez, wasn't it? – managed to swing public opinion so much he got 500 officers just to go after Raúl and friends. Time to move on again. Kind of wasted all the fun they'd had doing it live on air on an evangelical radio phone-in show. Pity. And she was very pretty and quite brave and almost peaceful right up to the end. Hard to make sense of, really. Overall it was a bit of a shame they'd had to mess her up. It took all the fun out of the original plan of dumping the body outside the church on a Sunday morning.

Anyway, Edinburgh – about the right size. A massive market but disorganized. He'd seen an episode of *Españoles por El Mundo* on RTVE in Madrid about Spaniards living in Edinburgh. Somebody mentioned the drugs problem as a downside of living there but Raúl didn't see it that way. It gave him an idea. Once they'd arrived it took some time to get established, but yet again Overwhelming Unreasonable Force did the job. A bit messy for a while but then it settled down.

The north side of Edinburgh was a total dump and it seemed to be constantly freezing even when the sun was out but there were always compensations. Like little Jen. Very cute in her own way. Cute and stupid, but then you didn't expect a fifteen-year-old to know anything about anything. And she was fun once she'd been given some encouragement. For some reason she seemed to be a very angry girl – almost as if she was looking for some excuse to do everything Raúl supposed she'd been told not to – which meant it hardly took any effort at all to pull her in. She started off being compliant and pretty soon was really quite enthusiastic. He only had to be a bit rough once; then she came crawling back and he knew he'd get everything he wanted. You just had to be a little patient sometimes. In fact, that made it better in the long run.

Anyway it all came right in the end. They went to her house when they were sure Mum was out at her cleaning job. She bundled the contents of a couple of cupboards into a case and walked right out with a smile on her face. Very good girl! There was a particular satisfaction in playing a little one and then seeing her jump right onto your lap. Funny how they could be so blind. Well, that was why he was worth a few million dollars and she and her Mum weren't worth worrying about. He thought he might see how long he could keep her going before he got bored. Miguel bet him six months. He took him on. He was sure he'd manage at least eight.

Chapter 10

SOUTHSIDE

By the time David was walking down over the Links on Sunday morning, the snow was beginning to melt and the air felt purified, as if the snow had caught every particle of dirt and grime on its way down and was returning them deep into the earth. He tried to put last night's events behind him. The girl would surely turn up, Mrs MacInnes would surely calm down, and Juan would come to see his point of view. Pausing to cross Melville Drive on the fringes of the Meadows, he preferred to think about dinner at La Hacienda. An evening of witty and attractive company was a rare pleasure and loomed larger in his mind than the problem of a missing teenager. Where it might go and what it might mean he chose not to think about right now. She was just lovely – sympathetic and sensitive. And he had good reasons to see her again in a normal way at Spanish class without considering the more complicated questions. It was enough to enjoy the moment. God knew there had been few enough to enjoy of late. He was feeling good and looking forward to church and the week ahead.

Just one thing kept niggling at the corner of his mind. Although he didn't want to admit it, the conversation with Juan had rattled him. Irene MacInnes's plea, his reaction to it, and Juan's challenge seemed to have crystallized something that up to now he hadn't allowed himself to consider. Is this what they call "thinking the unthinkable"? he wondered. Had he got to the point where he actually lost the plot in relation to faith – in relation to an active trust in a God who cared – or was it just temporarily misplaced? Was God in the dock with the verdict delivered or just subject to a final warning? And what did it mean to be even a part-time pastor, ministering to the faithful, if his own faith was hanging on a shaky nail in a house about to fall down? Juan had said that the story wasn't finished yet and that was true but he couldn't imagine what could change things now. Nothing could bring back the dead. That was for sure. And if he was somehow teetering on the edge, what would happen if he actually fell over? Where would he land, and who would catch him now if there truly wasn't a God you could trust? Finally, with all the activity of the past few days he'd never managed to get that sermon finished. What could he say about the Good Samaritan who took a risk to save a life? He felt the moment's euphoria steadily draining away.

"Good morning, Señor David!" a resolutely cheery voice called over the wrought-iron banister. His thoughts had taken him all the way from his own front door to the stairwell of their little rented upper floor room on automatic pilot. He could have passed a car crash, a bank robbery or an elephant on the way without noticing. He looked up, trying his best to be pleased and positive.

"Good morning, Mrs MacInnes. How are you?"

"Very well, thank you. Do you know, I slept so much better knowing you're going to help us. I've brought Alison along." David reached the landing and turned in through the double doors. A young woman in her mid-thirties was waiting for him dressed in what was very probably Sunday best. Her figure and face were slim to the point of looking pinched. Her complexion was pale, her hair fair and wispy, and her eyes red. She managed a weak smile as they shook hands.

"I'm really sorry to give you any trouble Mr Hidalgo." Her voice was husky and strained and did not sound like it would be much at home in Morningside. "It's probably nothing but Mum thought you might be able to help."

"Señor David," Mrs MacInnes corrected. "We all call him Señor David. On account of his being from Spain, you know. And *of course* it's no trouble. Señor David knows all about this sort of thing. That's right now, isn't it?" She was glancing from one to the other to make it clear that David and Alison were now part of a team.

"Well," David made sure to sound suitably cautious, "I really don't have many contacts in Edinburgh. I'm not sure I'll be very helpful."

Seeing Alison's hopeful expression drain away made him wish he had kept to a polite "Good morning". He could have explained to her later on in a calm and logical manner why he wouldn't be able to help at all.

"Humph." Mrs MacInnes let her feelings be known. "Nonsense. We'll talk about it over a cup of tea after the service." Alison bit her lip and allowed herself to be wheeled off. She sat down near the back next to the missionary prayer board and a pile of ancient hymn books. *Well done*, David thought, making his way grimly down the aisle. *That was nice. That's a lot of help.*

Juan was waiting at the platform.

"You'll have to use the stand mike," he said, adjusting it for height. "The tie clip isn't working again." He wrapped the cable round the boom and headed back to his mixing desk without once glancing up. Alicia at the keyboard caught David's eye and also looked down. *Great*, he thought. *That's unanimous. Everyone's mad at me.*

The band were in good form and led the couple of dozen of the congregation in a flowing, easy mix of lively celebration and quieter, more reflective worship. David led in prayer then looked up his reading. Luke 10:25–37 – the Good Samaritan. It was a well-known passage not encumbered with any tricky Hebrew names to navigate around or a pile of begats but as he read aloud, he found himself becoming increasingly uncomfortable. He'd got a few thoughts together during the singing and was hoping he could maybe wing it but it didn't feel remotely right. David read more and more slowly as the passage progressed. The parallels were unavoidable, the implications obvious. His mouth was dry and his palms sweating. He wanted to sit down but couldn't. He started feeling slightly dizzy then distinctly sick.

He took a sip of water, paused, then closed the Bible and looked out over the company. He'd only been here a matter of weeks and was still on honeymoon terms. For most there was a sense of satisfaction that they'd got a real pastor when the best they'd expected was a student internship. Here was a man of experience, a man who could be trusted, a man who had seen God at work and worked with him. He was the man for their moment who would sort things out. On the other hand Juan continued looking down. Alicia watched him with an expression of confusion and concern. Irene MacInnes pursed her lips, a steely glint in her eye. Alison looked hopeless. As the silence grew, the congregation started feeling a little uneasy. Some shuffling broke out and a cough or two. A low murmur was spreading as he folded up his notes and put them aside. He cleared his throat. He had made a decision. It had to be done.

"I'm afraid I have something of a confession to make this morning," he began. "I've recently found myself in a situation a bit like the Good Samaritan. But I haven't been handling it too well…"

After the service, opinions differed as to just what exactly had happened that morning. Some took the simple view that the ways of ministers are past finding out so further analysis was pointless. It was the sort of eccentricity congregations had to put up with from time to time. As long as nobody was asked to clap, cheer, raise their hands or otherwise interact then probably no harm was done. Group two – the minority opinion – took a dimmer view. They had never been in favour of an outsider and now they found they had only allowed themselves to be talked into it against their better judgment. "Señor David", as some insisted on calling him, had seemed a bit of a queer fish right from the start and now it was all coming out in the wash. Things like this should be nipped in the bud before we all end up being required to confess our sins to one another like Pentecostals. Finally, the largest group, while not entirely understanding what was going on, did sense something of the struggle and its outcome. These were the ones who shook his hand, squeezed his elbow, and wanted him to know they were with him, whatever it was all about.

Finally, tea and coffee were trundled out and people started milling around and chatting. David shook hands with those that had to go. Juan and Alicia were waiting for him as he came down for a coffee. Juan had a grin on his face and Alicia was looking as if she had just won the *Evening News* prize bingo. She threw her arms around his neck and squeezed till it hurt.

"*Estoy tan orgullosa de ti*. I'm very proud of you," she said. She reached up to kiss his cheek and whispered in his ear. "Well done. Rocío would have been proud." Mrs MacInnes bustled over the cups of tea, shepherding Alison along with her.

"Well, Señor David. I don't know if you were referring to our little problem today but in any case I've always had perfect confidence you would know what to do. So, what do you recommend?"

David may have been dimly aware he had turned a bend in the road but wasn't yet at the point of accelerating down the back straight.

"Well perhaps we need a little privacy first to let Alison tell her story." He was about to lead the way into the tiny back room when he felt a presence behind him and turned.

"Gillian? I didn't see you coming in. Welcome to Southside!"

"I had to see how things worked out after your call last night. Any news?"

"That's just what we're going to find out. Want to join us?"

With Alison's agreement they got together as the congregation began to disperse.

"Ok," David began directing himself to Alison, "I'm sorry there's so many of us here when it's such a personal matter. I can speak to you on our own if you want but we might need to work as a team to do any good. Is that all right?"

Alison shrugged and seemed to accept the need to tell her story to a meeting, not just to the pastor. Haltingly, with much encouragement, repetition, clarification, and summarizing, it all came out. Alison spoke of a marriage in trouble and Jennifer as a sensitive child who couldn't put up with the arguments and increasingly bitter atmosphere. Eventually when Ian had left there was an immediate sense of relief, but as time went on Jennifer missed her dad and Alison missed a partner in looking after a teenage daughter. Being evicted from the house and having to take a council flat in a tough area made things ten times worse. She hinted at a series of unsuitable boyfriends, debt problems, and finally worries about her health from all the stress. Jen was also getting to be a law unto herself. Schoolwork had gone by the board and she was keeping later and later hours, sometimes staying out for days. Then she started finding bits and pieces in Jen's room that pointed at experimentation with drugs. Alison tried being calm and understanding. Then she tried reading the riot act. Neither made much difference. Eventually, Jen was staying out all weekend and refusing to say where she'd been. Now she'd been gone for over a week with some of her clothes missing and Alison had done everything she could in terms of speaking to friends, teachers, and neighbours but without a clue.

"Ok," David summed up. "That's a lot of information. Normally missing persons are a matter for the police but your mum said you didn't want them informed." Alison glanced at her mum with a look of embarrassment.

"Yeah, I didn't really want Mum going to the police."

"So does that mean you *have* been to the police, you just didn't want your mum to know?" David asked. Alison was studying the floor.

"That's right," she muttered. "I went straight to the police when she'd been gone right over the weekend. I'm not daft, like. They've told me they'd be looking out for her but there's nothing more than that yet." Then, turning to her mum, she added, "I just wasn't wanting to worry you. It's my problem." Mrs MacInnes reached across and squeezed Alison's hand.

"I'm sorry you didn't feel able to tell me sooner. I know I should have given you more help. Once we find Jennifer I'll do better. I promise."

"Ok, so that leaves us with what to do now," David carried on. "In Madrid we knew all about the gangs – I'm sorry to say. Here I really have no idea."

"*No es verdad,* Señor David," Juan broke in. "That's not completely true. A lot of the *compadres* come into Hacienda. There've been more and more Spanish about in the last year."

"You mean more Spanish people moving to Edinburgh?"

"Yes, but not the sort we want. It looks like some of the bosses have maybe come to Edinburgh for a new market or something. Maybe the *Policia Nacional* have been making things harder for them so they need to make a new home. *Chicos* with too much money and big cars. They come to Hacienda and have a *fiesta* sometimes."

"Does that mean anything to you, Alison?" David asked. Alison shook her head, then, just as David was about to ask another question an idea struck her.

"Raúl? Is that a Spanish name? She's been talking about somebody called Raúl. It just sounded like a football player to me so I never paid any attention. Maybe he's a boyfriend or something?" David and Juan exchanged glances.

"Well, that might all be very interesting," Mrs MacInnes announced, sitting very upright and drawing her handbag in tight. "But there must be thousands of young people taking these drugs and dozens of these 'gangs' about. If the *Scotsman* is to be believed. How on earth are we to find out who they are and if anybody knows anything about Jennifer?" Nobody spoke for several seconds, then Gillian broke the silence.

"Soup," she said. "What about soup?" There was a mystified silence as they looked at her blankly.

"I help with a soup kitchen on Friday nights," she explained. "They go to Muirhouse and Pilton sometimes. They get lots of young people and homeless folk that need something to warm them up. Maybe somebody there might know something."

Chapter 11

DRYLAW

Dr Gillian Lockhart got in from a frantic day's teaching, marking, tutorials, and board meetings, made a quick pasta tea and ate it alone reading proofs of her paper on "changing vowel sounds in West of Scotland under 35s". The Radio Scotland six o'clock news chattered in the background. She quickly scanned the paper, noted one or two typos, added an additional footnote, then ran a bath. She turned the radio off, put *Blood on the Tracks* on her iPod then cleared away, tidied up the living room, undressed and took the latest McCall Smith through to the bathroom. Only when she had added some bubble bath, frothed it up a bit, closed the door, sunk into the bath and picked up her book did she realize that she hadn't stopped to think for a second all day. Then she remembered it was Friday and that Friday night was van night. They were hoping to run into someone who knew something about some missing teenager. She realized how keyed up she was but then noticed that it wasn't just about the kids on the street, the fights that sometimes broke out, the hostile drunks that pestered them or even the depressing, litter-strewn neighbourhoods. David Hidalgo was on her mind.

One week ago she had been quietly getting on with things, doing her job, trying to pursue a career, and telling herself divorce was not a failure. These things happened. Marriage had just been the wrong choice at the wrong time. Or maybe the wrong bloke at the wrong time – no more, no less. It was time to move on. And there were new interests to pursue, like improving her Spanish. Well, it had certainly turned into more than just a new interest. But how much more? She'd always thought meeting someone "quite unlike anyone I've ever met before" was a very nice idea for cuddling up with in the land of Mills and Boon but just not *realistic* in the real world. In fact "realistic" had become a bit of a comfort word. It helped you deal with one disappointing date after another. *There's nothing wrong with me*, she told herself resolutely. And nothing in principle wrong with the succession of blokes across the table at Prestonfield House or some other equally pretentious grazing spot. I'm just not being *realistic*. There was a very good reason why all her girlfriends in the "recently divorced – now looking around again" club used to grumble again and again about "the nice ones all being taken". But if you heard that long enough and then you came across what certainly looked like a nice one, not currently taken, it did make you suspicious.

She'd managed to piece together the basic plot partly from what he'd said, partly from what he'd not said, partly from Juan's hints, and partly from a bit of web sleuthing. Anglo-Spanish, brought up in Edinburgh, made his career in Spain. Got religion – seriously. Ended up a pastor in some sort of drugs rehab thing in a thriving church just outside Madrid. Then lost his wife. Just exactly how, she still wasn't sure, but it seemed to have been sudden and traumatic. So he came home to Edinburgh to try to put the few remaining pieces back together again. She'd come across "religious" people before of course – even one or two friends were a bit that way inclined. What she couldn't get a grip of was someone who really did seem genuine and open – hurts, heartaches, and all – but who still took seriously this other dimension to life. In fact it didn't feel like religion at all, more like just another normality. When he spoke about God he didn't seem embarrassed or ironic like most of her set. He spoke about things many people would probably see as coincidental or serendipitous or the power of positive thinking, but he thought they were miraculous. God, he seemed to be suggesting – fed up with being confined to the pages of philosophy essays or Sunday Supplement reviews of the latest Dawkins or Hitchens – was engaging in real people's lives and changing them for the better, his included. At least until recently. He may have been (probably was) sincerely deluded but he did not seem to be either a nutter or a crank. He wasn't proposing they live in a tent on the Meadows awaiting the second coming or hand out flyers on Princes Street. He was just a guy who had been doing what he thought was right, helping those that needed it, who had been brutally deprived, but was now somehow being asked to get back on the horse again and make some sense of what faith he had left. It couldn't be easy.

Confusing as all that might be, clearly there were also some personal implications – no point in denying it. But was it *realistic* to think this could have any bearing on her life, which in almost every respect seemed so different from his? In every respect except for one tiny little detail – they were both adrift and wondering what would come next. Had they been on a date? Surely not. Was there a possibility of "going out" with a minister? Ridiculous. But concluding it just wasn't realistic made her feel strangely disappointed. She did want to see him again – and not just to improve her Spanish conversation. Why? So she had found herself strolling down South Clerk Street, a mile and a half from home at eleven o'clock on a Sunday morning, when she was normally in bed leafing through the Sundays and enjoying a second round of tea and toast. Tiptoeing up the stairs and creeping in at the back of the hall had felt like infiltrating a secret society. Then that extraordinary sermon – if you could call it that. A mixture of confessional and exposition of a morality tale but actually applied as if it was supposed to change how you actually behaved in real life. Finally, to cap it all, when they had no idea what to do next, she had given them a suggestion that would draw her in even more deeply. Again – why?

Bob Dylan was singing "Simple Twist of Fate" as she climbed out of the bath, wrapped a towel around her, and went through to the bedroom to dress. It was often bitterly cold on the van so she usually wore thick jeans, an old work shirt of her dad's that she thought still smelled of him, a fleecy top, and a hill-walking jacket. Tonight she felt like a change. She might be venturing into the urban jungle but that wasn't any reason to look like a commando. Maybe some nail varnish too. An hour later, in black corduroys, a charcoal top from Next, and a puffy pink ski jacket, she was ready. She grabbed a pair of gloves, matching hat and scarf, locked up, and ran down the common stair. Her heart was beating a little too strongly to be from just the exercise. She stamped her feet and breathed smoke into the night air. Maggie and Jeff wouldn't be long. The temperature was falling fast.

The ancient Soup Dragon van, loaded up for a night's work, just managed the turn from Melville Drive into Marchmont Road, rattled up the hill, and squealed to a halt outside the delicatessen on the corner. The little man in the driver's seat seemed to consider wrecking the suspension a personal challenge. With his wispy van Dyke, earring, tattoos, and neckerchief, Jeff looked like a refugee from Dexys Midnight Runners. Maggie – big, blond, and brassy in a huge sheepskin-lined denim coat and shapeless jeans – sat next to him. Known to the regulars as "Big Maggie", she had patience with strugglers but the wasters and hangers-on got short shrift. Some wag from Granton had labelled her the "Soup Dragon" and it had stuck to the point that they painted it on the van. Maggie liked the joke, though she wouldn't admit it.

"You're all dolled up," she said, leaning back and taking a good look. "The punters'll no appreciate it y'know." Gillian rolled her eyes.

"I know," she said. "But you've got to make the effort."

"Ok," Jeff shouted over the belches and bellows of the engine. "Picking up your friend. Bruntsfield, is it?" Gillian gave him the address as they pulled up the hill onto Thirlestane Road. She really wanted David to make a good impression and not come over like a nut job. He was waiting outside, right on time, dressed exactly as for Spanish class – overcoat and fedora. Gillian wondered if he didn't have a very wide range to choose from, or maybe it just wasn't that important. He climbed in and off they went. They updated Maggie and Jeff on as much of the story as they knew speeding through Tollcross, past the old Methodist Central Hall now back in use again and apparently thriving after being empty for years, then down Lothian Road, round the elegant facades of Charlotte Square, and finally over the Dean Bridge and out Queensferry Road. Gillian felt a peculiar cocktail of excitement, anticipation, apprehension, and something else she couldn't quite place. They turned at the lights and plunged down Orchard Brae into the underbelly of the city.

"You haven't done this one before, have you?" Maggie remarked to Gillian.

"No, 'fraid not. Nights I've been on it's always been the Grassmarket or Leith Walk. Oh, and Craigmillar once."

"Once is enough," Jeff chipped in. Maggie ignored him.

"So, just to get this straight. The girl's been living in Muirhouse for about eighteen months. We think she's been shooting up for at least a year – in other words, plenty of time to make the acquaintance of every undesirable in the area. So there might be some connections. On the other hand we've no idea if she's even in Edinburgh any more – or in Britain for that matter."

"No, I think we know she's still in the country," David countered. "Her passport's at home. But, otherwise – Muirhouse, Macclesfield, could be anywhere."

"And there was that thing about Raúl, the possible boyfriend," Gillian added.

"Which could be significant or a complete red herring," Maggie replied. "I don't want to be negative, but I've been asked to look out for so many runaways and so few of them turn up. At least, so few turn up where you look for them. Plenty in London if you want to go that far. But a fifteen-year-old in London isn't going to do very well. In fact, I think as far as that's concerned, she's probably already in big trouble here."

With that gloomy assessment Jeff pulled the van off Ferry Road into the long strip of parking and run-down shops that made up the Drylaw Shopping Centre.

"Well – here we are. Welcome to my world," Maggie announced as they lurched to a halt.

"Weren't we were going down into Muirhouse?" Gillian asked as Maggie squeezed past her into the back of the van to start getting things organized.

"Ah, well. This happy spot lets us serve as a beacon to Muirhouse, Pilton, and Drylaw – not that Drylaw really needs it. It's amazing actually. Less than half a mile apart but in Drylaw you've got tidy gardens, second cars, new front doors, and nice kids. Just around the corner there's the new Axis flats – £375,000 apiece. Pilton across the road used to have more Alsatian dogs than people. I don't suppose the garden makeover shows go down so well here. And Muirhouse of course needs no introduction – specially if you've seen *Trainspotting*."

"But there's bound to be decent folk here as well," Gillian put in.

"Of course," Maggie agreed. "And maybe more decent than the bankers in Charlotte Square. But the fact is the area just hasn't been a priority for years. The housing's appalling, the kids have nothing to do, and there's very little for families. That means that if you have higher aspirations, you don't want to live here a moment longer than necessary. So people move out if they can, which leaves empty housing – which creates a vacuum for people that can't go anywhere else. They call it 'hard to let' so you really have to be desperate if you're willing to consider it. People that desperate often bring their problems with them. So it gets worse. Even the social workers don't want to be here. Can you blame them? They park their cars half a mile away and walk."

They began to get things organized. Jeff connected the gas, Gillian looked out the polystyrene cups and buttered the rolls, while David was detailed to fill the leaflet racks with handouts from Health Scotland, Social Work, and Telford College. Maggie had heard a bit about David before she'd agreed to allow him onto the van but now she took the chance to fill in the gaps. She listened closely as he described how Warehouse 66 had gone about getting kids off drugs and into jobs, houses, and relationships.

"So really it's community living with a bit of religion thrown in?"

"No, I wouldn't say that. Spiritual growth was the key. We found that without a change from the inside, outside things made very little difference."

"And what exactly do you mean by 'spiritual'?"

Gillian was listening in. She was hoping it might answer some questions but at the same time terrified it would show David up as just another religious fanatic. Instead he spoke quietly and sensibly about the kids that came in messed up and filthy, how they lived in the rehab houses, the successes and the relapses, and the number that went on to become leaders in other houses elsewhere, cleaned up to the point of being brand new people with new families and a purpose in life for the first time. And he put it all down to spiritual transformation. No hesitation. Maggie nodded from time to time. Gillian was relieved.

"Well," Maggie concluded when everything in the van seemed to be ready. "You're off your chump if you think religion is the answer for the nutters, bampots, and thugs we see. But whatever floats your boat. I'll give you this – from what you've said, you seem to see results. Can't argue with that. Far too much effort and far too little results most of the time."

"I'm curious," David remarked, while they were waiting. "Normally a soup kitchen is aimed at the homeless. But rough sleepers are in the city centre, not the housing schemes. So this isn't about soup at all, is it?"

"Quite right," Maggie agreed. "That's just for openers. We're here to try to get to know the kids, the dealers, the pushers, the runners, the addicts. They'll stop by for a cuppa when they'd never look twice at a welfare service. If we can gain their confidence then we can help them more when they need it."

"And they do come for help?"

"Sure, from time to time – some of them. When they're ready. We're well known to the Housing Department, even some of the GPs. We can try to work the system a bit in favour of those that are ready for a change."

"You keep saying 'we'," David said. "Who exactly is 'we'? There isn't an organization name on the van."

"Well done. The organization is Jeff and Maggie Ltd. We used to work for University Settlement. Then the Cyrenians. Then Edinburgh Action on Homelessness. I prefer being on my own. Nobody breathing down your neck and telling you what to do."

"And we fell out with every single one of them," Jeff added. "The last lot let us keep the van though so that was ok."

As they were talking, Gillian had a chance to look along the line of shops. Conspicuous by their absence were greengrocers, florists, electrical goods, and banks. Instead there was a full set of pub, off licence, bookies, criminal solicitors, two carry-outs, chemist, post office, loan agent, CAB, and a cheap supermarket – the complete opposite, in fact, from the cluster of shops at the bottom of Marchmont Road. She doubted whether her favourite delicatessen would do much business here. Not at what they charged for organic avocados and fresh pasta anyway.

Finally, Maggie gave everything the once over and seemed satisfied.

"Ok, Ladies and Gentlemen. We're open for business!"

David looked at his watch. Ten thirty. Jeff hopped out of the back door, hooked up a flap in the side, and they settled back for their first customer. It didn't take long. A group of giggly girls in strappy sandals and minuscule skirts appeared, apparently immune to the cold. It looked like their get-ups had come from a factory with a high-output target but not enough material to make complete garments.

"You girls out on the randan?" It wasn't clear if Maggie was posing a question or just making an observation. Either would have fitted.

"Aye. Party at Jools's the night," the blondest of a blond bunch replied. "Yiv goat tae look the part, 'n' tha'. Niven ken who ye might meet!" Even more giggling alongside some stamping and rubbing of bare arms to try to generate a little heat. One of the group produced a can of super lager and passed it round.

"Hey Maggie! Ken whit this is fur?" she said, holding a can of super lager up to the counter.

"Aye. Ah ken a' right. It's fur the girls on the game. Gets them in the mood."

A responsible adult using street talk seemed hilarious and the group fell about laughing.

"Gon' yersel' Maggie. Yir aw right!" the skinniest at the back shouted, holding up the can like a toast and gobbling down another swally.

"So, whit'll it be lasses?" Maggie adopted her posh voice now. "Tonight we have lentil soup, buttered rolls, buttered rolls and lentil soup. Oh aye, an' there's lentil soup."

"Goat ony lentil soup?" one of the girls shouted, cracking up again.

"Sorry hen. Wir completely out. There's lentil soup though."

"Ocht. Awright. Ge's wan o' them." More laughter.

Half a dozen soups and rolls were handed round as the group seemed to huddle closer to the van as if the open window were a source of warmth in itself. Maggie let them get comfortable then produced a plastic wallet with a 3-by-2 snap in it.

"So. Any o' yous lassies seen a girl wir huvin' a wee look fur. Hur mum's up to high doh and asked us keep an eye out."

"Who's that then?"

"Name's Jen. That's hur. Onybdy ken 'ur?"

Maggie handed down the photo while Jeff was passing refills around. Gillian dished out more buttered rolls and David kept well in the background pretending to be drying a handful of knives.

"Here, Chivon," the girl that seemed to be ringleader passed the photo back. "Is that no'…"

"Naw. That's no hur," Chivon replied, giving the snap the merest glance and handing it back. "Sorry, Maggie. Nae idea. Niver seen 'ur afore."

"So who did you think it wiz then?" Maggie tried but Chivon was having none of it.

"Dinnae ken. Naebdy."

"Well. Her name's Jen MacInnes. She's done a runner and her mum's climbing the walls so if onybody sees 'ur gaez a ring, right? The number's on the side o' the cup." The girls drank up and wolfed the rolls before mostly handing the cups back and heading off.

"Huv a gid nights, lasses," Maggie shouted after then. "Be good."

"An' if you cannae be good be careful," two or three of them sing-songed back to more giggling as they headed round the corner and disappeared.

"Well, no progress there," Gillian said, clipping the lid back on a big tupperware tub full of rolls.

"Not at all," Maggie countered. "They all know her but they're not talking. I'd call that progress."

So the night wore on as word spread that the Dragon was about. Their clientele consisted mainly of kids with nothing to do hanging round, guising, joking, pushing, play fighting till it got hard to tell if it was playing or real, some twenties and thirties at a loose end, one old man on his way back from the dogs, a couple of women heading home from a hen night complete with magic wands and flashing tinsel antennae. The story was the same. Those that didn't know sounded concerned and agreed to phone if they heard. Those that did weren't talking. Finally, at half past twelve, when most of the trade seemed to have either arrived back home or got to their party for the night, they started to pack up.

"Well, we did what we could," Gillian said, trying to sound cheerful.

"I think we can put it a bit more positively," Maggie replied thoughtfully, having lost her street twang all of a sudden. "The kids all know her and I think it's pretty likely she's still somewhere around here or there wouldn't be the need to protect her so much. If she was well away I think somebody would probably have said. What d'ye think Davie?"

It was years since anyone had called him that except his mum and he liked it.

"I think you're right. It's a neighbourhood where people know each other. But they know the authorities as well. All the soup in the world still doesn't get you across that line."

"Unless you get invited of course," Jeff put in.

"Of course. But we're not there yet. I'm sure you're right. Maybe that'll be helpful if we can give the police a bit of a clue."

"Oh no we don't," Maggie cut in. "We're here for the kids and the mum. She can talk to who she likes. We do not pass on what we get to the polis. Rule numero uno."

"Never?" Gillian asked.

"Almost never. I've had to do it a couple of times when it was life or death, but if it gets back to the street then we might as well sit at home and watch *Strictly*. That's the deal."

After that the rest of the assorted kit and leftovers were tidied up. They were just about to swing the window flap down and lock up when a friendly voice hailed them from the shadows.

"Haw! Maggie. How's it gawn? Missed ye last week." A thin, gaunt-looking young man with bleached blond hair and a wispy moustache, in a flimsy jogging suit despite the freezing air, popped his nose in at the hatch looking round for anything left. He could have been anything between nineteen and thirty-five. His companion was more heavily built, with short, jet black hair and a darker complexion. He wore a leather bomber jacket, expensive Levis, and cowboy boots. The collar of the jacket was turned up and one hand was thrust deep in a pocket – the other held a thin cigar. He was shivering.

"No bad Eric. Hoo's yirsel'? Fancy something warm? Lentil and bacon and rolls the night. There's just a wee bit left."

"Aye. Cheers. Magic. Man, it's absolutely baltic. Thanks. Ony chance o' annar roll? Cool." He stepped back and began to gobble down the bread and soup.

"What about yer pal?"

"Yes, me too." David immediately pricked up his ears. The accent was definitely not Scottish. He leaned forward as Maggie and Eric chatted.

"You're out late Eric. Whit's goan on?"

"Ah weel, ye ken whit it's like. Bit o' this, bit o' that. Miguel here's got some guys tae meet so we're jist heading doon the road." Eric's pal looked up uncomfortably and backed out of sight.

"Eric, I'm on the lookout for a lassie that's gone missin'," Maggie continued. "Think you might huv seen her?"

"Maybe. Whae is it, like?"

David offered a photo. "Her name's Jen," he said. "Fifteen. From Muirhouse." Eric held the photo up to the light.

"Oh aye. I ken Jen awright. Didnae ken she wiz AWOL though. Nice lassie. Nae idea whar she is though." Eric handed the photo back as Miguel muttered something under his breath. Whatever he said had an immediate effect on Eric.

"Right, we've got to leg it," he announced abruptly. "Best o' luck. See yiz." Eric planked his half-finished soup back on the counter, Miguel dropped his in the gutter, and they were off in the direction of Pennywell Road.

"Well, well," said Maggie. "A: he knows her and probably where she is. B: he has a good reason for not letting on – reminded by his mate. So whoever she's around with is somebody Eric doesn't want to get on the wrong side of. David, what did you make of Miguel? Spanish maybe?"

"Certainly. Or South American. I didn't catch everything but he certainly referred to their *jefe*. That's the boss. Maybe they're off to tell him someone's asking questions."

It took half an hour to get everything finally packed up. David was thinking of what he was going to tell Alison and her mum from their night out, Gillian was thinking of a warm bed, and Jeff about fish suppers and Irn Bru. Half-way back down Crewe Road, just past the Western General, Jeff noticed an untidy figure hunched up in the bus shelter. He was about to remark that there was a hopeful soul – the next night service bus wasn't for another hour – when the figure looked up, saw the van, and seemed to deliberately launch himself off the pavement right into their path. Jeff slammed on the brakes, sending every loose item hurtling forward. But instead of holding up his hand in the familiar mixture of greeting and apology of the meandering drunk, the man raced round to the passenger door, hauled it open, jumped inside almost onto Gillian's lap, and shouted at Jeff,

"Now drive ye daft bastard! Drive! Keep gawn!"

"Eric! What d'ye think you're doing?" Maggie bawled at him.

"Never you mind. Just keep gawn."

Jeff shrugged his shoulders, put the van into gear, and continued down the hill. Eric was a different man from the relaxed, bantering bloke of half an hour ago. Now he was seriously agitated. He kept looking out of both side windows and straining round behind them. Despite the heater going full blast he was shivering and seemed to be in a cold sweat. He had both hands gripped under his armpits, forearms clamped across his chest and would not put a seatbelt on. When Jeff made to retrace their steps towards Lothian Road Eric reached across to grab the steering wheel and had to be restrained.

"Naw. Head fur the park," was the only thing he would say. Maggie nodded curtly. So instead of back round Charlotte Square, Jeff took them along Queen Street past Robert Adam's grand facades and elegant doorways, down onto Leith Walk and out London Road.

Eric came to life again once they were in Holyrood Park. Jeff tried to turn right, up towards Pollock Halls and the South Side.

"No that way. The long way roon'."

Again Maggie nodded as Jeff shook his head and pulled the van round to the left. They drove through the velvet blackness of the park without a word. Arthur's Seat lay like a sleeping lion in front of them, masking half the starry sky. They followed the Queen's Drive down towards Jock's Lodge but at the turning Eric kept them in the park. Only when they were fully round the far side of Arthur's Seat at Duddingston Loch did he seem to relax.

"Right. In here. The car park." Jeff did as instructed, parking as far away as possible from the only other car. By the dim silhouette its occupants weren't interested in anyone else anyway. Jeff turned the key and the engine died. Maggie looked Eric full in the face.

"Right," she said, "just what exactly are you playing at?"

"Wait and see," said Eric, smiling for the first time. He had the look of a conjurer just about to pull a rabbit out of his hat. He took a *Daily Record* out of an inner pocket, unfolded it, crossed his legs, and turned to the football pages. Maggie stared at Eric, looked round at Jeff, back at Eric, then snorted with impatience, folded her arms, and stared fixedly out over the loch.

"This better be good," she muttered. "This really better be good."

Gillian began to tidy up the shambles caused by the emergency stop. David looked up at the stars and seemed unperturbed. Jeff glanced at the couple in the car across from them and wondered where he could get a chip shop open at this time of night.

Chapter 12

HOLYROOD PARK

That Friday started much like any other at Hacienda. Alicia had made arrangements to meet Julie from David's Spanish class for conversation over coffee at Beanscene on Nicholson Street, just round the corner. Actually the situation wasn't quite as dire as Julie had thought and she soon found she could understand most of what Alicia said and nearly everything when it was repeated a bit more slowly. Together they concluded that a big part of the problem was Julie's tutor's strong Argentinian accent, which changed a number of the vowel sounds, consonants, and even some grammar. Three cups later, once Alicia had explained the differences and got her to practise, it began to fall into place. Then they found they had a lot in common and agreed to meet the following week. Julie also heard all about Warehouse 66, David Hidalgo, and how Juan and Alicia had come to Edinburgh. She promised to bring a gang of student friends and sample the *tapas* and sangria.

Juan went in early to get things sorted out for that evening. Fridays were busy but it was the best chance to impress so that's when they tried new specials. Alicia's nephew Tomas was over from Madrid looking for work like so many more fleeing from *La Crisis* and had agreed to help in exchange for board and lodgings but some training was still required. He was sent out to buy ingredients and practise his English while Juan experimented with *Gallo de Campo a la Jerezana* from a new regional collection he had just bought. This involved browning chicken joints in olive oil with garlic, then adding green peppers and onions and sautéing till soft. Next a full bottle of oloroso sherry per eight portions. Once reduced by half, a similar amount of chicken stock, then reduced again. The chicken was removed and cut into filets and the sauce strained and reheated. Finally the chicken was covered in sauce and sprinkled with pine kernels and sultanas for a Moorish flavour. Juan tried it out a couple of different ways with slight variations until he got it exactly right. Delicious. Tomas got back with approximately what he had been sent for and Alicia came in from her meeting. They sat down to sample the new special and pronounced it fit for paying customers. Around mid-afternoon David dropped by and told them he had arranged to go out on the soup van with Gillian that night. Tomas eventually managed to get the coffee machine to work so they had a coffee together and prayed for a good outcome. David left them to get on with things while he did some visits.

The evening wore on about as normal with a few couples and one single family, until around ten when the door swung open and a large, noisy, mixed group swaggered in. The men were mainly in leather jackets and jeans except for one, a little older than the rest, in an immaculate camel-hair coat, beige trousers, and highly polished brown leather shoes. The women were in brightly coloured dresses and shawls. A few had flowers in their hair. They had a Latin American look with the exception of one younger, paler girl holding onto the man in the camel-hair coat. One of the men – tall, broad, and extremely muscular with a black shirt open at the neck and a variety of gold chains and rings – came up to the desk.

"You have a table for eight," he said. It was more statement than enquiry. This was Tomas's first customer.

"Eh, of course. Do you have a reservation?" he asked hesitantly.

"Álvarez." The man spoke with complete assurance. Tomas scanned the reservations book.

"I'm sorry, I – I can't seem to find anything in that name." The man grunted and narrowed his eyes.

"I think you must have lost it," he said. "Very careless." He turned back. "Hey – they've lost the reservation!" The man in the camel-hair coat held out his hands in mock disbelief and said something Tomas didn't catch.

"Ok. We made a reservation – now. You find us a table. Yes?"

"Of – of course, *momentito Señor*." Diving for cover, Tomas shot through the kitchen door. Juan appeared a few seconds later. He glanced round and summed up the situation.

"I'm sorry sir," he said. "We don't seem to have the reservation. But there's no problem. Over here. By the window?" The man looked back to the group.

"*¿Allá. A la ventana?*" he called over. The camel-hair coat looked up, wrinkled his nose, frowned, and shook his head. The man in the black shirt scanned slowly round then spotted another table against the wall about half-way into the dining room.

"There," he said. "That one." Juan forced a smile.

"No problem, Señor. *Está bien*." Tomas reappeared, ejected by Alicia. They brought two tables together and the group sat down. They studied the menu in a leisurely manner, the men pointing and joking and giving advice to the women who were giggling and adjusting their make-up. One or two were texting friends while the men chose for them. Only the younger, paler girl wasn't joining in until an older, strikingly glamorous woman next to her pointed out a few things which she seemed to be explaining. The girl smiled nervously and nodded. Once the hubbub had died down Juan came for the order. The man in the camel-hair coat questioned him about various dishes and wines then seemed satisfied and ordered for everyone.

"What was that all about?" Alicia asked as Juan came back into the kitchen.

"A big group. South American. Walking in here like they own the place! It's a good order but you sometimes wonder if we'd be better off without that sort. Do you know, there's something about one of them that seems a little bit familiar."

Despite Juan's misgivings and Tomas's nerves, the meal went off without further incident. The group were noisy and boisterous but not out of order. Extra wine was ordered then three large bottles of Cava. It seemed to be somebody's birthday. There was much chinking of glasses and calls of "*Salud*" and "*Feliz cumpleaños*". The pale girl produced a brightly wrapped package and placed it on the table in front of the man who by now had taken off the camel-hair coat and had it loosely arranged around his shoulders. He opened his mouth and eyes wide in mock surprise, smiled, put his arm around her, and kissed her hard – full on the mouth. The girl pulled back a fraction then seemed to remember herself and submitted. She giggled nervously as he unwrapped it. Whatever it was, it seemed to be expensive. He opened the jeweller's box, told her she shouldn't have – or something equivalent – and slipped it into an inside pocket.

Eventually, around 12:30, they began to wind up. The table was cleared, last sips taken from the coffee, and the bill produced. The man in the camel-hair coat took one glance at it then took out his wallet.

"*Estupendo.*" He glanced up at Juan. "*Muy rico* – delicious." He deftly counted out twenty-five ten-pound notes then thought better of it and added five more. Juan thanked him and gathered up the bill, the cash, and the empty coffee cups.

Half-way to the door, a mobile phone went off. One of the men pulled it out of an inside pocket and flipped it open. He listened for a few seconds, glanced at the pale-faced girl, then muttered a few words and snapped it shut. He took the man in the camel-hair coat by the elbow, pulled him slightly apart, and began to whisper in his ear. The older man nodded curtly a few times, also glanced at the pale girl, then smiled. He called the men back while the women hung around the door. An urgent, whispered conference took place. He was like a general giving instructions. Each man in turn was detailed for some duty. Then he stopped, half turned, and gave Juan a long cool stare before gathering up the group and ushering them out. As the door was about to swing shut he paused, turned, and called back.

"A very good meal. Tell Alicia she is an excellent cook. The secret is to concentrate on your work and not to become distracted. Then you can be good at it and avoid many problems. Is that not so? And you can tell Señor David he should do the same. Tell him it is a little advice from Raúl."

* * *

For the first twenty minutes, Eric sat quite happily reading his paper while the other occupants of the van dealt with the wait and his refusal to enlighten them with varying degrees of impatience. Jeff pushed his seat back and quickly fell asleep. Gillian kept busy washing and rewashing pots and utensils and tiding up the worktops. David stared at the stars. Maggie humphed and grumphed, muttering maledictions from time to time, twisting this way and that to get comfortable and keep warm. Eric seemed to be engrossed in the sport and was enjoying the whole effect. Celtic and Hibs had both won that week and Rangers and Hearts had lost, so the post-match analysis was particularly enjoyable. On the downside, the red hot favourite in the 3:15 at Musselburgh had come in fifth so that wasn't so good. Never mind. Win a few, lose a few.

Approaching half an hour, however, and even Eric began to get twitchy. He had read everything of interest in sport, news, and the health page – even cooking and lifestyle – and had nothing else to occupy himself. He was also beginning to worry about something and kept looking at his watch every few minutes. Eventually Maggie got to the end of her tether and gave him an ultimatum.

"Right Eric," she announced. "That's half an hour we're sat here freezing cold. Either you tell us what's going on or we all go home. Right now. No ifs or buts. And you can walk back to Muirhouse. How about that?" Evidently this last part clinched it for him. After a few seconds swithering he decided that whatever they were waiting for might not be happening so maybe he should cut his losses and at least get a lift back.

"Awright," he said reluctantly. "It's aboot that lassie ye said wiz missin'. I ken whar she is. She's wi' a dealer ca'd Raúl."

Suddenly nobody was complaining about the cold.

"So how come you couldn't just have told us that before?" Maggie demanded. "What on earth have we been sitting here for? And why couldn't you have told us in Drylaw? What's with the mystery tour?" Eric was incredulous.

"Huv yiz no' been listenin'?" he said. "I jist told you she's wi' Raúl. Huv you no' heard o' him? He's a total bampot. I'm no talkin' tae you onywhere I can get spotted by him 'n' his pals."

"Ok, I get that. But why the wait?" Maggie pressed him.

"Because she wiz supposed tae hav been here ten meenutes ago."

"Who? Jen? On her way here?"

"Well, probably no' noo. At least she might be but there's a fair chance she's no'." He was deflated. No rabbit in the hat after all.

"Eric," David took over. "Start at the beginning. What do you know about Jen and why do you think she should be meeting us here?" Eric took a deep breath and gave a long sigh.

"Have yiz no heard o' Raúl?"

"Only that Jen's mum had heard her talking about him," Gillian put in. "She thought he might be a boyfriend." Eric smiled grimly. David pursed his lips but said nothing.

"Well," he said, "that's wan way o' pittin' it. Raúl's fae Spain. At least ah dinnae ken if he's right Spanish or no' but he wiz runnin' a drugs thing in Spain. Then things wiz gettin' a bit tough an' tha'. The polis wiz out tae get him so the whole squad o' them moved ower here. Tae get the polis aff their backs, like. Start up again. So tae get his crowd in and the other crowd out he had tae rough things up a bit." Eric looked down at the floor and screwed up his paper. "Dinnae get me wrong noo. Ah'm no a wimp 'n' that but thon was brutal. There wiz folk shot, cut tae bits, and the bits left in a black bag outside their hoose. Folk that scared they moved oot. Onybody that tried tae fight back ended up in the Western. That's them that didnae end up aff their heeds in the Royal Ed." Everyone was silent now, intent on the story. Gillian had a hand to her mouth and David stared at the floor. Jeff had thoroughly woken up and was twisted round in his seat.

"And how does Jen come into this?" Maggie prompted him more sympathetically now.

"Well. That's the bit ah couldnae stomach. Ah take a bit o' smack mysel' noo and again so you kind o' get used tae hearin' aboot stuff that happens that shouldnae happen. But like ah said, this Raúl's a complete bampot. Dizznae ken when tae stoap." Eric paused as if trying to think exactly how to put the next bit. "An' he likes lassies. Wee lassies, if yiz get ma meanin'. Jen wiz livin' oan Pennywell Gardens. Just up fae me. So ah goat tae ken her a bit. Nice lassie. Then she started gettin' into dope and stuff. Ah tried tae tell her no' tae be sae daft but she wouldnae listen. Then she goat in wi' Raúl's mob. An' he sees her and takes a fancy tae her. She's only fifteen fur ony sake. He's aulder 'an me!" Eric paused for effect. "Probably pushin' forty! Ah tried tae warn her aaf but she wiznae listenin'. An' she likes the money, an' the cars, an' the claez an' bein' wi' the boss. So onywae, he's no' exactly the kind o' bloak yid take home tae yir maw so she does a bunk and moves in wi' him. But diznae tell naeb'dy whar she wiz. But then, now she's livin' wi' the guy she starts seein' things a wee bit different, ken? An' maybe she wiznae feelin' so smart at runnin' away. But she's wi' Raúl noo an' she kens whit he's like and it's no sae easy. Ken what ah'm sayin'? Then the polis are round lookin' fur her. Then you lot turned up and ah thought noo's ma chance. If ah can get a note tae her, we could get her oot and you could look after her an' that."

It all seemed so simple in Eric's mind. Whether she wanted to get out, whether she would drop everything just like that, and what might happen to whoever was harbouring her supposing she did get out – all questions he hadn't considered. There was silence as the implications sank in.

"So what did you do after you were at the van?" Maggie articulated each word slowly and clearly, as if asking a child how come the dog had eaten his homework yet again.

"Well, ah keep well away fae Raúl so ah couldnae jus' waltz in an' that. An' ah wiz wi' wan o' his crowd up at the van – Miguel – he's awright sometimes – so I gied him the slip an' wrote her a wee note and gie'd it tae wan o' her pals – Michelle – an' says fur her tae gie it tae Jen as soon as she could. Tellin' her if she wanted oot tae meet us in the park at wan o'clock in the mornin'. 'Shell has a wee Fiesta so she could run her. Nae worries." There was another pause as this latest bit of brilliant thinking sank in.

"Eric, you know you are just amazing!" Maggie said with feeling. Eric brightened up and smiled.

"Nae bother. Ah thoat yid be pleased!"

"Pleased? I'm ecstatic! Do you know, that is the stupidest, most ridiculous, most absurd, most ludicrous, least likely to succeed, half-baked idea I have ever heard!" Eric was stunned but Maggie was just warming up. She turned and bawled right in his face. "Do you know what you've done?" Eric's mouth was open but nothing was coming out. Evidently he did not. "For starters the chances of her getting a note from her best friend Eric are about zero. If this Michelle has any sense she'd roll it up and smoke it before she tried to pass it on. Second of all, assuming she does get it, how do you know she wants to leave enough to trust herself to you, ye big eejit! Then, let's assume she does get the note and she wants out, do you think Raúl is going to be ok with his wee girlfriend going for a drive in the country at one o'clock in the morning? That's if Michelle feels like taking her.

"Then, supposing all that and she turns up here, who's to say she's not been followed and we get asked in the nicest possible way why my soup van is offering a lift to the boss's wee bit of stuff in the middle of the night? And even if not, who the hell is going to take her in with big bad Raúl after them? Have you thought of that? What were you on when you thought this one up Eric? Whatever it was, it's only available in Muirhouse! It's you that's the crazy bampot – not Raúl!" Again there was quiet but this time it was a stunned silence as everyone thought through the implications of what Maggie had just said. Eric didn't even try to defend himself. Maggie sat and fumed. Gillian sat speechless in the back and Jeff was looking out of the window. David broke the silence.

"I think the sooner we get out of here the better. You'll have to take your chances back in Muirhouse Eric, but Maggie and Jeff are nothing to do with this. I think it would be good if we could get moving. Right now."

Just then Jeff looked out of his window back down the hill.

"Hey up," he said. "Here's the young lady now. Maybe." There was a pause as they watched headlights bouncing up the hill. Whoever it was wasn't sticking to the speed limit.

"I used to have a Fiesta," Gillian said quietly. "That's not a Fiesta."

"Start the engine, Jeff," Maggie said quietly. "Let's get out of here. Nice and easy."

As they began to back out of their space, a large black BMW 4x4 screeched round into the car park and pulled to an emergency stop about twenty yards away. Both near-side windows were down. A short, thick, stubby, black barrel poked out of each. Then the back of the van exploded. Chunks of metal and glass sprayed in every direction. Gillian screamed and was thrown against the counter. Everyone in the front seat flattened themselves below window height as the whole van rocked from side to side. Another bang, then a screech of tyres as the BMW took off. Suddenly everything was eerily quiet. There was blood everywhere. Jeff had his arms over his head and his head down against the steering wheel. David was on the floor at his feet. Only Maggie was sitting up. She was silent for barely a second then turned to Eric and started beating him with her fists.

"My van!" she screamed. "Look what you've done to my beautiful van!"

Chapter 13

LITTLE FRANCE

After years of overcrowding, traffic congestion, bad parking, trolleys in corridors, and lack of storage, the Royal Infirmary move from Lauriston Place backing onto the Meadows, down to the new site at Little France, south of the city, was welcome all round. Some thought the district was named after Mary, Queen of Scots' servants, while others said it was French cloth workers who had settled there in the seventeenth century. In either case, it was a pleasant, open site with brand new buildings, good parking, and the busiest A&E department in Scotland. It was also a straight run from where the radial route round Holyrood Park came out at the Commonwealth Pool at the top of Dalkeith Road. They reckoned that was what saved Gillian's life. The couple in the car next to them raised the alarm. The driver, a medical student, using his scarf as a makeshift tourniquet, slowed the loss of blood and braced an arm that might be broken. Eric, in a state of shock, sat there shaking. Maggie, though as white as a sheet, recovered quickly and got into the back to clear up some of the mess and make Gillian more comfortable. David phoned Juan to make sure there hadn't been an attack on Hacienda, Southside or his own flat – if Raúl had worked out the connections. They agreed to check everything and then meet at the hospital.

If Jeff was used to pushing the old van, that night he outdid himself. Half-way down Dalkeith Road they were met by police coming in the opposite direction who did a U-turn and escorted them right to the door. Even in Edinburgh an ancient Commer van with half of one side blown in couldn't be easily missed. A stretcher team was waiting and Gillian was immediately whisked off. The others – including Andy the medical student and his girlfriend Li Mei – were treated for cuts and shock. David and Maggie had been out of the line of fire but were badly shaken up. On the way to the hospital Maggie realized there was no point shouting at Eric any more and gave up. Now she sat in the waiting room in a daze, every few minutes wrapping her sheepskin denim jacket more tightly around her and walking out to the car park for another cigarette and a look at the remains of the van. The dragon motif had almost completely disappeared. The side of the van was a mess of tangled metal. One massive rend in the middle with mangled razor edges and a thousand pellet holes led up to the driver's window which was no longer there. Jeff had come close to having the entire right side of his face shredded like coleslaw.

David had cuts cleaned and pellets of metal and plastic picked out of his scalp. Physically he wasn't too bad but seemed to be in a complete daze. When Juan and Alicia appeared they gathered him up and held onto him. He had the expression of a man who could not take in what had just happened. It was as if he had woken up in the morning to find his bedroom furniture hanging from the ceiling. "It's impossible…" he kept saying. "Not again…" Juan put his hand on David's head and was quietly praying continuously in Spanish.

Although physically least hurt, Eric was in some ways in the worst state of all, convinced the devastation of the van was just a warning shot and that he could look forward to the full treatment as soon as he set foot back in Muirhouse. He was also desperate for a fix but could not convince any of the medical staff that this was an appropriate remedy. Sedation did some good but he just kept muttering to himself, swaying back and forward, and chewing his fingernails.

When everybody had been seen and patched up the police officers who had escorted them took statements and offered to take people home. The van was evidence and impounded so Maggie and Jeff got a lift home to Gorgie. Andy and Li Mei were able to get home under their own steam to try to explain to Li Mei's dad why they weren't in by 12:30 as promised. Juan and Alicia wouldn't hear of David going back to Bruntsfield and nobody had the heart to try to send Eric home to Muirhouse, so it was agreed all five of them would stay at the flat upstairs from the restaurant. Medics wouldn't let anyone see Gillian, but David insisted to the point of telling them he was her minister. Juan backed him up until he was allowed onto the corridor where he could see her through the tiny window in the door. One arm was in plaster, her neck was braced, she had a dressing on her scalp, monitors and wires seemed everywhere, and a drip went into the back of one hand. She was in a green hospital gown against snowy linen. Despite it all David still thought her jet black hair beautiful around the whiteness of her face and the pillows. She looked pale but peaceful and the registrar assured him she was out of danger thanks to a massive transfusion. The arm was set, metal in her back that had caused the bleeding had been removed, and otherwise it was cuts and bruises though maybe a cracked rib too – the X-ray wasn't conclusive.

David's face was a similar colour to the white linen on the bed. "*Gracias a Dios,*" he muttered.

Juan and Alicia's flat was comfortable for two but a squeeze for six, with Tomas already in temporary residence. Eric was given a foam roll and a sleeping bag, a generous shot of Lepanto, and bundled into the spare room. Juan, Alicia, and David flopped down in the living room. Hacienda would be closed the following day till they thought what to do next. Alicia disappeared to make a quick supper as Juan and David sat in silence. Twenty minutes later with something hot and a bottle of Campo Viejo on the table they finally sat together. Gentle snoring could be heard from the spare room.

"Well," David began, "it's the same Raúl. El Niño. No two ways."

"*Claro,*" Juan replied. "Do you know, I thought I recognized him when they came into the restaurant. I only saw him once in Spain, but of course he had a reputation."

"Now he's here to make a bigger reputation."

"Well, he's certainly succeeded," Alicia added quietly. "Your friend Eric was terrified to go home."

"If only I'd recognized his face when they came in," Juan reproached himself. "Maybe I could have warned you. Maybe all this wouldn't have happened."

"You don't need to feel guilty," David replied gloomily. "If I'd stopped to think for a second I would have guessed what was going on and gone to the police instead of trying to take it on myself – and getting Gillian involved."

"Don't forget the van was her idea," Juan reminded him. David grunted as if to say, *you may be right but that doesn't make it any better.* For a few seconds the only sound was that of tortilla and Rioja disappearing.

"You like her, don't you?" Alicia asked abruptly, looking at David.

"Of course. We all like her."

"That's not what I mean," she smiled at him. "You *really* like her." David was silent for a moment.

"I can't afford to *really* like her, as you put it," he said slowly. "She's not a believer – as far as I know. It wouldn't work. And I nearly got her killed tonight."

"And was Rocío a believer when you fell in love?"

"That was different. Neither of us had a spiritual outlook then. We both came to faith later."

"And is God able to bring Gillian to faith?"

"Of course. But she has choices too. What then? I'm involved with a woman who doesn't have faith? That just makes everything much harder. We've seen it too many times. The values, the outlook, the priorities – they're all just far too different. I'm not prepared to put myself – and her – through all of that."

"I've had a feeling about Gillian ever since you brought her in," Alicia continued thoughtfully. "From the first time I set eyes on her I've always thought of her like a sister. You're right together. Something'll happen. You'll see."

David cleared his throat. "Well, anyway, back to Raúl. What exactly do we know – besides the obvious and besides what Eric said? What's he doing in Edinburgh? You're sure it's the same man?"

"*De verdad*. Raúl Álvarez. *El Niño*. Part of Escobar's outfit in Colombia. They were hounded out when Escobar was shot and some of the gang moved to Spain. I'm guessing that when things got too hot there – remember Rodriguez and his five hundred *policías* – he had to move on again. So he must be setting up business in Edinburgh. It was definitely him in Hacienda last night with his associates and their women. There was a younger girl who didn't understand Spanish. I would bet this month's profits it was Jen. I just never thought at the time. *¡Cielos!* I was serving their meal. I never guessed!"

"I'm sure you're right. They were tipped off after Reckless Eric here basically wrote them a letter saying come and get us. Raúl's obviously not a man to do things by halves. The question now is – does the girl want to leave, as Eric thought, and if so, is there any way to realistically help her, without getting blown up again?"

"Do we have to see her *cara a cara* – to see what she says?" Alicia asked.

"Maybe. I suppose I have to speak to her mum first and let her know what's happened and find out what she wants to do. And of course the police will be more involved as well whether Maggie likes it or not. To be honest, I won't be doing anything more right now. I just can't put anyone else in the firing line."

"When do you think we'll be able to see her?" Alicia asked

"Jen?"

"No – Gillian, of course."

"No idea. I'll phone the hospital in the morning and see what they say."

It was now nearly five in the morning and everyone was worn out. David wanted to get some sleep before the sedatives wore off. Alicia brought out some bedding and Juan folded down a bed settee. Ten minutes later David was tucked under a warm double downie, another brandy inside him, but somehow sleep wouldn't come.

The banging at the door grew louder, gradually penetrating David's subconscious, then his conscious mind. It was light. He sat bolt upright and looked at the clock. Ten thirty. His first thought was whether the door would hold long enough to get everybody out a back window and down the fire escape. Bang, bang, bang. Even louder. Then a voice through the letter box.

"Police! Anybody at home?" David relaxed, threw the bed clothes aside, and shouted he was just coming. He pulled on trousers and a T-shirt and made for the door. Two solidly Scottish plain clothes officers could be seen on the landing in the fisheye peephole. They were holding up ID and certainly didn't look like they came from anywhere south of the Rio Grande. He undid the locks and opened up.

"Morning, sir – D.S. Thompson and D.C. McGuire. Are you Juan Hernandez?"

"No, David Hidalgo. This is Juan's flat though. Everybody's still asleep. It was a bit of a late night. Come in. We were told someone would be round for statements." Thompson and McGuire weren't exactly the Blues Brothers but did come in matching dark suits, white shirts, plain ties and thick-soled black shoes. Neither looked as if they would be much perturbed by fire, flood, murder or mayhem, which, in the current situation, was more reassuring than threatening. Having dealt with detective officers in Spain David found the degree of consistency quite comforting.

Alicia sleepily appeared as David was ushering them into the living room and tidied away the sofa bed. Then she went to wake Eric and get some coffee going. A few minutes later Juan appeared, swathed in a huge fleecy dressing gown. Tomas was rousted out and sent to spy on the tapas menu at La Tasca in the West End. Even Eric managed to join them still in the shell suit he'd been wearing last night and had slept in. As well as being shaky from the lack of his usual chemical start to the day, he was uncomfortable in the presence of CID and perched in a far corner, gnawing a piece of toast. Coffee and breakfast *empanadas* appeared and D.S. Thompson took over.

"Well, Mr Hidalgo, all I can say is you have all been extremely lucky." David remembered the last time he had been told something similar. This time it was no more convincing. "Ms Lockhart is comfortable this morning. Mr and Mrs O'Conner...," he consulted his notebook, "... eh... Maggie and Jeff, I think to you... seem to be none the worse for wear although the van's a wreck and I gather they sustained a few cuts. Mr Stoddart," he addressed himself to Eric who was trying to blend into the furniture, "you were furthest from the blast on the near side seat and were only treated for shock. That right?"

"Eh... aye. That'll be right."

"So," D.S. Thompson continued in formal tones, "you were aware we were making enquiries as to Miss MacInnes's whereabouts, but you chose to make your own investigations. Once the police are pursuing an enquiry we don't recommend members of the public to get involved. The reasons for that should be clear enough." He paused, loosened his tie, took another bite of pastry and a sip of coffee, and put his notebook down. Everyone understood this was not the Sherlock Award for Astute Detection.

"Anyway," he continued, relaxing, "that's the official line. As it happens, last night gave us some leads that may be helpful."

"Did you know all about Raúl already?" Alicia asked.

"We've had surveillance on them for about three months," McGuire continued. "Drugs enforcement is one of the priorities right now. We don't ignore the low-level users and dealers of course." Here he glanced ever so briefly at Eric. "But the main effort has to be centred on getting to the importers that control the trade. Spanish police alerted us to Álvarez about a year ago, but we only started hearing the name ourselves last March. He seems to have taken some time to get the lie of the land then went in really hard – beatings, knife crime, intimidation, that sort of the thing. At least two murders we're pretty sure about. Even attempts to buy off the local uniformed staff and launder cash into community projects."

"That makes sense," Juan put in. "The same tactics Escobar used in Colombia."

"Escobar?" McGuire asked.

"Pablo Escobar," said David. "He was head of the Medellin drugs cartel. At one time he was thought to be the seventh richest man in the world. He used a mixture of extreme violence, torture, and revenge killings to win control. But he also bribed judges and politicians and poured money into the poorer parts of the city. So rivals were terrified, judges turned a blind eye, and ordinary people protected him."

"What happened to him in the end?" McGuire asked.

"He was tracked down by electronic surveillance and shot."

"And you think there's some connection with Álvarez?"

"Raúl started working for him when he was a teenager. He learned how Escobar ran things and now he's using the same approach."

"Do you mind if I ask how you know all this?" D.S. Thompson eyed David suspiciously. "I was given to understand you are the missing girl's minister, and you," looking just as suspiciously at Juan, "run a restaurant."

"Well," David clarified, "firstly I'm not Jen MacInnes's minister as such. Her grandmother is part of Southside Christian Fellowship. I'm the part-time minister there. But before that I ran a church in Madrid. Juan and Alicia were part of the leadership team there. We did a lot of work with young drug addicts and came into contact with the gangs from time to time. We think Álvarez was part of the drugs scene there before moving to Edinburgh. We had a bit of..." David paused, trying to get the right words that wouldn't take him into a deeper explanation, "... a bit of personal contact with him." D.S. Thompson was making copious notes.

"You said you'd already been watching him?" Alicia asked.

"That's right," Thompson confirmed. "In fact, we've really only been waiting for something substantial that we can absolutely tie back to him before we go in. This is a serious assault, if not attempted murder. The student that treated Miss Lockhart took the make and number of the vehicle and we've got that linked back to the gang. Ballistics are at work on the van and want to match the ammunition to previous incidents. Then we'll have something to go on, as long as Álvarez doesn't disappear again in the meantime of course."

"And you won't forget about the girl?" Alicia wanted to make absolutely sure.

"Yes, the girl. Just what exactly is her connection?" Thompson had his notebook poised again.

"As far as we can tell, just the girlfriend," David said.

"But she's only fifteen or so, isn't she? Álvarez is...," he flipped a few pages back, "... thirty-seven according to Spanish police. That's a bit unusual..."

"Sixteen in a few weeks," David clarified. "But yes, unusual is one word for it." He glanced up at Eric but Mr Stoddart was studying his shoes and clearly did not wish to be cited as a witness. "As far as we can tell, she was only involved as a user – nothing to do with the business. Then she got too close to Raúl, who took a liking to her, and that was that. There wasn't any way out even if she'd wanted it."

"Also like Escobar," Juan put in.

"What do you mean?"

"That was part of Escobar's lifestyle as well. He was married and had mistresses but also he had the reputation for liking underage girls. It looks like Álvarez didn't just pick up business tips from the boss." Alicia shuddered, and then to everyone's surprise Eric spoke up with feeling.

"And that's whit ah couldnae pit up wi'," he said. "So onythin' that's gonnae get rid of that scumbag's awright wi' me!"

"Well, I'm sure we're all in agreement with that, Mr Stoddart," Thompson remarked dryly. "And you'll be willing to tell us what you know?" This was the Rubicon – or possibly the Water of Leith – for Eric. He hummed and hawed for a few seconds, then seemed to lose patience with his own hesitation.

"Ah. Course ah will. Whit d'ye think ah am?"

"Good. We just need to hope we can get to him before anything else goes wrong and he decides Edinburgh isn't as nice a spot as he thought. Anyway, we need some formal statements now. Reverend Hidalgo is it?"

Gillian woke up to birdsong outside the window, a nurse attending to the drip in her arm, and a pain in the small of her back as if she'd been hit by the London to Edinburgh express. The nurse leaned over to arrange her pillows.

"Good morning. How are you feeling?"

"Not too good. What happened?" Her voice was quiet and hoarse.

"You were involved in a gun attack on the van you were in. You had a fragment of metal in your back and lost a lot of blood. Your arm's broken in two places and a couple of ribs are cracked. You had a blood transfusion last night. Apart from that you're fine. You're making a good recovery."

"What about the others?"

"Cuts and bruises – nothing more. I'm afraid you got the worst of it. Do you feel strong enough for some visitors?"

"Who is it?" The nurse checked a clipboard on the side table.

"A Mr and Mrs Hernandez and a Reverend Hidalgo." Gillian was used to thinking of him as Señor David. Reverend Hidalgo seemed strange and formal. Mr and Mrs Hernandez she couldn't place at all.

"Sure – I'll be ok."

"Well, they'll only be allowed a few minutes each and one at a time. Any preference?" Gillian did have a preference but did not feel like sharing it.

"No. Anything."

As it happened David was ushered in first – the same ancient overcoat, the same battered grey fedora, the same beige trousers. *Somebody really needs to take that man shopping!* was her first incongruous thought.

"Hi," she smiled up at him.

"Hi. How are you?"

"Off the critical list apparently. I've felt better though. My back really hurts. And my side. And my head. Almost a complete set I think."

David pulled over a chair but kept standing.

"Gillian," he began, "I am so sorry you got mixed up in this. It's unforgivable." Weak as she was, she shook her head.

"No – I wanted to help. It was my idea – remember?" He

shrugged and didn't argue. "So I guess that wasn't Jen in the car?" she whispered.

"I think that's a fair guess." There was a pause while both of them thought what they might say next.

"I'm sure you can sit down, you know," Gillian suggested. "As far as I know a broken arm isn't catching."

He stepped round the chair and perched lightly on the bed, hoping he hadn't misinterpreted. Gillian naturally laid her hand on the covers palm upwards and David took it. Neither had planned it, but it just seemed natural.

"How's everyone else?" Gillian asked.

"Fine. A bit shook up. Not much compared to you."

"Well, I hope everyone's going to sign my plaster cast. Anything more about Jen?"

"We had a couple of detectives round this morning. They seem to think last night will allow them to move against Raúl if he stays put long enough."

David gave her the gist of what they had found out, putting all the pieces together. He left out his previous, more personal, dealings with *El Niño*.

"So maybe my soup van idea wasn't a complete disaster?"

"It was a great idea if we'd been able just to stick to the soup without any help from Muirhouse's answer to Maigret."

"How is Eric?"

"Terrified of going back home. He thinks he'll be next."

"What's he going to do?"

"Well, even though he brought the whole thing down on himself – and us – I do feel a bit responsible. Eric's going to be staying with me for a few days till we see how things work out." Gillian gave him a look as if to say, *Are you absolutely sure that's a good idea?* "I know, I know," David agreed. "If there was anywhere else he could go I wouldn't think of it. Turns out everybody he could normally camp out with has the same connections he has so he's convinced Raúl would find out where he was and send the boys round. Anyway, enough about that. Is there anything you need done? Does your work know what's happened?"

"No, not as far as I know. Would you mind giving them a ring and letting them know? I might miss a few classes."

"No problem. I just hope you're not going to be missing any of my Spanish classes."

"Well, maybe one or two. Actually, I was considering individual tuition." She looked at him deadpan, with only the merest hint of a smile.

"That *is* normally extra but I think I could maybe fit you in. Anything else?"

"There is something. You'll find my house keys in the bag over there. Would you mind popping up and checking mail and stuff? Water the plants. Turn the immerser off. Only if you've got time."

It was a small request and anything one friend might do for another but Gillian realized she wasn't asking just anyone – nobody from the department, not a neighbour, none of her friends from the chamber orchestra or the reading group, no former boyfriends. It was David she'd asked. That also seemed the natural thing to do.

"Well, since you're in here largely because of bumping into me, I think that's the least I can do. Don't be surprised if they're all dead when you get back though." David stood up and for a second they just looked at each other in silence.

"I am really glad you're ok," he said.

"I know. Me too."

David got Gillian's address, house keys, and work phone number. A kiss on the cheek seemed natural but was softer and took a fraction of a second longer than mere companionship called for. There was a definite squeeze before their hands separated. David disappeared and Gillian again brightened to find that Mr and Mrs Hernandez were Juan and Alicia. Gillian and Alicia did indeed get on like sisters, immediately talking about Eric, his antics, and the police visit. Juan hung about trying to look interested then excused himself and waited outside with David.

"She's looking good, Señor David. I was worried she would be worse."

"Me too."

"She looks very delicate but I think she is strong. You and she would make a good team."

"Yes, I know that's what you think Juan. Just stop thinking it."

"Ah Señor David! *En boca cerrada no entran moscas* – I can keep my mouth shut but you can't stop me thinking!"

Chapter 14

PENNYWELL GARDENS

Alison was pretty sure, all things considered, that the day they moved into Muirhouse was the worst of her life. Such high hopes – then it had all come to this. It was worse than the day Mr Hopkins, the music teacher, had groped her from behind in between movements of the clarinet concerto – and the following day when she'd been forced to agree it could have been an accident. And much worse than the day she'd discovered she was pregnant with Jennifer – though that had been troubling enough. Ian was a chemistry student and they had met at the Christian Union Freshers' Ceilidh of all places. After that they all repaired to the bar, then Ian's room in halls. When everybody else had left, they had a bit more to drink. Then she woke up in his bed in the morning. Six weeks later she bought a pregnancy testing kit in a panic from Boots in Princes Street. The wrong result came up.

Ian had done the decent thing under pressure but it had not been a success from the start. She dropped out of law and after the baby was born just couldn't seem to get back into things. Still, they had both tried to make a go of it. Ian graduated and got a job with Price Waterhouse and started studying for accountancy exams. They managed a two bedroom bungalow in Clermiston, near the zoo, and things seemed to be looking up. He passed on the second attempt and she got a job in the West End as a legal secretary. As Jennifer was growing up they seemed to be settling into a reasonable routine and family life wasn't too bad.

Then there was the day her dad died. That was bad. Dad had always been her hero, defender, and friend. He was the moderating influence on Mum's endless pretensions to middle-class gentility. He

131

was the one that made her laugh and talked her through the hard times. Then all of a sudden he was gone. For months after, she kept thinking of things she would have to tell him, only to be caught up short when she remembered he wasn't there any more.

The day she found out that Ian's many nights away weren't entirely work-related wasn't good either. She had met the woman once at a party – bright red hair and trendy thick-rimmed glasses. She was flirting even then. Alison started off furious then began blaming herself before ultimately realizing it wasn't her fault. That helped a bit.

Worse than all of these was the day the removal van arrived, collected her half of the furniture, and dumped it all off in front of a miserable flat in a miserable block in a part of town she – rightly or wrongly – associated with people at the very bottom of the heap. Now she was joining them. No doubt many were decent folk down on their luck – as she tried to think she was – but another part of the mix were the antisocial neighbours, the unruly kids, the users, dealers, pushers, and girls on the game. In a way she was almost glad Dad wasn't around to see it come to this. Now they were all her neighbours, saying hullo as she left for work, standing in front of her in the post office queue, and taking their bins out at the same time for neighbourhood wildlife to rummage through.

Sometimes she was convinced she was just as much of a snob as her mum. Who on earth was she to look down on any of them? Each of them was struggling in their own way to make a living, bring up kids, keep their lives together. Were they really so different? At least in Muirhouse there was less facade than in Morningside. People seemed to really be what they really were, not constantly pretending to be something else. Or maybe that was just Mum and her friends. So she had swallowed hard and tried to get on with it and keep on being who *she* was. She tried being friendly and in return found not just friendship but courage, resourcefulness, and a willingness to accept her without prying or judging. She felt ashamed of her own prejudices. It was possible, she found, to live life here after all and still keep the chaos at bay.

Unfortunately Jennifer – or Jen as she had started calling herself – didn't see the chaos as something to be avoided at all. She seemed to think that revelling in the worst she could get away with was a neat way of getting back at whatever and whoever. First there were meetings at school about her bad attitude and lack of homework, then temporary exclusions, then accusations of bullying. Being allocated to a school social worker seemed to be thought of almost like a badge of honour. She more or less gave up any pretence at schoolwork after a couple of months and there were times Alison felt like giving up as well. What was the point? Unfortunately there's a deal you do when you have kids. In exchange for this little pinkish bundle of potential you check your heart in. So giving up wasn't an option. Social Work and the Children's Hearing got involved after a spate of shoplifting. "Beyond Parental Control" was the neat-sounding legal jargon – the only neat thing about it. Nothing further was done to help though, as Jen was going to be sixteen in three months. Thanks a bunch, she thought. Jen sat chewing gum and staring at the ceiling throughout the hearing.

So life went on. Jen kept later and later hours, never went to school, and was constantly being brought back by the police. She treated the flat like a B&B and her mother like a domestic. The week she disappeared Alison actually spent the first two days in a state of relief. She could tidy up and expect it to stay that way. She could go to bed and sleep till morning. There was no one to fight with and she didn't have to take the mixture of sullen indifference and abuse that had become the norm. Then Jen didn't come back home on the Sunday night either – or Monday – and she started to worry.

When her mum turned up with a birthday present she broke her golden rule, cracked up, and told her how things were in a mixture of rage and tears. Actually it was a relief and Mum turned out to be surprisingly understanding: no condemnations, no told you so. Nobody's fault. She suggested they speak to Señor David – whoever he was. He would be sure to know what to do. Despite resisting every previous attempt to get her back to church, this time she was so desperate she had gone along that morning to the funny upstairs room and listened to that completely weird sermon, which might have been all about her, she wasn't sure. Nevertheless she was impressed. He seemed to have been through this sort of thing before and knew what he was talking about. Not at all what she had expected. Then they had talked about what to do and had come up with an idea that maybe could work. But whether it helped or not, she had felt listened to, taken seriously, and made to feel worthwhile. It was a long time since that had happened.

The night Señor David and the other woman were due to go out on the van she tried not to get her hopes up but couldn't quite stop herself. She could barely sit still and phoned her mum three times in the course of an hour, only finally going to bed after two when she thought they would have been in touch if there was anything to tell. Silly that – thinking they would just find out where Jen was, pop round for a cup of tea, and bring her with them. She had hoped for some information at least but was not prepared for what she discovered the following day. Señor David came to explain. She had thought Jen might be hiding out with a girlfriend from school, probably taking drugs round the back of the shops. Maybe she'd even run away with a boy. But to discover that she was now the girlfriend of a man as old as herself who seemed to be the boss of the entire North Edinburgh drugs operation – she couldn't believe it. Then she heard about the van.

"Gillian's going to be ok," David told her. "The van can be repaired. I'm just sorry it all worked out this way. None of us expected it so there's no need to feel bad." She wasn't sure if this meant she was supposed to be feeling guilty at this point. Dealing with all the guilt from what Jen seemed to have turned into was quite enough. She was not about to take on another bucket load.

"Ok – I'll try and remember. Thank Gillian when you speak to her."

"Will do. Maybe you should get back to work. It might take your mind off things."

"Yeah – maybe. It's just – what if I'm not here if she does come back – even just to pick up some stuff?"

As it happened, she needn't have worried. David had only been gone a matter of minutes when she heard the front door again. She thought he must have forgotten something and had come back. She stepped into the hall and froze.

"Jennifer! Thank God!" But her rush to put her arms around her daughter was held at bay. Jen twisted to avoid her and kept on going. She was wearing a crumpled black T-shirt and jeans – exactly what she'd had on the night she hadn't come home. She looked as if she hadn't slept for a week.

"I'm just back for my stuff," she said over her shoulder. Alison followed her into her bedroom where she had already pulled a suitcase off the top of the wardrobe and laid it on the bed. She stood in the doorway, stunned, unable to think of what to say. Jen started pulling open drawers and dumping armloads of tops, jeans, underwear, and shoes in the case.

"What are you doing?" was all she could manage, as if it wasn't obvious.

"Don't know. I think we're going away."

"Who? Where? You and Raúl?"

"Yeah."

"And where are you going?"

"Don't know. He's got a place. Something's happened." Alison thought about grabbing the case off her but simply hadn't the stomach for a fight. She flopped onto a tattered beige armchair in the corner.

"How can you do this Jen? He's more than twenty years older than you. And the police are supposed to be after him."

"Yeah, well, they're not going to find him, are they?"

"Stop and think what you're doing. He's a criminal. A drugs dealer. He's not someone you want to be with." Jen dropped an armful of stuff into the case then spun around.

"Do you think I don't know that? Do you think I'm, like, happy people are getting shot at? Anyone that tries to help me ends up in hospital." She paused. "I'm not even happy I can't come home."

"Why not? What's stopping you? I'm not stopping you. All I

want is you to come back and we'll try to work things through."
Jen laughed bitterly. "Do you think it's that easy? The hit squad was
out last night because somebody was trying to find out where I was.
Somebody's going to get killed if I stay here." She turned back to the
case, pulled it shut, and started fumbling with the clasps.

"Do I not even get properly introduced then and tell him to look
after you?"

Jen was struggling to get it to close.

"Believe me. You don't want to."

"Here. Let me help you." Alison held the lid down while Jen
pushed in the catches. Their shoulders touched. Suddenly Jen
grabbed her mother and started sobbing. Alison held her tight and
stroked her hair.

"There must be something we can do," she said quietly. "I'll
phone the police – or Señor David. There's bound to be a way." Jen
sniffed loudly and managed to collect herself.

"There's nothing you can do, Mum," she said. "You don't know
what he's like."

"So I've just got to let you go?"

"I've got to. I'll be fine."

Alison held Jen at arm's length then gathered her up again. They
both held on tightly, then Jen slowly eased away.

"I've got to go now," she whispered. "And he says I've to get my
passport."

"No!"

"I have to. If I don't he'll just send somebody round to get it and
that'll be worse." Alison saw the logic and reluctantly went through
to her own room and came back with it.

"Now, Mum – you've got to promise not to come looking for me.
I'll be ok. I'll find a way."

"Look, if you're going to take that, take this too." On impulse
Alison reached into a bedside cabinet and pulled something out.
"Granny gave you it. It's something from home. Take it." It was a
white leather Bible with her initials embossed on the cover.

A car horn blasted in the street. Alison looked out and saw a huge black 4x4. The windows were tinted so she couldn't see who was inside. Jen hauled the case to the floor, gave her mum a kiss on the cheek, and headed down the hall and out the door without looking back.

Chapter 15

MARCHMONT

The outside of Dr Gillian Lockhart's tenement block near the foot of Marchmont Road was not too different from Reverend David Hidalgo's in Bruntsfield – both quite plain compared with the more elegant, better known New Town facades. They shared a similar appearance of solid Victorian permanence and dependability without airs and graces. It was as if they had grown out of the slightly differing soils in their respective parts of town, a little grander here, a little more functional there, but more or less the same genus and species. New Town flats came from more refined stock and grew up with the shiny brass plates of advocates, architects and royal societies already in place. Bruntsfield was of humbler DNA and emerged only with Chinese restaurants and charity shops. Marchmont stood somewhere in between, with its urban professionals, delicatessens, and wine merchants.

Gillian's street was quiet with modest Saturday morning traffic, dog walkers, and joggers. David checked the number on the card, looked round to make sure the silver MX5 was still parked where it should be, and proceeded up the path. Unlike his Bruntsfield block, the Marchmont address had something that posed as garden space in front and did not open directly onto the pavement – just to let passers-by know they were entering an establishment a whisker higher up the tenement pecking order. He let himself in the outer door, squeezed past an assortment of bikes and buggies, and climbed to the first floor. The fact that Gillian didn't live up four flights was also a touch more refined than he was used to. As he fiddled for the right key, he was hoping that Eric, newly installed in his own flat, would not yet have lost the key, burned down the building, swapped his jazz collection for a fix, left the fire on and gassed the entire close, or otherwise made his indelible mark on David's only bit of personal space left. If he'd been Juan he'd be trusting the Lord. Right now the best he could manage was hoping for the best.

So what did that mean? Hoping for the best? No God? Or maybe "Yes God" but just not one you could rely on? Or was God up to something so far from human understanding that the questions were meaningless? He remembered Juan's remark "the story isn't finished yet" and tried to hold on to that as another key failed. He tried a third. How would God have fared judged by the stories of a handful of the former users and addicts of Warehouse 66? Very few got free without relapses, disappointments, even going to jail for offences committed in a past life. He thought of those who had contracted AIDS in their junkie days, dying with a certainty and a peace of mind that seemed entirely beyond human resources. They didn't make it either, but instead of blaming God for the final result seemed to be gloriously at peace in what they had, in the face of what might have been.

So if you made your final call at the lowest point, then no, God didn't seem to be shaping up very well. Rocío gone, Gillian in the Royal Infirmary, Jen – who knew where and in what sort of trouble – Alison bitter, angry, and worried, and David himself – not a very robust advert for faith at the present time. Then there was Raúl. *El Niño*. He seemed to be doing fine. A few unplanned changes of address but otherwise business was booming – no doubt a wealthy man indulging all his whims and amusements. Reprehensible in his habits so not the sort of person any normal human being would actually envy – you'd have to hope – but by his own lights seemed to be doing ok. He kept on happily sowing the wind – it was other people who were reaping the whirlwind. When would he get his? What was the phrase – "Justice delayed is justice denied"? So even if there was to be justice, when all the books were opened and the final court was in session, how many Raúls could get away with it all in this life, wrecking the lives of others with neither remorse nor retribution? He knew well enough that his biblical namesake

had been there long before him. How long, oh Lord, will you let
the wicked triumph? The Bible wasn't afraid of asking the question
but answers seemed a bit thinner on the ground. Too much, David
thought, as he finally got the right key and pushed it home. That's
enough. We've been round this block enough times already. Just live
in the moment. Sufficient unto the day is the evil thereof. He used to
have a university pal who called it the Lena Martell solution: "One
Day at a Time, Sweet Jesus".

Finally unlocking the front door, it struck David that he was
about to enter Gillian's world. So far almost everything had been on
his terms – his Spanish language class, a Spanish restaurant with his
friends, his church, his rescue mission. The only element of Gillian's
universe he'd touched so far was the soup van, which, thanks to
the problem he was trying to solve, was now in a police compound
waiting for analysis prior to being sold for scrap. This was *her* world
now. He went in with a mixture of curiosity, trepidation, and also a
sense of breaching the rules. It was like reading a diary or catching
a glimpse of a bank statement – something you'd better have a very
good reason for doing. Gillian had given him permission, but even
so, without her here he still felt like an intruder. Nevertheless, she
had asked and he had agreed. He *was* a friend not a burglar.

Stepping over the post his first impression was one of classic
Edinburgh middle-class chic. Wide borders of mellow golden
floorboards were worn with the impressions of at least four
generations of traffic. There were Turkish or Persian rugs in delicate
shades of blue, rose pink, and cream, with swirling geometric
designs. Wallpaper was plain cream but broken up with posters,
paintings, tapestries, calendars, and photos. One painting in
particular caught his eye – Edinburgh trams on Princes Street,
probably in the fifties, maybe a late winter afternoon. An impatient,
harassed mum was dragging her daughter either to or from a party,
judging from the frock, and stepping into the gutter to avoid a
bustle of shoppers. A younger man in a polo neck and sports jacket
was crossing the road, perhaps just off the tram for Churchill. The
Scott Monument was lit up like a beacon in the darkening sky. It was

a busy scene, superficially not too unlike the present day. Perhaps the real difference, David thought, was that these shoppers, office workers, and students were still broadly optimistic and expected life to get better. Health would improve, travel get quicker, educational attainment would rise with living standards and people would become more affluent, better informed and – yes – happier. For a similar picture today, he thought, you would have to add beggars, shoplifters, double the traffic, and adverts on the buses for the latest series of *Big Brother.*

David wandered round looking for Gillian Lockhart. Twelve volumes of the *Dictionary of the Older Scottish Tongue* stood next to Antonia Fraser's *Scottish Love Poems, Sueños BBC World Spanish,* the complete poems of Pablo Neruda (translated), *A Brief History of Time, Sherlock Holmes* and *Driving Over Lemons.* Jimmy Hendrix rubbed shoulders with the Mozart *Requiem* and the Grateful Dead, Gloria Estefan (in Spanish), and lots of Bob Dylan. Next to these was a photo album. Wondering whether this was off limits or not, David picked it up, changed his mind, and put it back. Get a grip, he thought. I'm here to water plants, not conduct domestic espionage. He filled a kettle then watered anything that looked in need of it – particularly a huge Swiss cheese plant and masses of tiny African violets. Gillian's bedroom had its quota of plants so he felt justified, indeed obliged, to go in. The bed wasn't made up but he didn't touch it. There were two huge antique oak wardrobes and a matching dresser covered in the paraphernalia of feminine presentation – what his mother used to call "war paint". David was impressed by the quantity and variety, but as to function, that was a closed book. Something on the bedside table caught his eye. A Bible. Open. The start of John's Gospel. Next to it a copy of *Alpha – Questions of Life.* Interesting.

Back in the hall, he gathered up the post and left it on the table then checked the fridge and emptied sour milk down the sink. He made sure windows were locked, bagged up the rubbish, and copied down a couple of messages from the answering machine. Having done everything he came to do though, he still found himself reluctant to leave. This was Gillian's space – her identity, her uniqueness, even her scent was here. He sat on what he guessed was an antique chaise longue in the living room and glanced round the high skirting boards, the heavy cornices and ceiling rose, soft furnishings and hangings, the wide bay window looking over the Meadows to the Castle. These helped describe but they didn't define. That was in the books, the music, the photographs, a half-empty bag of chocolate brazils, a silver flute on a stand next to a score of the *Brandenburg Concertos.*

God bless this woman, he thought. And help me not to mess her up even more.

For a few moments the silence, the scent, the very sensation of her being here made his senses swim. The garrulous, keeping up appearances Mrs MacInnes, the unlucky deserted Alison, and the angry and possibly now terrified Jen seemed distant. Even Juan, Alicia and Hacienda; Eric, Muirhouse and Raúl Álvarez faded. Maybe *El Señor* would work it all out after all. For the first time he admitted that this was what he wanted; he wanted it to work out and he wanted Gillian to be part of the finally completed puzzle. He wanted it a lot.

Suddenly the phone rang, shattering the moment. Should he answer it or not? He decided he would.

"Hello. Gillian Lockhart's flat…"

"Eh… is tha' David Hidalgo?"

"It's David Hidalgo speaking. Who's this?"

"Eric. Ye telt me tae phone ye if onythin' happened, like. Well… eh… this is me phonin'."

What on earth was it now? Had Raúl tracked down the elusive Eric and was now holding a gun to his head? Maybe it was merely that the chip pan had caught fire and devastated the flat.

"Ok Eric. What's happened?"

"Ye'll niver believe it. Ye ken ye telt me ah could read ony o' the stuff oan the shelves but no tae go into yir office?" Ok. That was it – Eric had accidentally pulled down a shelf of reference books and in trying to put it back had trashed all his sermon notes.

"Go on Eric…"

BENEFIT OF THE DOUBT

"Well ah fund this wee book aw aboot gettin' aff drugs – which is whit ah want te dae onywae, like."

"Fair enough."

"An' at the back o' the book it says Goad wid help ye an' that."

"Uh huh."

"But ye had tae say this prayer and gi' yir life tae Jesus, ken."

"Ok."

"So, if ye said this prayer, like, then yid be a Christian. An' Goad wid help ye get aff the drugs… an' look efter ye…" David couldn't quite believe where this might be going.

"So what did you do Eric?"

"Ah said the prayer! So that means ah'm a Christian noo – jist like you – and Goad's goat tae help us get aff the drugs. An' no let Raúl blow us up. Is that no right?… Is that no right Señor David… Hullo?… Ye still there?"

David locked up the flat, dumped the rubbish at the gate, glanced up again at the first-floor window, then set off down the hill, into Warrender Park Terrace and along Whitehouse Loan before cutting across the upper part of Bruntsfield Links towards the flat. Becoming a Christian was a major life decision. It involved a change of values and lifestyle, even for the most normal "good living" citizens. For Eric it would be as foreign as being set down in the middle of the Sahara, given a can of Coke, and told to get on with it. Who said God guaranteed to make cold turkey go away? And he normally didn't make the likes of Raúl Álvarez go away either. At least he hadn't for him. It would be sad to see someone genuinely wanting to make a change in their life so disappointed, but how could that not be the outcome? He had wondered if it might turn out to be a good thing that Eric was too scared to go back to Muirhouse. Maybe if he could somehow separate himself from his Muirhouse buddies and lifestyle, then he would stand a chance of getting his drug use under control. Maybe the church could have sponsored him through rehab. There would be ups and downs, renewal and screw ups, but eventually he might be ready to start thinking about spiritual issues not just the chemical ones.

But Eric was running remarkably true to form. He had somehow found an evangelistic tract aimed at drug users. He had read enough to get the gist of it. He had read he had to "give his life to Jesus" for a new drug-free life. He had accepted everything at face value, prayed the prayer, and was now expecting everything to be magically different – just like the man said. Which would be worse, David wondered, letting him go on in this simplistic illusion to crash when everything didn't work out like magic, or disillusion him now before he even got going? He'd never been a big fan of the snappy, happy, simple gospel tract. Now even less than before.

David unlocked the door to find Eric standing waiting for him with his life-giving booklet clasped to his chest. He was all smiles.

"Hullo there, brother!" was his opening remark.

David had absolutely no recollection of ever having seen the booklet Eric was proudly waving in his face: "Freedom in Christ: Recovery from Addiction through a Meeting with Jesus". It made it sound as if there was to be a public presentation in the Town Hall to which all were invited. The cover showed a junkie injecting heroin in an alleyway with three crosses in the background. It looked as if day were breaking, and the wasted figure slumped against the wall was looking up at the dawning light with an expression of longing and hope. David found the whole thing distasteful, shallow, and trite.

"Ok, Eric," he began, hanging up his coat and hat. "How about you make us both a coffee while I have a look at this, then we can talk?"

"Nae bother," said Eric and disappeared down the hall whistling the chorus from "Parklife". David got the impression that if he'd asked Eric to pop down and run the mower over Bruntsfield Links he would just have asked him where to put the clippings. He certainly seemed a changed man from the figure who had spent last night sat on the sofa with his arms clamped round his knees, shivering and muttering.

David popped the Buena Vista Social Club on and let the soothing tones of Eliades Ochoa singing about Chan Chan and his girlfriend on a Cuban beach calm his nerves. The booklet was much as he had expected, full of lurid stories of ex-addicts living lives of increasing depravity until drifting into a church service by accident, only to find the preacher speaking as if straight to the heart. Going forward at the altar call, they "prayed the prayer", found freedom in Christ, got rid of their dope, joined the church, got a job, met a beautiful girl from the Midwest, and were now happily married and active in missionary work. All this could be yours too for the small price of praying the prayer on the final page. David had rather expected a further invitation along the lines of "… and if you have found this message helpful please send $50 to the following address…" but instead, there was the offer of free literature, telephone counselling, a website, and the invitation to book a speaker for your own event.

Of course he believed in "freedom in Christ" – in principle. But right now he was finding it a bit tricky to match the simplicity of the message with the complexity of life. If he had learned anything in the twenty years of Warehouse 66 it was how long, difficult, and turbulent was the road to getting clean. He knew the temptations, the threats, the pressures, the triumph of each tiny step and the agony of failure. Actually, he was feeling a bit protective of Eric already. Despite his bull-in-a-china-shop antics, he was fed up with the way things were and wanted a change. And he obviously had a fair streak of basic Scottish decency to want to try to help Jen. Now a convenient straw had drifted by and he'd grabbed it with both hands. Maybe it might help if Juan could pop over and they could speak to Eric together. Juan knew more about how this worked from the inside than he ever would.

Eric reappeared with not only two mugs of coffee but also a plate of biscuits nicely arranged and a carton of milk.

"Didnae ken if ye took milk or no'," he explained, setting the whole lot down on a rickety coffee table.

"No, just black," said David. "What we call *café solo*."

"Right. Sounds like when ye go fur a cuppa and everybody gets up to leave when they see ye coming," Eric joked.

"What?"

"Solo," Eric explained patiently "Café solo. In a café on yer ain... Geddit?"

"Yeah – sorry. I didn't know there were any biscuits left."

"There wirnae. Efter ah phoned ye ah nipped doon tae the shoaps. D'ye ken there's some weird stuff doon there. Snails in a tin! See if ah tried to gie that tae Lorraine she'd get a fit o' the sceamin' abdabbs. Ken whit ah'm sayin'?"

"You know, Eric, here you are living in my flat, both of us kind of on the run, but I know almost nothing about you. I know nothing about Muirhouse, or Lorraine – the girlfriend? – or where you live or anything. How about I phone Juan to join us, then you tell us a bit about yourself? Then we can talk about what's happened."

"Fair enough." Eric was agreeable. "Just wan thing though. As soon as Juan..." (he pronounced it "Wan") "... as soon as Juan gets here I want a toilet service." He was emphatic. "The minute he gets in, mind."

"What's a toilet service?"

"D'ye no ken? I thought you wid ken bettern me. It's aw in the book. When ye become a Christian ye hufftae hae a toilet service. Ye aw cram in the lavvie like, then the junkie pits a' his dope doon the pan, then somebody prays and ye sing 'Shall we Gather by the River' an' the junkie pulls the handle and it a' gets flushed awa an' that's the end o' yir dope!"

"Of course." David tried to stifle a smile. "A toilet service. I must have forgotten. So you have some drugs with you right now?"

"Course. No' much though. Nae smack or ah widnae hae been in such a state. Just a coupla dozen pills an' a wee bit coke. Oh an' there's a spliff in ma jaicket poaket." David rolled his eyes at what the CID might have found had they fancied a closer look at Eric yesterday morning.

"I see. I'll phone Juan and put him in the picture, then we'll have a chat about things when he gets over. Anything you'd like to do in the meantime? Have a shower, wash some clothes? I could give you a loan of some stuff while it's drying."

"Ok – but no' till we've hud the service. Then ah'll hae a shower like and get rid of ma claiz. Ah'd like to dump the lot if that's aw right, but ah didnae think ah'd be your size." Eric was thin as a rake. A diet of illegal substances, pot noodle, and Pringles seemed good for the waistline if not the lifestyle. David left a message with Alicia, then they both headed round to the Bethany shop on Morningside Road to kit Eric out for his new persona.

The phone was ringing as they got back with three black bags full of cast-offs from the middle classes. Eric went to sort it out while David answered the phone.

"David Hidalgo."

"*Hola* Señor David. *¿Qué pasa?*"

"*Hola* Juan. How are you? *Bueno.* Now you're not going to believe this, but Eric has been browsing through some of my books, found something about drug recovery through Christ with a prayer of commitment in it and now thinks he's a Christian."

David was expecting something like his own cautious scepticism. Instead what he heard was a moment's silence, then whooping down the phone. Juan was shouting to Alicia in Spanish then back to David to check it was true.

"Well – that remains to be seen," David continued. "Could you come over and talk to him with me? I don't want him to think he's got everything sorted then come down to earth with a thump. Great. Well, as soon as you can. *Hasta pronto.*"

Eric was very pleased with his haul from the charity sector although it was something of a change of style. Out went shell suits and lycra and in came corduroy, brushed denim, and even a polo neck claiming to be cashmere. But not a stitch of it would he try on till they had done the deed and he felt his old life had been flushed away. David thought there might be some very spaced out haddock in the Forth that night.

Juan's face was beaming as David opened the door. He ran straight to Eric and threw his arms round him as if he truly were a brother.

"*¡Gracias a Dios!* That's wonderful. I am so pleased for you, Eric. Alicia and I have been praying for you. Tell me the story." They went through to the living room and Eric began to sketch out a bit about life in Muirhouse, finally repeating what he had told David on the phone. Juan took it in and seemed to have none of David's misgivings. Together they asked in a little more detail what he thought he had done. Although Eric was definitely theology-lite, from his point of view he had now handed everything over and was looking to "the man upstairs" to sort things out – drugs, relationships, and particularly Raúl. He was also keen to get home to tell off-and-on girlfriend Lorraine the big news. Lorraine, it seemed, had three kids – two of Eric's and one to another user who had since died of AIDS. Now there were plans for the future – first to get a job, then to look after Lorraine properly, getting them a house out of the area, and to take responsibility for the weans and generally get his act together. Somehow Raúl didn't seem to present as much of a threat any more – "An' whose goat the biggest gun d'ye think then – Raúl or the Big Yin?" He particularly wanted to come to Southside the following Sunday.

In all the tumbling rush of words David had forgotten the toilet service but Eric hadn't. As soon as there was a lull in the conversation he jumped up and said, "Cun we dae it noo then?", ushered them into the hall, and went to collect all his gear. Together they emptied it all down the pan, David said a prayer and really tried to mean it. Juan put his hand on Eric's head and prayed in Spanish. They did indeed sing "Shall We Gather by the River" although David had to tell Eric and Juan the words.

"That looks like hundreds of pounds' worth," Juan whispered to David as Eric pulled the flush. Juan shouted "Hallelujah!", Eric chanted "Here we go, here we go, here we go", and David managed a weak smile. Having never had a toilet service in Bruntsfield before neither David nor Juan were quite sure what came next but Eric wasn't in any doubt.

"Right boyz. Am awaw fur a shower. See yiz in a bit."

Juan and David went back into the living room. Juan was watching David closely.

"Is there something wrong Señor David?" he asked. "You do not seem very happy."

"You're right. I don't know what's wrong with me. Your attitude is exactly what it should be. All I can see is the problems. I can't seem to feel any enthusiasm. I just keep wondering whether it's real, how long it'll last, and what happens when things go wrong."

"Don't give yourself too hard a time, Señor David," Juan replied. "Two nights ago you were almost killed. So much has happened in the last week. You're bound to be feeling a little – *como se dice* – like a fish out of the water. You have a lot on your mind. You get to know a lovely lady then almost lose her – it's a lot to take in."

"But why am I not more excited for Eric? This is supposed to be the job, isn't it? If he had come in off the street, popped in and out for six months, come to an Alpha course, disappeared on a bender, got cleaned up again, gone for six months' rehab, then announced he'd come to faith, that would have been ok. That would have fitted the pattern. How come I don't think it counts, what actually happened?"

Juan pondered the question. He was a man of simple emotions and gut feelings and his response had been instinctive. He knew David was made up of more complex materials.

"Señor David. You think too much. You are thinking, 'What if this?', 'What if that?' God knows Eric. You believe this?" David nodded. "So, God knows what is coming next – the good, the bad things. The thief on the cross knew only how to trust. The Lord said, 'This day you will be with me in paradise.' So what that Eric knows nothing? What does he need to know, except that he has put his trust in God? God accepts him. You must too. He is like the children Jesus blessed. Maybe you are too grown up, Señor David. You have had so many worries. Things have been hard. You have seen things that didn't work out. Maybe this is something that is working. Let it happen. Bless it. I think God is at work, blessing Eric. Maybe Gillian too. Let him bless you." David leaned forward and let out a sigh.

"You're right. Do you know, I can barely remember what it was like when kids got saved at Warehouse 66. It's seems so long ago. We seemed to have miracles every week. Maybe I've forgotten what a miracle looks like."

"Well, I have another miracle for you. You want to know?"

"Of course. What?"

"Alicia is pregnant!"

"That's wonderful. You've been trying for so long. *¡Estupendo!* This needs a party."

"I know. We've closed Hacienda for tomorrow tonight and invited everyone from church. I phoned the hospital. They say Gillian can come out for the evening then back overnight. You're to go and get her."

If David had been having difficulty connecting the right emotion to the right event with respect to Eric, he had no problem now. They hugged, prayed together and must have presented a strange sight to Eric who had in the meantime showered and got changed.

"Well, boys," he announced. "Whit d'yez think?"

He had on brown corduroy trousers, a blue Fair Isle jumper, a cream jacket, and Chelsea boots.

"Well, they certainly won't recognize you in Muirhouse now," David managed at last.

Chapter 16

SOUTH CLERK STREET

"So you're turning into a God botherer too then?" Gillian's sister Ros was sitting at the foot of her bed munching on a nectarine, catching the juice in a tissue and reading a copy of *Chat*. Gillian had texted her to say she was in hospital after an accident but was ok. And she'd told her about David too.

Gillian didn't answer right away. She had never experienced a week like this last one. New people and new points of view had been challenging prejudices – then to find herself in the middle of drug gang violence and a possible kidnapping. Her head was spinning and she didn't know what she thought. She knew she was in a process but wasn't quite sure where it was taking her. And it all came against a background of faith. David, Juan, the church – they didn't seem to do what they did simply out of social conscience or habit. There was something they believed in – or Someone – and that made the difference. It was what made David take on another kid in trouble when he'd apparently lost his wife through too much of the same in another setting. But after a reluctant start he seemed willing to do it all again, even though she'd picked up that Raúl had been in Madrid himself before Edinburgh. It would be too horrible if he had had something to do with what happened to Rocío. Anyway, this faith thing was something she hadn't encountered in quite that form before. She wasn't willing to throw it out as irrelevant till she'd thought it all through.

"I don't know," she said finally. "Maybe. You make it sound like a disease though."

"Well isn't it? I heard this guy on the radio saying it's just like a virus. He wants everyone inoculated."

"That's ridiculous. David's church got kids off drugs and into jobs. They made them better, not worse."

She was surprised at the vehemence of her own response and a little embarrassed at how it had come out. She, as much as anyone, would have taken all the same views this time two years ago. Then she and Tony had separated. When they decided to divorce, Tony suggested they opt for unreasonable behaviour and he volunteered to make something up. They were both so sick of one another by that stage that anything that speeded things up seemed worth trying. But that had started her thinking. Here she was approaching middle age – single, no kids, reasonable career but nothing startling. What was it all about? Was there a point or was it just "live while you live and die when you die" and try to enjoy yourself in between? Even before meeting David she was feeling the need to delve a bit deeper.

"No," she continued, "there can be good reasons for believing or not. But just to say everyone who believes anything is ill really isn't fair."

Ros finished the nectarine and lobbed the stone neatly into the rubbish bin in the corner.

"Fair enough. Suit yourself. I just don't want you getting brainwashed or anything. Anyway, tell me a bit more about 'Señor David'. Sounds mysterious."

This change of tack irritated Gillian all the more. Ros had now hopped over to topic number two and was about to build a mental picture no doubt based on a similar degree of prejudice. Gillian was used to writing in block capitals in the margins of books that did the same and tearing a strip off students who tried to get away with it in essays. She did not approve of personal philosophies based on Sunday Supplement reviews of *The God Delusion* or the even shakier foundations of "what everybody knows". She wasn't sure she wanted to tell Ros anything, only to find it relayed to Dad mangled out of all recognition.

"Well," she said cautiously, "he's in his early fifties, wife died two years ago, he's part-Spanish – brought up in Edinburgh but had his career in Spain. Been back in Edinburgh a few months I think…"

"No," interrupted Ros. "What's he like? Dishy, ordinary, funny, boring?"

"He's quite serious, thoughtful – funny, sometimes – well read. I don't know whether you'd say good-looking. Needs a Marks and Spencer card though. He's a nice man. Sincere."

"Oh," Ros sounded disappointed. "Right, got to get going. Billy's working Saturday mornings so he'll be home soon and I've got to pick the kids up from swimming. I'll maybe manage in again next week."

"The doctors think I'll be home by the middle of the week."

"Ok then. Let me know if you need anything."

But whether Gillian needed anything or not, Ros had gathered up a handbag the size of a small suitcase and was off.

Gillian finished her coffee and tried to put the plastic beaker on her side table without twisting too much. It ended up on the floor. She felt tired and tried to lie back and relax but couldn't. That woman. They were about as unlike as sisters could be. Always had been. When they were children Ros had been bossy, always right, obsessed with Barbie, then her own wardrobe, then boyfriends, then having children. She couldn't say these were things a girl shouldn't be interested in; it just happened that none of them had interested her. Gillian had worked hard at school, ignored boys, dressed to her own style not the dictates of the fashion police, got her degree then her doctorate, met Tony, moved in with him, kept developing her career, married, looked after Dad, and arranged the nursing home place – everything a dutiful, diligent girl should do. Now look at her. Ros seemed content with her husband, kids, part-time job, caravan holidays in the West Country, helping at Brownies. Gillian was the one out on a limb, with drug dealers trying to saw it off. Maybe she should have been content not pushing all the time. Then she thought, no, that's not right. That's who I am. I'm not Ros and don't want to be. I do want to find out what it's all about and now I'm with people who think they know. Nice people. People I like. Why wouldn't I take that seriously? Just then the nurse interrupted her thoughts with the dinner trolley. Gillian had opted for vegetable soup, macaroni cheese, trifle, and coffee. As the smell wafted along she was beginning to wonder if she could still change to the salad.

Juan had insisted David borrow his car. Trying not to feel like a teenager using his dad's Cortina to take his girlfriend out on a date, David reminded himself he was over fifty, Gillian was not his girlfriend, and this was not a date. As it happened Juan had a Seat Leon not a Cortina. So while David was clear in his mind what was and was not going on, he just couldn't contain the cocktail of emotions bubbling around as he pulled into the hospital car park – nervousness, excitement, apprehension, uncertainty, exhaustion, even shyness. He didn't have a name for it but recognized the overall effect. He felt *exactly* like a teenager borrowing his dad's car to take his girlfriend out.

Gillian, sitting up waiting for him, lit up as David arrived. As instructed, he had gone over to Marchmont with Alicia earlier to get some clothes – neither prior sight nor input was allowed. Now he dutifully handed over a case he thought might have held enough for a long weekend. Gillian thanked him, then he was banished to the waiting room while preparations were made. It took a while. Two copies of *Classic Car* and one *BBC Good Food* magazine passed before his eyes without a word going in. Then she appeared. She looked fantastic, wearing a thin, floaty Indian print top with a warm shawl over ruby red velvet trousers. Her hair was up and she had somehow managed to get dressed over the plaster and perfectly made-up with nothing but a bedside mirror to hand. She was in a wheelchair on account of the stitches and the expression on the nurse's face pushing her along the corridor made it pretty plain what *she* thought was going on. Strict instructions were given. Eleven o'clock – no later. No excess excitement. Very limited amounts of alcohol. Absolutely no shotgun attacks. Gillian and David looked serious and nodded at the right times. This was so like a girlfriend's mum reading the riot act David found it hard to keep a straight face. A fit of the giggles hit them as soon as they were through the automatic double doors and into the cool night air. David opened the car door then helped

Gillian to her feet. Her perfume filled his senses. He gently lowered her into the passenger seat then pulled the seatbelt out.

"I'm sorry," she said. "I can't twist round. Could you?"

"Of course. Sure."

He reached across to clip it in. She laid her hand on his shoulder. As he was fiddling to fit the buckle Gillian found herself thinking, there isn't another man right now I would be comfortable doing this for me. But this isn't awkward at all. What does that mean? The clasp finally clicked and David stood up, straightened his jacket, closed the door, folded up the wheelchair, and popped it in the boot. It means, Gillian thought, David Hidalgo is a gentleman and I feel completely safe with him, shotguns notwithstanding.

They drove up to Hacienda chatting easily. Gillian told him about the hospital food and David told her Juan was threatening to impound his frying pan. She talked about Ros and how the visit had made her feel. He told her about phoning Maggie to see how she was and offering to have the van repaired and repainted. Gillian shared how she had met the larger than life Soup Dragon and her pixie husband and some of their adventures. David talked about Eric and how his unexpected news had caused him such mixed feelings. She told him about her Alpha Course and how she'd given up after a few weeks. David didn't try to find out why. Instead he recounted his feelings the day he left Spain, when half of Warehouse 66 had turned out to see him off – everyone in tears, including former dealers, prostitutes, and pimps. It made him feel the most loved man in the world and the most wretched coward at the same time. Neither felt they had to hide or explain. Gillian thought she could have told him anything and he would have known what to say. David felt they were like Adam and Eve before the fall.

Halfway up South Clerk Street they noticed a crowd outside the Queen's Hall, not in itself surprising, probably just the end of an early evening recital. What was strange though was how they were all looking up and a few were pointing. They found a place to park, joined the crowd, and followed their line of sight. A huge full moon, like a massive blue-veined cheese, was slowly being devoured by the shadow of the earth blocking the reflection of the sun. They watched for ten minutes, listening to the banter around them. David's hand moved onto Gillian's shoulder and she put her hand over his. The night was holding its breath. Would darkness triumph or life return? They both felt they might just ignore the party and stay there all night. Or forever. Finally, the moon re-emerged pristine and perfect. The crowd broke into applause then began to disperse. Gillian felt the light might be coming back in more ways than one.

Hacienda was crowded by the time they arrived. It was quite an entrance as David tried to negotiate the wheelchair through the doorway. Juan spotted them, leapt across, and ushered them in. Alicia, on the other side, saw them and waved. She was surrounded by well-wishers and had a pile of gifts next to her. Although this was her restaurant she wasn't allowed to lift or carry anything. Irene MacInnes had her pinny on and was bustling around, bossing Tomas about and dispensing trays piled with goodies. Multicoloured salads fought for space with plates of tortilla, trays of massive prawns, piles of calamares, and dishes of olives, *jamón ibérico*, chorizo, and *patatas bravas*. The centrepiece was a paella pan three feet wide with the most exotic mixture of colours, shapes, textures, and tastes the older ladies of Southside had ever seen. The air was full of the smell of good food. To some, it was not entirely clear that such self-indulgence was totally proper, but then the minister and that attractive woman with him seemed to be tucking in without too much hesitation so perhaps it was all right. The best of Juan's wine cellar was flowing and there were toasts, speeches, songs in Spanish and English, and any amount of good wishes. David rested his hands lightly on Alicia's head and prayed, for once without difficulty or embarrassment. Gillian claimed vociferously that she did not sing in public but dutifully recited "A Rosebud by my Early Walk" to big cheers. A couple of late diners, unaware that it was a private party, looked in hoping for a quiet table. Juan dragged them through the door, insisting they join the festivities and drink a toast to his beautiful wife and the new life within. Eric flitted around telling his story to anyone who would listen. There were some raised eyebrows but the major response was hand-shaking, back-slapping, and a few quiet words of advice.

Suddenly it was late and, like Cinderella, Gillian felt the approaching hour. Exhausted, she whispered it was time to go. Everyone seemed to be kissing everyone else in the Spanish way – even Mrs MacInnes taking a peck on the cheek from Mr Grant – and then it was over. Juan insisted that everything could be cleared up in the morning – looking meaningfully at Tomas – and hats, coats, and scarves were dished out. Soon David was pushing Gillian along the pavement past the Asian grocers, the video rental shop, the newsagents, and the pub. Then they were back in the car and on their way south. This time they were quiet. David knew all the reasons why he would never recommend young people to make serious relationships with those they couldn't share worship and prayer with. Gillian considered how she had known this man for just over a week. He was a minister for goodness sake – the last profession on earth she would have thought she could share a common outlook with. In neither case did it matter. David was thinking about Alicia's certainty that the Lord was in it. Gillian was thinking of the kindness David had shown all night.

They got back to Little France sooner than either of them wanted. David parked as near the entrance as he could, got the wheelchair out and opened Gillian's door. She was surprised how weak she felt. She had to put her arms round his neck to be lifted out. They stood facing each other, Gillian's arms still around his neck, her head tilted up. Without any premeditation David turned his head slightly, leaned forward and kissed her, lightly and delicately. She smiled up at him, letting him gather her up in his arms and gently ease her into the chair. The nurse, waiting in the foyer, smiled with some satisfaction at having guessed correctly.

Chapter 17

EDINBURGH

"So ah suppose ye'd huv tae say it's a miracle, like. As far as ah can tell onywae. Ken whit ah'm sayin'? So... eh... thanks fur listenin'. Cheers." Eric nervously cleared his throat, scrunched up half a page of scribbled notes, jumped down from the platform, and sat back in the front row. Silence ensued for a few seconds before David collected himself enough to get up and round things off.

"Well, I'd like to thank Eric for everything he's shared this morning. Can I encourage you to remember him and his friends in prayer? It's not going to be easy – I'm sure you'll understand. Now, please stay for tea or coffee if you can and remember to get a news-sheet on the way out. Mayfield small group are leading next Sunday. You know who you are! Thanks."

Southside Fellowship was a city church and didn't think of itself as leading a particularly sheltered life. They read the papers, watched the news, bought *The Big Issue*, occasionally had to navigate their way past drunks and beggars on the way to work, and thought they had a reasonable grasp of city life. What Eric had told them made many of them wonder. As David had gradually come to terms with Eric's conversion, he realized that if he had tended to a cynical first impression then others might too. Between the time Eric first turned up at the soup van and now there was already a marked change. He thought of the confident, streetwise junkie out with his mates, the terrified look on his face when he realized the lights coming up the hill were Raúl's men not Jen, the shivering, wasted figure on the sofa wondering where his next fix was coming from, and then the ecstatic sound of his voice on the phone. Which of these best represented the new Eric was still an open question. Even allowing for an absolutely genuine experience of something outside himself, he still had a long way to go. Key to that would be the support and encouragement of fellow believers. For that to happen, they would have to know where he had come from and what he was going to face.

So, just before the service that morning David had taken Eric aside and asked if he would mind sharing a bit about life in the North Edinburgh schemes and what had happened to him. Eric agreed but had gone much further. He told about his upbringing and family, his dad's alcoholism and violence, his mum's gambling and the predictable results of no money, no food, spells in care, neglect, sometimes actual abuse, falling behind in school, truanting, and a string of petty convictions. He also had them laughing about the times his mum would send him and his sister out with a shoplifting list then batter them if they didn't get everything on it, including the special offers – "Nick one, get one free" he called it.

Then he told a darker tale of drug use, dealing, and the confusion about who was the user or who was being used. He talked about the arrival of Raúl Álvarez and his bloody takeover. After the botched attempt to get Jen to safety there was the sickening feeling that the gun attack on the van was aimed at him and was just the beginning. Finally he told about his surprising Saturday morning and how he now wanted to live a new life.

After the Hacienda party he was so elated he had to go back and look up some old mates. The big news was that Raúl and his gang had disappeared. The rumour was that he had got wind that CID were about to move in and decided to move out first. The girl had disappeared with him. Nobody seemed to know where, but there were plenty of ideas – Spain, Portugal, Brazil, Colombia, Romania, Algeria or maybe even the US. Someone thought London and there was even one nomination for Prestonpans. Everybody was relieved – unless he turned up again, of course, in which case no one wanted to be too obviously overjoyed, apart from Eric who danced a jig and sang three choruses of "YMCA". Nobody knew what he was on but there was some interest in what it might be, how much it was, and where you could get some. Now he had a queue of Southside members wanting to shake his hand and wish him well.

That queue did not include Alison MacInnes. When the rest went forward to get their cuppa she sat with a blank expression, staring ahead. She had been so hopeful after the previous week and now it had all come to nothing. In fact things were now a great deal worse. Señor David had been so supportive as he explained what had happened that she felt duty bound to show up and tell him about Jen coming to the house in person. Now there was nothing left to tell. Eric had confirmed what she had guessed – the bird had flown and taken her little fledgling with him. She could guess for what purpose but tried not to think of it. Now, with everybody milling around at the front she was an isolated figure slumped in the back row. David approached her.

"Alison. Hi. How are you?" A pointless question, despair written all over her face.

"He's got her with him," she said with flatness and finality. They both knew what she was talking about.

"How do you know?"

"She came by the house to pick up her things and asked for her passport."

"How was she?"

"Horrible. She looked like she hadn't slept for days. He's forcing her to stay, you know. She doesn't want to. She'd rather come home but he won't let her."

"I thought that might be the case. I guess it just has to go back to the police then. I'm not sure there's much more we can do."

"Which means nothing's going to happen. Don't get me wrong, I'm grateful for what you tried to do and I'm sorry for what happened. I'm just worried sick. And there's nothing I can do about it."

David felt powerless to give her anything to cling on to. He was all too familiar with relationships everyone could see were toxic except the people in them. Sometimes it took a crisis to knock the juggernaut out of gear and allow the unwilling passenger to jump out before the whole thing tumbled over the cliff. Sometimes they were too late. Everyone could see it but Jen. So young, so dazzled by a bully with a flashy watch and a big car.

"Where do you think she'll be now?" Alison asked, looking for anything positive in the situation.

"I've no idea. Probably Spain. If I understand what's going on he still needs to be near enough to protect his business but far enough away to keep the detectives guessing. He'll have friends in the *barrios* of Madrid or Seville. Or maybe a place in the country where he can hide up for a while." Alison was quiet.

"Do you think there are any more miracles where that one came from?" she eventually asked, nodding in Eric's direction. David looked down.

"Alison, there is nothing I can say that's going to make things easier for you. Jen seems like a very single-minded girl. Maybe it'll turn out in her favour now. Sometimes help comes from the most unexpected sources. We need to keep hoping – and praying. I don't believe it's a waste of time. It's not all over yet." Even as he spoke David knew that he doubted every word.

Down the road in Edinburgh Royal, Gillian made good progress and by the following Wednesday – the fifth day after the attack – was told to go home, put her feet up, and get better. A nurse would call in and check on progress until the stitches came out. Did she have someone who could look after her? She thought she did. The first few nights after the shooting she'd had nightmares but these quickly faded as other emotions took over. The night after David dropped her off from the party she had lain still for hours feeling warm and complete, not wanting to sleep and lose the feeling. The background hum and rumble of the ward which normally kept her awake carried on, but now it felt distant and remote. Normally she loved to have her own things about her and felt disorientated when everything was so strange, but that night she was floating. She felt as if she was wrapped in a blanket or surrounded by a heavy perfume that filled her consciousness and dampened all other senses. Or maybe it was like the snowfall the first night they met. Everything sharp and abrasive was softened and everything ugly was covered over.

David came to take her home around mid-afternoon. He brought flowers and the scent of the lilies filled Juan's car all the way to Marchmont. He helped her out, supporting her with one arm and carrying her bag with the other. They took the stairs very gingerly, stopping a few times till she felt able for another few steps. He unlocked the door and pushed it open, then followed her into the living room. Having Gillian here in person made everything different. He no longer felt like an intruder – even a permitted one. She was the essence of the space that gave it a personality. She sat down gently on the sofa. David bent down and pulled her shoes off. He was about to go put the kettle on but she wouldn't let him. She gripped his hand and pulled him down. She laid her head on his shoulder and closed her eyes. They sat like that, quietly, almost drifting off to sleep. Eventually David spoke, barely audibly, not to break the spell.

"Hungry?"

"A little. Anything in mind?"

"I bought a few things. Why don't you sleep while I get something ready."

"That would be nice."

"Here. Let me." David got up gently and lifted her legs up onto the sofa. He eased a cushion under her head then took a throw from the back of another chair and laid it over her. He leaned over and kissed her lightly on the forehead. She reached up without opening her eyes, caught his neck, and pulled his head down. He knelt beside her. They kissed. Properly. Again and again. She was smiling in a dreamy sort of way. He finally kissed her through her hair then managed to get away. She let out a long satisfied sigh and turned her head to stare at the ceiling.

Over the next few weeks winter changed into spring. Alicia slept at Gillian's until she was fully able to look after herself, but otherwise David spent lots of time there till she was fit for work. Eric moved back to Muirhouse and back in with Lorraine, so the flat in Bruntsfield returned to normal, though still sparsely furnished and dismal. Gillian set about making it a place of comfort and life. David was amazed at what could be done with paint, paper, inexpensive fabrics, and a bit of taste. They went shopping for second-hand furniture and became regulars at Steptoe's in East Preston Street, holding hands and wandering through the clutter till they came on some undiscovered treasure coated in dust behind broken TVs, redundant record players, and musty piles of books. Repeatedly they surprised themselves and eventually racked up a very reasonable suite, a quite elegant table and chairs, lamps, rugs, a couple of kitchen appliances with three-month guarantees, and lots of occasional bits and pieces. Gillian gently suggested that perhaps a new washing machine might be a bit more functional than a tarnished old saxophone they found under piles of floor tiles and carpet offcuts – despite the fact that it claimed to be a 1948 Selmer Super Balanced Action. David put it back reluctantly. The concept of a colour and design scheme was something of a revelation to a man who normally considered magnolia a little bit racy and had no problem with dark green lino and powder blue walls. Gillian was careful, however, to seek his opinion and preferences at every stage. Together they decided on a Mediterranean feel and tried to hunt down dark wood, earthenware pots, and terracotta kitchenware offset with touches of olive green and pale cream. David felt the colour coming back into his home and his life. The flat was beginning to feel like somebody really lived there for the first time.

Gillian in turn was exploring more of the way David saw the world. He told her how he had come to faith as a sceptical, ambitious businessman in his early thirties. He was frank about his struggles to believe both then and now but also spoke about transformations in people's lives he could find no other explanation for. There was nothing they didn't talk about and no holds were barred. How did prayer work? How could God be in control if people still had free will? Would judgment be both conscious and eternal? How could God be in heaven watching himself dying on a cross? Did he really descend into hell, and if so how did he get out again? Do miracles still happen, and if so when and how? Was changing the water into wine not just a bit of showing off? David tried to answer as honestly as he could and where he didn't know, he said so. At one point he confessed it wasn't the parts of the Bible he didn't understand that gave him most trouble; it was the bits he did. The issue was not about having a foolproof understanding of every theological problem as much as trying to put into practice what he already understood perfectly well. It was a throwaway remark but made an impression. From that point on Gillian started thinking not so much about what she thought of God as what he might be thinking of her.

They talked about Rocío and how David and she had met, fallen in love, come to faith, and built the church together. Then she had gone on ahead, leaving him alone. Once he'd heard a friend refer to death as just a significant change of address – a nice phrase but not so nice for those left behind when the removal van leaves. Dozens of times he had decided, "That's it – I am no longer a believer – I am totally done with all of it. Either there is no God or whatever God there is, is unwilling or unable to help. Or else it's part of his divine recreation to torture and torment. In either case that's of no use to me." He could even have coped with God as the divine dentist, pulling away regardless of the pain until the rotten tooth popped out, but for a long time, this God had seemed more like an evil experimenter twisting teeth to see how much you could stand. But somehow, throughout it all though, there was still a feeling that God – whatever he was – wouldn't let him go. He kept intruding into his thoughts, even his dreams. Not with answers, just with a conscious presence as if to say I'm still here, still in you, still part of the world as much as the rocks, the air, and the sky. Eventually the pain receded enough for David to hear the still small voice again and begin rebuilding. Even so he had come to Edinburgh with little more than a nodding acquaintance left. In meeting Gillian and taking a step out in search of Jen something seemed to have shifted. They snuggled up together on the nearly new sofa, kissed, caressed, and grew together. Throughout this time David kept up a constant dialogue with whatever or whoever might be out there. He felt no sense of unease, just a strong and loving presence over everything they did.

Gillian told her story too. Duty and diligence, academic effort, and from time to time a little gratifying recognition in her chosen field. Then, when Tony and she had drifted apart, she found herself asking, "Is that all there is, then?" It wasn't really a traumatic break-up, just a gradual numbing of the senses until there wasn't anything left. She felt like a rag that had been soaked, wrung out, sterilized, hung out to dry, and left flapping in the wind. Now the wind carried a familiar scent like something you can catch a whiff of but can't quite place – like remembering a moment from childhood or a half-forgotten song. Nevertheless there was an authenticity about it, hinting at a richness and sweetness if you could only find the source. She was happy to be wafted along and see where it might lead.

They did other things together as well as decorating. In fact they did everything people who live in Edinburgh almost never do. They watched the firing of the One o'clock Gun from the Castle ramparts. They walked round, marvelling at the natural history exhibits in Chambers Street Museum. They risked the wrath of the attendants by taking their own picnic to the Botanical Gardens and eating salmon sandwiches and chocolate eclairs behind the bushes. They climbed Arthur's Seat and the Scott Monument and took panoramic photos from the top. They did the tour of the Royal Yacht at its berth in Leith with that peculiar mixture of curiosity and discomfort commoners feel peering into the lives of the rich. They went sailing from Port Edgar in a small yacht Gillian owned a part-share in with friends she'd met on a girls only sailing course. After David was sick the third time they decided he should start with a rowing boat on St Mary's Loch in Linlithgow.

David also made a welcome new addition to Scots Language social events. His Spanish background and occupation attracted attention but what got everybody talking was just how in love they both were. Colleagues were shocked to hear about Gillian's ordeal and ready to be very negative towards whoever had got her into such a fix. Immediately she got back to work, though, they began to notice a difference. Being shot at wasn't a trivial matter but she simply wasn't thinking about it. She seemed to float through turgid staff meetings, get on well with awkward colleagues, volunteer for unpopular lectures, offer to counsel and tutor failing students and even return her library books on time. At the same time, student grades seemed to be improving though nobody was sure whether this was due to more generous marking or simply more enthusiastic teaching. When Gillian and David turned up together at an end of term bash just before Easter, everyone was intrigued, then fascinated, and in some cases a little bit jealous. They simply *worked* together, as if they were parts of a machine designed to interlock, now finally turning in unison. They went to concerts. She got to like Latin and swing, coped with bebop but found free jazz impossible. David sampled Sting, Eric Clapton, and James Taylor with a reasonable show of enthusiasm. Then Salsa Celtica clicked for both of them so they started going to Pepe and Roberta's Latin dance class once a week. Gillian told him he needed tighter trousers to do the salsa but he wasn't ready to sell out altogether. David continued to teach Spanish and Gillian continued to attend – both of them trying to keep the secret with little success. When Julie passed all her essays and term papers the whole class went to Hacienda to celebrate. David kept on preaching, counselling, and leading at Southside, with Gillian sitting in the front row listening carefully and thinking it through. He tried not to let it remind him too much of Rocío listening to Paco.

Romance was in the air elsewhere as well. After Eric had decamped back to Muirhouse they didn't see him for several weeks which made everyone nervous. Had it really just been a flash in the pan? Had Eric had his spiritual shot in the arm then come down from the high and reverted back to normal? Then he started showing up at church and sometimes dropping by David's flat in the evening, at first a bit unpredictably then more and more regularly. Finally, he surprised them all – again – bringing Lorraine and the three children with him to church and announcing they wanted to get married. Could David do the service? Lorraine was a much quieter creature than Eric, not quite pretty but looking as if she could be with a bit more guidance and confidence. She was delighted with her new man. David was happy to officiate and they started looking at dates. Juan offered to do a very affordable reception, and Gillian and Alicia thought they could collaborate on flowers and decorating the hall. Senga, Tyrone, and Cameron made life more interesting for Sunday school staff that morning but improved with a clout round the ear from Eric while Lorraine looked on approvingly.

"Ah couldnae believe it when he turned up again," she told David over coffee. "At least, ah could believe he'd turned up aw right – ah'm used tae that – ah jist wisnae used to him turnin' up and staein' turned up, if ye ken whit ah mean. Then, when he wis aff the drugs and wisnae nicking money oot ma purse to buy smack aff aw these Spanish nutters, that wiz really weird – in a good way like. Noo he's even goat a part time joab an' that. It's magic."

So it was with a sense of surprising contentment and well-being that David sat down as part of three couples having lunch at Hacienda after church one day. The restaurant was normally closed on Sundays but occasionally Alicia cooked just for friends. Today she invited David and Gillian along with Eric and Lorraine and the children to celebrate the engagement. The normal menu was put to one side. Instead she cooked *Cordero Asado Castellano* in the style of Sobrino de Botin in Madrid – reputedly the oldest restaurant in the world, famous for roast lamb and suckling pig and where Juan himself had trained. It was crisp and succulent. Eric and Lorraine had never tasted anything like it and loved it after they got over their initial embarrassment. The older kids took more convincing and had to be provided with emergency pizzas or would have spent the day moaning and kicking each other under the table. Only Cameron took to Spanish eating. After finding out his name meant "shrimp", not even teasing from his older brother and sister could stop him wolfing down enough to make his bedroom reek of garlic for the next three days. Fresh-baked bread, exotic salads, and a Rioja reserva completed the ensemble.

David was enjoying the food, the surroundings, and the occasion and was able to reflect that at last things seemed to be going well. Numbers were up at church and not just on the back of students who had the loyalty and commitment of rabbits and were no foundation for long-term growth. Nor was it by dint of migration of the disaffected as with so much supposed "church growth". He squeezed Gillian's hand under the table and got a fleeting smile while she was supposed to be giving all her attention to talking about table decorations with Lorraine. The last three months had been a revelation. Without exaggeration he thought it must have something in common with heaven. Everything you wanted to do was allowed and things that weren't allowed you didn't want. Together they were slowly teaching each other to believe and live again. Now Eric and Lorraine were about to embark on a new phase of life as well, and he allowed himself to feel some satisfaction in their new start too. He still felt bad about his initial scepticism, but on the other hand it was looking for Jen that had made the connection. It could so easily have turned out otherwise, but this was how it was and he was glad of it. And that reminded him of Jen. They hadn't seen Alison at church since the week she turned up to tell him about the fleeting visit and the passport. Mrs MacInnes occasionally updated him on how she was doing. Normally it wasn't good news.

Just as they were finishing coffee and the party was about to break-up – at the point the kids were about to start throwing chips at each other – there was a loud banging on the restaurant door. Juan rolled his eyes in an uncharacteristic show of impatience. With Alicia expecting and Tomas back off to Madrid last week, more of the burden of running things was falling to him and Juan was jealous of his time off.

"*Cerrado significa cerrado,*" he muttered. "Do they not understand that closed means closed? This is our day off." Wearily he got up and went to the door as the banging continued. He hurried the last few paces. He quickly unlocked the door and pulled it open. As he turned, they saw who it was. Alison. White as a sheet. She rushed to the table, her lip trembling. She was only just holding it together. Without saying a word she pulled out a mobile phone, tapped a few keys and laid the phone down on the table, the speakerphone on full volume.

"You have no new messages and a saved message. Saved messages…"

A pause, then a young, female, Scottish voice. It had a deathly calm and control in spite of what was said.

"Hi Mum. This is Jennifer. I hope you get this. I'm in Spain but I'm not allowed out and I can't contact anyone. I stole this mobile to call you. Nobody tells me anything and I can't understand what they're saying but I know something's going on. Raúl gets really mad. He's… he's…" There was a pause. "… he's shot a couple of the gang and he's started… hitting me. And other things… I want to come home but I can't get away. We're in a country house. I don't know where. They've started packing things up. I think they're going to leave. Everybody keeps talking about 'Cali'."

Then she broke down.

"Help me," she sobbed. "Help me. I don't want to go. I want to come home. I think he's going to kill me…" Silence, followed by another sound in the background. Like a door slamming. A scream, then shouting in Spanish – *"Puta! Hija de puta!"* A thud, and another scream. The message stopped, then with jarring normality the recorded voice:

"To return the call key 5, to replay the message key 1, to save the message key 2, to delete key 3. For message details key 8."

Alison picked up the phone, closed the app, and laid it back down in the middle of the table. There was absolute silence. She sat looking from one to another with an expression drained of colour and life.

"What am I supposed to do?" she said. "What in God's name am I supposed to do?"

Chapter 18

MADRID

The landmarks of Madrid should have made it a very recognizable, attractive city from the air. As the Iberian Airways Boeing 737 banked, slowly circling, waiting for a gap in the holding pattern and space to land, David should have been able to make out at least the Las Ventas bullring, Real Madrid's Bernabeu football stadium and the Retiro park. Unfortunately, flight paths to Barajas don't cross over the city itself but come into the airport on the eastern side of town, over the unlovely industrial wastelands of the Corredor de Henares. But no matter; this wasn't a pleasure trip. David thought back to the moment the bombshell dropped: Jen was calling for help – literally. Alison had just sat there looking at them all. It might have been easier if she had become hysterical and started shouting for someone to do something. But the way she just sat there, white as a sheet, trembling, meant they had to focus on Jen. Was there anything that could be done to bring her back?

Alicia had suggested they pray, which they did, but that didn't seem like much in the face of the horror of what they had just heard. Alison excused herself for a few minutes to regain her composure as the others listened to the message again and again, repeatedly stunned and horrified.

"They're in Spain, but they're on the move," said David, groping for somewhere to start. "If they needed somewhere to hide out it would be natural to go back to Cali – back to Colombia."

"Unless the police presence is going to be too hot there as well," Juan suggested.

"But remember, when Raúl left Colombia he was just another

one of Escobar's minions. Not a big fish in his own right. That only happened in Spain," David countered.

"And if they take the girl to Colombia there'll be much less chance of finding her." Juan voiced the problem that had occurred to them all. There was a pause as they took in this even worse conclusion.

"What does *puta* mean?" asked Gillian. Juan and Alicia exchanged glances, then looked away. David answered.

"*Puta* is a whore. You know that *hijo* is son and *hija* is daughter. So *hija de puta* – well, you get the idea." Jen wasn't anybody's little darling any more. As might have been expected, Raúl – if that's who was speaking – had lost whatever attraction he'd had for the sixteen-year-old. Now she was just baggage, someone from outside the clan who knew more than was healthy about Señor Álvarez and his activities. David doubted very much if a ticket home would be part of the compensation package if things went wrong. So what then – simply abandoned or something worse? Raúl would be taking care of business for sure. And if Jen was bad for business…

Alison came back to a sombre gathering.

"Have you been in touch with the police?" David asked.

"Not much point in that," she said flatly.

"I know that's how it looks. But things have changed a bit now," David tried to point out as gently as he could. "In Edinburgh she was with Raúl by choice. Now it's clearly false imprisonment. That would give them something to go on."

"Ok," Alison agreed without enthusiasm.

"Did you try calling the number this came from?" Gillian asked.

"No reply."

"Was it Jen's mobile number?"

Alison shook her head.

"What about police in Spain?" Alicia suggested.

"I still have some contacts with the *Policia Nacional*," David offered. "I'll try first thing tomorrow."

"Can they no fund whaur a mobile phone call's fae?" Lorraine asked. In the moment of crisis the others had rather forgotten Eric, Lorraine, and the kids. Eric knew what was going on but with embarrassing memories of his last bright idea hadn't been offering any suggestions.

"No if yir no speakin' right then. It's no use unless yer awready lookin' fur it." He succinctly closed the door on that possibility.

And that exhausted their limited stock of good ideas. Alison would contact D.S. Thompson and David would get in touch with a friend in the Spanish police – if he still worked there, or remembered who David was. Juan made more coffee and juice for the kids. The adults sat round not saying much and wondering what on earth anyone could do now. The appalling words on the answering service were still hanging in the air.

Suddenly everyone jumped as Alison's mobile phone, still in the middle of the table, gave a beep. It was a text. Alison frowned as she read it.

"That's weird," she said. "It's not from a number I've got listed. It's just rubbish."

"What does it say?" Gillian asked.

"PS 59 1 2," Alison read out.

"Ah've pals that dae that," said Lorraine. "It's right annoyin'. Ye get a message wan day then three days later ye get a PS. An' ye've nae idea whit message it's a PS tae!"

"But it's not a number I've got listed," Alison was still frowning.

"They dae that in a'," Lorraine continued undaunted. "They run oot o' credit then borrow a phone fae a pal and send a text fae that. So ye've nae idea who it's fae or what they were sayin' afore. It's absolute murder, so it is."

"Maybe a promotion from your provider?" Juan put in.

"I don't know. Probably nothing." Alison shrugged her shoulders and put the phone in her bag as she got up to go. "Sorry I broke up the party. Maybe she'll phone again," she said, her voice empty of emotion. She had returned from desperation back to mere hopelessness. They would go through the motions but nothing would help. Nothing could be done. Nothing made any sense. If only she'd been a better mum. If only she'd been able to keep her marriage together. If only Jen hadn't got into bad company. If only she'd been able to do all the things she hadn't been able to do, then none of this would have happened. She smiled weakly and made for the door. As she was opening it to leave David spoke.

"Just a minute." He had a look of concentration as if trying to work out a tricky calculation or remember something he should know but couldn't quite grasp. "Can I see that message again?"

Alison shrugged her shoulders and came back in.

"Sure." She pulled out the phone, pressed a few keys, and handed it to him. He glanced at it briefly then laid it down. A black leather document case was on the floor beside the coat stand. He walked over, picked it up, came back, and sat down. All eyes were on him. He unzipped the case and pulled out a Bible. He glanced again at the message then started leafing through the book. He found the place, checked again then laid the phone down and read.

"'Rescue me from my enemies, O God. Protect me from those who have come to destroy me. Rescue me from these criminals; save me from these murderers.'" He laid the Bible down open on the table next to the phone. Juan picked up the phone, reread the message and nodded. Otherwise expressions remained blank.

"I don't understand," said Alison. "What's that all about?"

"It's not PS like in a letter," said David slowly. "It's PS for the book of Psalms. 'PS 59 1 2' is Psalm 59 verses 1 and 2. She must have a Bible. It's a message from Jen." Alison was shaking her head, mystified.

"I gave her a Bible. When she came to the house for her things. Just before she left I gave her the Bible my mum bought her when she started high school. I've no idea why. Maybe it was meeting all of you and coming to church again. I just thought it would bring her luck or something."

"No such thing," Juan muttered.

"Jen's a clever girl," said David, ignoring him. "She couldn't call you again but she's got hold of a phone she can text with. She can't send an ordinary message – whoever's phone it is would be checking. This is a code. She has the Bible you gave her and knows you could look up the same thing here."

"So she can say whatever she wants if she can find the right verse?" Alison asked.

"That's right. To a degree. Within the limits of the verses she can find. So we still have to be careful interpreting it."

"Jen's never been the least bit interested in the Bible. How would she know how to find anything or what to call the books?" Alison asked, still mystified.

"She's had a lot of time on her hands. She can't read Spanish or understand TV, so what does she do? All she's got to read is that Bible you gave her. She'll have done some RE at school. The abbreviations are very common. So she's reading the Bible and my guess is she starts thinking some of the passages are quite like how she's feeling. Lots of the psalms are about being in trouble and calling for help. It's not a great leap to think if she can get us to look up a verse we'll know what she's thinking. Jen is a very bright girl. She's thought it all out."

Alison was stunned.

"She was never interested in anything at school – after primary anyway – after, you know, we had to move. I suppose I just thought she wasn't very good at anything so she got bored by it all."

"Well," David offered, "I imagine she had so many other issues in her life that school was the last thing she was concerned about. But that doesn't mean she wasn't a bright girl. I think this is the proof. She's got it all figured out. If she can just find the right verses then she can say more or less she wants."

"And we can send her a message using another reference," Gillian suggested, completing the loop. "We'd need to make sure we're using the same version of the Bible though." Academic referencing was an everyday part of her job and so were the problems of incorrect, incomplete, and misleading references.

"So what version does she have and what version is that?" Alicia asked nodding to the open Bible on the table.

"This is a New Living," said David, then looking to Alison, "Do you know what version your mum gave Jen?"

Throughout this exchange Alison's expression had gradually

gone from blank, to dawning comprehension, to focused attention. Now she knew exactly what to do. She got her mum's number and hit call. When she spoke it was brisk and businesslike. There was some hope after all. There was something she could do.

"Hi. Mum? Ali here. Do you remember giving Jen a Bible when she started high school? No, high school. Four years ago. Yes? Ok. It's really important that you remember what version of the Bible it was. No, what version, like the King James or a modern one. Do you know?" It was a bit of an effort to make her meaning entirely clear. Mrs MacInnes seemed as confused by the question as she herself had been a few minutes before.

"Ok. That's fine. No, I'll hang on." Then covering the mouthpiece, "She's just going to look... Hi... Ok, so what was it?... Really... You're sure?... That's fine... Tell you later... Thanks, Mum. Bye." Alison was smiling. "New Living," she said quietly. "With a concordance at the back. Mum's just bought another the exact same for a niece's birthday. That was lucky."

"I told you. No such thing," said Juan, smiling.

"And whit's a concordance when it's at hame?" asked Eric, whose world didn't include anything you would find in the reference section of the library.

"A word list," David answered. "It means you can find all the verses that have a particular word in them."

"So she can find a verse wi' onythin' in it she wants?"

"Exactly."

"No bad!"

"So – ur we gonna say somethin' back, then?" Lorraine put in, very reasonably.

"What do we want to say?" Gillian asked. "We've got to let her know we've got the message and we know what she meant."

"But we also have to be careful whoever's phone it is doesn't guess it's a real reply," Alicia pointed out.

"So we use the same code in exactly the same form," Gillian said. Everyone was now looking to David. He had guessed the meaning of the text and would have the best idea where to look. He thought for a second, then picked up the Bible again. He flicked through a few pages with the air of knowing exactly what he was looking for and just checking it was right.

"Ok. Send this," he said. "'Jen' – except spell it 'G E N'. Now a space then '3' space '9'." Alison keyed it in.

"What does it mean?" she asked.

"GEN is the book of Genesis. It's pronounced the same so I thought that might be reassuring. Chapter 3 is after Adam and Eve have eaten the fruit God told them not to – they'd done what they knew was wrong. Then they ran away. Just like Jen. Verse 9 says, 'Then the Lord God called "Where are you?"' That's to say we want to find her but she's got to tell us where she is. That might work." Gillian shook her head with some disbelief.

"Amazing."

Alison sent the message and they settled down to wait. After half an hour there was still no reply so they decided it might take time for Jen to find a verse that said what she wanted then get a chance to send it. Rather than waiting fruitlessly all night they decided to split up but keep in touch. Eric, Lorraine, and the kids went home. Alison set off to see her mum and explain. Juan and Alicia cleared up, and David and Gillian headed for Bruntsfield.

"That was so clever," Gillian said as they walked over the Meadows arm in arm.

"Not really. Bible references are my job. If it was the *Dictionary of the Older Scottish Tongue* you'd have got it."

"Maybe – maybe not. Anyway. It was brilliant. Stop being so modest." She kissed him on the cheek and squeezed his arm. Far more brilliant to David were other events in his life over the past six months. Far better and just as unexpected. But he didn't feel he could take all the credit for these either.

Over the next few days a regular flow of messages started, haltingly at first, then more freely. It usually took Jen at least a couple of hours to reply, sometimes longer. They still had no idea how she was getting access to a phone but, however it was, it seemed to be holding up. The priority remained finding out where she was. Alison contacted D.S. Thompson, who confirmed of course that a crime was being committed. He would inform Spanish police. David tried to get in touch with his old contact but found he was on leave so there seemed nothing further they could do right then by official channels. Instead, David, Gillian, Alison, Juan, and Alicia met daily at Hacienda after work. Juan and Alicia still had a business to run so they used a back room and Tomas was imported again to help, with the offer of extra English thrown in. They agreed David should take over use of Alison's phone as communications officer and code breaker.

Following his first reply the next message they got was ROM 15 24: "I am planning to go to Spain, and when I do, I will stop off in Rome…", which confirmed that they seemed to still be in Spain and not yet South America. Then they got PS 121 1: "I look up to the mountains…", followed by PS 46 4: "A river brings joy to the city of our God, the sacred home of the Most High." So maybe somewhere in the mountains or with mountains in sight and with a river nearby. There was some discussion as to whether they could conclude she was or was not actually in a city. If the river literally brings joy to the city then perhaps it ran through it or surrounded it. Perhaps it was also a dry area so the river did indeed "bring joy". They tested this out by sending PS 1 3: "They are like trees planted along the riverbank, bearing fruit each season", but got back PS 63 1: "O God, you are my God; I earnestly search for you. My soul thirsts for you; my whole body longs for you in this parched and weary land where there is no water." So dry area but near a river. But actually in a city or not, and if so which one? If they were in a country district things might be harder either to find out where she was or let them know in a way that made sense. Álvarez had operated previously in Madrid and that might match with "the sacred home of the most high", which would have referred to Jerusalem when the psalm was written. It was a working hypothesis.

To check whether it was city or country David sent MT 9 26: "The report of this miracle spread throughout the entire countryside."

The reply to this took a long time. They assumed Jen must be finding it hard to get just the right verse. Then they got PR 9 3: "She has sent her servants to invite everyone to come. She calls out from the heights overlooking the city", followed by PR 8 3: "By the gates at the entrance to the town, on the road leading in, she cries aloud." David couldn't help but smile as he looked them up.

"Clever girl," he muttered.

Alison just shook her head. This resourceful, intelligent individual seemed so different from the daughter she thought she knew. The Jen she had lived with gave nothing away. At home she hardly communicated at all and seemed to be in a permanently bad mood. Her normal modus operandi was to treat the house like a badly run hotel and her mother as lazy staff. That made it ok to moan about when the laundry might be ready, why there was never the right kind of shampoo, and why all her stuff was always being deliberately moved if not outright hidden. It was a revelation to be in touch with such a different girl. The alternative Jen was ingenious, diligent, and communicative. True, the stakes were now different. Instead of just the everyday matter of who would win the battle of the bedroom – to clean or not to clean – this could easily be a matter of life and death. But even given that she had good reasons to keep in touch, the person they were now in touch with was showing surprising maturity and even some humour in spite of everything she was going through.

With all of these messages, David felt they might be getting somewhere so got everyone together after Hacienda had closed one evening with a map of Spain, a notepad, and a Bible. Alison cornered him as he was hanging up his coat. She paused and took a deep breath as if this was something she needed to take a run at.

"I just want you to know I appreciate what you're doing," she began, fiddling with a neck chain and looking everywhere except directly at him. David raised his hand as if to say – it's ok, you don't need to – but she ignored it. "No. Really. It's been a roller-coaster ride, you know – since Christmas. Or maybe more like the ghost train. Ever since Jen didn't come home that weekend... I... I've never known what was coming next. Was it going to be police, or the hospital or...

something worse? Gillian's been telling me some of what you've been through. It can't have been easy. I just want to say thanks. I feel at last there's maybe a chance now. It's the first time in ages."

David nodded. "I'm glad. I was worried we were behaving like amateur detectives without thinking about how you've been feeling."

"No way. And I need to say sorry for being so, well, not exactly full of confidence, you know." She stifled a nervous laugh. "Actually, it's really weird but I feel almost closer to Jen now than before. Before she went off with – that man…", she couldn't bring herself to say his name, "…we hardly ever spoke except for arguing. Just fighting the whole time. Back and forward. I was trying to get her to do things she didn't want to. She was trying to make me let her do stuff I didn't agree with. We couldn't do anything good together – you know, normal things – like shopping, going for a coffee. Even a film. Anything. Now at least we're talking – sort of."

They paused for a moment. A tray of coffees had appeared but neither of them moved.

"You know we never had children," David said.

Alison said nothing.

"So I have no idea what you've been going through. But maybe what's been happening here – maybe this could bring you back together somehow – even though it's been hard."

"I couldn't have heard that a week ago," Alison said slowly. "Now I think you might be right. I feel like I've been picked up, shaken about and don't know where I'm going to land. Know what I mean?"

"Exactly. That's what it felt like when I got back to Edinburgh last year. Now I feel I'm back on some sort of path again. I've just got to see where it goes."

"Me too."

"Ok – let's get some coffee before they finish all the *churros*."

Juan had already laid out the map as David and Alison joined the others round the table scanning towns, cities, rivers, and mountains, wondering which one might hold the key.

"Ok," David began. "Here's the situation. We think she's still in Spain. She's in a drier part of the country which would mean central or south and probably inland. She's in a mountainous area overlooking a city with a river nearby. So the question is — which city, which river? Any suggestions? Juan?"

"I would have said Madrid from the reference to Jerusalem," Juan started. "Also for the connections there. But Madrid isn't really a city on a river and I can't think of "heights overlooking the city". But if not Madrid then probably somewhere not too far away. *Lo siento* – I can't think of anywhere else."

"Ok," David said. "That's a start. Alicia?"

"The Guadalquiver is the most important river in the south but the main city it runs through is Seville, which isn't the capital, but I can't think of where you would say were "the gates at the entrance to the town"."

"Anyone else then? Alison? Gillian?"

Alison was looking even more confused than the others. She felt like they were trying to drop a line and Jen was trying to throw one up but neither one could quite catch on. And time was surely running out. She had no knowledge of Spain though so could only shake her head. Gillian was the only one left. She was frowning and concentrating. She spoke slowly and deliberately.

"I'm not sure about Madrid being a proper match for Jerusalem," she said. "The capital of Scotland has moved about quite a bit. Sometimes the most important city wasn't even the capital – it might be the seat of the church or the commercial centre or a port. Would that be true for Spain as well? During the Moorish occupation wasn't the capital in Granada or Córdoba or some other place? And what about where the verse says, 'The sacred home of the most high'? Does that have to be the capital?"

"Maybe not." David adjusted his glasses and took another look at the map. "The main cities that might fit would seem to be Granada, Seville, Córdoba, Toledo, Ciudad Real — and Madrid of course. I take it we can rule out Alicante and Barcelona because they're on the coast and Bilbao and San Sebastian because they're too far north and not in a dry part of the country. Seville has never been the capital, though it was a key trade centre in the golden age. Córdoba was the capital but more of the caliphs than the Spanish kings."

"Does that matter?" asked Alison.

"And what about Ciudad Real?" put in Alicia. "That was definitely a royal city – it's even in the name."

"Well, what about Toledo then?" Gillian asked. "Does it have a river?"

"Yes it does," David replied, "but I can't see how it would be the 'sacred home of the most high'." Juan interrupted him. "That's because you weren't brought up Catholic."

"What?"

"Your parents weren't Catholic – you didn't go through all the Catholic rituals."

"No. My mother was Church of Scotland. My dad was an atheist. Why's that important?"

Juan had a glean in his eye.

"Because every Catholic in Spain knows that Toledo is the seat of the Roman Catholic Church. Toledo Cathedral is the most important of all the cathedrals – where the bishops and archbishops are crowned. Jen must have found that out. I couldn't see it before because I was thinking of Jerusalem as the capital. *Momentito* Señor David. I have a road map upstairs. There might be a city map of Toledo so we can check it out."

Juan disappeared to retrieve the map from the flat. There was a muted excitement round the table. Maybe they were onto something. He reappeared with a road map and a laptop. He handed David the map and switched the laptop on. David found the page. There it was. The river Tajo flowed round the city of Toledo, catching it in a loop. Not only that, but the course of the river was through a steep-sided gorge crossed by a single main bridge – the gates of the city. And there were the mountains, the heights overlooking the city. It was a dry part of the country but with a river running through it. City gates. Even "the sacred home of the most high". While they were checking this out, Juan googled "Toledo Spain" and clicked the images button. In seconds they were looking over the city from the Parador Hotel on the hillside opposite the medieval town. Exactly as the texts had said – heights over the city, a road leading in, the cathedral standing out clearly against the skyline, and a river surrounding, protecting and indeed "bringing joy" to "the sacred city of the most high". This was it. It had to be. They could be looking at a view very similar to what Jen might be seeing every day.

But they had to be sure.

"Is there anything else that distinguishes Toledo?" Gillian asked. "Anything we could ask to let her know we think we've got it and are just checking?"

"Certainly," said Juan. "Toledo is the Spanish centre for working with steel – like Sheffield in England."

"Do you think Jen would know that?"

"Well, unless she's been kept a complete prisoner she'd be sure to notice. The old city is full of metal-working craft shops – swords, daggers, armour, pistols, that sort of thing."

"Ok," said David, looking up his Bible. "It's a risk. We might have got it wrong, in which case this'll just confuse her. Or even if we're right she might not have noticed, or might not have been out much. It's worth trying though. How about this – GEN 4 22: 'Lamech's other wife, Zillah, gave birth to a son named Tubal-cain. He became an expert in forging tools of bronze and iron'."

"*Perfecto*," said Juan. "Send it and see what we get back."

David keyed it in and hit Send. It was now after midnight. Jen might be asleep. She might not have access to the mobile; she might have been caught and forced to own up. They hardly dared expect anything before the morning – if then. After twenty minutes, spirits sagging, David was just about to get up and put his coat on when the message alert went off. He grabbed the phone.

"Look this up Juan," he said, struggling to keep his voice calm. "Exodus 31 4 and 5." Juan got there in seconds and read it out.

"He is a master craftsman, expert in working with gold, silver and bronze. He is skilled in engraving and mounting gemstones and in carving wood. He is a master at every craft!"

Hacienda's neighbours sometimes had to put up with quite a bit of noise when there were birthday parties, works outings, and business meetings that took in too much sangria; they usually managed to keep stoical about it. That night, though, there were definite murmurings about the dreadful racket, so late at night too. On this occasion the proprietors and their guests didn't care. There were cheers, clapping of hands and hugs all round. Toledo it was. They were sure of it.

Suddenly, in the midst of the celebrations the message alert went off again. Alison picked it up.

"PS 56 6," she read, "then PS 22 19."

David looked them up.

"'They come together to spy on me – watching my every step eager to kill me… O Lord, do not stay far away! You are my strength; come quickly to my aid.'"

This was not just a crossword puzzle. It was life in the balance. Whatever had happened before, Jen was now out of her depth and desperate.

"Now we've got something to go on," David said, "I think it's time for a visit to Spain. Anyone want to come?"

So it was they found themselves slowly circling Madrid in clear summer sunshine. Alison had been adamant: she didn't know what she could do but simply couldn't stand being left at home. In view of the circumstances she could hardly be refused time off work. Gillian initially thought she wouldn't get away with exams in full swing but when colleagues heard what was going on, they insisted. The common view was that the new Gillian had made things so much easier and more fun throughout the term that they owed it to her. Alicia felt torn. She wanted very much to come but knew someone would have to keep an eye on the shop. Juan was prepared to stay but she insisted he would be more use in Spain. With Tomas's help she would manage. Alicia had also kept on seeing Julie and they had become firm friends. The chance of a summer job speaking Spanish was just what was

needed for a running start into second year. So Julie joined the
staff of Hacienda too.

The seatbelt sign came on and David, Gillian, Alison, and Juan
buckled up and braced themselves. David knew he was bracing for
more than just a routine landing.

Chapter 19

TORREJÓN DE ARDOZ

"*David! ¿Cómo estás? ¡Que bueno! ¿Mucho tiempo, no?*" A tall, fair-haired man, perhaps in his mid-thirties, dressed in a pale linen suit and bright orange shirt was looking out for them as they came through international arrivals. He had a broad grin on his face and gathered David up in a warm embrace in the manner of friends who have been through a lot together.

"Mariano! Good to see you. You're right. It has been too long. Can I introduce you? Alison MacInnes – Mariano Segovia Lopez de Vega Serrano. Mariano is an aristocrat which is why he has so many names." Mariano just smiled, clearly used to such teasing and greeted Alison with a kiss on each cheek.

"*Encantado,*" he said. Alison thought she liked Spain already.

"It's Alison's daughter we're looking for," David explained.

"Of course. We have been praying for your daughter since David contacted us. I'm sorry your first visit to Spain is in such circumstances." Alison smiled weakly.

"And this is Gillian Lockhart, one of my Spanish language students."

"Again, *encantado Señora*. He is a good teacher? Yes?"

Gillian took a sideways look at David and thought for a second.

"Quite good," she said, considering. "*Su gramática es bastante buena pero pienso que su pronunciación podría ser un poco mejor.*" David raised his eyebrows and Mariano laughed as Gillian beamed and held onto David's arm.

"She says his grammar is quite good but his pronunciation could be better," Juan whispered to Alison who nodded and smiled.

"He's great," Gillian continued. "I've been learning all sorts of things I never expected."

"Well, sounds intriguing."

David cleared his throat and turned to Juan, changing the subject.

"And I think you've met this young man?"

"Juan, *mi hermano. ¿Qué tal?*"

"*Bien. Mucho mejor al verte.*" Again the two men embraced.

"Alicia – she is well? I hear you've had good news?"

"She's very well, *gracias. Si* – it's good news. An answer to prayer."

"Of course. *Bendiciones.* God's blessings on both of you, and the baby. Maria would love to see her. Maybe she can come to *Edimburgo* some time."

"Yes, Alicia would love it. And you are looking after Warehouse 66 without our help?"

"Ah, it is a struggle but we survive. No, I mustn't say that. Things are going very well. We miss David but we are growing again and planting some new churches. *Gracias a Dios.*"

"Mariano is senior pastor at Warehouse 66," David explained to Gillian and Alison. "He took over when I came to Edinburgh."

"He taught me all I know!" Mariano exclaimed. "Well, *bienvenidos a España,* everybody. I have a car in the shorter stay *aparcamiento.* This way please." Mariano took Gillian's and Alison's bags and led them off towards one of the exits. David recapped quietly to him as they went.

"The girl got involved with drugs in Edinburgh when the family had to move to a poorer *barrio.* Raúl Álvarez had started up a drugs cartel in the area and took a liking to her. When he moved back to Spain he took her with him though by this time she didn't want to go. Now we know she's being held against her will. You remember I said we've been in touch with her. It's a bit complicated but we think she's in Toledo. Unfortunately we don't know quite where. We also think Álvarez might be planning a move – maybe back to Colombia – so time's not on our side. Scottish police have been in touch with the *Policia Nacional* drugs team but we haven't heard from them yet. And that's basically where we're up to."

Mariano was looking serious as they exited the main building and headed along the walkway towards the car park.

"Álvarez is a dangerous man; you know this already. Many of our young people have escaped but they are still afraid of him. He can be very brutal. It would make a huge difference for Torrejón, Madrid and Spain if he were no longer in business."

"*De verdad,* but all we want at this stage is to get the girl out and back home in one piece."

"I understand. You know you will have every help we can give you. Warehouse 66 has grown a lot even since you left. We have people with some influence now as well as many who know the drugs trade. We can find things out. Anyway, you will stay with us till you decide what to do and come to church tomorrow?"

"*Absolutamente. Muchas gracias.*"

"And your friend, Gillian…" Mariano pronounced the name with a soft G like Gigi, "I think she is more than just your student. No?"

"Yes. More than just my student. She's been teaching me to live again. God is good. And I couldn't have said that six months ago."

"We knew how hard things were before you left and we were worried about how you'd cope away from your friends. It sounds like there was some kind of a plan going on after all." Mariano had led them to the ticket dispenser and was feeding coins into the machine one after the other.

"Yes. It's been very strange. I felt I was on the verge of losing everything. Then getting involved in looking for this girl brought Gillian into the picture. It's really saved my life I think. It's funny; none of the facts have changed – you know, about Rocío, Raúl, what happened. But at the same time everything is different. I'm a different man these last few months. There's a reason to get up in the morning again."

"*Bueno.* I'm glad. We pray for you often. Maria will be so pleased you have found someone. She is a *creyente*? A believer?"

"On a journey, I think you'd say."

"*Bueno*. We will continue to remember you both."

By this time they had stopped at a large van with *Warehouse 66: Un lugar para encontrar la Vida* in large letters on the side.

"I'm sorry for the primitive transport," Mariano said as he slid open the side door and lifted their luggage into the back. "We have a kids' club, the *Club de Amigos*, every Saturday morning so I have to be the bus driver for them before I come for you. I think we have emptied all the rubbish out. Señoras..."

Alison and Gillian climbed in the back while David and Juan shared the worn and faded front bench seat with Mariano. Juan explained the meaning of the signage on the van to Alison as they got in.

"It means 'a place to find life'. It's our logo. I helped choose it a few years ago. That's what Warehouse 66 means to me and many others."

Mariano started the noisy, smoky engine.

"Everyone is desperate to see you again." he said, "and to meet the Señoras. Patricio and Jorge suggested a barbecue, so I have left them getting things ready."

"Particio and Jorge are part of the leadership team," David explained over his shoulder to Gillian and Alison as Mariano got them going. "They're Chilean – all the South Americans are big carnivores, even more than the Spanish – so they think barbecuing is an art form. Any excuse."

"*Estupendo*," Gillian shouted over the noise of the engine. "I approve of men cooking. We need more of that in Scotland." Alison just nodded. She felt she didn't have much to say and remained preoccupied with what might be happening to Jen right now. At the same time she tried to get used to all the attention and support, painfully aware that the whole enterprise was on her behalf. Anyone giving her help or expressing support was such an unusual sensation it was a bit disorientating. Sometimes she felt "a lone parent" should be spelled "alone parent". Now here she was, in Spain, with people who had already put themselves in danger for her and her family and were willing to do so again. It was wonderful and frightening. She looked out of the window and hoped her make-up wasn't smudging.

The other weird thing was the Christian connection. Her mother's "churchiness" was always something she had despised. Yet the people who were helping her now were church leaders. If these people didn't genuinely believe what they said then they deserved an Oscar. Until she was disillusioned she was prepared to give them the benefit of the doubt.

By this time Mariano had navigated them onto an urban motorway. They were leaving the city behind. She guessed they were heading for the suburb where everybody lived – Torrejón de something or other. Just when she was about to ask how long they might be, she heard Mariano calling back that they were going to take a slight detour. Torrejón wasn't far but David wanted to drive by the Warehouse 66 building and Mariano also wanted to show him the site of their latest church plant. Alison didn't even know what a church plant was but assumed it wasn't an ornamental garden. They pulled off the motorway and into the teatime traffic. Wherever they were it was busy. Mopeds and motorcycles were buzzing everywhere, jockeying in and out of lines of cars and long articulated buses. Roadside kiosks were selling newspapers, cigarettes and lottery tickets on every corner. Open air cafés were crammed with young people hanging out with their friends or old men drinking *cerveza* or coffee. They twisted and turned through the traffic until they seemed to be moving into a more industrial area past furniture warehouses, construction yards, and vehicle depots. Pulling round one last corner they came to a large open area surrounded by a fence. Mariano got out, unlocked a gate, and pulled in.

"We'd love to pull the fence down," he said, "but we get enough vandalism with it up. There are those that do not like what we are doing. Anyway, there you are. The building we owe to the Americans but a lot of what goes on inside was built by David Hidalgo."

"Sorry for the detour everyone," David said quickly. "I know we'll be here tomorrow; I just wanted a quieter look round first."

He approached the front doors and peered in. Then he stood back and took in the whole facade. It was just a warehouse – no windows, no architectural merit, no presence, just a large sign with the name and the same logo as on the van. He walked along the parking area, past the separate entrance to *Semilla de Esperanza*, the Seed of Hope church bookshop, round the corner past the bins and utility installations, then round the back past bags of rubbish, left-over builder's waste and rubble and finally along the fourth side to the main entrance. Coming back in the morning would be a happy occasion, with old friends to reconnect to and relationships to renew, but there was a bit of unfinished business to be dealt with. As he walked he prayed, haltingly at first. It didn't come easily after so long. He prayed for all the people who met in there week by week, then for the leadership, then for the enterprise that had brought him back to Spain. *Please God, might they find the girl and all get home again in one piece.* But all the while he was aware of a deeper issue. It was something he'd been putting off for a long time. Raúl Álvarez.

What should his attitude be to such a man? It was Álvarez and his kind who had put him through the living hell of losing Rocío, losing his ability to do his job and right up to the edge of losing his faith. But praying for enemies was fundamental to the faith. *Forgive us our sins as we forgive those that sin against us.* Just as much and no more. So he *had* to pray for Álvarez. 'Please God, give him what he deserves' didn't seem to quite fit the spirit of the thing. What then? 'Father forgive them for they know not what they do' was Jesus' prayer but Álvarez knew exactly what he was doing. He just didn't care. Was a man like that worth goodwill? Was he even redeemable? Hard as it had been to imagine some of the changes David had seen in the life of Warehouse 66 he had to admit that none of these matched up to what it would take to change Álvarez. He wasn't a man in need, a victim desperate for freedom; he was the cause of the misery that the church tried to alleviate. So 'Show him the error of his ways' perhaps? Hard to imagine. The only change Raúl would want would be less police hassle and more buyers, which meant more misery for the young of Spain. Finally, though, David corrected himself. What Raúl thought, felt, and wanted wasn't his affair. He was only responsible for himself and his own attitudes. It was ironic that it was Raúl's reign of crime and terror in Edinburgh that had been the means of restoration from the harm the very same man had done in Madrid. So even despite the mayhem and misery, sometimes, somehow, there can be good consequences unintended. David thought of his favourite Old Testament story – Joseph and his brothers after they were reunited in Egypt. In spite of having every right and the power to carry out his revenge, what was it Joseph said to them? 'You meant it for evil but God meant it for good.' Unintended consequences. That's to say, unintended by them but a bigger plan seemed to be at work. Was he now in the middle of such a bigger plan? It was Raúl's liking for underage girls and the search for Jen that really bonded them. Unintended consequences. By the time he rounded the last corner he knew he was at least a little closer to where he should be.

"That's fine," he said. "That's all I needed."

Mariano shrugged.

"Ok. *Venga. Vamos.*"

From the industrial area of Warehouse 66 where nobody lived, they drove to a housing area of flats packed-in like left luggage. "This is Fronteras," Mariano said, nodding towards rows of six-storey flats, the alleyways between them, beaten up cars abandoned in front of them and small shops that had sprung up in the vacant spaces between the pillars that supported the flats. Slung across the balconies outside the flats were washing lines heavy with T-shirts, jeans, and underwear. Most vacant spaces within reach of a spray can were decorated with various messages, instructions, and advice. Alison felt sadly at home.

"I live somewhere like this in Edinburgh," she said.

"Oh," Mariano replied. "Well, you will not need me to tell you about it. We have a constant programme in the church to look for places like this and plant churches where we can. We have three already, two more planned, and this is the latest we're thinking about. It's where the immigrant families live. Immigrants and gypsies – if they decide to give up travelling. Drugs and crime are problems but not the greatest problem."

"What's that?" Gillian asked.

"Do you remember, Juan?" Mariano asked. Juan looked down then back at him.

"Hopelessness," he said. "When I lived in a place like this there was no one to give us hope. People got into debt, stole, cheated, took drugs – all in the hope that things would improve, but they never did. Bringing the good news to these people is what changes lives. Not just better education and welfare. This is a good work Mariano. May God bless it."

"Bien hecho Mariano," added David. "You'll have to come to Edinburgh and help us plan something new there."

"I know where you can start," Alison said.

"Bueno. Anyway, who is hungry? The *Chilenos* will have burned everything to ashes if we don't arrive soon. Or they will have eaten it, which is worse. What do the English say? 'Home James and don't spare the horses!'"

The barbecue smell hit them as soon as Mariano stopped the van and opened the doors. They came into the back yard of a modest suburban house with a large colourful garden full of guests all coming in their direction. David was squeezed almost to death. Everyone wanted to find out how he was, to say how much they had missed him, and to wish him God's blessing. Almost the same level of greeting was accorded to Juan and then in turn to the women. Mariano's wife Maria apologized profusely for the length of time they had been shut in the van. She was a petite, pretty girl with tight dark curls and a sunny smile that dominated her face despite a clear scar running from the corner of one eye down almost to her chin.

"You must forgive him," she said. "Warehouse 66 is his life and his hobby. Be careful not to ask him anything about it or you will regret it! Let me show you your rooms then you can freshen up and join us to eat."

By the time Gillian and Alison came back down Jorge had just announced that everything was ready.

An orderly queue formed at the grill as Patricio and Jorge stood like TV chefs dishing out steaks, sausages, chops, and chicken legs with great aplomb. Next was the salad table with fresh lettuce and peppers, olives, anchovies, roast vegetables, and potatoes done in the Spanish style, boiled with white wine and herbs before being deep fried in olive oil. Next were drinks – the ever-present *cerveza* plus freshly squeezed orange juice, ice cold water, and *vinos* both *blanco* and *tinto*. The dozen or so kids present had their own table with soft drinks and burgers. A cluster of what Gillian took to be Warehouse 66 leaders and helpers had already huddled round David and Juan, exchanging greetings and news. One of the women with quite good English was looking after Alison explaining different dishes to her. Gillian found herself next to Mariano and Maria.

"I'm amazed at what you're doing here," she said. "And I wouldn't have thought of Fronteras as an easy place to start a new church."

"And you would be right of course, Señora," Mariano replied, taking a bite out of a chicken leg. "It is not easy but at least people there know they have a problem. It's much more of a challenge with people who think everything's perfect. They have some money, a nice house, they go on holiday to Ribadeo, they get their children into a good school. They think they are well off but they don't know they need something money can't buy."

"And there's another problem too," Maria added. "The evangelicals – people like us who believe more in personal relationship than just a religion – we were banned under Franco so people are suspicious. They think we are a cult and are going to take all their money and brainwash them. Also they don't want to associate with the sorts of people who do respond – the drug addicts, prostitutes, gypsies, immigrants." Gillian nodded.

"That's funny," she said. "In Scotland people think of the church as something for the middle class. People go to church to be respectable and show off. Not so much now of course but it still has that sort of reputation."

"I understand," said Mariano. "I studied in Oxford for three

193

years, and that was what it was like there. We are different at Warehouse 66. We say 'theologically conservative but culturally liberal'. So you can wear what you like, have your hair any way you like, listen to what music you like, vote how you like, have any number of tattoos and piercings and we don't care. But if you're cheating on your wife or fiddling your taxes we do care. And we always invite people to make a personal commitment, believe the Bible and follow its teachings. So the exact opposite of what I saw in the churches I went to in England."

"Did you become a Christian in England then?"

"No, here in Spain. My brother got involved with drugs and we sent him to every rehab we could find. It was very expensive but my family had money so we paid. Nothing did him any good. When we could think of nothing else we sent him to Betel. That changed his life."

"I'm sorry, I haven't heard of that. What's Betel?"

"Betel is the Spanish word for Bethel, the place in the Bible. It is a Christian drugs rehabilitation ministry. They have more than a dozen churches all made up of former addicts and have planted something like thirty-five more. When you become a *Betelito* and get off drugs you are expected to help others like yourself. It is very successful but so many of their pastors are HIV positive they need more leaders all the time."

"And is your brother a leader in a Betel church now?"

"He was but he died of AIDS a few years ago. Before he died I decided to follow his lead. Then I got involved in Warehouse 66 and met David."

"Everyone here seems to think very highly of him, don't they?"

"David?" Maria smiled. "We love him. He was our leader for so long. He led the church to be the way we are. But he is terrible. He never thinks he has done anything important. And he worries. He always thinks it will fall apart tomorrow. So we have to tell him to be more Spanish and not so Scottish. Live for today – leave *mañana* to the Lord."

Gillian laughed. "I know what you mean. We Scots are always

thinking something horrible is just round the corner. I just hope we can go home with a good outcome from this trip."

"*Claro*," agreed Mariano. "And your friend, Alison, how is she? It is a difficult situation for her. I can understand a little of what she is feeling."

"It must be dreadful for her," agreed Maria, glancing over to where Alison was. Right then she had a group around her and was being well looked after.

"I think it is. I can't imagine what she's going through. But I think she appreciates all the support of everyone here and back at home."

"It's no problem," Maria said. "We want to help any way we can. You might meet some people tomorrow who can guide you what to do next."

"I hope so. I'm really looking forward to coming to church. I've heard so much about it."

"I hope we do not disappoint you."

The afternoon gradually turned into evening. People began to drift off and eventually only the party from Scotland and Mariano and Maria were left. Everything had been washed, tidied, and cleared away without anyone really noticing how it was done. All that remained was to make some coffee, pull some chairs together, and enjoy the relative cool of the evening as the intensity of a scorching Madrid summer day died down.

"So," asked Mariano, "what is the next step?"

"I'm not entirely sure," David admitted. "We need to make contact with the Spanish police. There's someone I used to know in the right department, but they've been on leave till now. I think they're back soon. If I can get in touch we can see what they've been told by the Edinburgh police, and then we'll find out what's going on. You know we've found a way of communicating with Jen?"

"Yes, I was impressed," Mariano exclaimed "Very ingenious. When was your last message?"

"Just before we left Edinburgh we sent REV 22 20: 'He who is the faithful witness to all these things says, "Yes, I am coming soon!'" but we haven't had a reply yet, so we don't know how things are right now."

Mariano nodded. "Ok. We'll see what the morning brings. Now, if you'll excuse me, I have a few things to look over. Unless you'd like to preach of course?" David smiled and held up his hand.

"*Muchas gracias* – perhaps another time." Mariano disappeared to do what preachers do the night before church. Alison said she was exhausted and turned in early. Maria went off to prepare a few things for lunch after church, leaving David and Gillian alone for the first time that day.

"So," he said, "*¿Qué piensas de España?*"

"Well, I don't know about the whole of Spain but I love your friends and the food's pretty good."

"They're a great group of people. You would hardly believe when you see them now what some of them have been through."

"I was talking to Mariano. He's really friendly – and Maria of course. What did you mean when you said he was an aristocrat?"

"Just that. I think he's a second cousin to Juan Carlos. Something like that."

"Juan Carlos? The former king? You're kidding!"

"No, it's true. The family disowned him when he joined Warehouse 66. He stood to inherit several million and all sorts of property but it didn't deter him. Now he's plain Pastor Mariano."

"That's amazing. The whole thing's amazing – Warehouse 66, Southside, Jen, Raúl, us. I can hardly believe everything that's happened in the last six months." Gillian took a last sip of wine and slowly breathed in and out, enjoying the balmy evening air.

"And all because of starting a Spanish class," David remarked. "It's a dangerous language you know. *Muy romantico*. You never know what's going to happen."

"Come on though. Neither did you and you were teaching the class."

"That's true. Do you know what attracted me to you that very first class – apart from the cape and the floppy hat?"

"I like that cape!"

"I know, so do I. It makes you look like the girl from the Scottish Widows advert."

"I can live with that. So what was it?"

"You were 'a woman of kindliness'."

"A what?"

"'A woman of kindliness'. Do you know the love story of Ruth and Boaz in the Old Testament? She's described as a 'a woman of kindliness'. She's aware of how others are feeling. Remember when Julie cracked-up in the class. I was useless but you took care of her. Kindliness."

"Hmm. And you, sir, are 'a man of integrity'," she said, giving him a playful poke in the chest.

"How so?"

"Same story. I've heard that one. Isn't Boaz described as 'a man of integrity'? See, I am learning something. The first Sunday I came to Southside you had decided not to get involved because of everything that had happened before. Am I right? Then you were going to speak about the Good Samaritan and couldn't do it until you had changed your mind and decided to help. I'm used to people who say and do what's convenient. You know, office politics, even relationships. You do what you know is right no matter how inconvenient. That's rarer than you think, you know."

"Well, do you think that makes us a good combination then?"

"Very good. I love you Señor David."

"I love you too, Dr Lockhart. Come here."

The evening light died over Madrid as David and Gillian kissed long and slow, held each other then went indoors. It would be a busy day tomorrow.

Chapter 20

WAREHOUSE 66

The sight that greeted them next morning at Warehouse 66 could not have been more different from the empty, lifeless building of the previous day. A long queue of cars filed in, church doors flew open, and hundreds of people were wending their way in. Stewards directed traffic and friends kissed and embraced in the Mediterranean way. The Scots got their share too, bumping into those who recognized them from the day before. Old aquaintances gathered round David, greeting him warmly and welcoming Gillian, who stood close beside him. As word of David's presence spread among the gathering crowd, the air echoed with shouts of joy and thanksgiving. Others were shyly interested but unsure in the way you might spot a celebrity in the street and hesitate.

Eventually Mariano and Maria managed to usher them in. Warehouse 66 may just have been what the name suggested outside but inside everything was different. Along one side of the foyer was an information desk like you'd find in a busy hotel. A team of young people in matching polo shirts with the church logo passed out information sheets and sermon notes. Opposite were a staffed cloakroom and a DVD desk. Finally, they made it through the crush into the auditorium. Nothing had the look of a traditional church. It reminded Gillian more of a concert venue. A huge sound desk dominated the back and behind it a glass windowed engineer's compartment. On the far side stood a café with seating for fifty or so and a long counter full of snacks and pastries. Round the walls were noticeboards, pigeonholes, and appliqué banners with illustrated Bible verses. The seats were fast filling up with all ages – though mainly at the younger end – exactly the age group most lacking in any church Gillian had ever been to before. She was hoping for somewhere near the back but Mariano ushered them right forward through the crowd.

"This is amazing!" Gillian whispered as they found their seats. "I never thought church could be like this. It's more like a James Taylor concert!" David squeezed her hand and smiled.

"Whatever we are, we try not to be boring."

Two huge video screens lit up as the worship band began to play. Gillian recognized some of the tunes and it reinforced a dawning thought. Although this was a different country and culture, the family identity was the same. Southside and Warehouse 66 were undoubtedly related – not surprising really.

"I know this one!" she mouthed as the band got going.

"It's like folk music," David whispered back. "Somebody must have written it somewhere but it ends up getting adapted all over the world," he added, clearly relaxed and at ease. Home at last. As the rhythm picked up, David, Juan, Mariano, and Maria were all on their feet, singing. Even Alison swayed a bit with the music, self-conscious but determined not to be left out. Everyone seemed to be enjoying themselves.

They were only into the second or third song when Gillian realized that something was wrong. The music was great, the people friendly, the leading relaxed, but somehow she was feeling increasingly ill at ease. The more they sang, prayed, worshipped and shared, the worse it got. What was wrong? She stopped singing then sat down, a knot growing in the pit of her stomach. Then it dawned. She had been so looking forward to being a part of it all. Now she realized she wasn't. It was fine as a social phenomenon, friendly, welcoming, positive. But there was a fundamental reality at the heart she couldn't share and she was determined not to pretend. They called themselves "believers" – *creyentes* – but she knew this was not just a matter of dutifully reciting some prayer or creed. This was relationship. You had it or you didn't. Everybody said it. Somehow it just hadn't sunk in. Not personally. The old chestnut all over again – not what you know but who you know. She could almost remember a time in her childhood when she had thought she had a connection but that was so long ago – before the pressure of "what everybody knows"; before studies, career, profession. The dominance of the rational. What you could prove and reference in a footnote. She knew enough to understand that couldn't be how you came to whatever God there might be. It was on *his* terms or not at all. She also realized that it couldn't wait till everything could be proved. Like almost anything of worth in life you had to put it into practice to know if it was true. And she really wasn't ready to take that risk.

Suddenly all the enthusiasm, sincerity, and engagement of the crowd became intolerable. She felt like a cork in the Cava bottles they'd been shaking up at the party; she had to get out. Without so much as a glance at David she simply grabbed her bag, pushed past Mariano and Maria, and almost ran down the aisle. David stopped singing and looked round. Mariano could only shrug. Maria took off after her. Then, before David had any more chance to react the band stopped and the leader turned in their direction. It would have to wait. Mariano jumped onto the platform, added his own welcome, then explained they had a special visitor that morning – the man they called Señor David. Applause and cheers rang out and David had to stand up and acknowledge it, still preoccupied with the image of Gillian running down the aisle. Mariano called him up.

"*Buenas Días*, Señor David. *Bienvenido!*"

"*Buenas Días*, 66."

"*Pues, como sabéis, Señor David*," Mariano continued, "*tenemos unos nuevos miembros desde que fuiste a Escocia. Puedes decirnos un poco sobre los días primeros de Warehouse 66?* And for our Scottish visitors, could Señor David tell us a little about the early days?"

What could he do? It felt like being grabbed for a High Street survey when your house is on fire. He swallowed, shuffled a bit, then began. Those who knew the story enjoyed hearing it again and others listened intently. It was a rare opportunity to hear the legend's story, straight from the legend's mouth. He told the story simply and factually – the obstacles, the small successes, the recoveries that seemed miraculous. Just being in the right place at the right time. And the opposition – Raúl and Rocío. He ended by explaining why they were back in Spain. At this point Mariano intervened and, much to Alison's embarrassment, brought her on stage as well where he prayed for safety, success, and a good outcome.

As they came down, David noticed Gillian had slipped back into her seat, her eyes red and cheeks streaked with mascara. She looked peaceful. Maria, next to her, was smiling. She squeezed his arm and mouthed, "It's ok", though this didn't clarify much.

Mariano spoke for nearly an hour. *"Vengan a mí todos ustedes que están cansados de sus trabajos y cargas, y yo los haré descansar."* The text was familiar even to Alison once Juan had translated. "Come to me all you that labour and are heavy laden and I will give you rest." David felt anything but restful. What was that all about and what did "ok" mean? Gillian simply sat looking forward seeming perfectly calm. It was maddening. Finally, Mariano drew things to a close, they sang a final song, and it was all over. But yet again David was waylaid, surrounded by people wanting a few words or to meet the man who started it all. It was impossible to move. As he tried to give sensible answers and concentrate on whoever wanted to speak to him his eyes were constantly flicking over to where Gillian was with Maria. Still a little red-eyed but she seemed to be smiling.

Finally, just as the crowd began to clear and it looked like he could begin edging down the aisle he noticed a distinguished-looking older man with short cropped hair, a neatly clipped moustache, and an upright military bearing hovering on the edge of the group. He waited patiently until the hand-shaking and blessing was over then rather shyly introduced himself.

"Señor Hidalgo, *perdoname*. We have not met but I believe you know my colleague, Captain Silvosa?"

"Yes, of course. I've been trying to contact him about the girl we're looking for. I was told he was on leave."

"He is back now but in another team. I think I may be able to offer you a little help. Esteban Rodriguez." He extended a hand.

"Mucho gusto. Forgive me Señor. Are you the same Rodriguez that

was in charge of anti-drug operations two years ago. Looking for Raúl?"

Rodriguez bowed slightly.

"*Sí*. I was aware of an enquiry from *Edimburgo* but I'm afraid I did not connect the name Hidalgo with yourself or the enquiry. If so, I might have been able to contact you sooner. Your forgiveness Señor David – if I may call you that."

"Of course. *No pasa nada. Muchas gracias.*"

"*Bueno*. The problem you referred to this morning, the missing girl – this falls within my area of responsibility. Señor Álvarez we know very well. We knew he had left Spain but we did not know where and also we did not know he had returned. We would very much like to have a conversation with him and some of his associates. How do you say in *Inglaterra*, 'to help the police with their enquiries...' Yes?"

"Yes – I think they do say that. But you didn't come to church just to look for me?"

"Not at all. My wife and I are regular attenders but we had no idea of your visit. I have worked with the national drugs team for some years now. I became aware of the work of the church through reports to the courts. When someone is convicted of a drugs offence in Spain they may be given a sentence involving some rehabilitation. We kept hearing about Warehouse 66 and the *Casas de Seguridad*. Very few of the programmes we refer people to seem to be effective but this was different. I made it my business to find out about it and that brought me to church." He paused, searching for the right words. "You must understand, Señor, I was brought up a good Catholic. We tend to be a little – how can I say – suspicious of other movements. It is hard to change the habits of a lifetime but I cannot ignore the evidence. In my opinion, to change the lifestyle of so many drug users is something out of the ordinary. So I had to find out how it works."

David nodded in agreement.

"As you might expect, to begin with, there was some reluctance to invite a chief of the police into the houses..." Captain Rodriguez had a twinkle in his eye, and David understood exactly what he was talking about. It brought to mind the unlikely meeting of Eric Stoddart and D.S. Thompson what seemed like ages ago in Juan and Alicia's flat in South Clerk Street.

"I can imagine," he said.

"Well, it took some time but I am a patient man. Once I understood what was going on, I was able to encourage the work and make more of a partnership. So then, I decided to come to church and see what is behind it all. And this," he gestured all round, "was a revelation. I don't need to tell you, there was much superstition and ritual in my background, as well as much that is good."

"I know," said David. "That's true of a lot of what we call religion."

"*De verdad*. To me this felt like reality, not a ritual. Real people and, if I might say so, a real presence of God. From my first week here I was convinced. My wife, Luisa, she took a little longer. Anyway, we must all have our meeting with God in our own way and our own time."

"Very true. I'm glad to hear the church has been of help to you. And you think you may be able to help us now?"

"I'm sure. Three things. Number one, a crime is being committed in Spain, one that is linked to criminal activities in another country. It gives us a bad reputation. I don't like that. Number two, this involves our friend Raúl, whom I've been trying to meet for some years. And number three, it is an obligation to help a brother, is it not? Particularly a distinguished brother who has been of such help to the drugs service – and the *familia* Rodriguez." The captain had a gracious but determined look that made David smile. He took an immediate liking to the man and yet again marvelled at the synchronicity of faith. Some people called it coincidence. Well, they were entitled to their view. As Juan was fond of pointing out, there was no such thing as luck.

"What do you think we should do next, Señor Rodriguez?"

"You must come to see me first thing tomorrow morning. If you can tell me what you know, the resources of our team will work to help you. Álvarez is what you would call quite a 'big fish' – a fish I would like to get my net around and remove from the water, if you follow me. So, until tomorrow? Here are my details. I will look forward to it."

David took the card, shook hands with the captain and thanked him. The problem of what to do next seemed to have been resolved. Just then he noticed Juan and Alison waiting patiently.

"Well, Señor David?" Juan began. "How does it feel to come home? A Spanish welcome – yes?"

"Very good but also exhausting. How are you doing Alison? I'm sorry you got dragged up."

Alison shook her head. "That's ok," she said. "You must feel proud to have started something like this."

"Ah well, as I keep saying, it was mainly Rocío's idea. Has anyone seen Gillian?"

"Over there," Alison nodded towards the café area.

Gillian and Maria were chatting like lifelong friends over *café con leche* and fresh *churros*. Gillian jumped up when she saw them coming, grabbed David, and almost squeezed the life out of him. Her eyes had a sparkle reflecting the spotlights.

"Ok?" David asked, not sure whether it might be better not to know.

"Yes, much better." She looked relaxed in a dreamy sort of way. "Just a few things that needed sorting out."

"So – eh – is that it?"

"Enough for now," Maria put in firmly. "Don't worry. It's all good!"

Chapter 21

SOUTHSIDE AND MUIRHOUSE

"I don't know what you think, Mrs MacInnes," Mrs Buchanan said, "but I'm afraid I just don't find it suitable. Not suitable at all. It's just not what we're used to, with all these other changes as well. I don't know what the minister must be thinking but us older folk find it harder to adjust you know. Allowances have to be made. Mr Grant here agrees with me, don't you Mr Grant?" The elderly gentleman next to her shuffled a bit, scratched his chin, and sucked his teeth.

"I do think she has a point, Mrs MacInnes," he said. "She definitely has a point. See for yourself..." He gestured round as if the point he had in mind would be self-evident if only she cared to look. Mrs MacInnes did indeed have a look, not because she needed to but just to make sure that she was seen to be more than reasonable before the time came to have her own say.

It just so happened that the first Sunday David, Juan, and the others had to be absent in Spain was also the first Sunday Eric and Lorraine had persuaded some of their friends to come with them to church. So, in addition to the normal congregation, the pews were filled that morning with a couple of dozen new faces, all definitely more used to the Ferry Inn than the likes of Southside Fellowship. While the norms of dress and decorum had loosened quite a bit in David Hidalgo's time, even these were utterly unknown to the visitors. Eric had warned everybody to be on their best behaviour. There was no question about actually taking anything in church but what could be wrong with a can of lager on the way up the stairs and a couple of rollups before things really got going? The fact was that most of Eric's friends were scared stiff of church, more so than a visit to court, given the correspondingly higher nature of the authority concerned and the greater rarity factor. So it was only reasonable that nerves needed settling a bit. Once that problem had been sorted out there was the more subtle issue of whether there should be a bit of a curb on "language". Wives and girlfriends generally thought so but some of the guys thought they should be able to effin' swear if they effin' wanted to. What were they gonna effin' say if they couldn't effin' swear all effin' morning? And so it went on. Putting your feet up on the chairs in the row in front, knowing when to stand up and when to sit down, singing something other than come on the Hibs and the Hearts are rubbish. There also had to be constant surveillance to make sure none of the kids were nicking stuff. Not that there was anything here worth nicking but all the same. It was all a bit weird, and they felt as much at home as Bay City Roller fans at the opera. Everything that was the norm in Muirhouse seemed to be the opposite here. But Eric was a mate. A bit of a nutter, but nevertheless a mate, and if he said it was magic then they were prepared to give it a go, however painful, awkward, and embarrassing it might be.

Mrs Buchanan and Mr Grant, however, did not appear prepared to give it a go. As soon as the service was over, even while the tea and coffee were being served and Eric and his mates were laughing and joking, getting to know a few of the regulars, letting the kids muck about on the drums and queuing up for a cuppa, the delegation approached Mrs MacInnes, officially left in charge in Señor David's absence.

"And what would you say the point was, Mr Grant?" Irene MacInnes drew herself up to her full height which, diminutive as it was, imparted additional gravitas. Ladies from Morningside are not to be measured in feet and inches when it comes to gravitas. Rather it is a quality born of a lifetime of telling the coal merchant that in no way does that look like three hundredweight of smokeless briquettes and would he kindly take them back to his yard or wherever smokeless briquettes are to be found, weigh them again, and next time bring the right amount? Ladies from Morningside are not to be trifled with and Mrs MacInnes now felt she was on the receiving end of the trifling. On this occasion it did not matter that it was her lifelong friend, Bella Buchanan, who was doing the trifling. There would be no trifling on her watch. Señor David had left her in charge and things would be spick and span when he got back.

"Well," Mr Grant shuffled, scratched, and sucked again. "You know how it is. They're just not our kind of folks. Not saying anything against them, of course, but it's just not what we're used to. I'm sure they'd be happier with their own sort as well. So it would really be much better all round."

"And what do you suggest, Mr Grant?" Mrs MacInnes was an old campaigner and knew very well the value of getting the enemy to set out their position in full before mounting a counter-attack.

"Well, I'm not entirely sure. I…" Mr Grant had, however, served his purpose in establishing that this was not a one-woman crusade but a mass movement and Mrs Buchanan no longer needed his limited input. She took over brusquely and made herself plain.

"There is bound to be a church somewhere nearer. This is far too far from their estate to expect people to come. Especially with the youngsters as well. I will contact the secretary of whatever church it might be and find out the details. Then I will advise the young man who seems to be in charge of all these…" she paused, searching for the right word, "… *individuals* and suggest that that would be more suitable by far. I'm even prepared to draw them a little map or something. You know, these people might not be used to following instructions. That will be much better for everybody, I'm quite sure."

Mrs MacInnes paused for a moment, just long enough to gather steam.

"So," she said, "am I to understand that although the Kingdom of God may have a place for sinners who have come to repentance, Southside Fellowship does not? That it may be easier to get into heaven than into this congregation? That when St Paul said, as I recall, there is now no longer Jew, nor Greek, slave nor free, male nor female, he should have added, 'but there remains a distinction between Southside Fellowship and the residents of Muirhouse'? The fact is, Mrs Buchanan, that young Eric has come to Christ and has sustained his calling over several months, now wishes to get married and make things right by his young lady, and is in other ways, it would appear, producing fruit appropriate to his confession – such as bringing his friends to church. And to their credit, unlike Nicodemus who was too ashamed to visit Jesus in broad daylight, they came right in, as a group, on the recommendation of their friend to see what we are made of. Well, I think I can see perfectly well what impression they would go away with if we were to follow your advice. No. Until Señor David gets back and comes to a different conclusion, Eric and his friends will be as welcome here as, well, as welcome here as you or I. Or indeed you, Mr Grant. I hope I make myself clear."

Mrs Buchanan had been gradually growing a deeper shade of red throughout this response and now looked like the human version of a faulty boiler at the old Portobello Baths.

"I see," she said between clenched teeth. "Well. This will not be the last you'll hear of this. Come on Mr Grant. I can see our views are not to be taken into account. Good day, Mrs MacInnes."

"Good day, Mrs Buchanan. Are you not going to join us for a cup of tea then?" Mrs Buchanan made a noise as if one of the boiler valves had suddenly sprung a leak and sailed towards the exit with Mr Grant meekly in tow. Mrs MacInnes shook her head. She did not enjoy such altercations for their own sake, though she knew some that did. But sometimes a church secretary has to do what a church secretary has to do. She joined the coffee queue behind a young man who seemed to be called Sniffy for some reason she couldn't quite understand.

"Well, Mr... eh... Sniffy..." she said, "What do you think of Southside Fellowship then?"

Jen slowly became aware of birdsong and morning light and opened her eyes. For a moment she had no idea where she was. It seemed too warm for Edinburgh and it certainly wasn't her bedroom at home. Then she noticed a high-backed wooden chair with a man's white shirt and trousers draped over the back and she remembered. She tried to move but found her hair was held tight at the nape of her neck. He was there behind her in the bed, one arm over her bare shoulder and another gripping the short curls tightly at the back of her head. Even in his sleep he controlled her every movement. The birdsong and sunlight had briefly raised her spirits but now she remembered everything and wanted to cry. She'd been doing a lot of crying lately. The anger, the violence, the hatred, the way she was treated, and the way everyone saw her as something disgusting with neither virtue nor purpose, just kept around till everyone had had their final fun – she felt worthless, stupid.

It was all so clear now but she couldn't understand how she had been so blind. Dazzled by the show-off cars, clothes, money, computers, drinks, and drugs. Fooled by an act designed for one purpose only – to get her to walk into hell of her own accord. All the jokes, the gifts, the smiles, the fun. All so clear now. She was a toy, an amusement. He had even called her "his little plaything" once and laughed. She had laughed along, thinking she was cherished like a favourite without seeing what it really meant. She'd been so intent on being grown-up, proving to everyone that she could take care of herself and make her own choices, that she hadn't realized until now that she'd been like a bird following a trail of breadcrumbs into a trap.

Anyway, the choices were over now. She was in, with no way out. A seed of hope had taken root when she got the mobile and thought of a way of sending messages. That had worked for a while. Then he had found out and beaten her so hard she couldn't move without stabbing pains for two days. It took more than a week for her face to go back to normal. She knew that some of the other girlfriends didn't like how he was treating her, but what could they do? They cleaned her cuts and bruises and tried to help her sleep but then he had come back for her, hauled her off by her hair, and done things she couldn't bear to remember. And she couldn't get the images and sensations out of her mind or her body. If none of this had happened she could see how he would have looked handsome in a photoshoot. Now she knew what he really was she couldn't think of him as a human being at all. He was a demon. All the demons rolled into one.

Finally, when the crying had emptied her of everything else, there was only one thing left to try. It's what Granny would have told her to do.

Chapter 22

POLICÍA NACIONAL

Captain Rodriguez sat behind his desk in a spotless, beautifully pressed uniform, a little more formal in his manner than the day before. David, Gillian, Juan, and Alison took chairs in a half circle round the desk. Another officer sat in a cramped corner taking notes. Rodriguez listened with the utmost attention and concentration. From time to time he asked a question for clarification or to check an unfamiliar English expression, but by and large, merely listened and nodded. David spoke most, with Alison describing the background and Jen's last visit to the flat. Finally, David read the most recent text – "PS 70 1 2: 'Please God, rescue me! Come quickly Lord and help me. May those who try to kill me be humiliated and put to shame. May those who take delight in my trouble be turned to disgrace.'" But that had been a week ago and nothing since.

"Well," the captain said at last, "that she knows we are coming is good, though the desperation and lack of contact for a week is worrying. We can only hope they will indeed be humiliated and put to shame. A remarkable story. But now we have limited time. I agree Toledo seems most likely, but I am concerned they may be planning a move. Colombia would make things much harder." He looked at David and seemed about to say something then changed his mind.

"In any case," he added, "the sooner we have the chance to have a '*charla*' with Señor Álvarez, the better. Since you have been in touch with the girl we need to work together. You will understand, not many of my officers could communicate in this way." He gave David a rueful smile. "To be honest, I would not be able to do so myself. Acceptable? Good. Well, we will need to set up a base in Toledo, while my men make enquiries. I know a location that will attract the minimum of attention. Álvarez will have his lookouts. Could I make a suggestion that may seem a little unusual? It may involve some risk. Please feel free to say no if this is too much."

Rodriguez looked carefully round to be sure they understood this included them all.

"I would like to suggest we set up our base at the Parador Hotel in Toledo. It is the best hotel in the city and the exact location where we would like to be. You would pose as tourists – my men will be in town on business. Señor David and Señora Lockhart would have to be a married couple. The same for Señor Hernandez and Señora MacInnes. But you are friends so you are in and out of each other's rooms. You go sightseeing in the town or visit some historical places and take photos. You know. My office will arrange your stay and deal with the costs. Would such an arrangement be acceptable to you?"

David and Gillian looked at each another – one of the top hotels in Spain... pretending to be lovers... at someone else's expense...

"I think we could manage that," David agreed. Juan shrugged and Alison nodded.

"Good. *Teniente* Espinosa here would normally be officer in charge of an active investigation but I have been looking for Álvarez for over ten years and therefore have some personal interest in the case. So I have approval to take personal responsibility. Now, we need to move as soon as possible. We can drive to Toledo in an afternoon. Someone will contact you later today to confirm. Our plan will depend on rooms but these hotels are government owned so perhaps we can bring some influence to bear. You will also need a vehicle." He looked to the *teniente* who nodded.

"Until we can start, then? *Buenas días.*" Captain Rodriguez stood up and formally shook hands with each of them. Espinosa took a note of their mobile numbers. Then, just as they were leaving, Rodriguez called David back in.

"Señor David. I did not wish to upset the Señora, but there is the possibility that even if Álvarez is planning to move elsewhere it may not be his plan to take the Señorita with him. You understand my meaning."

"Perfectly," David replied. "The possibility had occurred to me. I'm not sure if Alison has considered it. I imagine it would be just too frightening."

"Understandable. So there is some urgency. I would simply ask that you be ready to leave immediately we contact you and follow the instructions of my officers. I'm sure you see the importance of this. Also we have had some unfortunate – how do you say – leaks – in previous operations. Another reason why I will be leading this one myself."

"I see. Of course."

"*Muy bien*. We will be in touch."

And that was it. Two minutes later they were back on the street in the sunshine of a Madrid summer's day.

"What did you think of *El Capitán* then?" David asked as he and Gillian walked hand in hand, Juan and Alison following behind.

"What a polite man! It was so lucky... sorry Juan... I mean it was so good to meet him at church. What a connection. I had no idea what we were going to do once we got here. Now we've got all this help. And a Parador stay thrown in. *¡Estupendo!*"

"Rodriguez is one of a dying breed," said David. "He's an old-fashioned Spanish gentleman – a *caballero*. He believes in courtesy and good manners as a matter of self-respect as much as anything else. He'll be polite and respectful whether he's helping you put on your coat or a set of handcuffs. Part of the Spanish economic miracle followed by the crisis is the loss of a lot of these old-fashioned attitudes. People just need to survive now so everything has gotten a lot harsher."

"So a bit like Scotland except for the economic miracle?"

"I suppose so. Anyway," he turned to Juan and Alison, "we've got at least a couple of hours to spare in Madrid. Where do you want to go?"

"Oh, I've no idea," said Alison carelessly. "Wherever you think." She was in no mood to view the trip as a holiday. David hoped she would be able to keep up the pretence once they got to Toledo.

"Where do the tourists go?" Gillian asked. "If that's what we're supposed to be."

"Plaza Mayor," said Juan. "Puerta del Sol, The Prado, maybe the Retiro park. Casa del Campo if you have time."

"What's the Plaza Mayor?" Alison asked.

"The town square," David replied. "Almost every city in Spain has one; this just happens to be bigger than most."

"And the haunt of every pickpocket between Bilbao and Cadiz," Juan put in with a grin. "Don't forget, this was my workplace for years."

"You need to keep us right, then," said Gillian.

"Never let bags or cameras out of your sight. Money and credit cards in a zipped bag in front of you. Be suspicious of everyone. I'll try to keep an eye on things."

They all welcomed a distraction from Jen, Raúl, Bible codes, even Toledo. The Puerta del Sol was thronged with tourists, street entertainers, an anti-austerity demonstration, and a few beggars. Spiderman, Bart Simpson, and Spongebob wandered around waving at the crowds. At this time of year the visitors were mostly foreign besides a few Spaniards from the provinces come to see how the *madrileños* lived. Gillian queued up to have her photograph taken in front of the *Kilometro Cero* plaque from which all road distances in Spain are measured. She and Alison posed for photos next to the statue of the Bear and the Strawberry Tree. Then souvenir shopping as, for a few short hours, they joined Madrid town life in the open-air cafés round the town square. Only once did Juan have to grab a passing youth, relieve him of a misappropriated purse, and return it to an astonished American couple at the next table. In return he was obliged to accept their thanks, join them for a photograph, exchange email addresses, and see some snaps of their farm in Idaho. Eventually they paid the Bolivian waiter and wandered round admiring the architecture and murals, looking into the windows of shops set into the cloisters and listening to a South American pan pipe trio playing Abba's greatest hits. David couldn't help imagining, at the corner table in a particular bar, a girl with a raspberry beret and a younger version of himself. They were sipping Rioja and looking very pleased with themselves. But this time it didn't make him feel bitter. He strolled past hand in hand with Gillian and could have sworn the girl in the beret smiled at him.

Lunchtime rolled around and Juan suggested they all go to *Sobrino de Botin*, his former place of employment and famous as the oldest continuously functioning restaurant in the world. Eating early as suited Brits abroad they got in without a reservation and followed Juan's recommendations while he hobnobbed with former colleagues and friends in the kitchen. The *Cordero Asado* and *Cochinillo* were delicious. Then, just as they were feeling relaxed and comfortable, thinking they could get used to this, David's phone went off. It was Espinosa. Rooms had been booked at the Parador and a car was ready. Could they meet at Mariano's in one hour? He looked at his watch. It would be tight but they'd try. Sadly they had to forgo coffee, settle up (a discounted bill), and make their way to the nearest Metro.

Waiting on the platform Alison felt herself jostled by the throng of passengers all trying to find the best spot. Only once the train had arrived and they were in did she notice the missing purse and phone. The purse contained only twenty-five Euros and the mobile was a spare but she still felt stupid. Added to the sense that they were now embarking on the most hazardous part of the enterprise, she wondered if she should just have stayed at home and let more capable people take care of things. No. Jen was her girl. Her place was here.

Once again it made her trawl deep down for some hint she should have seen what was happening with Jen. Nothing. Just as there always was. She had done the best she could and that was that. Juan was also feeling stupid. Besides missing Alicia, it was his job to keep the women safe in a world he understood much better than they. How would things be now if it had been the other phone that had gone? Too horrible to contemplate. David and Gillian were the only ones who seemed at peace with themselves and the world. They hadn't forgotten the exploding van and why they were here, but somehow that night had taken on a distant ethereal quality. It might all have happened to someone else in a different world. What was real now was what was between them. David had explained earlier about his walk round Warehouse 66 the day they arrived. Now he needed to know Gillian's story. They found seats where they couldn't be overheard.

"So... can I ask about church yesterday?"

"Sure, ask away."

"Well – em – was it ok?"

"Yeah, ok." Gillian paused. "No – sorry – I shouldn't be making you work for it. It's just that – well – I'm not sure how to put it. God and I needed to get a few things straightened out."

"So I hope you've put him right."

"That's not even funny. All these months. I feel like I just haven't been paying attention."

"Meaning...?"

"I've been around so many people who've got it together and it's like I haven't even spotted the difference."

"Between?"

"Me and you of course. All of you. First of all I thought it didn't matter. You know, everybody just believes what they believe – we're all different – that sort of thing. Stuck to that for a while actually. Then it turned into – 'I can go with this – it kind of makes sense – but it doesn't need to change me – no problem'. That was stage two. But then there's a little voice somewhere saying, 'That isn't enough.'"

"Scary. I remember."

"You've no idea. It frightened the life out of me. I was thinking, 'What now?'"

"And you concluded?"

"Well all the time I'm thinking 'I do not want to turn into some weirdo', but then – you're not that weird. Well not really."

David made a half-hearted smile.

"So what would a weirdo look like?"

"Oh – I don't know. Adam and Eve, fire and brimstone, women with hats on – whatever. But the real problem is who's in charge. Since I was six *I've* been in charge of things. I told you Mum drank.

Dad used to rely on me a lot. I suppose it wasn't fair on such a youngster but it made me grow up quickly. So coming to faith means giving up control, doesn't it?"

"That's exactly what it means. Much more than the details of what you believe."

"Well, yesterday I just had to think that through."

"Any decision?"

Gillian squeezed his hand and kissed him.

"You'll be the first to know."

For a few moments they sat quietly listening to the metro car rattling its way under the weight of all the streets and avenues of Madrid. The squeal of the brakes, the hiss of the doors, carriages banging over a junction. Apparently random but with an underlying music if you knew how to listen to it.

They made it to Mariano's just a few minutes late. Espinosa was waiting. Parked outside was a silver-grey Jaguar XJ. David couldn't quite believe it.

"The captain's idea," Espinosa said in accented but good English. "You'll be in the best hotel in Toledo so you couldn't very well show up in a Kia Picanto." David passed the keys to Juan as the local boy.

"There's a map and some information in the glove compartment," Espinosa continued. "The SatNav should take you right there. You'll have new identities for checking in." He pulled a sheaf of papers from a briefcase. "Please read these and make sure you adhere to the instructions, for your safety and that of our officers." The lieutenant had little place for small talk and needed to be sure they were taking things seriously. He needn't have worried.

As Juan and Espinosa checked over the details, Alison, Gillian, and David went inside the house. In less than five minutes they were out again, cases in the car and ready to go.

"Well Señor David, I gather you've already had some success," said Mariano, glancing at Gillian. "God speed. Rodriguez is a good man. He's embarrassed about what Spain has become. In the eighties there were a lot of drugs around – you remember don't you? – but now in the crisis it's all got a lot more serious. It's not about freedom and experimentation any more. The business interests are only in it for the money. And with so many young people out of work and no chance of anything, what else is there to do but get high and forget the future? Now he feels he has a mission to clean things up. He takes it very seriously. If there is any way to achieve what you want, he's the man."

"*Muchas gracias, hermano,*" David replied. "For your welcome and all your help. I hope we'll have good news when we see you again."

"*Gracias por tu hospitalidad,*" said Gillian, embracing Maria and kissing Mariano. "And your prayers."

"*Un placer, hermana,*" said Maria, smiling.

And they were off.

"*En el próxima rotonda, toma la primera a la derecha,*" said a cultured female voice.

"I know my way to Toledo," said Juan and turned the SatNav off.

Chapter 23

PARADOR DE TOLEDO

If the Costa del Sol might be the cheap and cheerful Butlins of Spanish tourism, then the Parador network could be its Claridges. Somewhere in the depths of the ministry charged with travel and accommodation in the 1920s must have laboured an unusually far-sighted and visionary *funcionario*. Beavering quietly away he (almost definitely a "he" in those days) thought up the idea of a network of government-owned luxury hotels situated in some of the most historical, beautiful, and spectacular buildings in all of Spain. Gradually, over the years, monasteries, convents, hunting lodges, country mansions, smart town houses, even Moorish castles and fortifications, all found their way into the network to be lovingly restored, modernized, and equipped. Many were also visitor attractions in their own right for historically minded Spaniards to wander around and imagine the life of wealthy aristocrats in the golden age. Where no suitable historical location could be found a small number of modern Paradors were also built and a few existing hotels taken over. One of these is located on the slopes of the *Cerro del Emperador* or Emperor's Hill, on the south side of the ravine at the bottom of which runs the River Tajo, protecting three sides of the city of Toledo. Inside, perhaps inspired by its mountain eyrie, the building has something of the feel of a Swiss chalet resort with high-beamed ceilings, massive fireplaces, white plaster walls and polished, red-tiled floors.

Late that afternoon, Juan pulled into a car park occupied by BMWs, Porsches, Mercedes, and a bright red Ferrari.

"*Buenos días. Tenéis una reserva en el nombre de Gómez?*" David asked at the desk.

"*Buenos días, Señor,*" the clerk smiled. "*Un momento…*" He glanced through the register.

"*Si. Cuatro personas. Dos habitaciones con camas matrimonias. Correcto.*"

"What's he saying?" Alison whispered to David, a bit alarmed by the word "*matrimonia*".

"Just confirming our rooms – four people, two rooms, double beds."

"Oh." If the full implications of travelling as married couples hadn't already struck her it did now.

"What? Does that mean we… do we… I hadn't thought…" she stuttered.

Turning away from the clerk who was by now looking up at them under slightly raised eyebrows, David smiled, tried to look relaxed, and whispered back, "Don't worry, we'll sort it out. Just look calm."

She tried to compose herself as the paperwork was filled in. She was willing to do almost anything to get Jen back but hadn't expected it might come to this. She smiled weakly at Juan who was also wondering what sacrifices their endeavour might require.

The clerk confirmed room numbers, then handed over keys to rooms one and two and sent a porter out for the cases. Five minutes later they were upstairs, at the end of the long corridor, surveying the decor and fittings of Room One – the bridal suite. Furnishings were dark wood with white plaster and more red tile. The bed was enormous. French windows opened out onto a balcony with a stunning view over the ravine, the river, and the complete medieval city draped over the hill leading down to the water. The massive Alcázar fortress and Gothic cathedral stood out from a maze of winding streets, gently pitched roofs and mottled roof tiles, all set against a solid sheet of blue sky. The heat was intense but the colours of the city seemed more autumn than summer – creams, golds, russets, and a thousand shades of terracotta red. Here and there the sharp index finger of a cypress tree jutted upwards in mossy green. Below them the river wrapped itself around the city, cascading down through a series of weirs. They could hear its roar mixed with traffic noises and bells. To their right, round the bend in the river, bridges stretched over the gorge and into the city from the east.

"So, what do you think?" David asked as they took in the scene. "They say this is the best view over Toledo from any direction."

"It's fantastic," Gillian said. "I love it."

"And it fits perfectly with the texts," Juan added. "We're on the heights overlooking the city and these are the gates at the entrance to the town." He paused. "I wonder where she is." They stood together taking in the view Jen herself might have seen while hunting through a Bible for the ideal verse. If they were right, somewhere round the slopes of the very hill they were on, they would find her. Alison cleared her throat and brought things back to reality.

"Can we talk about bedrooms?"

"Of course," David replied. "I'm sorry. We should have sorted that out first. Maybe we should go back inside."

Inside the room the luggage was still in the middle of the floor where the porter had left it.

"Ok," David continued. "We're supposed to be travelling as two couples in case Álvarez has any contacts in the hotel. This does not mean we'll be sharing rooms as couples, but it does mean we have to keep up the pretence. So Juan and I will be sharing, and Gillian and Alison, are you happy to have this room?" They nodded in agreement. "Well, that's the sleeping arrangements but we'll have to spend the rest of the time as if we were couples. So Alison and I will have to change places quite early in the morning and quite late at night. Otherwise we just behave as normal. It's not ideal, I know, but I think it's necessary. How does that sound?"

"Good." Alison breathed a sigh of relief. "No disrespect to anybody but... well... you know..."

"That's fine," Juan agreed. "Alicia told me to behave myself this trip. Somehow I don't think she'd approve of any other arrangement."

"So that's agreed," David continued, much relieved as well. "We'll have to keep all of our things in the room we're supposed to be in. How you cope with the sleeping arrangements I'll leave to you. Just don't call for room service in the middle of the night."

"What's the next move from the police?" Gillian asked. "Do we know how long we're likely to be here?"

"Not entirely, no. Rodriguez said there's to be a conference first thing in the morning. We're to join in some of it. He says they've been concerned about leaks in earlier operations, so they're not using local police – which means they can't use local facilities. That means meeting rooms here. We'll just have to try to make sure staff don't link us up. And we treat the police as if they were just any other guests unless they approach us first. So, in the meantime, we're just on holiday."

That seemed all there was to say. Alison was relieved at the resolution of rooms but was still keyed up and finding it impossible to be "just on holiday". She took her bag and headed for the door. Juan shrugged, picked up the cases, and followed her with a look at David as if to say, "I'm doing this and I'm not complaining, just don't expect me to like it." David laid the remaining cases on the bed. This wasn't entirely straightforward. It was one thing to be conducting a relationship – another to find the pace dictated by a police investigation.

"Sorry things are… a bit awkward," he said. "Do you want me to leave you to unpack?"

"What do you think?" Gillian returned, half smiling. "I'm not feeling awkward at all. I'm here. You're here. So you and Juan have a bachelor pad next door and Alison and I share in here. The rest of the time we're together. *Me gusta mucho*." He smiled, mainly out of plain relief. As usual, Gillian did complicated emotions so much better.

"You're great," he said simply as they held each other, framed in the balcony doors as the evening sun began to slant long dark shadows over the honey-coloured stone of the City of God.

To maintain the illusion and "live the cover" (as Captain Rodriguez had mysteriously put it) they decided that everyone should unpack in the room they were supposed to be living in. The men finished first and with nothing else to do went downstairs to explore. Alison had packed light and was also soon done. She wandered over to the open balcony and looked out on the city. "Which direction?" she thought. "Which building? Which window?" Then, "No, I'll go mad if I start that. Better think about something else." She tried leafing through the Paradors magazine lying on the bureau but found she wasn't the least bit interested in Merida with its Roman amphitheatre or Santiago de Compostela, the oldest continuously functioning hotel in the world. "So what?" she thought, letting the magazine fall lifelessly on top of all the other unwelcome paraphernalia. This wasn't a holiday and nothing could make it into one. And these would not have been her natural choice of travelling companions. She was the odd one out and lately it had been getting on her nerves. She had spent most of her life studiously avoiding contact with Christians of her mum's particular flavour. Now here she was sharing her life with her mother's own minister and worship leader, for goodness sake. And sharing a room with his girlfriend! Despite feeling indebted she couldn't shake off the awkwardness and discomfort. Particularly since her only possible ally now seemed to have jumped ship. She remembered feeling her heart turn cold as Gillian and Maria came back into church all smiles. "That's it," she thought. "Everyone except me. This simply isn't fair."

She knew it was a probably a bad idea but couldn't stop herself. She had to say something. She walked through to the other room. Gillian was busy hanging up a mixture of summer dresses and floaty Persian print blouses, quietly humming to herself. She smiled as Alison came in.

"You were looking like I felt downstairs," she said with half a giggle. "I hadn't thought through the rooms thing either." Alison nodded, looked down to examine her fingernails, then again directly at Gillian.

"So, I just wanted to ask you. Are you a Christian as well then?" Gillian turned to Alison, a long silk scarf and hanger in her hand. She opened her mouth and made to speak but no words came.

"I know it's none of my business," Alison stammered, "but I heard you'd been praying with Maria. Is that not what it usually means?"

"I... uh..." Gillian began.

"I'm sorry," Alison muttered. "Forget I asked."

Gillian put the hanger into the wardrobe, sat down and rubbed her brow. "No, it's ok," she said. "It's a fair question. What am I? To be entirely honest, I really have no idea. I was a bit upset in the service. It's all been so new and confusing. I felt I had to do something. Look, I've finished unpacking. Shall we get some coffee sent up? Spanish police are paying, remember. Then we can talk."

The change of subject was like a lifeline. Alison nodded. They ordered a cappuccino and a *cortado* and took two wicker chairs out onto the balcony.

"I'm really sorry," Alison repeated. "I have absolutely no business interfering. It's just that... well... it kind of feels like just one more thing. Sometimes it's hard to always be the odd one out. My mum took me to a Billy Graham meeting once when I was wee. They were all streaming down the aisles, and the choir singing 'Just as I am' and all that. I know it would have made her really happy if I'd gone forward too but I just couldn't. I'd have been doing it for her, not me. And that's kind of the way it's always been. I'd like to believe but I've never been able to. Then you getting... you know... involved. It just kind of brought it all back. Sorry."

Apart from the story about Jen in the back room at Southside Fellowship, Gillian had never heard Alison string more than a couple of sentences together. Now it felt like a lifetime of frustration was pouring out. Frustration and disappointment. Disappointment with herself, with life, now maybe with someone who might have been a friend. There was a discreet knock at the door. Gillian got up, thanked the waiter, and brought a silver tray over to the balcony table. She took a sip of the *cortado* to compose herself, wondering where to start.

"Ok," she began as Alison nibbled a ginger biscuit. "I have no idea what you're going through and how all this must be feeling but I think I understand what you mean. It's all been a new world for me. I wasn't brought up with this like you. As far as I was concerned 'Christian' just meant that you weren't a Hindu or Jew or something.

So I never had that sort of pressure. Meeting David was my first real contact with someone who took it all seriously. He showed me it wasn't even so much about beliefs as... well... your whole direction really. As for Warehouse 66, I guess it all just came home to me that I had to do something, but I had no idea what to do."

"So that's why you went out?"

"Well, at that point it was all just getting too much. I guess I thought I would just sit in the foyer till it was all over, have a good greet, then go home. Then Maria came out and we talked for a bit."

"What did she say?" Alison put down the remains of the biscuit and was leaning forward.

"Not that much really. She got me a glass of water. I told her what I was feeling – in between blubbing – and she told me a bit about herself."

"What was that?"

"Well, she said she'd come from a traditional Spanish background but it was really just about going to Mass and remembering saints' days and so on. It wasn't a personal faith at all. Then she met Mariano and started seeing things differently."

"A bit like you and David then?"

"I know. Weird, isn't it? But anyway, she said leaving her parents' church was the hardest decision she'd ever made. She'd spent months worrying about it – how her mum would take it. Then she said she just got to the end of her tether and told God if he wanted her to change he would have to do something about it. And somehow things began to move. She didn't tell me the full story but somehow she began to see things a bit more clearly and know what she had to do."

"Hmm." Alison looked thoughtful. "Seems a bit too easy, that. Think of the thousands of people who ask God for a bit of help every day. I don't think things get that much clearer for them. And I know nothing magical has ever happened to me."

"Well, I suppose all we really know is our own story. Maria said I should maybe just ask to know what was right and then see what happened."

"So you didn't plan to actually become a Christian?"

"No, and I don't think I have. I'm still thinking it through. Maria said God can cope with our uncertainties and that seems enough for me right now."

Gillian took another sip and looked out over the city which had so much spirituality in its past.

"I have prayed a couple of times recently," she said with a ghost of a smile. "But it always seems to start with, 'If there's anyone there, I'm not sure I believe in you but…' or something like that."

"I've prayed like that too. Specially since Jen went missing. I've never got anything back though. It would be nice to know you're not alone. Some days I think it would be great to have everything tied up and no more doubts. Like my mum, for example."

"I know exactly what you mean. But I'm not sure your mum is in the majority there. David is full of his own doubts. He's told me. They're just different from mine right now. Or yours. Anyway, I'm still on the journey. I feel things are different. I'm not quite ready to put a name to it."

Alison looked down.

"I didn't mean to pry," she said quietly. "I just saw you go out and jumped to conclusions. It just felt like I was going to be the odd one out again. You know? Feeling kind of daft now."

"It's ok. Really. I'm not surprised. I can see how it must have felt."

"So, what now?"

"No idea. Just wait and see what happens, I suppose. No flashes of lightning yet." Gillian smiled. "I'll keep you posted."

"You don't need to. It's your business."

"Well, we're all involved in things that should be private to you. It's only fair. We'll just have to hope we both find what we're looking for."

David and Juan arrived back looking quite pleased with themselves having found the terrace café, the swimming pool and, predictably, the bar. They suggested a walk through the town. Gillian and Alison smiled politely, collected their things, and kept the conversation to themselves. Taking the Jag seemed unnecessary for such a short distance but it might be a long walk back so they compromised, ordered a taxi, and charged it to the room. Once over the bridge they were glad they'd left the car behind. Road blocks, diversions, and police were everywhere. They immediately thought it must be something to do with Raúl. Maybe the local force *had* got involved and something was happening. But the streets seemed full of happy people wandering about.

"*¿Que pasa?*" David asked the driver. It turned out they were right in the middle of the Fiesta de la Virgen del Sagrario, one of Toledo's major festivals. They got out and began to wander up towards the cathedral. The streets were a riot of colour. The toledana girls had their finest flamenco dresses on in vivid colours with polka dot patterns and swirly hems – including one teenager balanced precariously on the back of her boyfriend's scooter. The men were *caballeros* in tight black trousers, grey tunics, and wide-brimmed hats, or dressed as minstrels with period jackets and breeches. The children held balloons, sweets, and toys. Turning into the plaza they got their first close-up view of the cathedral, looking like a stone fountain frozen solid in honey-coloured pinnacles and archways. The complexity, intricacy, and scale were stunning. Draped around its feet was a full-blown medieval fair. Rows of stalls three deep were thronged with visitors and locals alike wandering about eating, drinking, touching, tasting, smelling, talking, and laughing. They joined the slowly moving lines strolling past the stalls. The atmosphere made Alison's senses reel. The fragrance of roast suckling pig from one *puesto* was so intense they could almost taste it. Piles of fabrics and furs were heaped up in such a variety of colours and textures Alison and Gillian couldn't resist reaching over and stroking them. The profusion was almost overwhelming – fresh bread baked in outdoor ovens, piles of spices and nuts, terracotta pottery, marzipan sweets and cakes, medieval armour, miniature statues of the saints like Hummel figures on their best behaviour, barbecue racks with chicken, pork ribs, and sides of lamb dripping over them, paella pans a yard across, strings of pungent peppers and garlic, antiques and bric-a-brac, replica firearms, racks of costumes, and finally an entire pig slowly turning over a pit of glowing charcoal. Round another corner a troupe of acrobats entertained the crowd to the sound of recorders and mandolins.

Suddenly, with a shock, Alison noticed that for some unaccountable reason she felt different. Without forgetting what they were there for some strange sort of peace seemed to have descended. She saw David and Gillian wandering ahead arm in arm and felt no resentment. Juan bought a box of sugared almonds and offered her one. It was perfect. A man in a jester's costume tried to climb a pyramid of acrobats and pulled the whole lot over. She laughed till the tears came. It was healing and refreshing. Then, equally unbidden and unexpected, she heard her own voice as she had spoken not much more than an hour before – "… nothing magical has ever happened to me…" A shiver ran up her body ending with a tingle on the top of her scalp.

Just when it felt as if the sensory overload couldn't get any more intense a trumpet blast split the air and a military band appeared round the corner, complete in blue fitted jackets with white lanyards and gold brocade, white trousers with a thick red stripe and silver helmets. They wheeled round in perfect time and headed for the cathedral entrance, sending the crowds scurrying to either side.

"So what do you think of a Spanish fiesta, Señora?" Juan shouted to Alison over the din.

"Awesome!" she shouted back. "But a bit noisy!"

"This is amazing!" Gillian shouted. "Did you know this would be happening?"

"No – no idea." David just managed to make himself heard. "The Spanish love a fiesta. Any excuse. Every *barrio* has its own patron saint and its own version of the virgin so any time from May to October there's always a fiesta somewhere." The band paused at the cathedral entrance, turned and played a loud, brassy fanfare, then put their instruments down and filed in, followed by a stream of dignitaries and ordinary folk in their holiday best.

"What's going on?" Alison asked.

Juan pointed to the mountains of fresh blooms on either side of the cathedral doors. "Blessing the flower offering,"

"'*Virgen del Sagrario*'," Gillian read the motto made entirely of flowers. "'*Ruega por nosotros*'. '*Por nosotros*' is 'for us'. What does '*ruega*' mean?"

"'*Rogar*' is to beg or plead," David replied. "It's asking the Virgin to pray on behalf of the people."

"Can't they pray for themselves?" asked Alison.

"That's part of traditional Spanish religion. God is too holy to be approached. Even Jesus was too good and perfect. So the thought is if you could get Mary on side he'd be more inclined to grant your request."

"Like getting the boss's mum to put in a good word?"

"I'm afraid so. Not very biblical but that's the tradition."

They turned and wandered on again, pausing opposite a barbecue stall. It made as much sense to eat here as go back to the hotel so they queued up and collected plates of ribs, kebabs or drumsticks, fresh bread and beakers of *cervesa* or *vino tinto*.

"This couldn't happen at home," Alison stated as a flat fact. "Even if it was warm enough."

"Why not?" Juan asked.

"Well, we'd all feel daft wandering around pretending we were medieval. Then the guys would all be wasted by half past one, the women would spend the whole day trying to keep them upright, and the kids would be nicking stuff off the stands. Anyway, the rain would probably come on halfway through and that would be that. Pity though."

After they got back to the hotel they stood on the terrace after dark and watched exploding cascades of colour over the city. "Nothing magical," Alison thought, the sky alight with fireworks. "Maybe I spoke too soon."

Chapter 24

CONFERENCIA

Next morning they had a Spanish breakfast of fresh fruit – oranges from Valencia, *piel de sapo* melon dripping with juice, fresh figs, grapes, dates, and pomegranates. For the carnivores there were a dozen different sausages and hams, supplemented by more kinds of bread and pastry than Alison had ever seen, with a choice of honey, jams, and of course *mermelada de Sevilla*. Top marks, however, went to the creamy scrambled eggs with asparagus and peas or avocado and prawns. These proved too much for the Scottish palate so Alison and Gillian stuck to the plainer alternatives. In the dining room, David picked out Rodriguez and Espinosa with a group of others he didn't recognize. The group got up to leave at the same time they did.

"Meeting room two, fifteen minutes," Rodriguez whispered as they met at the door.

The police team were as unused to Parador surroundings as the Edinburgh contingent. Comfortable wooden chairs upholstered in pink velvet surrounded a table draped in a deep green cloth. Hangings and ornaments decorated the walls and thick red and cream curtains framed the windows. Apart from Rodriguez, the police kept to themselves as the Scots came in, talking together and shuffling papers. They had the solid, slightly cynical, go-on-surprise-me look of detectives the world over. David wondered what sort of businessmen they might be taken for – travellers in lie detectors and listening devices perhaps? The captain, however, was warm and welcoming. Once the door shut he spoke to each of them in turn, thanking them for coming and apologizing for the inconvenience the investigation was putting them through. After a few minutes, he took the chair at the top of the table. In English he welcomed the civilians, then, in Spanish, explained who each of them were. David noticed that he did not introduce his own men, who remained anonymous. Other comments were translated by a young officer on his left.

"You have seen something of the city?" Rodriguez asked.

"A bit," David said. "We had a meal in town last night and were able to walk round a bit."

"It's a beautiful city," Gillian added. "I'd like to see a bit more of it."

"Ah well, that brings me to my first point," he said. "Our task is to locate Álvarez and recover the Señorita. My team have been briefed on your means of communication. We now have information to support your view that they are in Toledo. However, we have yet to identify the specific premises. If your guesses are correct then it's likely to be somewhere on the hill, perhaps nearer the bridges. There are a limited number of locations so this may not take long. Then we must decide how we can get access to the girl – pardon me Señora, your daughter Jennifer – and remove her before apprehending the others. But in the meantime, I'm afraid I must ask you to restrict yourselves to the hotel. Álvarez and his associates will no doubt be around the city from time to time. We have no idea if any of you is likely to be recognized – Señor Hernandez, you had the group in your restaurant, I believe. So, we cannot risk further contact. I apologize for the restriction but there may be worse places to be confined. If you would be so kind as to charge all expenses to your rooms, this will be dealt with in due course. Now, assuming we can identify the location, how can we make contact? Señor David? You may still be able to pass a message?"

"I don't know. It's more than a week since we were last in touch. I could try to send instructions but we might have no way of knowing if they got through. If I knew what you were planning I could try to find a way to tell her to get out beforehand. Even to the garden or the pool."

If Rodriguez was irritated by having a civilian intrude on his plans he didn't show it.

"Ah. I regret this may not be sufficient. We will be surrounding the area. It would not be safe within the cordon. And it will depend on the layout of the premises. Anyway, we will continue with our discussion now, if you please, and meet again this evening. Briefings every day at ten a.m. and eight p.m. unless there is a change of plan. This is acceptable? Good. Many thanks again." Rodriguez spoke in Spanish to one of the detectives near the door who jumped up and opened it for them. Their part of the proceedings was evidently at an end. Even before they had all left, the conversation had already begun in Spanish and different voices could be heard with different points of view. David wondered if not everyone was as pleased to have the pleasure of their involvement as *El Capitán*.

"What did you make of that, then?" David asked Juan once they had moved out onto the terrace overlooking the town.

"Either they have no idea how they'll get Jen out or they have an idea but nobody wants to share it with us." Juan summed up what everyone was feeling. No one answered him as the waiter arrived with three milky coffees, one black, and four slices of deep-filled apple pie and cream. Toledo was again looking fantastic just over the river. From here they could see even further round in both directions than from the balcony above.

"I keep looking at the buildings round the hill and asking myself which one it is," Alison said.

"I know," Gillian agreed. "It feels like this has been going on for so long. Now we're so near. We just need to know the next move and get on with it."

Suddenly Juan seemed to go rigid in his chair.

"*Dios mío*," he said under his breath. "Nobody move. Try to look casual. Turn away if you can."

Through the doors from the indoor salon a group of men were advancing. They strolled easily, confidently, even with a trace of a swagger. Most were young but one older man talked on a mobile. He was smiling and whatever he was dealing with seemed to be under control. David and the others sat at a table at one end of the terrace. The group chose a table towards the other end, grabbed some chairs not being used by an adjoining group – and sat down.

"Don't get up. Don't look round. Do nothing that attracts attention," Juan hissed. The temptation to look was almost overpowering.

"What is it?" Gillian whispered back.

"You're not going to believe this. Alison do *not* look round. That's Álvarez and his men. I'm sure of it!"

A stunned silence followed. It seemed incredible, the very individual they had just been talking about was now less than fifty feet away. Their mixture of intelligent guesswork, coded texts, and inspiration had indeed been good – Toledo they had thought and Toledo it was. On the hill overlooking the city. Here was their quarry, though now hunter and hunted might have changed places. What to do now? If any of them made a move it might attract attention. If they sat stock still there was a chance Rodriguez and his team might appear. For the next half hour they sat almost completely rigid and in silence. Waiters were waved away. The coffee got cold. Nobody had an appetite for the food. Suddenly the delights of Toledo no longer held any fascination. Alison was almost dying from frustration to catch sight of the man who'd been filling her nightmares for the past six months. She might hear her daughter mentioned by name. David knew that it would more likely be simply the *chica* or even the abusive *puta* they'd heard once before. But instead they were talking about *a casa* – back home, *a patria* – in the home country, and *mi tierra* – my homeland. And they weren't shy. They were laughing and joking, slapping each other on the back and shouting for more coffee. Perhaps they were on the brink of moving and in high spirits at the thought. The only consolation was that Álvarez' back was to them and he wasn't looking in their direction. After what seemed an eternity, the bill was brought, a few notes left on the table, and the group got up to leave. The Scots tried to shrink into their chairs and keep their eyes down. Concentrating on the unfinished coffee and cakes, they failed to see Álvarez turn on his way out, pause, look slightly quizzical, shrug, then continue to the door.

The instant they were gone, David and Juan raced to the conference room. Officers were packing up papers, rolling up a flipchart and chatting. David told them the news. Rodriguez immediately gave orders and a group of officers grabbed jackets and took off along the corridor.

"This may be a godsend or ruin everything," the captain murmured. "It all depends if you have been recognized." They sat in silence and waited. No more than two minutes later a pair of the officers came back all smiles. Two black BMWs had been just about to leave the car park as they got to the foot of the stairs. One pursuit car had got in behind them and was now following, ready to peel off at the first junction, leaving a second to continue before returning control to the first. Rodriguez pulled a radio out of his case and flicked it on. A running commentary came from the car. Given the geography of the hill, if their guess was right, they would have less than a mile to go to any of the properties they thought possible. Twenty minutes later both teams were back. High fives and handshakes were exchanged. They had a result.

"I really find it hard to believe we're going to be this lucky – or whatever Juan thinks the word should be." Gillian sat at the mirror putting on make-up. David was changing his shirt for dinner.

"I know. It seems incredible." He shook his head. "I couldn't believe it when Juan said they'd come in. Rodriguez wants to bring everything forward. He's had watchers and listening devices trained on the house. He even thinks he knows which room Jen's in. You know, we've been so keen to get to this point, now it's about to happen there's part of me that feels it's all too sudden. I thought we'd be here for three or four days at least. Now it's all come in a rush." David sat down and leaned forward, hands clasped in front of his face and elbows on his knees. "I'd give a lot to know what we'll be thinking twenty-four hours from now."

"Well, I have an idea what's going through Alison's mind."

"How?"

"She asked me to sit with her for a bit after you got back from speaking to Rodriguez. She's finding the tension very hard. She's got no one to share it with. Her mum's... well, Mrs MacInnes, and Jen's dad don't seem to be on the scene at all. We're keyed up but it's not our daughter and we have each other to talk to."

"How is she?"

"Not great. She had a bit of a cry then started telling me all about what Jen was like as a youngster. She was always getting into scrapes. When the drugs thing started Alison thought she'd lost her altogether. Now she might be getting her back – or losing her completely. She's a complete bag of nerves."

"Understandable. At any rate I've a feeling we won't have to wait long. Rodriguez wants us all to meet again at eight tonight."

Dinner was a sombre affair. Not even the *perdices con chocolate* or *truchas a la navarra* could breathe much life into the party. David felt the weight of his own past. He tried not to think that this time it was somebody else's loved one, not his – not a very worthy thought but nevertheless true. They had had their moment of drama on the terrace – now they were spectators. Still he had a feeling there was a plan or a guiding intelligence underlying everything. How else to explain the chance gift of a Bible, the coded messages, the meeting with Rodriguez, now the location? For that matter if it hadn't been for a girl about to fail first-year Spanish, Gillian might have been nothing more than another student in the class. So many chance events and what ifs. Calling it fate seemed inadequate. He looked at his watch and waited for the hands to drag their way to eight o'clock.

Like the meal, the evening's conference was a solemn event. Little was said in English. If Alison already felt events were out of her hands this made it worse. The police team seemed to be going over times and events in infinite detail. The flip chart showed five- or ten-minute intervals starting from 3:30 a.m. next morning. But what exactly was to happen at each of these times she had no idea. Grab bags were issued and contents checked. Guns, ammunition, and what looked like grenades and flares appeared on the table. Some officers had body armour and helmets. There were handcuffs enough to detain a small army. Perhaps that was exactly what they were about to tackle. The briefing dragged on and on. At times there seemed to be differing points of view. One officer would come back at something Rodriguez had said and seem to question it. Then another would weigh in, though whether in agreement or not she couldn't say. The only other one she knew – Espinosa – said little, simply looking round under heavy brows and occasionally making a note on the pad in front of him. At times the briefing became almost a shouting match between officers on different sides with Rodriguez quietly watching. Finally the noise, the disagreements, the detail, the guns, the concentration, and the sense of utter powerlessness became too much. Alison covered her face with her hands and shouted.

"Will you all just shut up! Whose life are we talking about!" Such was the buzz it took a few seconds for everyone to realize who had spoken. They stopped in mid flight. She took just that long to get a deep breath.

"Excuse me! I'm not a police officer. I have no idea what you're planning but this is my daughter! I've been sitting here for the last hour and I haven't understood a single word. Now would somebody please tell me what is going on!" There was a second of silence, then Rodriguez spoke.

"Señora. My deepest apologies. We asked you to attend in case there were questions we might need to ask you but you have not been kept informed. This is unforgivable. This is a complex operation and there have been... how can I say... some differences of opinion. But someone should have been explaining to you. Again I can only apologize. As it happens I think we have now arrived at a conclusion." He looked round the table. No one disagreed.

"The situation is this. We know the premises Álvarez is using. We know the gang are intending to leave the area though not exactly when. They have been loading equipment and boxes all day. So we must act quickly. Our operation will begin at four forty-five tomorrow morning. Our priority is the safety of your daughter. Officers Correa and Torres," he indicated the men immediately to his left, "will go in first. Their job is to locate and remove your daughter. Álvarez will then be given the opportunity to surrender, but we do not consider this a likely outcome. We are then prepared to do what is necessary.

"I'm sorry if that seems such a quick summary from all of our discussions but we have been considering how this is to be achieved. The aim is not in doubt. Once again, I regret this has not been made clear to you. My sincerest apologies, Señora, and I trust this is satisfactory."

Alison nodded. With so much frustration and stress no answer could really be enough. On the other hand, she could not imagine how else things could be arranged.

"Ok," she muttered. "How do we know how things are going?"

"Officer Sanchez here," Rodriguez indicted another member of the team, "will stay with you all of tomorrow. He will wake you early – if you wish – and will have access to all of our communications. He can explain to you what is happening. I trust that before the day is over you will have your daughter back again and we will have removed a danger to the state." Alison nodded again, and at that, the meeting broke up.

"There was more going on there than Rodriguez said, wasn't there?" Gillian asked quietly on their way back upstairs.

"Absolutely," David confirmed. "Some of them – I think maybe even the more senior guys – felt it was so important they get Álvarez that Jen should be expendable. They basically wanted to go in all guns blazing and take out any and everyone they could. Rodriguez overruled them. Jen will be the first objective but I guess not everyone is totally happy with it. I wouldn't like to be the first one in."

"So we just wait for tomorrow morning then?"

"Not much else we can do."

"Well, somebody needs to be with Alison. She must be climbing the walls. I'll go and look for her."

The evening dragged on. To maintain the fiction they had to

avoid the police and couldn't talk about the events of next day but that was the only thing on anyone's mind. They sat in the bar for a while, never less like holidaymakers. Gillian suggested they should get an early night. An early start was the only thing they could say with certainty about the next twenty-four hours.

The sound of the telephone took a while to penetrate David's consciousness. He fumbled for his watch – 4 a.m. They weren't supposed to be wakened for another half hour. This was supposed to be Juan and Alison's room, though, so he couldn't answer it. He shook Juan awake, grabbed the handset, and passed it to him. Groggily, Juan managed to mutter something, listened, then sat bolt upright in bed.

"Si... Si... No. Seguro... Si... Inmediatamente." He put the handset down and rubbed his eyes. He was looking puzzled.

"What's going on?" David asked.

"There's someone at reception asking for Alison. I have no idea what's going on."

"Ok. I'll go downstairs and you go next door and get Alison. We'll all have to be up in half an hour anyway. It's probably just one of the police team wanting an early start."

When David came downstairs he expected to see Rodriguez or maybe Sanchez or one of the others, but the night porter was standing in the middle of the foyer with a girl in jeans and a flimsy T-shirt. David looked at the porter who gestured towards the girl.

"Are you Señor David?" she asked. He nodded. "I was told to ask for you if I couldn't get my mum. I'm Jennifer MacInnes."

David's jaw fell but before he could say anything, Juan came down the stairs two at a time. He grabbed David's elbow and pulled him aside. He wasn't looking puzzled any more.

"They've got her," he said. "Alison's been drugged and Gillian isn't there." David looked back to the girl.

"I was told to tell you I'm a swap," she managed to say with a trembling lip. "Raúl says he's looking forward to meeting you."

- - -

Chapter 25

OUT AND IN

Juan was amazed that David could keep functioning at all that day. Either it was autopilot or simply "grace to help in time of need". As David had gone downstairs, Juan knocked on Alison and Gillian's door, then, getting no reply, went in using his spare key. There was no sign of Gillian, which seemed strange so early in the morning. Maybe she hadn't been able to sleep and had gone for a walk. Alison seemed to be fast asleep, though she was lying in an awkward position. He tried to rouse her. No response. He noticed an empty bottle on the bedside table and read the label: Rohypnol. Juan knew the name but on the Edinburgh streets they called it "roofies". *Edinburgh Evening News* readers knew it as the "date rape drug". Then he ran along the corridor and down the stairs to find David standing at reception with a girl beside him. Juan told him what he had found and the girl gave her message. It took some seconds to sink in, then the whole terrifying situation became clear. David pelted back upstairs. The bedclothes were in disarray. One red leather sandal lay in the middle of the floor. There was no sign of Gillian's clothes and a chair had been knocked over. Alison was breathing but could not be wakened. He ran back to reception. Juan was sitting with his arm around the girl as she wept and shook. The night porter was exactly where David had left him, watching the whole proceedings like a movie.

"*Es una emergencia,*" David told him slowly and clearly as if speaking to a child. "*Necesitamos una ambulancia. Rápidamente. ¿Donde está Sñr Rodríguez?*" The small, tubby *portero* finally grasped that something was wrong and roused himself. He checked the computer and gave David a room number, then dialled the hospital and handed him the phone. Juan was amazed at how calmly he was able to describe the situation despite the frustrating slowness of whoever was taking the call. He shot back upstairs and hammered on Rodriguez' door. The captain was already up, brushing his teeth at the bathroom mirror. When he saw the look on David's face he stopped in mid stroke.

"Jen's downstairs. They've taken Gillian."

A quick *Dios mío* was Rodriguez' only sign of discomposure before moving into command mode. They went into Alison's room. The facts were quickly confirmed.

"Take the girl out of the foyer," he ordered. "Get her something to drink. I'll get someone to accompany the Señora to hospital."

Since secrecy was now pointless, contact would be made with the local police. Two of his men would check out the property Álvarez had been using, though probably more as a formality. Road blocks would be set up and descriptions circulated. A helicopter would be sent for. He would interview the girl. Within minutes the meeting room was transformed into an incident room. Hotel management were roused from their beds and left in no doubt of police requirements.

David went back downstairs and managed to get a basic breakfast for all three of them. In the midst of the panic and horror he had to force himself to register that this was Jennifer MacInnes sitting in front of them gulping down cereal and coffee – the girl they had come all this way to look for. He had hoped, maybe even expected, this would be a moment of triumph. Now it was his worst nightmare. His brain knew what had happened but his spirit was numb. Rodriguez spoke to Jen in private then took David aside.

"It seems Álvarez has been aware of our presence for some time," he began.

"The terrace! He must have recognized Juan. Or maybe remembered Alison and recognized her as well. We should have guessed!"

"Well perhaps, but I think not. Apparently they had been planning a move, then a few days ago things became more urgent – more men, more vehicles, more packing. This was before the day you saw him. I think he knew we were here and could not resist coming in for a look."

David let out a sigh and shook his head in amazement.

"You almost have to admire his audacity," Rodriguez mused. "He has been very successful and he is a confident man. This can become overconfidence. Perhaps he will be tempted until he makes mistakes."

David was in no mood to admire anything about Raúl. He kept to the point.

"What else did do you know? Do we know why they took Gillian?"

"I'm afraid that remains a mystery. There seems to have been a lot of excitement in the house last night – drinking, laughter, you know the sort of thing. The vans were loaded up then the girl was locked in her room. The convoy left, then at about two a.m. she was woken, shoved in a car, and brought here. She was told what to say and made to repeat it. Then she says four of Álvarez' men came into the hotel and ten minutes later came out with a bundle. We have to assume this was Señora Lockhart." Rodriguez paused as David looked down. "I am very sorry, Señor David. None of us anticipated this development. We will do everything in our power. Now I'm afraid I have to meet with my team. Perhaps things will become clearer in due course." Then he was off down the corridor, still ramrod straight but, David thought, perhaps slightly less assured in his gait.

The sunlight was beginning to strengthen outside. Day staff were arriving, talking quietly in little groups, and looking over in his direction. None of it mattered. David felt weak and slumped in an armchair. It made no sense. Jen back and Gillian taken. Why? And here he was again. Another loved one in danger. It was like the poster for *Jaws*, he thought bitterly. Just when you thought it was safe to go back in the water... He needed to know everything – anything that could be relevant. Maybe Jen had more to say. Maybe there was something Rodriguez hadn't asked – something more that would give them a clue. She had said, "Raúl says he's looking forward to meeting you." What was that all about? It was like being given a formula but not being told what calculations you could use it for. God knew, it was almost more than he could bear to get involved in the first place. Now this – history repeating itself. It seemed like anyone he loved was destined to be ripped away from him and lose their life.

It was still only 5:30 a.m. and the breakfast room was empty except for Juan and Jen huddled at a table in the corner as David came in. Jen was shivering despite a cardigan round her shoulders but was still managing to dispose of breakfast between dabbing her eyes and nose with a tissue. David couldn't help reflecting on Alison's description of a girl with no respect for home and no fear of the big bad world. All she wanted was to break the rules with no thought for the consequences. Now the world had gobbled her up, chewed and spat her out again. But for Raúl's twisted sense of humour, at that very moment her body might have been lying crumpled on some waste ground slowly cooling in the morning air. Maybe an early dog walker would have come on a twisted bundle in the bushes. The dog might have been sniffing with curiosity, then the owner might have bent down for a closer look. Later that day, depending how easy it was to identify the body, depending on whether her face was still recognizable, the word might have come through to Rodriguez and his team who by this time would have drawn a blank at the house. Then Alison would have had to go to the morgue to identify the corpse. Gillian, Juan, David himself, Rodriguez and his team, and in due course Mrs MacInnes and the entire church – even Eric and his mates – everyone would have been hit with a sense of loss and defeat, then begin blaming themselves and asking if they could have done more. But as it was she was here. Alive. Tearful and traumatized but alive. It was Gillian's life that might be hanging in the balance. David poured more coffee as she scooped up the last spoonful of cereal. Neither he nor Juan was able to touch a thing. Finally, when she was finished he began, as gently as he could.

"Jen, I know you've spoken to Captain Rodriguez already but I need to speak to you too. I may have some different things to ask you. Do you know who I am?"

Jen sniffed and dabbed again and Juan gave her a clean tissue. She nodded.

"You're Señor David. Granny's minister."

"Do you know who this is?" She shot a tiny glance at Juan, then looked down again and shook her head.

"This is Juan Hernandez. Juan and his wife are friends of your mum's from Edinburgh. Do you remember being out for a birthday meal at a Spanish restaurant the night the van was attacked? Juan and Alicia run that restaurant. We were out looking for you that night. Raúl heard about it when you were in the restaurant and ordered the attack on the van. Do you remember that?" She sniffed and nodded again. "When you came into the hotel you said you were to be a swap. What does that mean?"

"They brought me back and took someone else."

"That's right. Gillian was part of our group. It was her idea to go out on the van that night to look for you. She was involved in the attack and was badly hurt but still wanted to keep on looking. When you left that mobile phone message and we knew you were in Spain she insisted on coming along. Now Raúl has her. We have to do everything we can to get her back. I'm sorry I have to ask you more questions, but the sooner we get some idea what to do or where to look the better. Is that ok?" She nodded, then broke down again.

"I'm sorry," she sobbed, hardly coherent. "I'm so sorry. I never thought any of this would happen." For some moments there was nothing further to be said. David pulled his chair round the end of the table and put his arm around her as she continued to cry, huge sobs shaking her whole body. David knew this would be a slow journey to recovery. Finally, she fell silent, more through exhaustion than resolution.

"Is my mum going to be ok?" she whispered.

"We don't know. We hope so. She's in hospital so they'll be doing everything they can."

"I'm really sorry," Jen whispered again.

"I know. Everybody makes mistakes. We're glad we've got you

back. Your mum'll want to see you as soon as she's recovered. But in the meantime we've lost someone else. Someone dear to all of us. We need you to help us find her. Can you do that?" Jen nodded again. "Ok. After you said that you were to be a swap, you said that Raúl was looking forward to meeting me. Do you know what he meant by that?"

"Yes. He gave me another message but he said I was only to tell you." She looked up at David then across to Juan.

"*¿Quieres quedar solo?*" Juan asked.

"No. I need you right here." David was emphatic. "Juan is my friend, your mum's friend, and Gillian's friend. He's your friend too. Anything you need to tell me you can tell him." Jen shuffled in the chair and pulled her cardigan more tightly shut.

"This other message," David continued. "Have you told Captain Rodriguez?" She shook her head. David and Juan exchanged glances. "Ok Jen. What are you to tell me?" There was another pause as she tried to concentrate and collect her thoughts.

"He said you're like his travel agent. Every time he hears your name he has to move out."

"Are you sure?" Juan asked, incredulous. She nodded more confidently this time.

"I don't know what it means but he made me repeat it three times. He says every time he hears your name he has to move. First it was to Edinburgh, then back to Spain, now somewhere else. They were planning to move anyway, but when they found out you were here they had to bring everything forward. He was very angry, then he started laughing. I don't know why. I got locked in my room. I could just hear them all laughing downstairs."

"Is that it or is there more? You said he was looking forward to meeting me."

"He said he thought last time would have been enough but you didn't – sorry…" She corrected herself as if it had been learned by heart. "You don't learn very well." Jen looked embarrassed and blew her nose. "I'm sorry. I don't know what it means. He just told me to tell you."

"That's ok. Don't worry about it. We just need to know exactly what he said."

"He said this time he needs to tell you himself. He said if you want to see the girl again... I think that's the other person, not me..." David nodded. "Well, if you want to see her again you have to meet him."

"And how can I meet him?"

"He says you should leave the hotel this morning and drive east. He'll contact you. He says he has your mobile number." David took a deep breath and let out a long sigh.

"Is that everything?" Jen looked down and frowned for a second, thinking.

"He says you have to go alone and not tell the police. If you tell anyone or anyone knows where you're going the Señora will die." She stopped and looked down again. "I'm really, really sorry," she said. "I didn't think..."

"*Es loco*," Juan said under his breath. "*Imposible. No puedes ir.*" David said nothing then looked up at Juan.

"I know, but I've got to go. It's my fault Gillian's here at all. I've no choice. You'll have to cover for me with Rodriguez. He's been so good I hate to deceive him but there's no other way. If he finds out he'll want to put a tracking device on the car or something. If Raúl finds that he'll just kill Gillian and probably me too. At least this way she may get out alive."

"You better get out alive as well." Juan smiled ruefully. "Alicia won't let me home without you. *¡Vaya con Dios hermano!*" David smiled and gripped his hand. They sat for some moments, hands tightly clasped, and looked steadily into each other's eyes.

"One other question," David finally asked, looking back to Jen. "You said Raúl knows my mobile phone number. How?"

"I don't know," Jen replied, shrugging her shoulders. "There were lots of people who came to the house but there was one visitor only Raúl would see. He used to come late at night or early in the morning. There was some sort of signal, then everybody had to get out of the way. Nobody was allowed to be there. Raúl would take him into a side room and when he went away Raúl would tell his men what they were going to do. I think that's who told him you were in the hotel. Maybe he gave him your number somehow." Juan and David exchanged glances again.

"Does Captain Rodriguez know about this?" Jen nodded. "He asked me about everyone that came to the house and if there were any unusual visitors. I told him about this one but I wasn't able to tell him what he looked like or anything."

"But how did you know about him if it was all so secret?" Juan put in.

"Carlos told me."

"Who's Carlos?"

"He was the only one that was nice to me. He gave me his phone to send the messages."

"And who did he think you were sending messages to?"

"I told him it was a lottery game. He made me agree to give him half if I won." For the first time Jen managed a weak smile. "I told him it was for *El Gordo*. That's the big prize, isn't it? We used to talk about what we would do if we won."

"Do you think he believed you about the codes?" David asked.

"I don't know. He never tried to stop me but he told me not to tell Raúl or any of the others. He said if he had enough money he would get out of the gangs and buy a hotel in Ferol – that's where he's from. He said he'd get a big house by the sea, far from Madrid and all the pushers and addicts. He'd make it into a hotel and we would sit on the rocks and fish in the evening. Or we could take guests out in his fishing boat. Then we'd have barbecues on the beach with fresh fish." Jen's eyes were bright, for the first time not with tears. "He was supposed to keep watch on me but then we got talking. I suppose we were both bored. I helped him with his English and he taught me some Spanish."

"And how did Carlos get involved with Raúl in the first place?" Juan asked, thinking back to his own childhood.

"He's Raúl's nephew. He told me his mother told him to have nothing to do with his uncle but he wouldn't listen. Then he got involved and couldn't get out." Jen looked down again and twisted her paper tissue. "Just like me."

Incredible. A guardian angel right in the heart of the gang. Who the late night visitor was seemed more of a mystery. David remembered Rodriguez talking about leaks in previous operations, which was why he was leading this one himself. Maybe one of his aims was to find out where the leaks were coming from. It was classic Escobar – greasing police palms as insurance – like reinvesting some of the profits to keep one step ahead of the enforcers and free to do more business.

"And how did you come up with the idea of the codes in the first place?" David asked now that Jen had settled a bit and was talking more freely.

"My mum made me take the Bible Granny gave me when I left. It's all I had to read. Once things… changed… I read it the whole time. It's all there was to do. But I couldn't really understand it and I was just going to throw it out when I found the book of Psalms and it just seemed to be all about me. Whoever wrote it was in trouble the whole time and wanted God to help him. They were praying, just like me. I didn't have anyone else to turn to. Carlos was great but there wasn't much he could do. He couldn't stop the other ones… the older ones…" What he couldn't stop them doing David could guess. Now was not the time to ask.

"Then I thought about you," Jen continued looking at David. "Granny used to talk about her minister. She was so pleased you'd started helping them at church. I started wondering, like, if you knew all the bits I was reading and could explain them to me. Then I wondered if Granny might be reading the same bits I was reading at the same time. I just thought if I could tell you what I was reading then you would know what I was thinking. Then I had the idea of the lottery codes and asked Carlos if I could send a text. He was bored too and that was when he made me promise to give him half if I won. So he let me have the phone whenever I needed it. And he used to tell me when a message came in. I told him it was the winning code they sent out to everybody that had entered but I don't know if he believed me."

Clever girl, David thought again, just as he had that day at Hacienda, which now seemed so long ago, when the first code had arrived and he had almost missed it. Very clever.

"Ok Jen, that's great. You've done really well. Is there anything else you can think of that might help us?" She shook her head. "Well, if you remember something you can tell Juan and he'll decide if the police need to know. Maybe you should get some sleep now. You can use your mum's room. Then we will get you to a doctor, as soon as possible." Jen understood and nodded. They took her upstairs and Juan managed to find a big T-shirt of Alison's for her to wear. When he knocked gently and put his head round the door ten minutes later she was already asleep.

"What are you going to do?" Juan asked as they sat together next door. "You don't mean to go ahead and meet him? It would be suicide."

"Maybe so. But how could I live with myself if I get home in one piece and Gillian doesn't? I think you might be right but I have to go. And I can't hang about. Rodriguez is still busy. If he gets any idea of what's going on he'll want to stop it. The sooner I can get away the sooner Gillian might be free. It's not her they want. I'm sure of that.

"So," David got up, pulled down a small case, and started throwing a few things in. "I don't know where I'm going or how long I'll be away but you'll have to keep the captain happy and not have him looking for me as well. It would be best if I can get to one of the cars without having to speak to him. Anyway, I'll have to try my luck." Juan was about to come back with his usual rejoinder but this wasn't the moment for splitting hairs. He knew what David meant and his part in it. He nodded.

"Make sure you take your Bible so you can send us a message," he said.

David laughed with a release of tension.

"I hope that won't be necessary!"

Less than five minutes later they were crossing the lobby and heading out to the car park when Rodriguez suddenly appeared out of a side room. "Oh no," thought David, "now we're in trouble." But the captain merely smiled at them.

"You're leaving us?" he asked.

"Just for a few days, I hope," David answered truthfully. "I don't know if you know what happened to my wife but I'm afraid this is all too much like history repeating itself. Anyway, I don't think you need me any more. I really just need to get away and calm down a bit. Juan will know how to get in touch. He can look after Alison and Jen if need be."

"I see," said the captain. "I hope that's a wise decision. I am aware of the history a little. It is most regrettable. *Déjà vu*, I think the French call it. I'm afraid we do not have a better term in Spanish."

"Nor do we in English," David agreed. "At any rate I hope I'll be back before long."

"Of course. Now, I have some other matters to deal with. *Vaya con Dios*, Señor David," he said, still smiling. He gripped David warmly by the hand, then he was off again striding purposefully across the red-tiled floor to another meeting. Strange – he had used the very same words as Juan, "*Vaya con Dios*". Did the captain know more than he was letting on? Anyway, David had enough to occupy his mind without that as well. They made it out to the car park without being further accosted, Juan handed over the keys and set up the SatNav. They embraced, maybe for the final time.

"Good luck!" Juan shouted as the car moved off.

"I didn't think you believed in it," David shouted back.

"God knows what I mean!"

Chapter 26

VALDEPEÑAS

David pulled onto the long, winding downhill drive to the roundabout then right to join the *carretera de circulación*. This took him past the bridges into the town – the gates of the city – then up to the major roundabout out of town. Now the first dilemma. There is no main road that runs due east from Toledo. The N400 would take him north-east towards Aranjuez then on in the direction of Cuenca. Or, according to the SatNav, he could take the south-east road, the CM400, initially towards Mora then bending more east to Alcazar de San Juan or south to Valdepeñas. Neither was exactly east, but if Raúl had his number no doubt he would be put right. He remembered that first evening when he and Gillian had shared a meal and talked all night at Hacienda. After the Albariño they had had a Gran Reserva from Valdepeñas. In the absence of any other guidance he turned south-east.

Now, for the first time all morning, he had time to think. Where was Gillian? How was she? Was she alive? Realistically he thought it was unlikely she'd been harmed – over and above the shock of being abducted in the middle of the night. Even Raúl, psychopath as he might be, had no reason to deliberately ill-treat her. She was the bait and he was the fish. Now he was swimming onto the hook. Or, to put it another way, she was being held to ransom and his life might be the price. Well, he was prepared for that. He was sick of the whole business and just wanted it to end. After finally feeling he was getting his life back together, here it was all slipping back through his fingers like sand. Funny, the Spanish word for sand is *arena*. The arena where the ancient Christians were ripped apart by wild beasts was covered in sand to soak up the blood. Here he was, walking up the tunnel to face whatever lay ahead, perhaps with as much chance of survival as they. The best he could do might be to make a good death. "Precious in the sight of the Lord is the death of his saints," said the psalmist. Sometimes it felt like, whether or not his death would mean something, his life was of little worth. After the worst seemed to be over, having made it to the surface, here he was about to go under again.

He knew a long time ago it was Raúl who had been responsible for what happened to Rocío. The message confirmed it. But he had grappled with that already. Bitterness and hatred was doing him more damage than it was doing Raúl so he had to let it go. Now this morning's events brought everything back – more real, more immediate, and more horrific than before. Without Gillian he felt he just couldn't start all over again. If he had to go home without her, how could he cope? Where would that leave him? And in the meantime it was hard not to blame it all on a teenage girl who thought the world was her plaything. After treating her mother with complete contempt she had put other lives at risk as well. Even so, it was hard to feel angry in the light of how she had been that morning. And that brought him back to Gillian. It seemed highly unlikely that both of them could come out of this in one piece. Raúl thought he had a score to settle – or maybe more like a fly he had to squash. One more life would mean little to him. But if Gillian didn't survive, David thought in a matter-of-fact way, then his life was over too. It was a bridge too far – a mountain too high – whatever. But in the meantime – *oh God, please let her be alive. Let me find her. Let her be ok.*

His mobile phone rang, cutting across his thoughts. His heart sank as he flipped it open.

"David Hidalgo..." A pause.

"Señor David. How are you? I feel I know you though we've only spoken once. Do you remember? On the radio?"

"Raúl?"

"Of course. I apologize for getting you out of bed so early this morning. But I understand you and *El Capitán* had it in mind for me to get an early morning call of another sort."

"These are entirely different things. All I wanted was the girl back. If you've broken the laws of Spain that's your problem. You would have been given the chance for a fair trial."

Raúl snorted with disgust.

"Fair trial, fair trial! Don't talk to me about a fair trial. If Rodriguez could have taken me back to Madrid in a body bag he would have been delighted. Anyway, I did not phone you to exchange insults. I would like us to have a civilized conversation. You have caused me a great deal of disruption over the years. I need to persuade you this is in neither of our interests."

"Nothing would please me more than never to hear your name again. All I want now is to get my friend back and leave you alone."

"And so you shall, Señor David. So you shall."

"Can I speak to her?"

"Of course. Do you think I have no human feelings? But let me remind you, any attempt to place my operations in jeopardy and you will neither speak to her nor to me nor to anyone else again. Is that understood?"

"Of course. I'm coming alone. The police think I'm taking a few days out. Nobody knows where I'm going."

"*Bueno*. The Señora..." There was a pause, then David heard Gillian's voice.

"David, is that you?"

"Gillian. Thank God. How are you? Are you all right?"

"Yes. I'm fine. Splitting sore head but I haven't been hurt. Where are you?"

"Coming to get you, I think. Jen turned up at the hotel when they took you away. She gave me a message from Raúl. He says he wants to meet me. This is his way of making it happen. I'm so sorry you got mixed up in any of this."

"My choice. Remember?" She sounded tired but coherent. Not hysterical, not blaming, not angry, amazingly not even sounding frightened. Serious, but matter of fact. She was made of sterner stuff than David gave her credit for.

"How's Alison? It was horrible when they came in. I couldn't see what they were doing to her."

"She was drugged but she's in hospital now. She's going to be fine. I love you."

"I love you too. I…" But at that moment the phone must have been dragged away and Raúl's voice came back on.

"Yes, yes. Very touching," he said. "If you follow my instructions – *exactly* – you can whisper sweet nothings in person. Where are you?"

"About twenty-five kilometres out of Toledo. Just passing Mora. Your instructions said east but there isn't a road due east."

Raúl again let off a snort of disgust and impatience. "Stupid girl!" he said. "I told her south-east. Never mind. You are on the right road by good luck." If Juan was right and there was no such thing as luck then he was meant to be on the right road. It was his first sign of hope and raised his spirits a little.

"Keep going. Continue south towards Valdepeñas. You should be there by noon. Find somewhere to stop and wait for my call. Remember, do not try to inform anyone else. If you make any attempt neither of you will live." With that the line went dead. Valdepeñas again. Another good sign. David thought back to that conversation with Juan in his freezing Edinburgh flat so long ago, when Juan had said that the story wasn't finished yet. That was true then and still true now.

Despite everything going through David's mind, anxieties over Gillian, and the surge of adrenaline that came from speaking to Raúl, as he calmed down, there was something liberating in a strange sort of way in being out on the road, on his own, without any other demands on his time or attention. The sky was a solid dome of blue softened at the horizons. The hills and slopes slipping by were of baked red earth or rough scrub of parched greys and browns. The day was getting hot but the air conditioning kept the car cool. David wasn't used to such luxury. He adjusted the angle of his seat and tried to relax. Orderly rows of olive trees or almonds marched up the slopes away from the road. Here and there, Moorish towers and castles looked down from the peaks by the roadside, still on guard more than 500 years after the *reconquista*. The modern Spanish road network was now second to none thanks to European funding, and between that, light traffic and SatNav instructions, little concentration was needed. It was the oddest feeling. Here he was, quite possibly driving to his death, but instead of a rising feeling of panic he was, if anything, feeling more and more at peace. Where was that coming from?

The thought struck him incongruously that this was very much like a day out doing sales calls in the early days of Warehouse 66 before he gave up his job. He had had so much optimism at that time of his life. Nothing was impossible. Young people were coming to faith in amazing numbers and soon the older group who had started the effort were in the minority. These were the pioneer days – no rules and no limits. If God seemed to be in it, they did it. That was even before they were Warehouse 66 – when it was just plain *Torrejón Iglesia Evangélica*. It was only when they had gathered the first 150 and needed bigger premises that the idea of turning an old American Air Force warehouse to better use came up. Number 66 was on the market. It had a huge concrete apron ideal for parking, any amount of space inside, and most importantly was cheap. To start with they felt like refugees at a welfare centre huddled together at one end of the shell singing into the echoey heights with no decoration, heating or anything else. But as the new church grew, money came in. People who had next to nothing gave more than they could afford and God blessed both them and the church. They never took an offering but simply left out a box, and time and again the treasurers would empty it out at the end of a service to find it stuffed with notes, cheques, and promissory letters. Gradually, bit by bit, they were able to buy sound equipment, build a stage, have the building plastered, put up a ceiling and partitions, make a suite of smaller rooms, buy Sunday school materials, add an adult baptistery, buy chairs, and make what started off as a bare shed suddenly feel like home. Meanwhile everyone he met on his sales calls kept asking him what had happened to make him so cheerful. Was it a new contract or a big bonus that plastered that permanent smile across his face?

Most of them thought he had gone a bit *loco* but others were interested and a few came to church. One or two went all the way. Then they got a dose of the stupid grins as well and had to explain that to their girlfriends and colleagues. So the bandwagon rolled on. Then it jumped off the tracks when Rocío disappeared. But many more came on because of what happened to her. Now Gillian was coming nearer to faith. And there was Eric – despite David's own lack of conviction about the process. Maybe Jen herself would find a better reason for living in time to come. It wasn't a bad thing to give your life for. He felt a shiver up his spine and looked at the dashboard clock. Still only 11 a.m. as the car coasted effortlessly up and over the Sierra de la Rabara, giving him a panoramic view out over the plain to the south then more wooded slopes in the distance. In spite of everything he was smiling. For the first time in years, despite everything, live or die, he once again felt that a power was in control beyond his choices and beyond his understanding. There was certainly nothing he could do now, so it was absolutely and completely "over to you".

The kilometres slid by and David drove on as if in a bubble. The demands of other people looking to him for a lead were behind. What that day and tomorrow would bring hadn't yet arrived. He hummed a tune, turned on the cruise control, and unwound the seating angle a few more degrees. Around 11:30 he found a roadside café and stopped to join the truckers, farmers, and business travellers for a *café solo* and a *tapa*. The big screen TV was showing highlights of last night's Champion's League with Sevilla running rings around Inter Milan, which made everyone feel even better. Even David found himself getting caught up in the cheering at a Luis Fabiano goal from forty yards. Back on the road again he joined the main *carretera* just past Consuegra then let the miles roll by. Soon he was passing Manzanares and onto the long straight main road almost due south across the sun-baked plains of La Mancha. The nearer to Valdepeñas he came the greater the expanse of vineyards stretching in all directions. This was claimed to be the largest single extent of vineyards in the world and so it seemed. By 12:30 he was nearing the outskirts of the town but instead of driving in and getting clogged up in roads he didn't know, he turned off slightly to the north, climbed to a viewpoint over the town – and waited.

Chapter 27

CALATRAVA LA NUEVA

The morning was wearing on at the Parador de Toledo and some sense of normality returning. Juan got an emergency GP appointment for Jen then took her to the hospital to visit her mum while they were waiting for the results of her tests. In the meantime he went off to wander around town to calm himself down and pray. He would pick her up in an hour and a bit and take her shopping. At the hospital she was ushered into a side room to find her mum still groggy but smiling.

"Hi Mum," she said quietly. "They let me go."

"I know," Alison whispered. "They told me. I'm so glad to see you. Are you ok?" Jen nodded and took her mum's hand. They squeezed together but Jen's grip was stronger.

"Mum, I'm so sorry for everything. I never thought it would happen like this…" Alison shook her head.

"Shhh… It's over now. You're back and we can all go home." Jen knew that wasn't true but couldn't bring herself to explain. The consequences were still working themselves out – not so much like ripples in a pond as an avalanche still gathering speed downhill. She desperately wanted it to be all over so she could get back to plain, simple, boring normality. She wanted to go to school and sit with her friends in a maths class. She wanted to moan about school dinners or get asked to the youth club disco. She wanted to do her homework by the fire and watch some pointless soap. Above all she wanted to go to bed at night and know she could sleep till morning without a drunken Latino gangster barging into her room and pulling her bedclothes off. She knew that she could never go back to how it was before but hoped there might be moments, then hours, then maybe even days, when she wouldn't be thinking about the horror and wanting to forget.

"How long will they keep you in?" she asked.

"Not long. The doctor's English isn't too good but I think he said another day. So maybe tomorrow sometime. What will you be doing?"

"I don't know. Juan said he'd take me shopping."

"That would be nice. Have you met Señor David?"

"Yeah," Jen nodded but said no more. She didn't want her mother to ask about David or Gillian. She changed the subject.

"I've learned a bit of Spanish."

"That's good. What can you say?"

"Just the usual stuff – hullo, how are you, what's the weather like. And I can say things I like and don't like and ask where things are. I can even play Mus. It's a Spanish card game, so I know all the numbers." Alison smiled.

"Well done," she said. "And you're a Bible expert too now."

"Look, I've still got it." Jen smiled back and pulled a very dog-eared, scuffed, white leather Bible out of her hip pocket. "I didn't know why you gave me it. I suppose it saved my life."

"I suppose it did. You were very clever to work it all out. I didn't catch on but Señor David guessed. You'll like him when you get to know him. Gillian's lovely too. Have you met her?"

Jen ignored the question and looked at her watch instead.

"Sorry Mum. I've got to go. The nurse said just five minutes and I've got to meet Juan." She leaned forward and kissed her mum on the forehead.

"Love you, Mum." Alison smiled again. She felt completely at peace.

"I love you so much," she murmured. "I'm so pleased you're back. Now we can all go home." Jen kissed her lightly again then squeezed her hand and jumped up. She did a tiny wave at the door, mouthed "see you later" and was gone. She knew her mum ought to be stronger before she found out that things weren't quite as simple as she thought.

She let the door softly shut then meandered down the corridor in no particular hurry – Juan might be another hour yet. Like any hospital, anywhere in the world, every junction seemed to have a dozen different signs guiding visitors to various departments and services. Some of them were almost the same as English, others she could guess, and some she had no idea about. A middle-aged porter with a neat haircut and pencil moustache passed her, pushing an elderly lady in a wheelchair. He wished her *buenas días* and smiled. She smiled back. A few yards on she stopped and looked at a framed display of children's posters encouraging healthy eating. Probably a primary school project. The bright colours, childlike figures, and funny antics made her laugh. She wandered on till she got to the waiting area at reception. A drinks machine stood in the corner and she had just enough money for a can of coke. She felt proud that she had managed to follow the Spanish instructions and was rewarded with the dull clunk of a can landing in the tray at the bottom. She took it out, pushed back the tab, and took a long drink. Here she was, doing an ordinary thing in an ordinary place without anyone to fear for the first time in months. It felt strange but good. She could hardly remember what normal life was like and even found it hard to remember the "good times" before Raúl started to get angry with her all the time. Anyway it was over. She felt bad for the others but in herself she felt free. When she was younger she liked listening to her mum's old records and teasing her about how Noah must have had a record player in the ark. The Who were her favourite. Now she could hear Roger Daltrey singing "I'm free" in her head. She drained the can, dropped it into the recycle bin, and even lifted another empty one out of the litter basket and dropped it in too. She was going to be a model citizen from now on. She looked around for a vacant seat. The small tables built into the rows of plastic chairs had piles of Spanish magazines. She found a seat next to one and began to look through them in the hope of finding something familiar. Maybe she'd recognize some of the Spanish celebrities. It was so normal. She loved it. And maybe she would be home soon.

Suddenly there was a terrific commotion at the entrance. Two burly men in jeans and denim jackets came barrelling in half carrying, half dragging a third and shouting at the tops of their voices. Somehow they lumbered the man up to the reception desk and started demanding something or other. He was severely overweight and not easy to manage. He was also unconscious and Jen guessed the other men were his friends and had brought him in as an emergency. The receptionist seemed to be telling them to go to another department and was pointing back outside but they were having none of it. They kept shouting and pointing to their friend. Suddenly he seemed to regain consciousness for a second, groaned, and was slightly sick. Along with everybody else Jen was mesmerized. After more shouting one of the men banged his fist down on the desk and the receptionist gave way. She picked up the phone and gestured to the men to sit down. She must be summoning a doctor. They turned round to carry their friend to the row backing onto Jen's. For the first time she got a good look at the patient. It was Sebastian, Raúl's cook! What on earth was he doing here? He never looked well at the best of times but now his lips were blue and his face as white as a sheet. Beads of sweat coursed down his forehead. Maybe a heart attack or a stroke, or even a drugs overdose? Thankfully he was drifting in and out of consciousness and in no condition to notice her. She didn't recognize the other men but in any case quickly turned back round and slumped in her seat, heart thumping. A wave of panic swept over her and her palms were sweating. The other men were too preoccupied to pay her any attention. Less than two minutes later a doctor appeared with two porters, spoke briefly to the men, and had the patient manhandled onto a trolley and wheeled off down the corridor at top speed. The two men tried to follow but were sent back. This time they complied and sat back down immediately behind Jen. She slid even further into her chair and tried to make herself invisible. Now Sebastian was somebody else's problem, they calmed down. Soon they were laughing and joking, maybe wondering if it was one of his own "specialities" that had done the damage. Then they seemed to change the subject. Although she was terrified of being identified she was also fascinated to see what she could learn. She heard Raúl's name mentioned several times.

From their tone of voice they seemed to be discussing something that seemed uncertain. It was almost as if they were weighing up pros and cons. Then she heard the names "Gillian" and "David" – Gillian with a soft G and David with an "ah" an "ee" and a "th". Then one of the men spoke.

"*¿Dónde esta la cita?*" Jen knew that *dónde* meant "where" and she'd heard the word *cita* plenty of times. It was a date or a meeting. Raúl had them all the time. She held her breath and strained to hear.

Before long she noticed Juan approaching the door. She got up as casually and naturally as she could and made her way out. The double doors opened with a hiss. Juan was smiling and about to ask if she was ready to go shopping but Jen spoke first.

"We've got to get back to the hotel. I know where Gillian is."

Captain Rodriguez listened carefully to everything Jen had to say.

"Are you sure you weren't recognized?" was all he asked. She was as sure as she could be. The men who brought Sebastian in weren't part of Raúl's core group and she'd never seen them before in Edinburgh or Toledo.

"And have you told anyone else about what you have heard?" Rodriguez was looking from Jen to Juan and back again. They both said no. He looked relieved.

"Well that is something, I suppose."

"What happens now?" Juan asked, leaning forward.

"Now? Well, I would say that depends a bit on where Señor David is," Rodriguez said with a smile. "He should certainly be consulted, don't you think?" That stopped Juan in his tracks. He was on the point of making up an excuse when something in the captain's look made him stop.

"He's on his way there right now," he said flatly.

"Ah. I did wonder at him leaving so soon. A great shock, of course, but to disappear, with an overnight bag, when a loved one is in danger…? Not what I would have expected. Not of Señor David."

"Raúl gave Jen a message for him. He was to go to a meeting. They would tell him where. All we know is that he was to head east."

Rodriguez leaned forward, placed his elbows on the table, and clasped his hands. He spoke quietly but seriously. "Thank you, Señor Hernandez. I appreciate you are all concerned for your friend but if we are to be successful then we must work together. If you had failed to give me this information then I could have told you nothing further. But you have chosen to trust me – a little late perhaps, but trust all the same – and so I will also trust you. This is fair, no?" He turned to Jen. "Thank you for that information, Señorita. My main concern is that you have not told anyone else what you have found out. This is essential. You see, I already know where the Señora is. And I know Señor David is on his way there. Not only do I know where the meeting is to be, but in fact I suggested the location." Juan half rose out of his chair.

"You?" he said, incredulous.

"Well," Rodriguez continued, unmoved, "not exactly. I made the original suggestion but someone else actually put it into Raúl's mind."

"Just exactly what's going on here?" Juan was red in the face now and on his feet, leaning over the table. "Are you saying you've known all along and still let David go off on his own?"

"Calm down, my friend. Which question would you like me to answer first?" Juan sat down and controlled himself with difficulty.

"How do you know where Gillian is?"

"I told you – I suggested it. Let me go back a little. You remember our discussion in Madrid. I mentioned to Señor David that we have been experiencing a certain – how should I put it – lack of security, in operations concerning Señor Álvarez. This is why I have taken responsibility here. None of the men in this team has ever been involved in an operation concerning him before. But his way of working is always to make sure he has inside information."

"Like Escobar."

"Just like Escobar. He is used to corrupt policemen and indeed expects it. So perhaps he might not be surprised if someone in the new team were to contact him and offer a little information for some suitable reward? And this is just what happened. For a fee, Raúl was given information from the very heart of our operation."

"And how... I mean who..."

"*Momentito* Señor." Rodriguez held up one hand and with the other picked up a phone. He spoke rapidly in Spanish. A few seconds later the door opened. Espinosa came in and took a seat next to Jen. He looked briefly round, then back to the captain.

"Espinosa happened to make the acquaintance of your host, Señorita. He offered some information and appropriate assurances and, I am glad to say, got a positive response."

"The man nobody was allowed to see!"

"Señorita," Espinosa replied with a nod.

"So you had someone feeding information to Raúl? And that's how he knew when the raid was going to be?" said Juan. "But why would you tell him about a raid you yourself were planning?"

Rodriguez paused for a second.

"Do you remember the discussion within my team? Matters grew, shall we say, a little heated? Well, we could not agree that evening. Where possible I aim to have an agreement among my team before we act. In what we do it is essential to trust one another. We could not agree on how to get the Señorita out of the house before the gunfire began. Any way we thought of was going to be too dangerous. So I suggested we invite Señor Álvarez to do it for us. Espinosa was able to give him the details of our plan and suggest there would be a great deal less police attention if Jen was returned before they left. Maybe they would even be allowed to leave the country without too much fuss. It was not our intention that Gillian should be taken in exchange. That was a surprise and most unfortunate. However, when we found out he wanted a meeting and that Gillian would be there, then naturally he would want somewhere he could be sure was far away from the city and any police presence. So Espinosa was able to introduce an idea to him, based on his knowledge of the region and police deployment. He is from southern La Mancha. Again we were lucky, pardon me Juan – *gracias a Dios* – he took the bait and so, I regret to say, while of interest to us, what you heard this morning was not strictly news. But it is very useful to confirm that there has not been a change of plan."

"So what are we doing here then?" Juan again insisted. "If you know where Raúl and Gillian are then why don't *we* have a plan? Why didn't you tell David you knew before he went?" Rodriguez smiled again but sounded a little less patient this time.

"In the first place, we do have a plan," he said. "And secondly it is essential that Señor David does not know what is happening. I understand your concerns," he held up his hand to fend off Juan's objections, "but he must appear completely convincing. Any hint that he knew more than he should could ruin everything. Please, trust me in this. Nothing in life is certain but I am confident that Gillian and David together will be returned to us." Juan leaned forward and put his head in his hands.

"I hope you're right," he said. "I only hope you're right."

With the engine turned off, the heat of the day building, the stuffy car, and overwhelming exhaustion, David began to doze. He dreamed he was lying on his back staring at the sky, a Spanish flag fluttering over his head. When he looked around he found he was on a Spanish treasure galleon sailing home.

The sound of a text message arriving woke him up. The instructions were terse and to the point. He was to turn west towards Almagro then south to Calzada de Calatrava. Once there he was to wait. Well, he thought, so be it, wound up his chair and pulled back onto the highway. The SatNav identified towns, villages, and features as they drove. Almost everything for miles around seemed to be Calatrava this or that. He passed through Moral de Calatrava and on to Almagro. To the north was Bolaños de Calatrava, further west Valenzuela de Calatrava. Before long he was passing through Granatula de Calatrava. The vineyards of Valdepeñas had given way to drier, more arid scrubby hillside and the Sierra de Calatrava rose up on the horizon. He was travelling deeper and deeper into the Spanish countryside. Wherever Raúl was taking him, it was off the beaten track and far from any police attention. Probably that was the point – to get him somewhere unknown to anybody but the village constable and far from the reach of Rodriguez, Espinosa or anyone else. He would be completely on his own. No cavalry would be coming over these hills. But where exactly would the meeting point be? A house on the outskirts of a village, a hunting lodge halfway up some mountainside or maybe just a parking place by the roadside? He imagined a couple of Raúl's henchmen lounging outside a wooden shack halfway up a track, as he pulled up outside. One of them was going in to report his arrival. Then Raúl came out holding Gillian roughly by the arm. Would she be bound, gagged, and blindfolded? They spoke. Raúl had a smooth, almost silky tone but an unmistakable undercurrent of malice and violence. He gripped Gillian more tightly and made her wince. David felt powerless to stop it. Suddenly he realized what was happening. Letting his imagination free flow like this brought a rising panic and made his stomach churn, in place of the peace of mind he had felt up to then. He would leave the outcome to the same power that seemed to have set up so many coincidences already. Deliberately he handed the situation back and let the countryside go by without questioning where he was going or what would happen next.

As he approached Calzada the next message arrived. Were they simply estimating his journey time or were there lookouts at every turn? He should continue south-west then turn right up to the monastery castle of Calatrava la Nueva. So that's where he was going; it was a destination he knew something about. Calatrava la Nueva had been the fortified base of the Knights of Calatrava – an order of warrior monks who claimed to worship God mainly by attacking the Moors. How ironic that this site should witness the outcome of his own small war.

It didn't take long to get there. He could see the castle from miles away, which probably meant Raúl could see him – and any reinforcements he had been foolish enough to bring. It stood on a high rocky outcrop of honey-coloured stone, dominating the landscape. Approach was by a track of rough cobbles hammered in, worn down by countless generations of feet and hooves and snaking round the mountainside to the battlements. He was not surprised to see the telltale 4x4 at the turning, with Raúl's men lounging against it and keeping cool with cans of San Miguel. He ignored them and started slowly up the track. At the top was a rough, gravel car park with three more of Raúl's convoy parked together. He stopped as far from them as he could and got out.

The walls of Calatrava were plainly made for war. They seemed to grow organically out of the solid rock to withstand the fiercest of assaults. His heart pounded in his chest as he started up the path. Two men appeared from their vehicles and fell in behind. A flag fluttered from the ramparts and David felt that he too might blow away in a strong enough breeze. The path wound up for eighty yards or so towards huge double doors. It felt like a ladder to the gallows, and he, the condemned man leaving everything behind – both debts and assets. Well, if Gillian came out alive that was enough. A makeshift sign was nailed to the main door – *cerrado por obras*, closed for repairs – but as he approached a smaller access door creaked opened. He took one last look around the world outside. A clump of delicate mauve flowers that might have been crocuses had seeded into a crevasse in the rock and were flowering despite the heat, drought, scorching wind, and baking sun. David swallowed, felt the dryness in his throat, and walked through the doorway.

Inside, two men with automatic weapons were his welcoming committee. Another couple stood guard at the door of a long low shed to his left. Through the open door he could see a dejected group in yellow safety jackets sitting or standing around. These must be the custodians, archaeologists, and construction workers who looked after the monument. Being held at gunpoint in their own office was not in their job description and it showed. Strangely, now David was inside the castle walls and knew this was where whatever had to happen would happen, he again felt a strange peace of mind. It began as a tingle on his scalp then seemed to flow through his shoulders, down his spine, and fill his body.

"Sigue caminando," said a voice behind him. Keep walking. He made his way through the courtyard towards the higher levels. In some places the walls were roughly mortared medieval stone. Others had been hewn straight out of the rock. Orientation boards were dotted around explaining the history and architecture. There was no sign yet of Raúl. With occasional encouragement from a gun barrel in his back or shoulders David made his way up a flight of steps towards the ramparts, then through a thick arch onto a platform about ten metres square bounded by the outer wall. The Spanish flag he had seen from below fluttered from a pole set into the rampart wall. Raúl – it couldn't be anyone else – was dressed in a pale linen suit and was lounging in a richly upholstered high-backed wooden chair that looked as if it had been taken out of the castle museum, which it had. In front of him was a low table of a similar style. He was speaking on a mobile and ignored David's arrival. Three gang members with weapons leaned against the wall. Raúl felt no need to hurry his business and spoke for some minutes, occasionally taking a sip from a glass of *Jerez* but never even glancing in David's direction. His conversation seemed to be about quantities, delivery, and penalties for late arrival. It didn't seem to matter that anyone else was listening. Finally, the call came to an end with Raúl making his wishes perfectly and painfully clear. He closed the phone, shook his shoulders, looked up, and grinned.

"Señor David!" he said. "How are you? I feel we ought to know each other. We seem to have been circling round each other for so long – you know, like the matador and the bull. But which is the matador and which is the bull, eh? That is the question! You know you have caused me a great deal of inconvenience. Many times life could have been easier without Señor David." He beamed again as if expecting David to smile in acknowledgment or share the joke.

"Your inconvenience is of no interest to me," David replied perfectly calmly. "Where is she?"

"Where is she? Where is she?" Raúl parroted back at him. "You are so careless with your women. Is that how the Scottish behave? Your wife, the child of a church member, now your girlfriend... It's shocking! Well, before we have a touching reunion there are some matters to discuss." He nodded to the men with him, two of whom exited through the arch, leaving only one young man standing behind the chair while Raúl took out a large, heavy pistol and laid it on the table in front of him next to his glass.

"Carlos," Raúl said over his shoulder, "a chair for Señor David." The young man made a move but David interrupted him.

"I prefer to stand."

"Something to drink then?" David shook his head and Raúl shrugged.

"You know, Señor David – if I can call you that – I'm not a monster. I'm simply a businessman. And in business you sometimes have to take action to protect yourself."

David said nothing.

"So what has happened between us in the past – none of it has been personal – just business, you know." Raúl paused but David stayed silent so he continued. "I appreciate it may not have felt like this to you, but nevertheless – you have your church, I have my organization. We both need to protect what we have created."

"An interesting point of view."

"You disagree?"

"There is not the slightest point of comparison between what we do. Your business involves conning your customers into thinking they can take drugs and stay in control. Then it turns on them and they have to lie, cheat, steal, and kill to keep it at bay – all of which is profit for you. Usually they can't feed it fast enough so it consumes them as well. They lose, their families lose, their children lose, their friends lose, and their communities lose. But you win so long as you can find another customer to take their place." David took a deep breath and continued. "I work with people who have had enough of death and want life instead."

"A point of view," said Raúl with a shrug, taking another sip of *Jerez*. "But not *my* point of view."

"Evidently."

"However, you are correct in one respect. To put it another way, the market is under some pressure. Customers have many sellers to buy from. I have made some profit over the years. However, it's becoming harder to – how can I put it – harder to find a stable niche in the market."

"By which I take it you mean you were hounded out of Spain, hounded out of Edinburgh, now you're back in Spain and under pressure again."

Raúl shrugged again. "Your analysis is not even close to correct. But nevertheless it is time for a younger man to take over. Carlos here," he indicated the young man behind him with a twist of his head, "Carlos is my nephew. There are very few people to be trusted in my profession. So family bonds are strong. Carlos will take over from me in a year or two. But he is young and he has grown up in a different world. Perhaps his ways will be different from mine. And that might please you." Carlos looked down and adjusted the grip on his weapon. Right now he wasn't looking much like a *jefe de drogas*. David tried to catch his eye but he wasn't looking.

"So, what do you want from me?" he asked. "Why return Jennifer and take Gillian? Why am I here?"

"Why indeed?" Raúl mused, dabbing his brow with a white handkerchief as the midday sun grew stronger. "As you say in *Inglaterra* – it seemed a good idea at the time. No, the girl was of no consequence. She was getting in the way. There was nothing she knew that could make any difference. I appreciate you felt an obligation to make an effort for a member of your church but really she is of no value to either of us. I wanted us to have this little conversation and I guessed that only the Señora would be a sufficient encouragement for you to meet me without police interference. And so it has proved."

"What do you want from me?" David repeated.

"I've told you," Raúl snapped. "I want to pass my affairs on to someone else. I want to go back to Colombia. And I want to do so with the minimum of obstruction. Now I know you are a man of honour and a man of your word. And you have influence. In return for your life and the life of the Señora you will pass on certain information to Señor Rodriguez. You will lead him to believe I have planned a certain course of action. He will direct his attention in one direction. I, in the meantime, will leave the country in another direction and be no further trouble to the Spanish Crown. My entire operation will leave Spanish soil and we will not return. The *chicos* and *chicas* of San Blas will never hear from me again. Of course," he glanced behind him again, "I cannot speak for Carlos and how his business will evolve, but you will be rid of me for good. Which is what you want, isn't it?"

David was stunned then shook his head in disbelief.

"I'm astonished."

"No doubt. But surely pleased as well? You get what you want; I get what I want. There is no further trouble for either of us. Surely a suitable outcome all round. You should be gratified I think so well of you."

"I am amazed that you have so little grasp of the kind of man I am." Raúl started to speak but David left him no space.

"Do you think I've been through everything to make a deal? Your operation isn't to be passed on like a corner shop. You, your suppliers, your dealers, the policemen and judges you've bought and sold, the drivers, the couriers, the bankers and lawyers who've colluded with you – every single last one of you needs to be somewhere you can never sell so much as a bottle of pills again. Forget it. Rodriguez is on your tail and that's the only way you'll get out of the business. Let Gillian go. She's nothing to do with this. But I don't care if I leave here in a box. I will never help your business, wherever and however it's to be carried on."

Raúl leaned forward and took another sip from his glass, then put it back on the table. He picked up his pistol and casually fired a single round, shattering the lamp mounted on the arch above David's head into a thousand pieces. Fragments of glass and metal showered down on his head and shoulders. The sound of the gun was deafening. David jumped involuntarily.

"Brave words," Raúl said quietly. Then, without turning his head, added, "Get the woman."

Carlos walked past him as David was trying to shake fragments of glass out of his hair and off his shoulders. The noise had made his ears ring. Before long he heard footsteps. Gillian was running up the steps under the arch and into his arms, crying with relief. He held her tight and stroked her hair which was untidy and unbrushed.

"It's ok," he whispered into her ear. "It's ok. We're going home."

With a gesture from Raúl, Carlos took Gillian's arm and pulled her away, his weapon levelled at David. He was stood to one side, while Raúl lifted his pistol and pointed it at Gillian.

"Now," he said, "let's try that once again. Your life and the life of the Señora in exchange for your cooperation." No one spoke. The flag above their heads still fluttered in the breeze. Two black specks were wheeling on thermals high above the citadel. Gillian had her hands clasped together covering her mouth, all colour drained from her face. She trembled as if shivering on a Madrid winter's day. David looked at her and couldn't turn his eyes away. Finally, he spoke.

"Let her go and tell me what you want me to do," he said quietly.

"Oh no," Raúl replied. "She stays with me till we're home in Cartagena. You fulfil your part of the bargain then she goes free."

David's shoulders sagged. He could weigh the lives of the street kids in the suburbs of Madrid and Barcelona and Bilbao against his own but not against Gillian's.

"Don't do it David. Don't agree to him!" Gillian cried out, but the battle was over.

"*Vale*," he said. "I'll do it." Raúl looked at him curiously.

"You know something, Señor David? I'm surprised at you. I suppose there's part of me that hoped you might be a more honourable man – even though that would make things harder for me. Now we've had this little conversation I'm beginning to have my doubts. A man with so little integrity… I don't think you'll stick to it. It's too big a risk." He turned to his henchman. "Carlos. Kill them both."

The young man looked steadily at David and Gillian and adjusted his grip on the gun. Gunfire pierced the air. But David was still standing, untouched – the sound had come from the courtyard below. Now a shot rang out on the platform. David spun around. A gleam of sunlight glanced off a rifle sight high on the bell tower behind them. In a flash Raúl gripped his gun, then grabbed Gillian, and, pointing the barrel at her head, dragged her into a corner under cover from the tower.

"Carlos!" he shouted. "Kill him! Then cover me." For a moment the young man stood rooted to the spot while Raúl kept shouting at him. The sound of gunfire from below was intensifying. As if in slow motion he lifted the barrel of his machine gun and pointed it at David. "Do it, Carlos! Kill him!" Raúl ordered. David closed his eyes. This was it. His time was up, and with him he would take yet another innocent life. A burst of automatic fire, then a scream. David opened his eyes. Carlos was standing where he had been with the gun at his hip, pointing not at David but to where Gillian and Raúl were still standing. Gillian was covered in blood and Raúl was behind her, still holding her round the neck. Slowly his grip slackened and the gun fell. She grabbed the now limp arm, unwrapped it, and let him sink to the ground before running to where David was and clinging onto him, shaking and sobbing. Carlos seemed to be in a daze as if he couldn't believe what had just happened. From the courtyard below there was more shouting and gunfire but it seemed to be lessening. Suddenly David caught a glimpse of something bright out of the corner of his eye. A burly man in a yellow safety vest ran through the arch, also with a gun in his hand. Raúl lay on the ground. Carlos was standing with a loaded weapon now pointing vaguely in their direction. The marksman's eyes narrowed as he took aim.

"No!" David shouted and lunged at him. The gun went off as their bodies collided. Shots rang out as they crashed against a flight of steps. David's head made contact with a sharp edge and the lights went out. The last thing he saw was the Spanish flag shivering as a line of gunfire passed through it.

Chapter 28

THE CITY OF GOD

The medieval walls and battlements of the castle of Calatrava were no strangers to the sounds of combat – automatic gunfire, however, was something new. The comings and goings of horses, donkeys, mules and, more recently, cars and vans were also normal, but the rhythmic whirr of a helicopter landing in the car park seemed completely out of place. It could hardly have added to the surreal quality of the day if it had been a spaceship instead. The start of the madness was when Timo, the heritage officer in charge of restoration, got a call from his boss the day before. He was told to expect contact from a senior officer in the Policía National drugs squad and was to give them his full cooperation. He was not to discuss the matter with anyone else. Sure enough the call came through. Calatrava was to be the site for apprehending a notorious drugs gang. He shouldn't worry about why or how. Early next morning a SWAT team would arrive. They would take charge of the site and he would brief them on the layout of the buildings and duties of staff so they could pose as custodians and construction workers. The remainder of his staff were to take the day off. Who or what a SWAT team was he was only vaguely aware of from dubbed versions of Steven Seagal movies.

Next morning when he turned up early for work they were already there. Heavy cases of arms and ammunition were manhandled up the ramp and stowed in the makeshift huts and sheds the restoration team used for artefacts and tools. They already had work clothes and yellow reflective safety vests on with body armour underneath and now spent several hours combing over the entire citadel and making plans. Just after ten, when a convoy of black 4x4 vehicles made their way up the hill, the site was exactly as any outsider would expect except for an absence of admin and clerical staff and a greater number of construction staff. When Raúl and his henchmen came bursting in, machine guns locked and loaded, the staff reacted exactly as they would have expected – with shock, horror, and stunned compliance. A woman the gang brought with them was hustled out of sight. Timo didn't see her again until it was all over. Normal visitors were thereafter turned away and told to come back tomorrow.

Early in the afternoon, a silver Jaguar could be seen creeping painfully up the access track and into the car park. Its solitary occupant made his way slowly, but with an air of determination, up the path to the double doors guarding the entrance. Instead of being turned away like the others, however, he was escorted in. Site staff – at least those the gang were aware of – were kept in the reception hut under guard while the visitor was marched at gunpoint through the courtyard to an upper platform. Time passed. Suddenly, based on some prearranged signal Timo wasn't even aware of, all hell broke loose. One of the team grabbed him and he was bundled without ceremony behind a set of filing cabinets and told not to move until someone came to get him. He was happy to oblige. Gunfire seemed to be coming from all directions at once – the sharp crack of pistol rounds, the clatter of machine gun fire and the piercing whine of high-velocity sniper shots. The windows of the shed were shot out almost immediately. Then, within minutes, it was over except for one persistent exchange coming from the chapel. Soon that too was stilled and he was fetched from his shelter.

Outside was a scene of carnage. Bodies seemed to be everywhere, some groaning and some lying still. The SWAT team leader, the one they called Kris, was already speaking on a VHF handset and reporting on the day's events. He had an air of quiet satisfaction. Finally, he came over to Timo, thanked him politely for his cooperation, and explained that a helicopter would be arriving to evacuate the wounded. Ambulances would remove the dead as soon as could be arranged. Then, incongruously, he asked if some coffee could be made. And did they have a bottle of brandy anywhere? While Timo hunted around for these, Kris led three individuals into the hut and sat them down. The woman Timo had seen earlier seemed in a bad way, her face and hair splattered with blood, her eyes red, and her face streaked. She was walking on her own though and didn't seem to have been hit. She was holding onto the man who had come in the Jaguar. There was a bandage round his head, his shirt was soaked with blood, and his arm was in a sling. He walked with support on both sides, his face pale. The third was a young blond-haired man that Timo had noticed earlier as part of the gang. He was also pale-faced and shaking, and although uninjured seemed bewildered, unsure of where he was or why. A female member of the team came in as Timo was putting coffee things on a makeshift trestle table and helped the woman get cleaned up. Kris added a large measure of brandy to each of the coffees and passed them round.

As they sat in the office, Timo could see loaded stretchers being carried through the courtyard and out of the castle gates. Vehicles came and went. The injured man managed only a few sips before the sound of a helicopter was heard in the distance rapidly growing clearer, then, finally, almost deafeningly loud as it set down outside. The three civilians were ushered out and Timo didn't see them again. He helped himself to what was left of the coffee and brandy and ripped open a box of souvenir biscuits. For the next hour or so SWAT officers continued crawling over the entire site, measuring, taking photographs, picking up cartridges and other bits and pieces and dropping them into sealable bags. Then, as suddenly as they had arrived, they were gone. Kris shook Timo by the hand, thanked him again for his cooperation, and told him he would find out about it on the evening news. That was it. No explanation, no clarification, no identification. Over and done with.

At home that night he and girlfriend Marta watched mesmerized as the newsreader told the nation about the capture of the notorious Raúl Álvarez and his gang in a shoot-out at the Calatrava la Nueva Castle in La Mancha province. Six gang members had been shot dead, two seriously wounded, and five given themselves up. Police casualties were minor. Raúl himself was now in hospital under armed guard. The programme cut to a reporter outside the new Toledo General Hospital. How ironic, it was pointed out, that one of the new hospital's first patients should be a man who had so seriously damaged the health of so many Spanish young people. As soon as he was fit he would be standing trial and, as another gang was taken out of circulation, perhaps the overall health of the nation would benefit. Apparently the operation had also involved inside help from a younger member of the gang who, it was suggested, might be given a sympathetic hearing by prosecutors for his part in bringing Álvarez to justice and, it was believed, saving the lives of two hostages who were also receiving treatment. Drugs enforcement agencies particularly wanted to thank the Department of Historical Monuments for their cooperation. Timo and his girlfriend sat open mouthed as the report concluded and the anchorman went on to introduce a new high-profile Madrid fashion show. It was as if the day's events had happened to someone else. Timo went to make two cups of coffee and added a generous measure of brandy to one.

The operation to remove a bullet from David Hidalgo's right shoulder took place that afternoon. The bone was shattered but the bullet had missed all major veins and arteries, and with appropriate osteosyntesis a full recovery was expected. The fact that it was a round from one of the SWAT team's weapons that had caused the damage was a source of some embarrassment to the police team. By the next day he was sleeping peacefully. Gillian was merely kept in overnight for treatment for shock and observation. So the next morning it was a sizeable party who turned up to see the invalid. Alison was now fully recovered. She and Jen were getting acquainted again and had spent the morning on the shopping trip Jen should have had with Juan. Alison felt like a new mum all over again having got a new daughter back. Rodriguez was in meetings all morning but free early in the afternoon. So Juan, Alison, Jen, Gillian, and Captain Rodriguez all found themselves in the waiting room. Everyone had something to thank David for – Alison and Jen for a new beginning, Juan just for coming back alive, Rodriguez for helping to neutralize a dangerous criminal, and Gillian for coming to get her. She was already thinking of him as her white knight in a silver Jag. For David, however, it was all too exhausting. He felt weak, but worse than the physical effects he didn't feel at all that he deserved any thanks and appreciation. He had put Gillian at risk, attempted to deceive Rodriguez, abandoned Juan, ignored Jen and Alison and, worst of all, caved in to Raúl's intimidation. He wasn't sure what else he could have done other than standing up to the bully then turning belly up as soon as the danger was directed at his loved one. It didn't feel good. He was able to smile weakly, squeeze Gillian's hand, graciously accept Rodriguez' apologies, and wish Alison and Jen all the best. But behind it all was Raúl's voice, "...a man with so little integrity. It's too big a risk. Carlos. Kill them both."

As the group left, Juan saw the look on his face and knew it wasn't a patched up gunshot wound in his shoulder that was causing the pain.

"*¿Quieres hablar amigo?*" he asked.

David nodded, waited till everyone else had cleared the room, then told him everything that had happened. He talked about the doubts, the anxiety, the resignation, the handing of things over to God, the fragile but timely peace, then the cold fear and finally the shame.

"You know, Señor David," Juan said after they had sat in silence for some minutes, "when I was young I sometimes used to go to confession in San Blas. I used to feel so dirty I had to tell someone about it and get some relief, but I hated going because the old priest seemed to love to punish us. He would listen to your confession then tell you what a wicked person you were and how God would never accept you unless you changed your ways. But there was never any power to change. God was far away sitting on his throne. He didn't care. All he wanted to do was judge and punish, judge and punish. It seemed that no one could live up to what he wanted so no one could be accepted. And the old priest was here to tell us how angry God was. Then at Warehouse 66 we spoke about a forgiving God. So which one are you thinking about today? The forgiving one or the angry one?"

David lay looking up at the ceiling and said nothing. Juan continued. "You came to Spain despite what happened to Rocío to try to find another lost one. She is now safe and happy. Raúl is in custody. Most of the gang are dead or in jail. You've got Gillian back again and your arm will be better soon. Maybe you won't be able to use the frying pan for a while but that's a good thing. Look, Señor David, I've been telling you for months, *El Señor* is at work. Remember in the garden he said, 'It is not good for the man to be alone.' So he gave you Gillian. She is finding out about faith for herself now too. Tell me how this could have been better? You don't think you've covered yourself with glory? Does God care what you think? Does Gillian care what you think? Do I care what you think?" By now they were both smiling. "So. God has been at work. This is how he has allowed it to happen. You should be grateful. Get well, go home to Edinburgh, and ask Gillian to marry you. That is my advice!"

David didn't know whether to laugh or cry. In the end it was a mixture of both. He had a smile on his face but his body was shaking. Juan squeezed his hand, carefully kissed him on both cheeks, then winked and turned to go. Gillian, who had been waiting outside, came back in. Neither said a word. With complete disregard for hospital decorum she stretched out on the bed beside him and held him in her arms.

As soon as David could be discharged from hospital he joined the group back at the Parador Hotel. Despite the millions likely to be recovered as the proceeds of crime, now that the operation was over there wasn't an unlimited budget and they would have to leave as soon as David could travel. Thankfully that still gave them a few more days. Rodriguez, however, had to disappear back to Madrid to tidy up the paperwork. A lot more work would still be needed before the case could come to court. That was mostly a matter for the lawyers but police evidence would be needed, which meant paperwork. It was, as much as these things can be, a happy task, so he was in a good mood when he joined the group for dinner in the dining room on his last night. The *perdices con chocolate* were back on the menu and he ordered with relish. As a last gesture he personally provided a couple of bottles of excellent wine. David noticed it wasn't a *Valdepeñas* but he had had enough of that part of the country for the time being.

"So Señor David, we must both go back home to take care of business, no?"

"I guess so. Maybe a bit of a break first though. And you. How long before Raúl is in court? Will we all need to come back to Spain to testify?"

"If it does come to court, yes of course, but the latest news is that it may not."

"Why would that be?" asked Juan. "He's not going to wriggle out of it like Escobar, is he?"

"No, of course not. It is the medical reports that suggest some doubt."

"Is he going to die?" Jen asked quietly. It didn't take much to guess what was on her mind.

"No, he seems stable. But the bullet Carlos fired went into his brain. It is likely he will have severe brain damage. He may never be fit to stand trial."

"That seems so unfair!" Alison said, putting down her knife and fork. "After everything he's put us all through. Why should he get away with it? He should get what he deserves."

"Ah well, Señora, which of us would be happy with what we really deserve? In any case, if Raúl cannot stand trial it will be because he has already received a life sentence. Instead of flashy cars it'll be a wheelchair. Instead of the best restaurants – like Hacienda perhaps? – he'll be on baby food now. Personally I would prefer the prison. At least you still have yourself. What he used to be may be no more than a memory – if that."

"So he could be in the same ward as people who have suffered brain damage from overdoses or contaminated drugs," Gillian said thoughtfully. "All due to him."

The captain inclined his head.

"As you say Señora. And in any case he will have to answer to a higher court than merely the Spanish Crown. Anyway, we must not allow Señor Álvarez to spoil our dinner. What is it you call it in English – the last supper?"

"One thing I don't understand though," said Gillian, pausing between bites of a succulent roast lamb. "How did you manage to turn Carlos against the gang – against his own uncle in fact – so much that he was prepared to shoot him to save us?"

"This is something I would love to take the credit for," Rodriguez smiled, "but alas it is not possible. We have the young lady to thank." He raised his glass to Jen who blushed, sank down in her seat, and pulled the neck of her sweater over her chin but was obviously pleased with the attention.

"Jen and Carlos have, how should we put it, plans for the future."

"What?" Alison almost choked on a mouthful of chicken. Jen looked embarrassed and clearly didn't want to upset her mum all over again. Rodriguez took up the tale.

"You remember Jen told us it was Carlos who loaned her a phone to send the messages? They got to know each other. Once Jen was brought back and Gillian taken…" again the captain gestured with his glass "… Carlos decided he had to do something. Unless he acted he knew he would never see Jen again and he could be implicated in a kidnapping, perhaps a murder. We know he was wanting out by this time."

"So what happened?" Gillian persisted.

"He contacted me."

"You mean he just phoned you up?"

"More or less. He phoned my office, said his name was Carlos, that he was part of Raúl's group, and wanted to talk to me. Naturally they don't give out mobile numbers carelessly. In this case they made the right decision. He called me up early in the morning. He offered some information and I chose to trust him. Time was short so I told him we would have men at Calatrava by the time Raúl got there. He said Raúl was training him to take over. He was expecting to be involved in the meeting with David and the Señora. He said he would protect them. I conveyed this to Kris and his team. Plans were made accordingly. Carlos was clear that he would do whatever was necessary. And so it proved."

"Wasn't that leaving things a bit to chance?" Gillian sounded dubious. "What if he had been discovered? Or wasn't there when Raúl met with David? Or was there and couldn't do anything?"

"But he was and he did."

"*And* almost got shot for it in spite of everything."

Rodriguez inclined his head.

"That was unfortunate, I admit. My men were briefed, but anyone with a gun pointed in David's direction could have been a threat. In any case, all the possibilities you mention didn't happen."

"Which was a bit of luck for us!"

There was only a slight pause before Juan said, "No such thing."

Chapter 29

SCOTLAND

The flights back to Edinburgh were mercifully and beautifully mundane. No delays, no lost cases, the in flight food was fine, and the Iberian staff were polite, efficient, and good-looking. In Edinburgh it was raining but it soon cleared up so it was overcast but dry as Alicia met them. Tomas and Julie, who had been seeing quite a lot of each other under the pretext of language lessons, came too and brought a second car. Rather than immediately splitting up, Gillian offered to have everyone round for tea but it was a half-hearted affair. Alicia wanted Juan home, Alison wanted Jen home, Tomas and Julie were set for dinner at the Tapas Tree in Forth Street followed by salsa dancing, and David was tired and weak from the travel. So they sat round, drank coke, ate pizza and chatted a bit, then as soon as it was polite to do so got up to go. The results of Jen's tests were clear – no physical infections and emotionally she seemed to be making a good recovery. All the same Alison felt they just needed time doing normal things to get back into a healthy routine and was keen to get started. As everyone was leaving David took his coat down and started struggling into it one-handedly. Gillian saw everyone else off, shut the door, took the coat back off, and hung it on its peg. Then she did what she had been wanting to do for a long time – took his fedora off and sent it spinning down the hall. David himself was turned around, firmly headed back into the living room and sat down on the sofa.

"Do you remember when I came back from hospital?" she asked. He only nodded, partly out of exhaustion and partly out of doubts about what might be coming next. "We came upstairs, you helped me in and we sat on this sofa. Do you remember I could hardly move, I was that tired and sore?" Another nod. "Well, if I remember rightly, a handsome man took advantage of my incapacity. Now it's my turn..." She leaned over, kissed him on the forehead, and undid his tie, then went for a blanket, manoeuvred him round, lifted his feet up, took his shoes off, snuggled up beside him, and pulled the blanket over both of them.

Thanks to Irene MacInnes's good offices and a certain amount of arm twisting David was given indefinite leave of absence from Southside duties. Since they weren't paying him anyway this sounded more substantial than it was, but in any case it was one less pressure. Everyone was pleased to have him back in any capacity and delighted Jen was back with her mum. Collective hair stood on end as the story spread. Apparently it involved drugs gangs, machine guns, a secret code, exotic locations, a medieval castle, helicopters, and kidnapping. Nothing as exciting had been heard of since... since... well, since never actually. Mrs MacInnes wanted exclusive rights for the church magazine and David happily agreed. Despite being relieved of preaching duties he did manage along the next Sunday morning, Gillian driving. She, Juan, Alison, and Jen were all there. Jen seemed like a new person, so unlike the girl that Alison had remembered from only weeks before. She was bright, enthusiastic, cheerful, polite, communicative, and considerate – everything Alison had feared was missing in the teenage stage of MacInnes family genes. Alison didn't mind being reminded of what she was like as a teenager, just smiled and nodded.

Alicia was healthy and glowing in her pregnancy. She had already had to extend her range of clothes – in every sense of the word – and Juan was helping her up and down, bringing her glasses of water and trying at every turn to make up for the time away. Gillian was besieged by well-wishers who were scandalized by the horrors of a reported abduction and – would you believe it – a shoot-out in a medieval fortress. "Well I never," didn't quite seem adequate but it was the best respectable Edinburgh had available and was offered with feeling. Gillian smiled, fended off further questions, and kept an eye on David and how tired he was looking.

For David himself the strain of the past few weeks was real, but right now he felt in the grip of some sort of weird god-like, dreamy, disconnected feeling – exhausted, happy, peaceful, almost floating up above it all. In fact, quite a bit like some of the chemistry he'd ingested in the eighties but this time strictly kosher. It felt ok. Eric and Lorraine didn't quite get the mood of the moment and insisted on updating him on their wedding plans, oblivious to his lack of capacity. Mrs MacInnes had advised him the night before on her run-in with Mrs Buchanan so he was forewarned and forearmed. Mrs B. was expecting "words" to be had and tried to keep a low profile; however, David sought her out. Soon she was gulping like a goldfish as he killed two birds with one stone by recommending her to be in charge of wedding decorations. The attraction of organizing other people soon overcame her reservations about "that sort of people".

Finally, after all the hymn singing, something entirely inappropriate and immediately forgotten from a visiting speaker, and coffee and biscuits after the service, Juan finally caught David by the elbow and guided him into a corner.

"So that's it then *amigo*," he said with a grin.

"Well it's certainly something," David conceded, wondering what was coming next.

"What I mean is," Juan pressed home his point, "mission accomplished. Here we are. Home. With the girl. None of us dead. And your *novia* too. Gillian is a lovely girl. *El Señor* has given you just what you needed. Even when you didn't believe, he was planning it all along."

"I imagine so. Can't complain. Six months ago I thought it was all over. I just couldn't see my way back. It's all worked out better than I could have hoped."

"So was I right? *Sí* or *sí*?"

"About what?"

"About trusting God again, *tonto*."

"I suppose so."

"Suppose? What's 'suppose' about it?"

"Ok. You're right. Things *have* worked out well. I thought we were rescuing Jen but in the end I suppose she rescued me. But still. It changes you, you know, something like this. Gillian isn't Rocío. It's not as if it didn't all happen. Trusting has a lot to do with knowing what might happen next. About things being predictable. Life just isn't like that. I know that more than ever now. So God knows what's coming but I don't. I'm sorry Juan. It's just going to take me some time to be able to completely trust again."

Juan made a sound like a lottery player who had missed *El Gordo* by just one number.

"You want my honest opinion, Señor David? You're crazy. If one of my customers was as grateful for dinner as you sound now for all God's been doing I'd ban him for life. Just stopping thinking for once, can't you? God is good. Whatever happens next. Now take that lady home and start enjoying life again. And stop worrying."

Gillian came up, hats and coats in hand.

"Did I hear the word home?" she asked, looking pointedly at David and passing him his hat. "Enough talk for one day. Doctors are supposed to give orders, you know. Even doctors of literature."

David didn't complain and they didn't do a big farewell, just slipped quietly outside and downstairs. It was a sunny Edinburgh summer day. Crossing the road to the car they both noticed a huge *CLOSING DOWN – 50% Off Everything* in the window of Rings and Things and stopped to have a look as if by unspoken agreement.

The last thing Rodriguez had said to David before they left Spain was to keep alert. Just because the *jefe* was out of action didn't mean that some young blood lieutenant out to make a name for himself wouldn't want to take a pot shot and consign the great David Hidalgo to history. But South Clerk Street – on an Edinburgh Sunday afternoon – in the sunshine? So he didn't see the glint of the rifle sight in the window of the black 4x4. Hardly heard the sharp crack like a broken twig. Didn't notice anything until he felt a weight fall against him. It wasn't a cry, more like a cough. Then a sigh.

Dumb disbelief. Tiny flecks of red glinted on the jeweller's window. Trays of diamonds sparkled behind shards of shattered glass.

THE STORY CONTINUES IN...

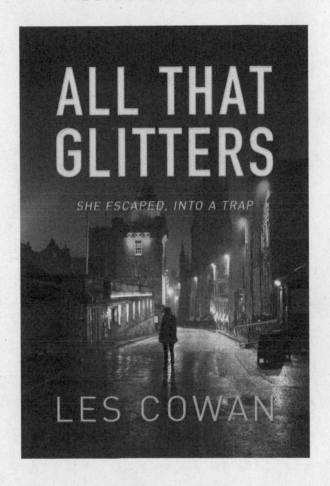

ALL THAT
GLITTERS

SHE ESCAPED, INTO A TRAP

LES COWAN

OUT MAY 2019